Roots of Evil

Also by Sarah Rayne

A DARK DIVIDING
TOWER OF SILENCE

Roots of Evil

Sarah Rayne

SIMON & SCHUSTER

LONDON • NEW YORK • SYDNEY • TORONTO

First published in Great Britain by Simon & Schuster UK Ltd, 2005
A Viacom company

Simon & Schuster UK Ltd
Africa House
64–78 Kingsway
London WC2B 6AH

Simon & Schuster Australia
Sydney

ISBN 978-0-7394-7341-2

Typeset by Palimpsest Book Production Limited,
Polmont, Stirlingshire

AUTHOR'S NOTE

The film and story of *Alraune* referred to in *Roots of Evil* come from a book written between 1911 and 1913 by a German author called Hanns Heinz Ewers.

Several versions of *Alraune* have been filmed over the years, most recently by Erich von Stroheim in 1952, but a number of silent versions were made between 1918 and 1930, mostly in Germany, Austria and Hungary. The eroticism of the earlier films was decried and deplored by many people at the time, and this, of course, served to ensure their commercial success.

For the purpose of this story, a late-1920s version has been created – a silent film starring an infamous film-actress called Lucretia von Wolff.

CHAPTER ONE

It is not every day that your family's ghosts come boiling out of the past to disrupt your ordinary working day. Lucy Trent had not been expecting ghosts to appear today, and there had been no warning of their imminence. It had, in fact, been years since she had even thought about the ghosts.

She had reached her office early and had spent most of the morning engrossed in a presentation for silent horror films from the 1920s: Quondam Films, who specialized in the restoring and marketing of old films, were putting together a marketing package aimed at the satellite TV networks, and Lucy had been given the task of setting up the presentation. She had only worked for Quondam for about six months, so it was quite a coup to be trusted with this project.

She had been immersed in writing a summary of a fourteen-minute film from 1911 called *The Devil's Sonata*. Quondam had had this in their archives for several years and had been trotting it out unsuccessfully at regular intervals, so it would be particularly good if Lucy could flog it this time round. She was just describing how the charismatic violinist lured the kohl-eyed heroine into the deserted theatre, when reception phoned through to say there was someone to see her. A lady called Trixie Smith.

No, she had not said what she wanted, but whatever it was, it seemed that only Lucy would do.

The rather dumpy female in the small interview room shook hands with Lucy in a brusque, businesslike way, inspecting her from bright brown eyes. She was wearing a plain mackintosh and sensible shoes, and her hair, which was turning grey in pepper-and-salt fashion, was cut in a pudding-basin style. Lucy thought she might be a games mistress of the old style, or an organizer of therapy-type workshops for people to make raffia baskets. Intelligent, but possibly a bit tediously over-emphatic when it came to her own field, whatever her own field might be. She had probably brought in an ancient reel of ciné film that would turn out to be smudgy footage of great-uncle-somebody's boating holiday from 1930, and Lucy would have to find a tactful way of telling her that Quondam did not want it.

But Quondam's policy was never to ignore a possible acquisition, so Lucy sat down and asked how she could help.

Trixie Smith said, 'Can I make sure I've got the right person before we go any further? You are Lucretia von Wolff's granddaughter, aren't you?'

Lucy thought, oh, blast, it's something to do with grandmamma. Another weirdo wanting to write an article or even a book. But she said, guardedly, that yes, she was Lucretia's granddaughter.

'Ha!' said Ms Smith. 'Thought I'd found the right Lucy Trent. Can't always trust reference books, though. *Who's Who* and all the rest of them – they often get things wrong. The thing is, Miss Trent, I'm doing a postgraduate course.' She named a smallish university in North London. 'Useful to have a doctorate in teaching, you see. More money.'

'You're a teacher.' It explained the brisk authority.

'Modern languages,' agreed Trixie. 'But the subject of my thesis is, "The Psychology of Crime in the Nineteen-fifties".'

'And,' said Lucy, 'you're going to use the Ashwood murders as the cornerstone.'

'Yes, I am.' A touch of truculence. 'I don't suppose you mind, do you?'

'Not in the least. Half the rainforests in South America must have been cut down to provide paper for books about Lucretia. She was a celebrity almost before the word was invented, and the Ashwood case was one of the biggest *causes célèbres* of its day.' Lucy paused, and then said, 'Listen, though, Ms Smith—'

'Call me Trixie, for goodness' sake. Life's too short for formalities.'

'Uh – Trixie, if you've got any wild ideas of solving a mystery, you should know there truly isn't one to solve. In the late twenties and thirties my grandmother was the original sultry temptress of the silent screen. The men adored her and the women disapproved of her. Her lovers were legion and her scandals were numerous. She got somehow tangled up in the Second World War – not very creditably by some accounts – and then afterwards she tried to make a comeback.'

'Ashwood Studios,' said Trixie Smith, nodding. 'She was making a film at Ashwood, wasn't she, and two men – both of them supposed to be her lovers – got into a jealous argument. Upon which Lucretia flew into a tantrum, killed both of them, and then killed herself – either from remorse at their deaths, or from panic at the thought of the hangman's noose.'

'Two murders, one suicide,' said Lucy rather shortly. 'And clearly you've found out most of the facts already. I don't think there's likely to be anything I can add to any of that.'

'Don't you care that your grandmother was branded as a double murderess?'

Bother the woman, she was like a steamroller. But Lucy said, 'I don't know that I do care very much. I wouldn't have chosen to have a grandmother who was a murderess, and I'm not very happy about the alleged spying activities either – but it all happened a long time ago and it was years before I was born. I don't think any of the family is particularly bothered about it these days. I'm not; I never even knew Lucretia – oh, and I'm not named for her in case you wondered. But I hope your thesis works out well, and I hope you get your doctorate out of it.' She stood up, hoping this would end the interview.

It did not. 'What I really want,' said Trixie, 'is to talk to any members of your family who might actually remember Lucretia. She had two daughters, didn't she?'

'Yes. They changed their surname after Lucretia died – or their guardians or trustees changed it on their behalf or something like that. My mother was the younger daughter—' Lucy hesitated briefly, and then said, 'She died when I was eight. The other daughter is my aunt – Deborah Fane.'

'The books all mention her, but I hadn't got a surname.' Trixie Smith wrote it down industriously and Lucy thought, Damn, I didn't mean to give that away. 'And she's still alive, is she?' said Ms Smith hopefully. 'Deborah Fane? How old is she? Would she agree to see me, d'you think?'

'She's certainly over seventy and her heart's a bit tottery – a touch of angina – but she's pretty lively. She might talk to you.' This was quite possible; it had been Aunt Deb who had told Lucy most of the stories about Lucretia, and she had always seemed to rather enjoy Lucretia's smouldering legend. Lucy rather enjoyed it as well, although she was not going to admit this to a stranger. The rest of the family had always found Lucretia slightly shameful, of course; and as for Edmund . . . Lucy repressed a mischievous grin at the thought of her cousin Edmund's probable apoplexy if he discovered that Lucretia was being dragged into the spotlight again.

She said carefully, 'I could ask Aunt Deb if she'd talk to you. I can't promise anything, but give me your phone number and I'll call you later this evening. It's just background stuff you want, is it?'

'Mostly background. Although there is one other thing—'

'Yes?' There was no particular reason why Lucy should feel a sudden butterfly-flutter of apprehension, but she did feel it.

'I want to find out about Alraune,' said Trixie Smith.

Alraune.

The name dropped into the small room like a heavy black stone falling down a well. There were several possible responses to it; one of which was for Lucy to say, with extreme flippancy, 'Yes, wouldn't we all like to find out about Alraune, dear,' and then escort Ms Smith out of the building faster than a bat escaping hell. After which Lucy could forget this entire discussion, leave Lucretia with the brand of Cain on her sultry white forehead, and shut Alraune firmly back into the stored-away memories along with the rest of the ghosts.

The second option was to look faintly bored and slightly disdainful, and to act as if a rather embarrassing gaffe had been committed. ('Oh, we don't talk about *that*, Ms Smith, not in *public* . . .')

The worst thing of all would be to say, in the kind of aggressive voice that positively invites an argument and a discussion, that Alraune had never existed, and add that the whole thing had been a publicity stunt dreamed up by journalists.

Lucy said, 'But you must surely realize that Alraune never existed. It was all a publicity stunt dreamed up by journalists,' and Trixie Smith, with the air of one who has finally heard what she has been waiting for, said,

'Are you sure about that?'

As Lucy made her way home that night, she hardly noticed the stuffy, crowded tube and the rush-hour jostle of people.

She reached her flat, threw her coat into the wardrobe, and went through to the kitchen. She lived in the upstairs, left-hand quarter of a rather ugly mid-Victorian house on the edge of Belsize Park; the house was not quite large enough to warrant the term 'mansion' but it was not really an ordinary family house either, and the inside was very nearly palatial. It meant that Lucy had a huge sitting-room, which had originally been the house's master bedroom, and a tiny bedroom opening off it, converted from a dressing-room. The original landing, which was vast, had been partitioned so that she had a kitchen and bathroom at the front half, and the flat on the other side of the house had the back half. This worked reasonably well, although the dividing wall between the two bathrooms was a bit thinner than it should have been.

Aunt Deb had always thought it rather a ramshackle set-up and Edmund had never understood how Lucy could live here, but Lucy liked it, partly because she had the feeling that it had once been a very happy house. She liked the feeling that over the years entire families had printed their cheerful memories on the old timbers, or that contented ghosts had pasted their shadows on to the walls.

Memories and ghosts . . .

She liberated a bottle of sharp dry wine from the fridge, and took it to the uncurtained window to drink. It was dark outside: the rooftops beyond the windows were shiny with rain, and there was a long, snaking bead-necklace of car headlights from the Finchley Road, which always seemed to be in the grip of its own rush-hour, no matter the day or the time.

Alraune. It was years since Lucy had even heard the name. Her mother had always maintained that Alraune had genuinely been nothing more than a publicity stunt. A ghost-child created by the gossip-columnists, the conception and birth deliberately surrounded by mystery. It had just been something that would sell newspapers, and bring people flocking to see the films, she had said; Lucretia had always had an eye to a good story, and she had never had much regard for truth. But there had never been any such person as Alraune – why, the name alone went to prove that it was only fantasy. *Mandragora officinarum*. Mandrake root. For pity's sake, said Lucy's mother, who had lived a bright mayfly existence with her husband and small daughter, would even Lucretia name a child after a mandrake root!

'But it was a *film*!' Lucy had said to Aunt Deb years later. '*Alraune* was the title of the first film Lucretia ever made! Didn't mother ever understand that?'

Aunt Deb had said yes, of course, the name had come from the film – and a very outstanding film it had been in its day, by all accounts. But other than that, she would never talk about Alraune, although she once said that if even a tenth of the stories had been true, it must have been a childhood so bizarre and so bitterly tragic that it was best not to re-tell any of it. Alraune, either living or dead – and most probably dead – was better left in peace.

Lucy frowned, and picked up the phone to ring Aunt Deb to explain about Trixie Smith. Aunt Deb would probably talk to Edmund about it all – she talked to Edmund about most things – and Edmund would be strongly disapproving of the whole thing, but Lucy could not help that.

After she had done that, she would cook herself some supper and have another glass of wine, in fact she might even finish the bottle. Why not? Hearing Alraune's name again after all these years surely warranted it.

Edmund Fane did not have to cope with rush hours or crowded tubes. He lived within two miles of his office, and he drove himself there and back each day.

He liked his life. He was due to turn forty in a couple of months' time, which a great many people would have found vaguely alarming, talking about landmarks and watersheds, planning slightly hysterical celebrations or starting rigid exercise regimes that they would not keep up. Edmund had no intention of adopting such extreme behaviour; he viewed his fortieth birthday with quiet confidence and thought it was not being vain to look at his life with satisfaction.

On the material side there were a number of pleasing credits. There was his house, which, although small, was two hundred years old, and not only carefully maintained but very tastefully furnished. No one realized what a kick Edmund got when guests complimented him on his possessions.

There was his small solicitor's practice, which he had built up almost single-handed in the prosperous little market town, and there was another kick to be got there. 'Mr Fane,' people said. 'One of the town's leading solicitors.'

People liked him, Edmund knew that. When he was still in his teens, they had said, Oh, what a nice boy! So responsible, so clever. And such beautiful manners. When he got a first at Bristol University people told Aunt Deborah how proud she must be of him. A brilliant future ahead, they said, and expressed surprise when he chose to come home and set up his own law practice, because wouldn't you have expected Edmund Fane – Edmund Fane with that first-class honours degree in law – to have aimed for something more high-flying? Rather odd that someone with such a brilliant mind should bury himself in a small country firm – why, it was barely five miles from the place where he had been born. Ah, but perhaps he wanted to remain near to Deb Fane who had been so very good to him, almost a mother to him, in fact. Yes, that would be the reason. Dear, thoughtful Edmund.

On the strictly emotional side, the score was not quite so healthy, in fact Edmund admitted that if you were going to pick nits, you might say that the one shortfall in his life was the lack of a wife. But he had fostered a small legend about having carried a torch for some unspecified lady all these years, and it had worked very well indeed. (Poor Mr Fane, so romantically good-looking, and is it true that he never recovered from losing the love of his life . . . ?)

Aunt Deborah had once or twice wondered if Lucy and Edmund might one day get together – such good friends they had been in their childhood, and only cousins by marriage, and wouldn't it be nice? – but Edmund knew it would not be nice at all; Lucy would drive him mad inside of a fortnight.

At around the time Lucy was drinking her wine and thinking about Alraune, and Edmund was reviewing his life with such satisfaction, a sharp and incisive mind was remembering a very particular childhood fear.

It was a fear that still sometimes clawed its way to the surface, even after so many years and even when a degree of prosperity had been doggedly achieved. Even today, the fear that had ruled the life of a lonely child and that night after night had filled up a house had not completely faded.

The house had been in Pedlar's Yard, once the site of an East London street market, once a busy little world of its own. The original cobbles were still discernible in places, but the market had been abandoned a century and a half earlier, and the houses and the surrounding areas were sinking into decay. No. 16 was squeezed between two larger buildings whose frontages both jutted out in front of it, so that it was always dark inside and there was a squashed-up feeling.

On some nights in that house it was necessary to hide, without always understanding why. But as the years went by, understanding gradually unfurled, and then it was necessary to be sly about the hiding places, changing them, sometimes doubling back to earlier hiding places, because if you were found on the nights when fear filled up the rooms – the nights when *he* stormed through the house – terrible things could happen.

None of it must ever be talked of. That had been one of the earliest lessons to be learned. 'Tell a living soul what I do in here and I'll break your fingers, one by one.' And then the thin angry face with its cold eyes suddenly coming closer, and the soft voice whispering its threats. 'And if you do tell, I'll know. Remember that. If you tell, I'll find out.'

On those nights not my pleas, not mother's frightened crying – nothing – ever stopped him. She covered up the bruises and the marks and she never talked about the other wounds *he* inflicted on her in their bed, and I never talked about it either. She sought refuge in the tales she had stored away about the past; they were her armour, those tales, and they became my armour as well because she pulled me into the tales with her, and once inside we were both safe.

Safe.

But have I ever really been safe since those years? Am I really safe now?

CHAPTER TWO

Lucy supposed that she would get to hear the result of Trixie Smith's researches eventually. Probably Aunt Deb would phone, which would be nice, because she could tell a good tale, dear old Deb, and Lucy would enjoy hearing all about the delvings into the squirrelled-away memorabilia. (Would the delvings turn up anything about Alraune . . . ?)

But at the moment she was not thinking about Alraune and she was not thinking about her disreputable grandmamma; she was concentrating on Quondam's presentation for the silent horror films.

There were going to be three films in the package. As well as *The Devil's Sonata* there was a version of Du Maurier's *Trilby* which Quondam had recently picked up somewhere, and also a very early edition of *The Bells* from 1913.

Lucy had finished the precis of *The Devil's Sonata*, and was now immersed in writing one for *The Bells*. It was not the famous Henry Irving version but it was still a wonderful story of the murderer haunted by visions of his victim; in fact all three of the films were terrific stories. You could see why they were classics, each in their own way. Lucy rather liked horror stories, especially the dark-house, killer-prowling-up-the-stairs kind; she liked the way they reinforced your own sense of safety.

She re-read what she had done so far and thought it was reasonably all right but that it needed a lift, a sparkle, a bit of pizzazz to make it stand out. Such as what? Well, maybe such as setting the whole presentation against some sort of spooky Gothic background. Would that work? They would not want to use any of the actual film footage they were hoping to sell, of course, on the principle of the Victorian tart's cry: If you don't want the goods, don't ogle them, dearie. But they might achieve some good effects with lightweight screens and graphics, or even with slides.

Lucy considered this. The mechanics would have to be kept extremely simple; a roomful of TV programme-makers would become impatient if there was too much scurrying about with extension leads, or propping up of wobbling display screens, and slides coming out upside-down, so that would have to be carefully planned. She was inclined to think they should pitch everything just very slightly over the top: maybe have a cobweb-draped mansion as back projection, and appropriate sound effects. One or two creaking doors, a few hollow echoing footsteps. All tongue-in-cheek stuff. If you wanted to grab people's attention, it was a good ploy to make them smile at the beginning.

She typed and sent an email across to the technical department to see if there was anything in the archives in the way of creaking doors and sinister footfalls, and then passed on to the idea of music. Music as an intro for *The Devil's Sonata* would be a terrific scene-setter – wasn't there a piece that was supposed to have been actually devil-inspired? She scooted across to the small library section and rummaged through a couple of musical dictionaries to find out. Yes, there it was: *The Devil's Trill* by Giuseppe Tartini. A violin sonata, supposedly inspired by a dream in which the composer sold his soul to the devil for the music. Tartini had woken from the dream with the music firmly in his mind, and had written it down, or so the story went. Story or rumour, the music ought to be beautifully eerie; Lucy would try to get hold of a CD.

She had just got back to her desk when the phone rang, and Edmund's voice said, 'Lucy? Thank goodness you're there.'

Edmund would not ring her at the office unless there was something serious. Lucy said, 'What's the matter?'

'There's some very bad news,' said Edmund in his solemnest voice. 'I'm afraid it's Deborah.'

'Oh no—'

'I went out there last evening, and I found her lying in her chair—' A pause. She's dead, thought Lucy in sudden panic. That's what he's going to say. And then – no, of course she isn't. People don't die just like that, out of the blue. In her mind, she could already hear Edmund saying that no, of course Deborah was not dead.

But what Edmund said was, 'Yes, I'm afraid she's gone. A great sadness, isn't it? A heart attack, they think. But apparently it would have been almost instantaneous.'

So dear, slightly scatty Aunt Deb really was dead and Lucy would have to find a way to bear it. And at some point Edmund would say wasn't it a mercy she had had a quick death, and Lucy would hate him for saying it because Deb ought not to be dead at all. She had been so full of life, so warm and kind, always so pleased when Lucy came to spend part of the school holidays in the big rambling old house . . . She had always wanted to hear about Lucy's life; encouraging her if work became difficult, staunchly partisan if a romance went wrong . . .

A hard desperate loneliness closed down on Lucy so that she had to fight not to burst into floods of tears at the rush of memories. But Edmund would get huffy and embarrassed if she did that, and after a moment she managed to say, a bit shakily, 'Oh Edmund, how awful.'

'It's a great shock,' said Edmund conventionally. 'I shall miss her very much. I'm going out to the house later on – there's a lot of sorting out to do, of course.'

'Yes, of course.' Lucy tried to match Edmund's tone. 'Could I help with that? Shall I drive up?'

'Oh no,' said Edmund at once. 'I can manage perfectly well. And I'd quite like to be on my own in the house for a day or two. To say goodbye, you know.' This came out a bit embarrassedly.

'Edmund, are you sure you're all right? I mean . . . finding her dead . . .' Edmund had not exactly lived with Aunt Deb, but he had shared all the holidays, and he had lived near to Deb for a long time. Lucy said, 'You must be absolutely distraught.'

'I'm extremely upset,' said Edmund politely.

Edmund was certainly upset, but he was not what Lucy had called distraught because he would never have permitted himself such an untidily excessive emotion. What he was, was deeply saddened at Deborah Fane's death, although not so much that he could not focus on the practicalities.

He was, of course, the person to take charge of things – Deborah Fane's dearly-loved nephew, living in the neighbouring market town, barely five miles distant – and his staff at the office said that of course they could manage for the afternoon; it was Friday in any case, and bound to be quiet. His secretary would take the opportunity to catch up on some filing while he was gone. Yes, they would make sure that everywhere was securely locked up and the answerphone switched on.

Edmund drove to the house, and parked his car at the side. It was ridiculous to find the sight of the blank unlit windows disturbing, but then he was not used to the place being empty. Still, everywhere looked in quite good condition, particularly considering that Aunt Deborah had lived here alone for so many years. Edmund tried to remember how long it was since William Fane had died. Twenty years? Yes, at least that. Still, he had left Deborah well provided for. Comfortable if not exactly rich.

The house was comfortable if not exactly rich as well, although it might not look as good when subjected to a proper professional survey – Edmund would commission that right away. But in the half-light of the November afternoon everything looked reasonably sound. The paint was peeling here and there, and the kitchen and bathroom were a bit old-fashioned for today's tastes, but all-in-all it was a spacious family house and in this part of the country it would fetch a very satisfactory price indeed.

Edmund allowed himself a small, secret smile at this last thought, because although Aunt Deborah had refused to let him draw up a proper businesslike will for her – eccentric old dear – she had been no fool and a will of some kind there would surely be, just as surely as Edmund himself would be the main beneficiary, although there might be a legacy for Lucy, of course. It was just a matter of finding the will. People had always said indulgently that since William's death, Deborah had lived permanently in a muddle, but it was such a happy muddle, wasn't it? This point of view was all very well for people who would not have to clear up the muddle now that she was dead.

Edmund unlocked the heavy old door at the house's centre. It swung inwards with a little whisper of sound – the whisper that was so very familiar, and that in the past he had sometimes fancied said, *welcome* . . . Did it still say that? Mightn't the whisper have changed to *beware* . . . Beware . . . Yes, he would have to beware from now on. Still, surely to goodness anyone was entitled to feel a bit nervous on entering a dark empty house where someone had died.

He pushed the door wide and stepped inside.

The past surged up to meet him at once, and the memories folded around his mind.

Memories . . .

Himself and Lucy spending holidays here . . . Lucy very much the small cousin, but determinedly keeping up with everything Edmund did. Long summers, and log-scented Christmases and glossily bronze autumns . . . Picnics and cycle rides . . . Berries on trees, and buttercup-splashed meadows, and misty bluebells in the copse . . . The time they had set the stove on fire making toffee when Aunt Deborah was away for the weekend and they had had to call the fire brigade and repaint the kitchen after the fire was doused. Lucy had been helpless with laughter, but Edmund had been panic-stricken.

He set down the small suitcase he had brought, and went back out to the car for the box of provisions he had picked up on the way. He would have to spend most of the weekend here because he would have to sort through the magpie gatherings of an elderly lady's long and full life, but there was no point in going out to a pub for his meals (the White Hart charged shocking prices even for bar meals) when he could quite well eat in the house while he worked.

He carried the groceries through to the big old-fashioned kitchen, dumped them on the scrubbed-top table, and reached for the light switch. Nothing. Damn. He had not bargained for the power having been switched off. He rummaged for candles and matches, eventually finding both in a kitchen drawer, and set several candles to burn in saucers around the kitchen, with a couple more to light the hall. Huge shadows leapt up at once, which Edmund found slightly unsettling. He found the house's silence unsettling as well. Once upon a time, he had lain in bed in the room at the top of the stairs and been able to think, That's the old lime tree tapping its branches against the window of Aunt Deborah's bedroom. Or, That fluttering is the house-martins nesting in the eaves: they always go there at this time of year. But the house's sounds were no longer familiar or reassuring. He would make himself a cup of tea to chase away the ghosts; he usually had one at this time anyway, and there was no reason to change his habits.

The kitchen range was cold, of course, but the gas was still on for the cooker. Edmund set a kettle to boil, and then wondered if the lack of power was simply due to a mains switch being off. He picked up one of the candles, thinking he would check the fusebox, and he was just crossing the hall, the prowling candle-flame shadows walking with him, when he heard, quite unmistakably, the crunch of footsteps on the gravel path outside. He stopped, his heart skipping several beats, because the footsteps had been rather slow, rather careful foot-steps – they had walked around the front of the house and then paused. Exactly in the way an ageing, but still-agile lady used to walk across the front of the house, dead-heading plants as she went and pausing to prune the wisteria growing near to the front door. (Aunt Deborah, returning to the house where she had lived for so many years? Of course not! Snap out of it, Edmund!)

But as Edmund glanced uneasily at the narrow windows on each side of the front door, a shadow appeared at one of them and a face swam up against the glass, peering in. Edmund prided himself on his unemotional temperament but fear clutched instantly at his throat. There *is* someone out there!

And then the shadow stepped back from the window, and there was the crunch of footsteps again, and then a sharp, perfectly normal rat-a-tat on the front door. And after all, it was barely five o'clock in the evening, and ghosts would not knock politely on doors, and there was no reason in the world why someone should not have come out here on a perfectly legitimate, entirely innocent, errand.

But Edmund was badly shaken and it took a moment for him to recover and open the door. When he did so, on the threshold stood a completely strange female, four-square as to build, sensible as to garb.

'Mr Fane?' said the female. Her voice matched her appearance. 'Mr Edmund Fane?' She held out her hand. 'I'm Trixie Smith. I spoke to your aunt on the phone a few days ago. I'm very sorry to hear she's dead – please accept my condolences.'

'Thank you,' said Edmund. 'But—'

'And I hope you won't mind me turning up like this, but Mrs Fane promised me some notes about her mother and they're very important to my research. So I thought, Better drive out to collect them before they're destroyed in the clearing-out process.'

Edmund could hardly believe this was happening. He could scarcely credit the pushy impudence of this bossy female, or the fact that she had driven all the way here without even the courtesy of a phone call first.

'I went to your office first,' said Ms Smith. 'Best to be businesslike, I thought. They said you were here, so as it was only a few extra miles to drive I thought I'd come along and see if it could all be dealt with on the one trip. But please say if this is a bad time – I shan't be offended, I prefer people to be straight. And I can easily come back, or you can post the stuff to me.'

Clearly she was not going away, and equally clearly she would have to be asked in. Edmund did so, forcing a degree of politeness into his voice. No, he said, it was not especially inconvenient – he laid some emphasis on the especially – although not having any electricity at the moment was making things a touch difficult. But he was afraid he could not really help; his aunt had certainly told him about Miss Smith's approach, although he did not know anything about any notes on Lucretia's life. In fact, said Edmund, he doubted there had been time for her to make any notes, since she had died so very suddenly.

'I really am sorry about that,' said Trixie Smith again. 'I'd have liked to meet her. We got quite friendly on the phone – she was very interested in my thesis.'

'"Crime in the Nineteen-fifties"?'

'Oh, she told you that, did she? Yes, I'm hoping to use Lucretia von Wolff as the central case study. Remarkable woman, wasn't she?'

'I never thought so,' said Edmund shortly. 'Greedy and manipulative, I always thought.'

'Yes?' She sipped the cup of tea he had felt bound to offer. 'Well, whatever she was, I'd like to find out what drove her that day at Ashwood Studios. Psychologically, it's a very interesting case. See now, that one man who was murdered, Conrad Kline, he was your grandmother's lover, wasn't he?'

'She wasn't my grandmother,' said Edmund shortly. 'I'm from another side of the family. Deborah Fane married my father's brother – William Fane. So Deborah was only my aunt by marriage.'

'Oh, I see. But you know the stories?'

Edmund admitted that he knew some of the stories. His tone implied that he disapproved of what he did know.

'How about Alraune? Do you know anything about Alraune?'

Alraune . . . The name seemed to shiver on the air for a moment, and Edmund frowned, but said, 'The film?'

'The person.'

'There was never any such person. Alraune was just a legend. Everyone agrees on that.'

'Are you sure? The police records show that a child, listed simply as "Allie", was at Ashwood that day and—'

Edmund was not normally given to interrupting people in mid-sentence, but he did so now. 'I'm afraid you're starting to become enamoured of your theory, Ms Smith,' he said. 'Twisting the facts to suit it. That could have referred to anyone.'

'—and I've talked to your cousin, Lucy Trent, about Alraune.'

Dear God, had the woman been working her way through the entire family! But Edmund said, 'And what did my cousin Lucy have to say?'

'She said Alraune had been created by journalists, purely for publicity. Only I had the feeling that she didn't entirely believe that. I'm good at picking things up like that,' said Ms Smith. 'In fact somebody once told me I was a bit psychic. Load of rot, of course, but still. I went to your cousin's office – Quondam Films, interesting set-up, that. In fact—'

For the second time Edmund cut her off. 'Ms Smith – I wonder if you'll forgive me if I close this discussion. I've got an awful lot to do, and I'm only here for two days.'

'You'd like me to go. Quite understand.' She drained the tea and stood up. 'But if you should come across anything that I might make use of . . . And if you could post it to me I'd be grateful. I'll give you my address and phone number.' She scribbled this on the back of an envelope. 'You won't forget? I mean – if there's anything about Lucretia . . . Anything at all . . . '

'I won't forget,' said Edmund politely.

*   *   *

After he had seen Trixie Smith to her car, Edmund went back into the kitchen and rather abstractedly began to prepare a meal from the groceries he had brought.

His mind was replaying the conversation with Trixie, but he was already thinking: faced with this situation, faced with Trixie Smith, what would Crispin do?

Crispin.

Even the thought of Crispin made Edmund feel better, and he knew at once that Crispin would say there was only one way to deal with this meddlesome female. You've shouldered this kind of responsibility before, dear boy, Crispin would say. Do so again. You know what needs to be done.

Crispin was an irreclaimable gambler, of course; Edmund knew that and he more or less accepted it, even though he privately deplored it. Still, there were times in life when a gamble had to be taken, and this looked like one of them. There was also the fact – and Edmund would not admit this to anyone, not even to Crispin – that the taking of a gamble was deeply and excitingly satisfying.

He went on preparing his food, his mind working.

*

In Pedlar's Yard, Mother's tales had almost always been spun at bedtime, because that was when *he* was out of the house. The warp of the stories had been threadbare and the weft was frayed and thin, but the tatterdemalion tales had still been the stuff that dreams could be made on, and they had been the cloth of gold that had tapestried a child's unhappy life.

Once upon a time . . .

The glowing promise of the phrase had never failed to work its enchantment. Once upon a time there had been a family in an old city, full of romance and music, and they had lived in a fairytale house among the trees, where princes had visited and ladies had danced, and where life had been wonderful.

'The city was called Vienna. It's in Austria, and it's the most romantic city in the world, Vienna. And your grandmother lived in that house – she was maid to a lady called Miss Nina. It was a very important position, and it meant she saw all the grand people who came to the house for dinners and balls and concerts.'

'Because they were very rich, that family.'

'Yes. You like rich things, don't you?'

'Yes. So do you.'

'Oh yes. Once I thought I would be rich. Perhaps I still will be one day. And then you'll be rich as well.'

'That would be pretty good. But tell what happened to the family in Vienna.'

'Well, when your grandmother was seventeen, a handsome young man came to the house, and he saw her and fell in love with her. But they wouldn't let him marry her, because she was a servant and he was important – perhaps he was a lord, or a duke . . . he might even have been royalty—'

'And so they had to part? And it was very sad and very romantic.'

'Yes, it was. You always ask that when we reach this bit of the story.'

'You have to tell stories exactly the same every time. It's like – um – like a jigsaw or painting. If you change anything, next time you tell the story there'll be a wrong piece somewhere.'

'You look like a worried pixie when you say that. A ragamuffin pixie. Have you brushed your hair this morning?'

'I'll brush it in a minute. Why don't we ever go to see my grandmother?' People at school often talked about going to visit grandmother; it always sounded a good thing to do.

'Well, families are odd things, you know. If you marry someone your family don't like—'

'Oh. Oh, yes I see.'

'I wonder if you do.' Almost to herself Mother said, 'But he could be very charming when he was younger.'

He could be very charming . . . But that was years ago, and now you're terrified of him. This could not be said, of course, and it was a relief when Mother said, in her ordinary voice, the voice that always dispelled the fear, 'But one day we will go. Just the two of us.' This was said with a wary glance at the door. 'One day we'll do it.'

One day, when I can no longer stand the brutality . . . One day we'll run away, just you and me . . .

'Where does she live? Do you know exactly? Is it miles and miles?'

There was a pause, as if Mother was trying to decide whether to answer this. Then she smiled, and said, 'Yes, I do know. It's a place called Mowbray Fen. That's in Lincolnshire. You have to go through Rockingham Forest, and along by Thorney and Witchford, until you come within sight of Wicken Fen.'

The names were repeated softly, as if they might be a spell; a charm that would take you on to a golden road. Like Dorothy in *The Wizard of Oz*, or like the children who went through a wardrobe into a magic land.

'There are marshes there, with queer darting lights that the locals call will o' the wisps – they say if you can capture one it must give you your heart's desire.'

'What's a heart's desire?'

'It's different for everyone. But once you'd gone through all those places,' said Mother, still in the same far-away voice, 'you'd come to the tiny, tiny village called Mowbray Fen. There's a house there standing all by itself and it's called the Priest's House because it was built at a time when people could be put to death for believing in the wrong religion, and there are legends that priests hid there before being smuggled out of England and across to Holland. We'll find the places on your school atlas in the morning.'

The names had been like a litany. Thorney and Witchford and Rockingham Forest. Rutland Water with the place called Edith Weston that sounded like an old lady, who knitted things and smelled of lavender water. And there was Whissendine and Thistleton.

'They're like the places in that book I read at school. *The Hobbit*.'

Books could only be read at school, because there were no books in Pedlar's Yard. But the school had a small library where you could sit at dinner-time or in between half past three when classes finished, and four o'clock when the teachers went home and the school was locked up. It was quiet and there was a nice smell from the books and on Mondays there was a polish smell from the weekend cleaning. When I'm grown up and when I have a house of my own it will always, *always* smell of polish.

'You're a hobbit,' said Mother, smiling.

One day they really would run away: they would probably do it at midnight which was when people did run away. They would go to the house where the will o' the wisps danced, and the lady from the stories would be there.

It was a good thought; it was a thought to hold on to when *he* came slinking into the bedroom, and when he said that if you told anyone what he did to Mother with his belt and with his hands, he would break your fingers one by one, or maybe hold your hand over the hotplate in the kitchen. And so you never told what happened, not once, not even on the night you were physically sick, doing it in the bed because you were afraid to attract his attention by going across to the bathroom.

When *he* did these things, all you could do was lie there with your eyes tightly shut and pretend not to know what was happening on the other side of the bedroom wall, and cling on to the knowledge of the house where the will o' the wisps danced. One day you would find that house.

CHAPTER THREE

Lucy thought it was grotesque for the sun to shine at a funeral. Funerals ought only to happen in the pouring rain, so that the weather became part of the misery and the dreariness. It would not be any use trying to explain this to Edmund, of course.

Still, at least he was putting on some kind of hospitality after the service, although he would probably measure the sherry with a thimble. He had told Lucy on the phone that he was still searching for the title deeds to the house, and also for the will.

'Is there a will?' said Lucy in the sepulchral tones of one of their elderly great-aunts who, with true Victorian relish for all things funereal and fiscal, unfailingly asked this question whenever anyone died. But Edmund had no sense of the absurd, and he merely said that of course there would be a will and it would eventually turn up. He would see Lucy at twelve o'clock sharp, he said, and they had better drive to the church together. Lucy thought that by the time she arrived Edmund would have found the deeds and the will, and have everything else filed and indexed and colour-coded.

She was taking along a copy of Jenny Joseph's poem, *Warning*, hoping that there could be a reading of it. 'When I am an old woman I shall wear purple/With a red hat which doesn't go . . .'

It was purest Aunt Deborah, and Lucy thought Deb would have liked it read today. She would ask Edmund about it when she got to the church; she thought she might manage to read it herself if no one else would, although she might dissolve in floods of tears halfway through. But Deb would not have minded that.

Edmund was certainly not going to let Lucy or anyone else read some outlandish modern rubbish today. They were going to have a proper decent service, with Bach for the music, a reading from the New Testament, and 'The Lord is My Shepherd' and 'Praise my Soul the King of Heaven' for the hymns. It had all been arranged with the vicar, and it would all be very tasteful and entirely suitable.

'Oh, very,' said Lucy, and Edmund looked at her sharply because she had almost sounded sarcastic. Still, at least she was dressed more or less conventionally; Edmund had had a bad few moments last night visualizing the kind of outfit Lucy might wear today. But it was all right; she had on some kind of silk two-piece which he had to admit looked very well-cut and also very expensive. It was not black, but it was suitably dark – a deep rich brown, the colour of an old mahogany table. It made her hair look very nearly auburn, and if you bothered to notice such things you might say it emphasized her good figure as well, not that Edmund was really noticing such things on the day of Deborah's funeral. And now that he looked at Lucy again, he had to say it was a pity she had added that trailing tortoiseshell-coloured scarf to the outfit.

A lot of people thought Lucy was very attractive – my word, they said, that Lucy Trent, what a stunner! All that hair and those eyes – very sexy. It was to be hoped no one thought this today because it was hardly acceptable to look sexy at a funeral, although to be fair Lucy had pinned her unruly hair up into a chignon.

Everyone had been invited to Deborah's house after the service, of course. This was what you did at funerals, and although there were not many actual relatives from Deborah's side, there were Lucy's father's people, and also Edmund's own side of the family. They had all had to be asked and most of them accepted, and it had added up to quite a lot. Edmund had called in a contract cleaning firm to sweep and scour and polish so that everywhere would be spick and span. A small local caterer had delivered sandwiches and rolls and wedges of veal and ham pie a short while ago.

Before leaving he had checked the house one final time to make sure that everything was satisfactory. Yes, the rooms were clean and bright and pleasantly scented with furniture polish; there were fresh towels and soap in the first-floor bathroom and the little downstairs cloakroom, and the food was neatly laid out in the dining room, covered with clingfilm to keep it fresh. Plates were stacked at one end of the big table, and the caterers had provided two large urns, one of tea and one of coffee. There was also sherry and madeira for those who wanted it. All very civilized and correct, and people would tell one another that you had to admit Edmund Fane always did things properly. Elderly aunts would kiss him effusively – poor dear Edmund who had been so devoted to Deborah – and uncles would gruffly shake his hand.

He had set Aunt Deborah's jewellery out on a little table downstairs, and he was going to ask the ladies in the family to each choose a piece as a keepsake. ('How thoughtful,' the aunts would say, pleased.) There were some really lovely amber beads that Lucy might like – amber was expensive these days and it did not date. Edmund suddenly had an image of Lucy wearing the amber beads with her hair cascading over her bare shoulders . . . And firelight washing over her body . . . He pushed this image firmly away, and rearranged the pieces of jewellery more neatly.

Crispin would be present today, of course, although he would dim some of that charm because he knew how to suit the manner to the occasion. He would be deferential to the older ladies – the aunts and Aunt Deborah's friends, who all loved him – and he would be man-to-man with the younger men, and extremely polite to the younger females. Everything would be perfectly all right. Most of the people who were coming were family or long-standing friends, and there would be no surprises.

But there was a surprise, and it came shortly after the funeral.

People were dispersing from the graveside and there was the customary slightly over-eager, goodwill-to-all-men atmosphere that pervades any after-funeral assembly. The aunts were telling one another what a nice service it had been, but oh dear, poor Deborah, who would have thought – and at her age, because she had not really been as old as all that when you counted up . . . The sprinkling of men who were there hoped they would be given a decent drink; Edmund Fane was a bit tight-fisted, in fact he was downright penny-pinching. Probably it would be viewed with disapproval if some of them nipped down to the White Hart, would it . . . ? Oh well.

With the unpredictability of English weather, clouds had already started to gather, and the rain that Lucy had thought should accompany the proceedings began just as everyone was setting off for the parked cars, flurrying people into searching for umbrellas and scarves. Elderly ladies were helped along the wet path and sorted into the various vehicles, and there was much talk of soon being at the house where it would be warm.

Lucy, who had dashed back to retrieve someone's gloves, saw Edmund helping people into his car; she saw him turn to look for her, and then to indicate that he would come back to collect her in about fifteen minutes. Lucy waved back to tell him not to bother because there were enough cars around for her to get a lift to the house. She delivered the errant gloves to their owner, who was an elderly great-aunt, and then helped her along to the car she was travelling in.

'We'll see you at the house, Lucy, will we?' said the aunt, getting carefully into the remaining passenger seat of an already-crowded car.

'Yes, of course.'

'Do tell me, dear,' said the aunt, lowering her voice. 'Is there a will?'

'I believe,' said Lucy gravely, 'that it's missing.'

'Missing? How dreadful.'

The car drove off, the aunt twittering happily to the others about the missing will, and it was only after they had gone that Lucy realized all the other cars had left as well. She muttered an oath quite unsuited to the occasion and the surroundings, scooted back to the sketchy shelter of the lychgate, and foraged in her bag for her mobile phone. Or had she left it in her own car, parked at Aunt Deb's house? Damn and *blast*, yes she had!

They would realize what had happened, of course, and somebody would drive back to the church for her, but it might be a while before that happened, and in the meantime the rain was coming down in torrents. Lucy was just wondering if she could sprint back to the church and find the rector to ask to use his phone, when she saw a man coming around the side of the church, his coat collar turned up. He stopped at the sight of Lucy, hesitated, and then came towards her.

'Are you stranded?'

'It looks like it. I was part of the funeral, but there seems to have been a mix-up over the cars.'

'Deborah Fane's funeral? I could give you a lift to the house.' He was thin-faced with dark brown hair and expressive eyes and hands.

'Could you? I mean, are you going there anyway?'

'I wasn't especially going, but I can take you. I know where the house is. My car's parked in the lane over there.'

Lucy had no idea who he was, but he had a nice voice. He was probably somebody local; a teacher from the local school or one of the village's doctors.

'Funerals are always harrowing, aren't they?' said her companion as they drove off. 'Even for the elderly, and especially when they hand you all that ghastliness about resurrection and only having gone into another room to await friends.'

This was so precisely in tune with Lucy's own sentiments that she said, without thinking, 'And that panacea they always offer about, not dead, merely sleeping. That's quite grisly if you interpret it literally. Um – I'm Lucy Trent, by the way. Deborah Fane was my aunt.'

'Do you read Edgar Allen Poe by any chance, Ms Trent?'

Lucy smiled involuntarily. 'Today I wanted to read a modern poem about a lovely dotty old lady who got a kick out of being old and dotty.'

'Was it called *Warning* by any chance?'

'Yes, it was! Aunt Deborah would have adored it, but my cousin Edmund thought it wasn't suitable.'

'I met your aunt a few times,' he said. 'And I think you're right that she'd have liked the poem. Oh – I'm Michael Sallis. I'm from a Charity called CHARTH. Charity for Rehabilitating Teenagers made Homeless, if you want the whole thing. We pick them up off the streets, dust them down, teach them a few basic social skills, and then turn them loose again, mostly on a wing and a prayer. Sometimes it works, sometimes it doesn't.'

'Was CHARTH one of Aunt Deb's pet charities? I know she had a couple of particular favourites. She used to do quite a lot of voluntary work.'

'I don't know about voluntary work,' said Michael Sallis. 'But she left her house to us. That's why I wanted to come to her funeral. As a courtesy.' He clearly sensed her shock, and took his eyes off the road for long enough to look at her. 'Didn't you know about the house? I assumed you would.'

'I didn't know,' said Lucy, staring at him. 'And I've got a feeling my cousin Edmund didn't, either.'

Edmund certainly had not known, and he was very much inclined to question this stranger, this Michael Sallis who had turned up, cool as a cat, and who appeared to consider himself Deborah Fane's main beneficiary. Well, all right, not himself precisely, but his company or charity, or whatever it called itself.

But people did not blithely make over their entire properties to tinpot charities, ignoring their own families, and Deborah Fane would certainly not have done so. CHARTH, for goodness' sake! An outlandish name for a charity if ever Edmund had heard one. What did it stand for? Was it properly registered? He, Edmund, had never heard of it, and it would not surprise him to find that this Michael Sallis was nothing but an adventurer. It would not surprise him to find that there had been undue pressure, either. This would have to be looked into very carefully.

Still, the conventions had to be observed, and Edmund beat down his anger and took Sallis into the small downstairs study. The subdued murmur of the funeral party was still going on across the hall; it was infuriating to remember that he ought to be out there, handing round drinks, talking to people, gracefully accepting sympathy. Being admired for his control and his efficiency at such a time.

Michael Sallis said, 'I'm extremely sorry about your aunt's death, Mr Fane. I only knew her slightly but I liked her very much. As a matter of fact I spoke to her on the phone only a few days before she died.'

'About the homeless teenagers?'

Michael Sallis took that one straight. 'Yes. She was very interested in CHARTH's work. I only meant to attend the service today, though. But then your cousin Lucy missed her lift outside the church, so I drove her here and she asked me to come in for a drink.'

So it was 'Lucy', was it! And on five minutes' acquaintance! Edmund said coldly, 'I suppose this bequest is all in order?'

Michael Sallis's cool grey eyes met Edmund's angry blue ones. 'Oh yes,' he said. 'Perfectly in order. But this is hardly the time to discuss the legalities, is it?'

And now the man was putting Edmund in the wrong, and on Edmund's own terrain as well! Arrogance, you see!

'Quite,' said Edmund, and added offhandedly that he dared say there was no objection to his having given out some pieces of his aunt's jewellery to various members of the family. Only a few trinkets, really.

'I suppose that strictly speaking there ought to be a probate inventory before anything's actually taken,' said Michael Sallis. 'But that's your terrain, more than mine. I do know that it's only the bricks and mortar that are left to us, though.'

Well, of course Edmund knew there should be a probate inventory, but he had not bothered to get one because he had assumed everything was coming to him. But he could not actually say this, so he merely said, frostily, that if Sallis would leave a card, they could be in touch in the next week or so. After probate was obtained.

'Yes, certainly. I'll give you our legal department's direct number, as well.'

So it was not such a tinpot set-up after all. This annoyed Edmund even further, and he remarked that it was all very unexpected of his aunt. Of course, elderly widows were given to such enthusiasms, most people knew that.

Sallis looked at him thoughtfully for a moment, and then said, 'Mrs Fane asked a lot of very searching questions about our work. About exactly how we would make use of the house if she decided to leave it to us. It was all quite carefully tied up.' He paused, and then said, 'I wish I had known her better than I did; she was a remarkable lady. It must have been an immense shock to you when she died so suddenly.'

Edmund said, in his silkiest, politest voice of all, 'Yes. Yes, it was a great shock. But everyone has to die some time.'

Everyone has to die some time.

Even though Deborah had been over seventy, Edmund was very glad to know that he had not fumbled or bungled things. A swift, painless death, it had been. Anything else would have felt almost discourteous.

'Of *course* you wouldn't have fumbled it,' Crispin had said, afterwards. 'A gentleman to the last,' he had added, smiling the secret smile that Edmund always found so fascinating, and that he thought – hoped! – no one but himself ever saw.

Nobody had suspected anything wrong about Deborah's death, and even if they had, they would not have dreamed that respectable Mr Fane would have . . .

Go on, say it.

Would have committed murder.

Murder. An old, old word that had smeared its bloody pawprints on the history of humankind. A word whose dark origins derived partly from the Middle English word, *murther*, taken from the Old English *morthor*. Akin to the Old High German word, *mord*.

No one would have suspected trustworthy, reliable Edmund Fane capable of committing *mord*.

The post-mortem on Deborah Fane had been held within a couple of days – that was one of the advantages of living in such a small place, of course – and the conclusion was a myocardial infarct. Sudden and fatal heart attack. Perhaps there had been a slight puzzlement on the part of Deborah's GP, who had told Edmund that apart from the angina which they were controlling well with the medication – oh, and a touch of arthritis – Mrs Fane had been in fairly good general health. But then he had said, oh well, you could not always predict when a heart was about to give way. Still, she would be a great loss to everyone who had known her.

'She's a great loss to me,' said Edmund sadly. 'I shall miss her very much.'

CHAPTER FOUR

Short of the occasional domestic disaster – 'Water pouring through *all* the bedroom ceilings, Edmund, and I cannot get a plumber to come out before *Thursday*!' – Aunt Deborah had hardly ever phoned Edmund at the office.

'I don't believe in intruding into business hours, Edmund, dear,' she had always said. 'It's important to respect a person's place of work, and you have clients to consider.'

It had been a surprise, therefore, to hear her voice, shortly after nine fifteen one morning. Edmund had been engrossed in the complexities of a boundary plan relating to a right-of-way dispute for a farmer, and he had just been brought his coffee; he liked a cup while he looked through his morning's post and generally arranged his day. Decent coffee, of course; he could not bear the instant powdered stuff. He had bought and installed a good filter machine for the office, and he paid for properly ground coffee and fragrant Earl Grey tea. Considerate Mr Fane, such a generous employer. He did not expect his staff to swill the stuff indiscriminately, though. Two cups of coffee in the morning and two cups of tea in the afternoon were enough for anyone. If his staff wanted more than that, they could bring their own.

Into the phone he said, 'Good morning, Aunt Deborah.'

'I tried to reach you last evening,' said Aunt Deb, without preamble.

'I was at a Law Society dinner.'

'Oh, I see. Well now, listen. Lucy phoned me at the weekend.'

'How is Lucy?'

'She's perfectly fine except for that wretched neighbour who sings rugby songs in his bath – I do *wish* she wouldn't live in that crazy flat! – but I haven't phoned you to talk about that, Edmund. I've phoned you because Lucy's been approached by a woman called Trixie Smith.'

'Yes?' Edmund spoke rather absently, his attention still being more than three-quarters on the farmer's assertion that not a soul had walked the alleged right of way for seven years.

'This Trixie Smith – are you listening, Edmund? You sound very vague, I hope you haven't got a hangover. Your father was always much too fond of a drink, and you don't want to go the way he went— Anyway, this Trixie Smith is a teacher somewhere in North London, but she's been studying for a doctoral thesis, and she wants to use the Ashwood murders as a main case study.'

The quiet, well-ordered office blurred for a moment, and Edmund had to take a deep breath before replying. Then he said, 'Oh, not again. It only needs it to be the anniversary of the murders or for somebody to resurrect one of Lucretia's films, and they come crawling out of the woodwork. You aren't going to do anything about this one, are you?'

'Yes, I am,' said Deborah. 'I've already phoned Ms Smith, as a matter of fact.'

'You have?'

'Yes. Rather an odd-sounding person. Abrupt. I said I didn't know how much help I could give, but you know, Edmund, I was in my teens at the time of the Ashwood murders, so I remember quite a lot about it. Ms Smith – they all like to be called "Ms" these days, don't they? – says she'd like to talk to me about

Lucretia.' It was typical of Deborah that she never referred to Lucretia as 'mother'; or perhaps, thought Edmund, that was due to Lucretia herself.

He said, 'She'll be a sensation-seeker, that's all.'

'I don't think she is,' said Aunt Deb. 'She wants to talk about all the people involved in the Ashwood case, not just Lucretia. I was there that day, and so—'

This time the room did not just blur, it tilted as well, and Edmund had to grasp the edges of the desk to stop himself from falling. From out of the dizziness, he heard his voice say, 'I didn't know you were actually there when – on the day it happened. You never told me that.'

'Didn't I? But I used to go to the studios with Lucretia sometimes – you knew that.'

'Yes, but . . . Don't you think,' said Edmund after a moment, 'that it might upset you to talk about it all? I mean – Lucretia's death and everything . . . Won't it be dreadfully painful?'

'Oh, not at this distance,' said Deborah. 'It all feels as if it happened to someone else. You'll understand that when you're older, Edmund.'

A pulse was beating inside Edmund's head, each hammer-blow landing painfully on the exact same spot, rapping out a maddening little rhythm against his senses, over and over. *She-was-at-Ashwood-that-day, she-was-at-ASHWOOD* . . . said this infuriating rhythm. *She was there when it happened, she was THERE* . . .

He forced himself to take several deep breaths, but the pulsating hammer blows continued. *What-did-she-see . . . ?* they said. *What-did-she-see-that-day-at-Ashwood . . . At ASHWOOD . . . ?*

'And it isn't as if any of this is going to be published and made into a best-seller or anything like that,' Deborah was saying. 'It's a – a scholarly thing that Miss Smith's going to write. She'll be dealing mostly with the psychological aspects.'

'How very modern of her.'

'Don't be sarcastic, Edmund, it doesn't suit you. I suppose you ate too much rich food at the Law Society dinner last night and it's given you indigestion: it always did make you disagreeable, indigestion . . . '

'I do not have indigestion—'

'. . . a good dose of Andrew's liver salts, that's what you need. If you haven't got any you'd better get some on your way home tonight. So now, here's the thing: I'm almost sure Trixie Smith is genuine, but I thought it might be better if you made the call setting up the meeting. You wouldn't mind doing that, would you? She's perfectly agreeable to driving up here at the weekend, and I can give her some lunch while we talk. But just in case she has got a – what d'you call it? – a hidden agenda, I thought a call from a solicitor would let her know that I'm not some half-witted old dear, all on my own.'

'Nobody would ever call you half-witted,' said Edmund automatically, and without warning the pulse stopped. An enormous silence flooded the inside of his head, and he saw, quite clearly, what he must do. From out of this huge silence, his voice said, quite calmly, very nearly absent-mindedly, 'Still, now that you mention it, it would be quite a good idea for me to make the call. Give me the number and I'll ring now. Or – no, wait a moment, I'm going out to a client's house later this afternoon, and I'll be driving past the end of your lane. How about if I call in and phone from your house? I'd rather do that; they're such a gossipy lot here, and if anyone overheard—'

Deborah said certainly they did not want any of Edmund's staff to hear such a conversation, not even that nice secretary who was so very reliable, or the good-looking young man who looked after the conveyancing work. If Edmund was not expected anywhere later, perhaps he would like to stay on to supper, she said.

'That's an offer I can't refuse,' said Edmund and rang off.

It was important to remain perfectly calm and not to give way to nerves, although Edmund thought he might have been forgiven for doing just that; you did not expect to be confronted with the dangerous resurrecting of your family's ghosts while reading your day's post, and you certainly did not expect those ghosts to come packaged, so to speak, with warnings about indigestion and a throwaway remark concerning the infamous *locus in quo* of a murder.

(*She-was-there* . . . said his mind, starting up its maddening tattoo again. *Deborah-was-there . . . What-did-she-see . . . ?)*

As he drove to the house Edmund's mind was working furiously. There must be no investigations of the Ashwood case – no prying researches so that some unknown female could write MA after her name, no books written by sensation-seeking chroniclers, no idle delvings by anorak-garbed enthusiasts, or journalists constructing Fifty-Years-Ago features . . .

There must be no elderly ladies growing garrulous with increasing age, reliving memories, talking about the past to anyone who might listen.

The past . . .

The truth about Ashwood's past must never surface, no matter the cost.

Tea and scones were set out for Edmund with the slightly slapdash generosity that had always characterized Aunt Deborah's hospitality.

Edmund, accepting the cup of tea, said, 'What I think I'd better say to this woman is that . . . Oh, keep still a moment, Aunt Deborah – there's a spider crawling on your neck—' He set down the cup and went over to her chair.

'Ugh, how horrid – flick it off for me, Edmund, you know how I loathe spiders—'

There was no spider, of course; what there was, brought into the house in Edmund's pocket and now carefully concealed in his hand, was a hypodermic syringe, unobtrusively taken from a medicine cabinet years earlier, when Deborah Fane's husband had had to be given intravenous injections of heparin and nitroglycerin for his failing heart by a nurse who came in every day. Edmund had taken the syringe after William Fane died, and had kept it at the back of a drawer in his own house. You never knew what might come in useful; Crispin had instilled that in Edmund shortly after that last university term, and it was a good maxim.

Carefully kept, as well, had been the memory of a conversation with the nurse, who had still been called a district nurse because people were old-fashioned in this part of the world. You had to be very careful with intravenous injections, she had said, that was why she had to come in each morning. The syringe had to be correctly filled, so that you did not inject air into a main vein and risk causing an embolism.

Embolism?

Air bubble in the system, said the nurse, rather flattered to be sought out and talked to by Mr and Mrs Fane's attractive nephew, pleased at being able to impart information. Mostly the body could adjust to a small air bubble and absorb it, but if you introduced a big enough pocket of air into one of the large veins – the femoral vein, say, or the jugular – that pocket of air could travel to the heart inside of a couple of minutes, and the heart would stop. The nurse had noticed that it was a murder method sometimes utilized by writers of whodunnits. It was probably not quite as cut-and-dried as the books made out, but the principle was perfectly sound. Hadn't Dorothy L. Sayers used it in a book?

Edmund had said, with polite regret, that he did not read detective books – 'Too busy studying, you know' – and the nurse went off thinking what a charming young man he was, so obviously grateful to the relatives who had been so kind to him. She wondered if he had a girlfriend at university. Or he might be gay, of course; the really nice-looking ones often were. Ah, well.

Edmund did not read detective books, but he could and did read the encyclopaedia, and he had looked up embolism at the next opportunity. Sure enough, there it was.

'Embolism, from the Greek, *embolos*, meaning stopper or plug. Obstruction of a blood vessel by material which has been carried along in the bloodstream. Commonest cause is detachment of a blood-clot, portions of growths on heart valve, pieces of tumours, fat, masses of bacteria, and in some instances, air bubbles . . .'

Air bubbles. Airlock in the system, just as the nurse had described it. The same thing you sometimes got in a car or a central heating system, bringing the car or the heating system to a full stop. Bringing the human body to a full stop . . . ? That was how it sounded. Introduce a big enough bubble of air into one of the large veins – for instance by jabbing in an empty hypodermic syringe and pressing the plunger – and the chances were that death, swift, painless, silent, undetectable death, would result within minutes. That was interesting. It was something to tuck into your mind and remember. One day it might be necessary to find out if it really did work.

It had worked that afternoon all right. As Edmund pressed the hypodermic's plunger, Deborah Fane had given a little gasp, as if of surprise, and then her head had fallen forward. Edmund stared down at her, and after a moment felt for a pulse at the base of her throat, and then beneath her ear. Nothing. But let's be absolutely sure: this was not a time to take risks or make assumptions. He felt for a heartbeat. Nothing. She was dead, the embolism thing had happened, and presently Edmund would phone the local GP, slightly panic-stricken at coming in to find dear Aunt Deborah apparently dead in her armchair.

The tiny pinprick on Deborah Fane's neck had not even been noticed, because no one had thought there was anything that needed noticing. Aunt Deb's angina, a known and existing condition, had already taken the pathologist three-quarters of the way to a verdict of heart failure caused by a severe angina attack. In reality, it had been *murther* – the Old English *morthor* – but no one had realized this. Edmund had not really expected that anyone would, but it was still gratifying to know that he had not overlooked anything, and that he had foreseen everything.

He had not, it was true, foreseen that the house would be willed to Michael Sallis's absurd charity, and he did find it sad that Aunt

Deborah had not told him about this. Edmund had thought there had been better trust between them – it just went to show you could not rely on anyone. But losing the house was not disastrous, and it would take a few weeks for probate to be granted so there was plenty of time for Edmund to make a thorough and orderly search of the house – several thorough and orderly searches in fact – to assure himself that there was nothing incriminating anywhere.

Still, as he moved about the empty rooms after the mourners had left, he realized that he was constantly glancing over his shoulder as if he expected to see Aunt Deborah watching him from a doorway, her head twisted a little to one side where he had jabbed the hypodermic in . . .

Sheer nerves, that was all.

*

The shameful ghosts from the early years in Pedlar's Yard did not often return, but when they did they always brought back the old fear and the memories of all the nights spent shivering under bedclothes, helpless with fear and misery and despair. How did I stand it for so long?

The fear had not always been there. To start with it had only been a question of avoiding the anger and the drunkenness – and of escaping from the belt with the hurting buckle which was sometimes used on your back and which was used on Mother more often than anyone ever knew. She had never complained, and she had never told anyone about it because there had not been anyone to tell. In those days – it had been the early 1970s – and in that environment, there had not been such things as battered wives' refuges, or brisk, well-meaning social workers, or even telephone numbers that could provide help. In any case, the Pedlar's Yard house did not have a telephone. And Mother had had an odd streak of stubbornness. When you married, she said, you exchanged vows, and vows ought not to be broken. Your father married me when no one else wanted me and I was grateful. (And he was very charming when he was younger . . .)

But Mother had made that other promise as well – the promise that one day they would escape from Pedlar's Yard, just the two of them.

'You do mean it, don't you? We'll really go there one day? To the house with the lady from the stories?'

'Yes. Yes, one day we really will go there.'

But Mother had hesitated – she had quite definitely hesitated, before replying, and a new fear presented itself. 'She is real, isn't she, that lady? I mean . . . you didn't make her up?' Mother was good at telling stories; once she had said she might have written books if she had not got married.

But it was all right. She was smiling, and saying, 'No, I didn't make her up, I promise. She's real, and she lives exactly where I told you. Look, I'll show you—'

'What? *What?*' It might be a photograph, which would be just about the most brilliant thing in the world.

But it was not a photograph, it was a letter, just very short, just saying here was a cheque.

'But there's the address at the top. You see? The Priest's House, Mowbray Fen. That's a real address.'

'She sent a cheque?' Cheques represented money in some complex, barely understood grown-up way.

'Yes, she does it quite often. Does that convince you that she's real?'

'I think so. Yes. Only real people can send cheques, can't they?'

'Of course.'

So that was all right. The lady was real and the house was real, and one day they would make a proper plan and escape.

It had been too late to escape on the night that *he* erupted into the house, his eyes fiery with drink. He was not an especially big man, although he was quite tall, but he seemed to fill up the house with his presence on these nights.

There had not been a chance to make for one of the safer hiding places – the old wash-house or even the cupboard under the stairs – so there were only the sheets and the thin coverlet for protection. Sometimes, though, it was possible to force your mind away from the shabby bedroom and away from Pedlar's Yard, and to delve down and down into the layers of memories and dreams . . . Like summoning a spell, a charm, that took you along a narrow unwinding ribbon of road, studded with trees and lined with hedgerows, and through the little villages with the Hobbit-like names that were strung out along the road like beads on a necklace . . . Far, far away, until you reached the house on the marshes, where the will o' the wisps danced.

But tonight the charm did not work. Tonight something was happening downstairs that made that dreamlike road unreachable. Something was happening in the little sitting-room at the back of the house that was making Mother cry out and say, 'No – please not—'

There was the sickening sound of a fist thudding flesh, and a gasp of pain, instantly cut off. Oh God, oh God, it was going to be one of the nights when he was hitting her: one of the nights when the neighbours would listen through the wall, and tell each other that one night that cruel monster would kill that poor woman, and someone ought to do something.

One night he would kill her. What if this was the night? What if Mother died, down there on the sitting-room floor? The horror of this very real possibility rose up chokingly. Someone ought to do something . . .

I can't. I *can't*. He'd kill me.

But what if he kills her?

There were ten stairs down to the sitting-room and they creaked a bit, but it was possible to jump over the third and then the seventh stair so that they did not creak at all. It was important to jump over those stairs tonight, and it was important to go stealthily down the little passage from the front of the house to the back, not noticing how cold the floor was against bare feet. It was important to open the door very quietly and peer inside without being heard. Because someone ought to do something, and there was no one else . . .

The room was filled with the tinny firelight from the electric fire, and shadows moved in an incomprehensible rhythm across the walls. They were huge shadows and it took a moment to sort them out because at first it seemed as if there was one monstrous creature, sprawling across the little gateleg table under the window . . . There was harsh rasping breathing in the room as well, like someone running very fast, or like someone sobbing and struggling . . .

The shadows moved again, and it was not one person, but two: two people fastened together, the larger shadow almost swallowing the thin frail one.

Mother was half-lying on the small sofa, her hair tumbled about her face – she had nice hair, dark and smooth – and her skirt pushed up to her waist. Her legs were bare and *he* was standing right up against her, pushing his body into her – pushing it in and then out and then in and then out, over and over, the muscles of his thighs and buttocks clenching and unclenching, his face twisted with concentration and with savage pleasure.

You did not grow up in Pedlar's Yard and not know what men did to women in bed – or what they did in the backs of cars and vans, or up against the walls of the alleyways. This, then, was what the playground sniggers were about: it was what some of the older children at school whispered and giggled over, and boasted of having done, or having nearly done.

Neither of them had heard the door pushed open, so it would be possible to creep back upstairs unheard. But Mother was gasping with pain, and her mouth was swollen and bruised, and bleeding from a cut on one side, and what if this really was the night he killed her? The firelight was showing up angry red marks across her face from where she had been hit – they would turn blue tomorrow, those marks, and she would not go out of the house until they faded so that no one would know. (But what if she was no longer alive tomorrow to go anywhere . . . ?)

He had moved back now, swearing at Mother, calling her useless, and shouting that she could not even give a man a hard-on these days. He was not shouting; he was speaking in a cold hating voice, and his eyes were cold and hating as well, the way they always were on these nights, and he was nearly, but not quite, ridiculous, with his trousers discarded and the shirt flapping around his thighs.

'That's because you're too pissed to fuck anything tonight!' Mother's voice was thick with crying and anger, but it was stronger and shriller than it had ever been before, and there was a stab of shock at hearing her use words like *fuck* and *pissed*, even though they were words people did use in Pedlar's Yard. For a truly dreadful moment, Mother was no longer the quiet familiar person who spun stories and talked about one day escaping. She was a screaming red-eyed animal – a rat – no, a shrew, like in the play at school! – and she was clawing and yelling at Father for all she was worth, and she was ugly – *ugly!* – and as well as that she was also suddenly and confusingly frightening . . .

'Get off me, you useless bastard,' she screamed. 'Get off me and let me get out of this place for good and all!'

She pushed him away so that he stumbled back and that was when he saw the half-open door. Before there was time to dodge into the little hall, he had already crossed the room and he was reaching out. His hands were rough and there were callouses on them because he worked all day shifting loads on to lorries in the yards. He hated his work – in some incomprehensible way he was bitter about having to work at all.

He was saying that snooping children had to be taught lessons – they had to be taught not to snoop – and then there was the feeling of his hands – hard and strong – and he was reaching for the leather belt with the buckle . . .

That was when Mother moved across the room, one hand raised above her head, the light turning her eyes to red like a rat's. But she's not a rat, she's not . . . Yes, she is, because I can see her claws . . .

They were not really claws but they were glittering points of something hard and cruel, turned to red by the fire . . .

Scissors from the sewing basket by the hearth.

The points flashed down and *he* threw up his hands to protect himself, but it was too late, because Mother was too quick.

The scissors came glinting down and where his eyes had been were the steel circles of the scissors' handles.

The points of the scissors had punctured both his eyes.

CHAPTER FIVE

Incredibly, it did not kill him. He stumbled backwards with a bellow of pain, the handles of the scissors still sticking out of his face. Blood ran down his cheeks, a thick dark dribble, mingling with a watery fluid where his eyes had burst and were leaking all down his face. The sickness came rushing back at the sight of it.

He was trying to pluck the scissors out – one hand was already feeling for them – and then he found them and with a terrible animal grunt he pulled them out. There was a wet sucking sound – dreadful! – and then another of the cries of pain, but the blades came out, and more blood welled up and spilled over.

Mother had backed away to the wall. There was blood on her knuckles from where she had driven the scissors home, but she was watching the blind, blood-smeared face and it was impossible to know if she was horrified or frightened, or what she was feeling at all.

The mutilated head was turning from side to side – after what had been done to him, was it possible he could still *see*? No, of course he could not. He was going by sound, by smell, by instinct. He knew Mother was still in the room, and he was going to smell her out like dogs did. Could humans do that? Oh God, yes, he's starting to move across the room, and he's holding the scissors over his head, and I must do something, *I must do something* . . .

But it was like being inside a nightmare. It was impossible to move, and it was impossible to call out a warning because the words would not come out, just as words would sometimes not come out in a nightmare, no matter how hard you tried.

And now he had reached Mother and he was grabbing her arm, lifting the dripping scissors over his head with his other hand. Curses streamed from his mouth – you could almost see the words coming out, wet with the blood and the eye-fluid . . . Kill you, kill you, bitch, murdering bitch-cunt, and then kill the child as well, kill both of you . . .

She was fighting him off, clawing at his face – yes, her hands *were* like claws! – but he had too strong a grip. The two of them fought and struggled, and just when it seemed that Mother was about to push him away, he brought the scissors flashing down, stabbing them deep into her neck. The blood spurted out at once, like a tap turned full on, splashing the floor and the walls, and Mother was crumpling to the floor, a look of surprise on her face.

Time seemed to run down and stop completely, so that it might have been hours or only minutes before there was a wet rattling sound in Mother's throat, and she fell forward. Dead? Yes, of course she was dead, it did not need a second look to know it. Like a light going out. Like something collapsing deep inside.

The man standing over her remained absolutely still: it was impossible to know if he was recovering his strength or fighting his own pain. Then the terrible *listening* movement came back. He turned his head from side to side, and the dreadful face with the two wet, bloodied sockets seemed to search the room. He's still holding the scissors! He pulled them out of her neck, and he's *still holding them*! And now that he's killed her, he's searching for *me*!

The realization brought a fresh wash of terror. He's mad with pain, but he's still as cunning and as brutal as ever. And he's searching for me because I saw what he did. If he can get me, he'll kill me so that I can't tell people he's a murderer.

There was surely nothing easier than escaping from the murderous hands of a man whose eyes had been destroyed. It was the kind of thing people made jokes about: a blind man on a galloping horse would never see that, they said. Or they said that something was about as much use as a blind man in a coal-hole on a dark night.

But when you are eight years old, and when the two outside doors of your house are locked, the escape tips over into a macabre cat-and-mouse game. It begins with the need to move silently across the room, trying not to make any sound at all – quenching a shudder when you step in a slippery patch of blood – and then slipping out into the dark little hall beyond. Had he heard that? Had he sensed the movement – perhaps felt the cold breath of air from the opening of the door? Yes, he was following – there he was, horridly silhouetted against the red glow from the electric fire, already starting to feel his way along the passage to the stairs. He knows the hiding places, of course. He knows about the cupboard under the stairs, and he knows about the little space between the kitchen and the old wash-house . . .

But he can't see them any longer. And he must be in agony – surely he won't be able to search for very long? So where would be safest to hide? The stairs – yes, the cramped cupboard under the stairs with the smothering smell of old raincoats . . . I can close the door tightly and fold up into a tiny creature, as if I'm not really there at all . . . He'll go past the door because he won't know exactly where it is, so I'll be perfectly safe. He'll grope his way into the kitchen and once he's done that I can be down the hall and I can unlock the front door and be outside . . .

The front door. It would be locked and the keys would be upstairs, on the chest of drawers in the front bedroom, where they were always kept. Then I've got to get upstairs and get them, and come back down and unlock the door. Panic rose up, because it surely could not be done without being caught.

The door of the stair-cupboard was jerked back, and the blinded face appeared in the opening. The blood was still wet on the cheeks, but a crust had started to form over both eyes, and it was still a nightmare thing, that head, it was still something to shrink from and scream, only a scream must not happen because it would give the hiding place away. *I'm-not-here, I'm-not-here* . . .

A hand came reaching out, groping in the little space, so that it was necessary to shrink right back against the wall and to stop breathing so that he would not hear . . . Please don't let him find me. Please don't let him know I'm here . . .

The raincoats swished around and the world shrank to the tiny damp-smelling cupboard, and to the nightmare face. And then – oh, thank you God, thank you! – the head moved back and the cupboard door swung in again, and the shuffling footsteps went stumbling down the two stone steps into the kitchen. I ought to feel sorry for him, but I don't, I *don't*! And if I can get upstairs and snatch up the keys, I can be out of the door and away. Yes, but where to? Where is 'away'?

Again there was the rush of panic, and then, like the unfolding of a secret, like the soft, silken drawing back of a curtain, the answer came, and with it a deep delight.

'*She lives in a place called Mowbray Fen*,' Mother had said. '*It's a tiny village on the edge of Lincolnshire. You have to go through Rockingham Forest, and along by Thorney and Witchford until you come within sight of Wicken Fen* . . . '.

Thorney and Witchford and Rockingham Forest. The litany came as easily and as smoothly as ever it had done. The house on the marshes. The house called the Priest's House, whose owners had helped to smuggle priests out of England hundreds of years ago. Could it be found? Would the lady from the stories still be there? How long ago had that letter with the cheque been sent? Months? Years?

At eight years of age there are times when the mind can move with nearly adult precision and clarity, and the instinct for self-preservation is inborn rather than instilled – as strong in a child as it is in an adult. Later, there would be grief for Mother, who ought not to have died, but for now there was only the recognition that to stay here – to summon help from neighbours or from the phone-box at the corner of the street – would mean doctors and policemen and hours upon hours of questions. The truth might be believed, or it might not – *he* might very well manage to shift the blame. But whichever way it went there would either be an order for a care home or a remand home or young offenders' hostel. Children in Pedlar's Yard knew about being taken into care, and they knew about remand homes and hostels as well. And if any of those things happen, I shall never see the marsh house, I shall never see the lady of the stories . . .

Decision made – in fact, there was no decision to make. He's blundering around in the kitchen, and if ever there was a moment to make the attempt, this is it. *Now.* Into the hall, along to the stairs, and straight up them. Remember the two stairs that creak and avoid them . . . Good. Now into *their* bedroom, snatch up the keys. Good again. What about money? To travel anywhere you need money. Would it be stealing to open the tin money-box kept in the chest of drawers, and take whatever was in there? If it is stealing I can't help it. And he's still crashing around downstairs, so there's time.

The money-box held thirty pounds. Was that enough for the journey? It would have to be. And now school satchel from my own bedroom to carry things, and a thick coat and woollen gloves. Toothbrush and comb from the bathroom, but get them quietly – Is that him coming upstairs? No, I'm still safe. Anything else? The money-box was still open on the top of the chest of drawers, and inside it was a brown envelope. Mother had kept important things there. Documents. Birth certificate? You had to show your birth certificate sometimes. Better take it.

The birth certificate was inside the envelope; it was simple enough to fold it carefully, and tuck it into the side of the satchel.

Anything else in there? What about the letter with the address of the Priest's House on it? I ought to take that if it's here. Then she – the lady – will know I'm really who I say I am.

The letter was in the envelope, folded up, a bit creased, but readable. Also in the envelope was a photograph – a small snapshot of Mother and Father together, both of them smiling straight into the camera. There was a moment of absolute rejection of it: I don't ever want to see him again! – but almost instantly was the knowledge that to take the photograph would be like taking a tiny fragment of Mother. And she looks happy – I'd be able to look at her and think of her being happy. The photograph went into the satchel with the birth certificate. And now I'm ready.

The front door had to be unlocked very stealthily indeed, but the key turned quietly enough, and it did so with a soft whisper of sound that said, 'You've escaped!'

At this time of night there was no one about, and it was easy to run to the phone-box. It smelt disgusting, but at least it had not been vandalized like a lot of phone-boxes these days. Dial 999, and ask for an ambulance. And don't worry about sounding panicky – they'd expect a child to sound panicky.

The call was answered at once. 'Emergency – which service do you require?'

'Ambulance, please.'

The space of four heartbeats, and then a different voice. 'Ambulance service.'

'Please – someone's dreadfully hurt. My – father. He's been stabbed – I don't know what to do—'

'What's your name? And your address?'

Pretend not to have heard the first question. Cry a bit. You're allowed to be frightened and confused, remember? 'This is my address.' It came out clearly. 'Please come quickly.' And replace the receiver. Enough? Yes, they would not dare ignore it; ambulance people did not even ignore obvious hoax calls, everyone said so. And the person at the other end had seemed to accept the information as genuine.

So now I'm ready and now I've done everything, and now I'm leaving Pedlar's Yard – horrid, hateful place – for ever. I'm leaving all the bad memories. Later on I'll be sad about Mother, but I can't think about that yet.

Thirty pounds. Enough for a train journey? Would the railway station sell a ticket to a child? Why not? And if a train did not go all the way to Mowbray Fen, there would be buses for the last miles; buses were usually very cheap.

And from now on I am nothing to do with Pedlar's Yard, and I am nothing to do with North London. I am somebody who has a normal life and a normal family, and I'm going to visit my grandmother.

The prospect was exciting and terrifying. It was an adventure like children had in books. It was the four Pevensie children going through the wardrobe into Narnia. Hadn't they eaten apples to survive on one of their adventures? I'll buy apples and eat them like they did. Or I'll buy hamburgers and chips. Nobody looks twice at a child buying chips. And orange juice to drink.

Surely the journey could be managed, and at the other end of it, beyond all those villages with their ancient English names, would be the house surrounded by the will o' the wisp lights that could give you your heart's desire.

And the lady from all the stories would be there.

*

'I don't know if this will be of any help,' said Edmund on the phone. 'But I rather think I've got permission for you to actually go inside Ashwood Studios.'

Trixie Smith sounded as brisk and down-to-earth on the phone as she had face to face. 'Very good of you,' she said. 'Lot of trouble for you as well, especially after your aunt's death. Always a lot to do after a death, I know that. How did you manage it? I was going to see if I could trace the owners, but I didn't know how to go about it.'

'I haven't actually traced the owners, but I have contacted a solicitor who holds the keys,' said Edmund who had, in fact, done this by the simple process of consulting an Ordnance Survey map and then ringing Ashwood's appropriate local council. 'He acts as a kind of agent for the site, and he's just phoned me to say you can have access to the place for a couple of hours.'

'When?'

'Well, that's the thing,' said Edmund slowly. 'The solicitor wants me to be there with you. As a kind of surety for you, I suppose.'

'In case I'm a sensation-seeker, likely to hold a seance on a wet afternoon, or a potential arsonist with a grudge against film studios in general?'

'Your words, not mine, Ms Smith.' Edmund pretended to consult a diary. 'I think I might manage Monday afternoon,' he said, with a take-it-or-leave-it air. 'I could probably get there around four – it's a couple of hours' drive from here, I should think. But nearly all motorway, so it would be straightforward. You said you lived in North London, so you're fairly near the place anyway. Would Monday suit you?'

Trixie said gruffly that Monday afternoon would suit her very well. 'Have to admit I hadn't expected to hear from you, Mr Fane,' she said. 'In fact I thought you were giving me the brush-off that day at your aunt's house.'

'Surely not,' said Edmund politely.

'And I'll reimburse you for your time, of course. Never be beholden, that's my maxim.'

'Oh, that's all right,' said Edmund. 'It'll be quite interesting to see the place, although I gather it's been derelict for years, so I don't know what value it'll be to you.'

'Atmosphere,' said Trixie at once. 'Background details. And you never know, I might even pick up something the police missed.'

'After more than fifty years? Oh really—'

'Why not? History teaches us perspective, Mr Fane, and hindsight gives us twenty-twenty vision. And wouldn't it be satisfying to discover that the baroness wasn't a murderess after all?'

'She wasn't a baroness. The title was just another of the publicity stunts.'

'Even so.'

'Yes,' said Edmund politely. 'Yes, it would be marvellous.'

On the following Monday Edmund gave himself a half day's leave of absence, issued his staff with instructions as to how various clients should be dealt with were they to turn up or phone, and set off. It was barely two o'clock, but it was such a grey rain-sodden afternoon that it was necessary to drive with full head-lights on. This meant he almost missed the Ashwood sign, which was obscured by overgrown hedges. But he saw it just in time and turned off on to a badly maintained B-road, so narrow it was very nearly un-navigable. Edmund winced as the car's suspension protested, and frowned as bushes scratched against the doors and painted sappy green smears on the windscreen.

A couple of miles further on he came to some tall rusting gates, sagging on their hinges but with the legend 'Ashwood Studios' still discernible. Edmund, peering through the car's misted windows, thought he had never seen such a dismal place. Astonishing to think that London was only about twenty minutes' drive from here.

There was a small security guard's booth on the right of the gates, and on the other side were what appeared to be a series of neglected airfields strewn with single-storey, corrugated-roofed buildings. Edmund sat for a moment, the car's engine still ticking over, and stared at the straggling dereliction. So this was Ashwood. This was the place that once upon a time had spun silvered illusions and created celluloid legends.

Trixie Smith was waiting for him, in a weather-beaten estate car. Edmund reached for his umbrella, switched his car's engine off, and shrugged on a quilted rainproof jacket before getting out to walk across to her. She was wearing a long mackintosh that in the damp atmosphere smelt slightly of dogs.

'I hadn't realized it would be quite so tumbledown,' said Edmund, peering through the grey curtain of rain.

'It looks to me,' observed Ms Smith as they plodded across the squelching mud, 'as if the whole lot's about to sink into the mud anyway.'

'It's a mournful place,' agreed the person propped against the inside of the security booth, clearly waiting for them. 'Practically the end of the world, and myself I wouldn't waste petrol on coming here. Still, that's your privilege, and I've brought the keys to let you in as you wanted.' He came out of the sketchy shelter of the booth and introduced himself as Liam Devlin. He was dark and careless-looking, and he looked as if he took the world and its woes very lightly indeed. He also looked as if he might be wearing yesterday's clothes and had not bothered to take them off to go to bed last night.

'I thought,' said Edmund severely, 'that your firm acted as site agents.'

'So we do. But if,' said Mr Devlin, 'you can find a reliable contractor who doesn't mind the ghosts, and who's prepared to tidy this place up and keep it tidied, you'll have done more than I ever could.'

'Ghosts?' said Edmund sharply.

'Lucretia von Wolff. Who else did you think I meant?'

'Oh, I see. You know Ashwood's history, then?'

'Everyone in the western world knows Ashwood's history, Mr Fane. This is the place where the baroness killed two people and then committed suicide.'

'She wasn't a baroness,' said Edmund, who was tired of telling people this.

'You believe the official version, do you?' demanded Trixie of Liam Devlin.

'Isn't it what most people believe?'

'I don't. I've been doing some delving,' said Trixie. 'And I'm becoming less and less convinced of Lucretia's guilt.'

'Is that theory or fantasy, Ms Smith?' Devlin appeared perfectly happy to enter into a discussion in a field in the middle of a rainstorm.

'Neither. The facts are there, and the reports about Alraune fall into a coherent chronological pattern. The birth at the beginning of World War II – the disappearance before the war ended. And,' said Trixie, 'I'm perfectly used to people scoffing at my theories, Mr Devlin, so you needn't raise your eyebrows like that. I'm particularly used to men scoffing. And usually,' added Ms Smith pointedly, 'they're men with inadequacies.'

'Ah. In that case I stand chastened and rebuked.'

'Well, don't stand too long, because if we stay out in this rain any longer we'll all catch pneumonia,' said Edmund crossly. 'How far is Studio Twelve from here? That's the one Ms Smith wants to see.'

Liam glanced at Edmund's shoes, which were leather, and with what Edmund could only feel was a slightly malicious air, said, 'Well, now there's the unfortunate thing. Studio Twelve's on the very far side from here, wouldn't you know it would be.'

'Can't we drive across to it?'

'You can try,' said Liam cordially. 'But in this quagmire you'll probably get bogged down within about ten seconds.' Again there was the faintly mischievous look to where Edmund had parked, as if he found the meticulously polished car rather amusing. 'Come on through the gates and we'll view the terrain, though. They're not locked nowadays, not that there'd be any point because as you can see the hinges have long since rusted away. And they say the gates are always open to those who ask.' He surveyed the rain, and then turned up his coat collar. 'Have we enough umbrellas? Good. Do you believe in ghosts by the way, Mr Fane?'

'Of course not.'

'Do you?' demanded Trixie.

'Not at all,' said Liam cheerfully.

Studio Twelve was a long low building, exactly like all the others, windowless and weather-beaten, with narrow windows that had probably once had screens or shutters, but that had all been firmly boarded up, giving the place a blank, blind appearance.

Edmund was not in the least surprised when they had trouble getting the door to open; he had never seen such a collection of worm-eaten shanties in his life.

'It's only warped by the damp,' said Liam. 'It's a new lock – all the buildings had new locks on after some teenagers got in last year and held a seance on the anniversary of the murder. Wait now, while I try a bit more force—'

This time the door swung protestingly inwards, and old, dank air gusted into their faces. They stepped warily into what appeared to be a dim lobby area with the floor covered in dead leaves and bird droppings, and then through a second door.

'It's very dark,' began Trixie. 'We shan't be able to see much.'

'I don't suppose there's any electricity on anyway,' said Edmund.

But Liam had found a battery of switches just inside the door, and was pressing them all in turn. The first ones brought forth a sputtering crackle from the defunct light bulbs, but one lone bulb near the wall, apparently made of sterner stuff than the others, gave out an uncertain illumination.

'Good God Almighty,' said Edmund.

'Dismal, isn't it? But this,' said Liam, 'is what you wanted to see. This is where a legend died and a fable began. The stuff that good theses are made on, Ms Smith, isn't that so?'

'I did say I wanted background atmosphere,' said Trixie, sounding slightly doubtful. 'But I'd have to say that after the build-up this is a bit of a disappointment.'

'Isn't that always the way with life.'

Studio Twelve appeared to be little more than a massive warehouse-like structure, perhaps seventy or eighty feet in overall length, its walls mottled with damp and grey fingers of cobwebs stirring in the draught from the opened doors. Edmund tutted and brushed the cobwebs aside before advancing deeper in. The floor creaked badly under their footsteps, but it seemed fairly sound which was one mercy. The amount of dust was deplorable though, and it was probably as well not to look too closely into the corners, or into the dark void beyond the roof girders overhead. There were huge shrouded shapes looming out of the dimness as well, and it took a moment to realize that they were only the discarded junk of years: pieces of scenery and furniture and odd stage props, and cumbersome-looking filming equipment. But most of them were covered in dust-sheets or lightweight tarpaulins, which gave an oddly macabre appearance to the place. As if someone had deliberately blinded the eyes of this place . . .

'What's over there?' said Edmund, abruptly.

'Doors to the dressing-room section, I should think.' Liam's footsteps echoed uncannily as he walked to the far side, threading his way through the dust-sheeted shapes, and moving around the jumbled piles of furniture. After a moment he called back, 'Yes, I think they are dressing-rooms – there're four, no, five of them. Two fairly small ones – star dressing-rooms, I should think – and three large ones. Probably communal. Loo and washroom in between. Oh, and there's what looks like an abandoned wardrobe-room as well, but I wouldn't recommend going inside that unless you feel like being sick: the smell's appalling.'

'Mice and damp, I daresay,' said Trixie briskly. 'Especially if there're any clothes still stored in there.'

'I daresay you're right,' said Liam, coming back. 'Listen now, I'm going to leave you to it if that's all right. You've got the address of my office, haven't you, in case you need it? It's only a couple of miles from here.'

'I'll bring the keys back,' said Edmund.

'No need. It's a Yale lock, so you can slam the door when you leave.'

'You don't suspect us of having a van parked discreetly outside to load the entire contents on to it and flog them in a street market?' asked Edmund.

'I hadn't thought about it. Do you have contacts within street markets?' inquired Liam politely, which was a remark Edmund chose to ignore.

'How late can we stay?' asked Trixie.

'You can stay here until the last trump sounds for all I care. But it'll start to get dark around four, and you won't be able to see much at all then.' He moved to the door. 'Also,' said Liam, 'I'm reliably informed that the ghosts come out when the darkness closes down.'

CHAPTER SIX

Trixie Smith was glad when that buttoned-up iceberg, Edmund Fane, rather pointedly consulted his watch, sighed a couple of times, and finally said if she wanted to stay for a while he would leave her to it. He really should be getting back, he said. Was there any reason why Trixie could not pull the door to when she left, making sure that the Yale lock clicked down?

There was no reason at all, and Trixie would far rather make her notes and scout around, working out who had died where, without being watched by Mister Fish-Eyes. So she said she reckoned she could manage to close the door securely.

'You won't mind being on your own in here? It's a bit eerie.' He glanced round as he said this, and Trixie even thought he repressed a slight shiver. Ha! A gleam of humanity at last. But she said briskly that anywhere would be a bit eerie in the middle of a field on a dark November afternoon. 'I'm not expecting to encounter any lurking ghosts if that's what you mean.'

'Ah. No, of course not. Well, in that case,' said Edmund, 'I'll leave you to it. Goodbye. Good luck with the thesis.'

'Thanks. Thanks for setting this up, as well.'

'It was my pleasure,' he said, which was a whopping great fib if Trixie had ever heard one because it had not been his pleasure at all, in fact he had stonewalled her from the start, and she would just like to know what had caused his change of heart: Edmund Fane did not strike her as a man who would do anyone a favour without first calculating what return he was likely to get. She watched him go out, and heard him close the outer door, and then turned her attention to plotting the exact layout of Studio Twelve. The thesis was going to incorporate a plan showing where the murders had actually happened. Neat and businesslike and informative. Now then. Conrad Kline had been killed in the wardrobe-room; Leo Dreyer in Lucretia's dressing-room. Better look at both places. Wardrobe-room first.

Liam Devlin had been right about one thing at any rate; the wardrobe-room stank of damp and decay. Even so, Trixie stood for a moment looking into the dark cavernous interior, remembering that this was where Conrad had lain dying and that his bloodied handprints had been smeared over one of the walls. He was supposed to have dragged himself to the wall dividing this room from the baroness's dressing-rooms, and tapped feebly on the wall, in the hope that someone would hear and come to his aid. But no one had done so because they had all been scurrying around summoning ambulances and police.

Leo Dreyer had been the financier for the film they had been making, and Trixie, reading the reports, had received the impression of a rather calculating man, probably given to patting the bottoms of wide-eyed would-be starlets, and lubriciously murmuring in their ears, I could do a lot for you, my pretty dear . . . She had not much liked the sound of Mr Leo Dreyer, although you would not wish his death on anyone.

Measuring up so that the plan would be to scale was difficult in the near-dark. There was a faint glimmer of light from the boarded-up windows, but even at high noon they would not provide more than a thread of daylight. Trixie had brought a tape measure, but she had not brought a torch. There was one in her car, but it was still raining hard and she did not fancy trekking back across the mud-fields. She would try to manage with the light there was.

She came back into the main studio and looked around. It really was an appallingly desolate place. Before she set off, Francesca Holland, who was staying with Trixie at the moment, had asked if it was really worth making the journey – all that way, and in the middle of a November rainstorm, Fran had said, peering doubtfully at the weather. Still, if it had really been such a *cause célèbre* . . .

Trixie had at once said, God, Fran, your *accent*! at which Fran had replied defensively that it was all very fine for Trixie and her posh education, but not so fine for people who had only attended Brick Street Junior School! She could be a bit prickly at times, that Fran, although there was a definite touch of the spaniel-eyed romantic several layers down.

Here was the baroness's infamous dressing-room, next door to the wardrobe. It was not quite as dark, but Trixie had to feel around to locate the door handle, and even when she found it and opened the door, she could not see very much. But she set to with the tape measure again, going more by feel this time than anything else.

One of the versions said that Conrad Kline had caught Leo Dreyer making love to Lucretia in here, which in Trixie's view would have been a mad thing for them to have done, what with people milling around outside and anyone likely to come in. But maybe Lucretia had got a kick out of the danger; Trixie believed some people did get kicks in that way.

But what had really sparked the Ashwood murders had been a version of the eternal triangle, or so the police had finally decided. The story that was afterwards pieced together – the one that was put out as the official verdict – was that there had been a monumental row between the three main characters, with everyone accusing everyone else of any number of debaucheries. Leo Dreyer had apparently said Conrad Kline was a shameful libertine from whom no female was safe – which taunt Kline had not minded – and that his music was rubbish, which Kline had minded very much indeed, retorting that he, at least, stipulated that his women should be over the age of consent.

After this, Lucretia, never one to stay out of the action for long, had flown into one of her celebrated tantrums and had snatched up a stage prop which somebody had left lying around and which unfortunately had been a stiletto or a knife that the props department had not yet blunted. She had gone after Kline, who had stormed off to the wardrobe-room to sulk, and had stabbed him and then returned to Dreyer and stabbed him as well. Then she had slashed both her wrists, either out of an extravagant burst of remorse or as a means of escaping the ugliness of the gallows. Either way, you could not say she had no style, that Lucretia, even if the style was *Grand Guignol.*

Whatever the truth of it, it all made for a damn good case study. Trixie sat on the floor directly beneath the solitary light and marked the salient points carefully on her plan. One body *here*, a second *there*. Cameras and technicians presumably grouped about *here* – she would take an educated guess at that. And then Lucretia's suicide *here*. Lying gracefully on the floor of her dressing-room it had been; trust the baroness to be gracefully arranged, even in a blood-dripping death, thought Trixie, and added a note to explore and if possible analyse the complexities of an ego that cared how its mortal coil looked after it had been shuffled off.

She came back to where the solitary light bulb cast its sullen glow, and sat down to make some notes about the actual studio – the floor was cold and disgustingly dusty, but sitting on it was preferable to burrowing under one of the shrouded piles of furniture to find a chair. She was trying to ignore those pallid shapes under the dust-sheets and tarpaulins, and she was also trying to ignore an increasing sensation that she was not on her own in here. Ridiculous, of course, although it would be a bit of a laugh if she did turn out to be psychic after all! She could just see Mr Edmund Fane's face if she was able to give him an action-replay account of the murders! Oh sure, said her mind sarcastically.

But there *is* something here, I can feel that there is. What is it, though? Lucretia von Wolff . . . ? The kohl-eyed baroness, still bound to the scene of her crime, resentful of intruders? Suicides did not rest, most people agreed on that.

But the murdered did not rest either. Was it Lucretia's victims whose presence she was sensing so strongly? Lot of rubbish, all this ghost business, but still—

But still, she was hearing *something*. Soft creakings and rustlings. Mice? Or even (shudder) rats? Or was it the dying Conrad Kline butchered and mutilated, left to die in the dark, but scrabbling on the wall for help . . . ?

Tap-tap . . . Help-me . . . Tap-tap . . . Help-me . . .

For a moment this last image was so vivid that Trixie almost believed she could hear him.

Tap-tap-tap . . . I-am-dying . . .

Who had really killed Dreyer, and who had really killed Conrad Kline? The question sounded slightly absurd, like the old rhyme about Cock Robin. How did it go? All the birds of the air/Came a-sighing and a-sobbing/When they heard of the death/Of poor Cock Robin . . .

So, who killed Leo Dreyer? Not I, said the baroness, with my stiletto. And all the ghosts of Ashwood/Came a-sighing and a-sobbing/When they heard of the death/Of poor Leo Dreyer . . .

Except that ghosts did not sob, any more than they existed, and there had been nothing poor about Leo Dreyer, in fact it was Trixie's guess that no one had especially sighed or sobbed at his death. But the method of his dying, yes, that had been bad. And quite a number of people had probably both sighed and sobbed for Conrad Kline.

The rain was still beating on the roof, sounding for all the world as if somebody was throwing hundreds of tin-tacks on to a metal tray, but beneath it, Trixie caught a sound from beyond the inner door. Someone out in the lobby area, was it? Or perhaps Edmund Fane had not closed the outer door properly and it was the wind. No, she had heard him slam the door herself. But he might have come back for some perfectly innocent reason, or Liam Devlin might have done so. Something to do with the keys or the parking of the cars. But surely they would not creep around out there; they would come straight in, calling out to her.

The sound came again, a little more definitely this time, and Trixie's heart skipped several beats, because what if there was someone out there – someone who had been watching her as she paced out the murder trail and scribbled her notes, occasionally muttering to herself as you did when you believed you were on your own? Someone who had stolen in after Edmund Fane left, or even someone who had been in here all along. She turned to look towards the door leading to the lobby. Was it moving? As if someone was inching it cautiously open, trying not to be heard?

Trixie set down her pad and pen, got stealthily to her feet, and began to step back because like this, standing directly in the fly-blown circle of light, she was as vulnerable and as exposed as if she had been on a spotlit stage. And the door was definitely being pushed open, she could see that it was.

Before she had taken more than a couple of steps away from the light, the door opened more fully, and for a split-second a dark shape was framed there. And then whoever it was closed the door softly and moved into one of the patches of darkness. Damn! Had he seen her? Yes, almost certainly he had.

She dodged deeper into the shadows, but before she could decide what to do next, there was a sudden darting movement near the door and then a soft click. The friendly illumination from above shut off and the entire studio was plunged into darkness.

This was certainly no spook; ghosts did not switch off lights for goodness' sake, and she could hear the brush of human clothes against a wall as he – it would certainly be a 'he'! – began to make his way towards her. She could hear the creak of the sagging old timbers as he trod on them as well: like a hoarse voice saying, I'm creeping across the floor to get to you, my dear . . .

With her heart pounding and sweat forming between her shoulder blades, Trixie started to back away from the sounds, keeping near to the wall because if she could circle around the edges of the studio, she could get to the door— And if she could do that before his eyes adjusted to the darkness . . .

On this last thought she dropped down on to all fours so that she would not be in his sightline – ha! he would be searching for her on his own eye-level, and that would fool him! She was shaking with fear, but if she kept her nerve she could reach the door and be out into the night before he realized it. And then across the waste ground – never mind how muddily squelchy it was! – and into her car, still parked near the old gates. She began to crawl stealthily towards the door, the wall comfortingly on her left, but she had not got more than a couple of feet when a blurred face suddenly swam up in front of her, the eyes huge dark pits, the hair a grey cobwebby veil.

Trixie gasped and recoiled, her stomach clenching in panic, but she had already realized that it was only her own reflection in an old looking-glass propped against a pile of discarded furniture, her features distorted by the green depths of the mirror's surface. And now he *will* know where you are, you wimp! Of all the stupid, uncontrolled things to have done— But it was too late for regrets; Trixie had already felt the sudden burst of triumph from him.

OK, no need to pussyfoot around any longer. She stood up and in a voice sharp with fear called out, 'Who's there? What do you want?' There was just the faint possibility that it was simply someone setting her up: someone laughing quietly to himself, and saying, I'll take the piss out of that daft old Trixie Smith . . . One of her own students? One of the middle years who had found out about the thesis and followed her down here? Yes, she could think of a couple of possible contenders very easily! She was gratefully aware of a little curl of anger, and when she caught another of the furtive movements over to her right she took a deep breath and lunged forward. If this really was some malicious joker, he had picked the wrong person to play jokes on!

She was halfway across the floor when a figure with smoky

darkness where the face should be stepped out of the shadows, and there was another of those moments of frozen terror – *ghosts after all?* Before she could recover, he had moved behind her, grabbing her arms and twisting them halfway up her back. Pain shot through her so that she cried out, but she struggled against him because she was damned if she was letting some weirdo over-power her! But he had imprisoned her wrists now, and he was jerking her arms even higher; his hands felt like iron bands and pain was shooting through her shoulders, but Trixie was still clutching on to that burst of anger, and she managed to kick out backwards. She encountered solid bone and flesh – his shin, had it been? Good! But wherever the blow had landed, it had drawn an angry grunt of surprised pain from him as if he had not expected her to resist. Serve you right, you bastard!

But then he pulled her back against him – she felt the hot hard excitement of him pressing against her body. God, this was obscene! One of his arms hooked around her throat, slamming into her windpipe and driving the breath from her body. She gasped, and struggled again but he still had that half-stranglehold on her, and before she could kick out again, he released his hold slightly, and a split-second later something hard and hurting smashed down on her skull. The world exploded in starbursts of light before she tumbled down into a spinning blackness.

Edmund had been careful to open and close the outer door loudly enough for Trixie Smith to think he had gone. In fact he had remained just inside, standing quietly in the shadows of the lobby, his heart racing with anticipation, his muscles taut with nervous tension.

But he was already imagining that Crispin was with him – if he could surround himself with Crispin's personality, he always felt so much stronger. Like chanting a spell to make you brave. (How flattering, Crispin had said, amused, when Edmund had once tried to explain this. I've never been compared to a magic spell before.)

The initial plan had been to use the empty hypodermic syringe on Trixie Smith, as he had done on Aunt Deborah. Quick and simple and relatively painless, and the verdict would be heart failure exactly as it had been with Deborah. It would be a gentlemanly way to commit a murder, if you could have such a thing. A coroner might say that Ms Smith was rather young to suffer a heart attack, but these things did happen; it was very sad, and deeply unfortunate that she should have been on her own at the time, but there you were.

But Crispin, with that devastating logic Edmund could never quite master on his own account, had pointed out a flaw in this plan. Yes, he had said, fine, dear boy, very good indeed, to go for that verdict of heart attack. But here's the thing, Edmund: mightn't such a verdict cause people to ask *why* a young and presumably healthy woman should succumb to a heart attack? In such a place? And how about the danger of tabloid newspapers picking the thing up and speculating as to what, precisely, Trixie Smith might have seen inside Ashwood to terrify her into it? A series of headlines had flashed across Edmund's mind at this. *'Death inside haunted studio . . .' 'Ashwood claims another victim . . .'* Perhaps even, *'Was schoolteacher frightened to death? . . .'*

It would be very newsworthy indeed, Edmund had seen that at once. It could mean that the whole Ashwood tale would be rehashed all over again, and Lucretia's name would be splashed across the newspapers once more. People would become interested – worse, they would become curious.

Edmund had been aware of self-anger, because he had not seen any of this – he, who was so methodical and so meticulous, had almost bloody *missed* the great gaping flaw in his plan!

All right, so you didn't see it, Crispin had said. But it doesn't matter, because I saw it for you.

Yes, but what do I *do*? What do I do instead of shoving a prick into the bloody woman?

There had been the familiar ruffle of amusement from Crispin at the slight *double entendre* – he loved it when the normally prim

Edmund occasionally became risqué – but he had said very coolly that for goodness' sake, Edmund could surely make it appear that the Smith female had been attacked by a tramp or a drug-addict. Hit her over the head with an empty whisky bottle and leave the bottle there for the police to draw their own conclusions. And then, said Crispin, you can jab needles into her to your heart's content.

Edmund had taken a moment to weigh this up. Both methods together?

Certainly. Blows to the head are unpredictable things, said Crispin. But this way you're making sure. The verdict can be heart failure after a severe blow to the head. So set the scene for that, dear boy.

Set the scene. Edmund took off the rain-jacket he had been wearing, and retrieved the empty whisky bottle and the hypodermic from its capacious pockets. He was already wearing gloves, which were important because of not leaving fingerprints on the bottle, but he took a knitted balaclava helmet from the jacket's inner pocket. A touch dramatic this last, perhaps, but you never knew.

He left the bulky rain-jacket on the floor, and when he stepped quietly back into the main studio the Crispin-spell was already working, and the feeling of Crispin's presence was so strong there was even a moment when Edmund thought he glimpsed Crispin's outline, slender and young, the glossy reddish hair tumbling over his forehead.

The light switches were on the left of the door – he had marked their position earlier – and he took the two steps that brought him within reach of them. A quick movement and a soft click, and the single overhead light was quenched.

The instant the darkness closed down, Edmund was aware of a hard throbbing excitement engulfing him. And instead of inhibiting his movements, the lack of light was heightening his senses and even lending him other senses he did not normally possess. The ability to sense his victim's presence, in the way of hunting animals . . . Edmund could not see Trixie Smith and he could not hear her, but he knew exactly where she was; he knew she had backed away to the far wall on his left, and that she was kneeling down, hoping to evade him.

She did not evade him, of course. When he stepped out of the darkness, he felt her bolt of fear and surprise and he was aware of a deep triumph because after all she had not known he was so close to her. Strength poured into him – his own and Crispin's together – and he knew himself strong enough and confident enough to kill twenty prying schoolteachers.

He twisted her arms tightly behind her back – the bitch kicked him quite hard but he knocked the breath from her by hooking his right forearm around her throat. And then he lifted the whisky bottle high and brought it smashing down on her head.

CHAPTER SEVEN

As Trixie slumped to the ground, the whole of Ashwood's past seemed to jump straight at Edmund; ghosts stirred and slithered within the darkness, and a confusing jumble of echoes swooped and spun around his head.

Ghosts.

Deep within the swirling echoes he could just make out a soft whispering voice; distant and blurred at first, but then becoming more distinct.

Well done, Edmund . . . said this whispering voice. *Oh, well done . . . And now you're going to kill her, aren't you . . . ?*

It was a very young voice – almost a childish voice, and Edmund knew it was a voice he had never heard in his life. Was it the voice of a child who had not lived to grow up . . . ?

He stood very still, concentrating intently on this light, young voice, and gradually he understood that it was asking why he did not forget that careful precise plan he had made – that murder committed by a fictitious drunk or a convenient tramp. Why did he not use Ashwood's legend in his plan . . . ?

Ashwood's legend. With the words came a sudden thump of such searing excitement that for a moment Edmund thought he was going to lose consciousness under its impact.

But of course he could not use Ashwood's legend. It was far too dangerous. It would make people remember.

Scaredy cat ... said the voice mockingly. (Yes, it *was* a child's voice.) *Couldn't you cope, Edmund, if people did remember ... ?*

The excitement was pulsating through Edmund's entire body, and the darkness was throbbing and becoming laced with the fear that still lay on the air from when he had stalked Trixie Smith a short while ago. Fear was the colour of crimson, like old blood; Edmund could feel the lingering fear and he could almost see it.

Ashwood's legend. Dare he use it? But the possibility was already zinging around his brain like arcing electricity, setting up little sparks of shivering anticipation. *Ashwood's legend* ... But could he cope with the memories being resurrected?

Oh, of course you could ... said the whisper. *Do you really think that anyone has ever forgotten what happened here, once upon a time ... ? The story will be dug up again anyway when Trixie Smith's body is found ... And this always was the Murder Studio, Edmund, let's not forget that ...*

The words hissed lightly to and fro, like silk being spun in the dark. I'm imagining it, thought Edmund. I'm not really hearing anything at all. It's just the rain outside. Yes, but *'A child, listed simply as "Allie", was at Ashwood that day ...'* Could that child have been Alraune? Was Alraune here now? But Alraune had never really existed ...

Didn't I, Edmund ... ? Are you sure about that ... ? The whisper was so light and insubstantial – it was like the dry husks of flies in a spider's web. Was this really Alraune's ghost, Alraune's voice?

I don't believe in you, said Edmund, half-angrily, half-pleadingly. I don't dare believe in you.

You don't need to believe in me ... All you need to believe in is the practice of morthor ... *Remember that, Edmund ... And remember, as well, that it's akin to the ancient High German word of* mord ...

Mord. Edmund still did not believe in Alraune, but he could not stop thinking that something that might be Alraune was very close to him. He found that he had already crossed the floor to the light switches, and that he had reached up to switch the single light back on. Trixie Smith lay in an ungainly huddle where she had fallen. Still unconscious? Yes. But breathing. He walked towards the suite of dressing-rooms and the wardrobe-room.

You're going to do it, aren't you, Edmund . . . ? There was a sudden burst of glee.

Am I? thought Edmund.

The wardrobe-room, when he pushed the door open, was dark and evil-smelling – Liam Devlin had been right about that – and it was smaller than Edmund had been expecting. Clothes rails were still fixed to the walls, and although some of them had fallen away from their moorings it was not difficult to imagine the rows and rows of costumes and hats and shoes that would have been stored here. Lucretia would have known this place very well, of course; she had probably sailed imperiously through here, demanding expensive outfits for her scenes, refusing to wear anything that did not meet her exacting standards. Self-centred bitch, thought Edmund.

But there would be something in here that would chime with the legend, and he was starting to see that Alraune was right about using it; he could not think why he had been so chary of the idea. He would meet it head-on, that legend; he would take the history of this place by the scruff of its neck, and make use of it when he killed that snooping Trixie Smith. He would teach her not to disturb his calm, well-ordered life, and it would be a warning to anyone else who might try the same thing.

He was still alert for any sign that Trixie might have regained consciousness, but almost his entire mind was focusing on what he might find in here. Trying not to breathe in too deeply because of the disgusting stench, he wedged the door open so that there was a spill of light from the main studio, and began opening sagging old cupboards and worm-eaten drawers, deeply thankful for his leather gloves as he did so. Nothing. I'm not going to find what I want, thought Edmund.

Yes, you are . . . Again the sly amusement came.

And quite suddenly, there it was, exactly as he had hoped, and exactly as Alraune had known. It was lying at the back of a small drawer, probably pushed in there by some long-forgotten wardrobe mistress or make-up girl, and it was black with tarnish, but the thin spiked point was still cruelly sharp.

A spike, a skewer, a gimlet. *A stiletto* . . . The one used all those years ago? Probably not, but close enough to the original.

He came slowly out of the wardrobe-room, the thin sharp instrument in his hand. Stay with me, Alraune.

Oh yes, Edmund, I'll stay with you . . . And Edmund—

Yes?

Remember the eyes, said Alraune's voice. *Remember the EYES, Edmund . . .*

Trixie came swimming and struggling up out of the sick-feeling darkness, and for a moment had no idea where she was. And then memory rushed painfully in – yes, of course, she was in the old Ashwood studios, and some maniac had hit her on the head, and it must have knocked her out.

She was aware of a banging headache, but she was also aware of bitter fury because she had been so easily attacked – she, who had so often boasted that it ought to be child's play to foil an assailant or a mugger! A swift kick in the balls and most men were disabled, that was what she had always said!

She sat up carefully, aware now that the light had been switched on again. Did that mean he had gone? Dare she hope that he had got his horrid kicks by knocking her out, and had simply scuttled out into the night? Was she going to be able to get away? Her senses were still spinning from the blow and she had a three-aspirin-headache, but that would not matter if she could just get back to her car. Car keys? Ah, in her bag, and there it was, lying on the ground barely four feet away. She was just reaching out for it when several of the dust-sheets stirred slightly as if someone had walked past them.

She had not heard his footsteps this time, but he was already standing on the edge of the pool of light cast by the single overhead bulb, and for the first time Trixie saw that he was wearing one of those woollen helmets, like you saw on members of the IRA. His eyes glittered through the slits – it was extraordinarily eerie to just see someone's eyes. Did she know him? Was there something familiar about him after all?

But then she forgot about who he might be, because in one hand he held something that glinted sharply, and the sight of it brought the panic rushing in all over again. A knife, was it? No, much thinner than a knife. She tried to get to her feet but she was still dizzy and uncertain from the blow, and even before she was halfway to standing up he was bending over her, one gloved hand curling around her throat, forcing her back down on to the floor. There was a smell of mildew and dirt from the hard floor, and he was raising his free hand high above her head, and whatever he was holding had flashed evilly in the overhead light . . .

There was a split-second – barely the space of a heartbeat – when Edmund felt the throbbing excitement falter.

But the childish whisper came in at once. *Go on, Edmund! This is right! This is what you have to do! So do it, Edmund, do it NOW! And I will help you*, said Alraune's voice.

Incredibly there was the feeling of a small firm hand curling around the stiletto, and of Alraune's hand guiding the glinting point downwards.

Down and down and down . . . Yes, thought Edmund, breathing fast, as if he had been running hard for miles. I can do this and I will do this. I am a giant, a titan, and I am invincible.

As Trixie began to scream and struggle, the person that most people knew – the polite, slightly pedantic Mr Fane – seemed to shrink into a tiny insignificance, and the other Edmund, the secret Edmund, the one whom only Crispin had ever known, surged uppermost. When the stiletto's point punctured Trixie's eye, this Edmund did not feel repulsed or disgusted, and when viscous eye-fluid spilled out over his gloved fingers he only felt the bursting strength urging him on.

He straightened up at last, looking down at Trixie. She was no longer screaming, but she was still moving which he had not expected. Could you survive with a steel point thrust into your brain? You could not tell with these things.

But dead or not-quite-dead, there was something not quite right about what he had done to her. What was it? Edmund studied her carefully. The right side of her face was grotesque; it was slicked in blood and not-quite-colourless fluid, and the eye socket was a wet dark wound . . . But the left side – Ah yes, of course, that was it. The left side of her face was untouched, unbloodied, and it was the lack of symmetry that was bothering him. He could not bear anything to be lopsided or uneven.

Edmund raised his hand again, and this time the stiletto came down with more intensity and more assurance. He felt the deep shudder go through the prying snooping creature, and he saw a spasm wrack her body. And then she was still. Ah, she had not been quite dead, then. He straightened up for the second time. Yes, that was better. Both eyes gone now. Now you really won't be able to see anything that might be dangerous, my dear.

Her body would be found eventually, of course. Someone would miss her and make inquiries, and backtrack to her journey here; her car, still parked at Ashwood's entrance, would be spotted. That was all perfectly in order, and it did not matter who found her; what did matter was whether Edmund had left any telltale traces.

But he was certain he had not. Any fingerprints or traces of his hair found here would be ascribed to his earlier visit, and he had worn gloves for the return. The stiletto was still in the left eye, though; he was uncertain whether it would be better to remove it.

But the point was embedded so deeply in the bone behind the eye socket he could not get it out. The gloves which he dared not take off slid over the smooth steel surface, and although he made several attempts, it resisted him. But did it really matter? The thing had been here all along; it was not as if he had purchased it anywhere and brought it with him. No, it would be all right to leave it in place.

The crackling starbursts of energy were gradually dimming and he was aware of a dull ache across his temples and of his hands trembling. No matter, he would overcome that sufficiently to drive home. But he did not move yet. He stayed where he was, looking down at the crumpled thing that had been Trixie Smith. Something still not quite right. Something that still needs doing.

And then he knew what it was. On the day Lucretia von Wolff died, the people who had broken down her dressing-room door had been greeted by a macabre tableau. If Edmund was really going to echo that day, he must re-create that tableau as closely as he could.

He walked cautiously around the studio again, and after a few abortive explorations beneath the dust-sheeted mounds, he found a large, high-backed chair near one of the walls. On closer inspection it turned out to be a rather elaborate affair, ornately carved. The satin or velvet upholstery had long since gone, of course, but it was still an imposing-looking thing. Edmund smiled to himself as he dragged it clear and set it in the centre of the studio. It was exactly right. It might even be the original chair Lucretia had used that day. Your chair, Madame von Wolff. Your stiletto. Who would have thought it?

He turned it to face the main door, and then he arranged Trixie Smith so that she was sitting upright, her hands lying along the carved wooden arms, her head turned slightly as if she was watching for someone to enter. It took longer than he had expected because Trixie was heavier than he had allowed for. Dead weight, of course. But in the end it was done and he stepped back to consider the effect. Yes, very good indeed.

And now there was one final thing. It must seem as if the killer had had to break in. The police were not fools; if there were no signs of forced entry, they would instantly start suspecting anyone who knew where the keys were kept. That would mean Liam Devlin, and possibly his staff if he had any: presumably Devlin employed other people at his office. Edmund would not lose any sleep if Devlin came under suspicion, but he was not going to risk coming under suspicion himself.

It was clearly impossible for the door to be broken in or the lock snapped off, but what about those nailed-up windows? Edmund walked across to examine them. They were a bit more solid than he had previously thought, but he managed to prise a corner free, and saw that there was a second board nailed on outside. Awkward, but not insurmountable, although he would need something to use as a lever. He hunted around again, and found a section of steel that appeared to have fallen off some sort of structure – it was impossible to know what it had originally represented, but the steel piece would do very well for Edmund's purpose.

He went out into the lobby, propping the outer door carefully open, and around to the side of the building. Ah, here was the first of the windows. It was quite high up, but Edmund was fairly tall, and by dint of levering the steel under it, he managed to lever a whole section free. The plywood was brittle with damp and age, and it came away without too much difficulty. It would be easy enough for someone to clamber through and drop down on to the floor on the other side. Edmund was not going to attempt this, of course; he was not going to risk leaving fibres from his clothes or shoes on the window frame because they might later be found by the police, and identified as his. He could scatter fibres and hairs inside but it would look very questionable indeed if such things were found on a high-up window-sill outside.

He went back in, and levered an equivalent section of plywood from the window, then stood back to consider. Yes, it looked all right; it looked as if someone had got in, and had afterwards tried to replace the boarding to hide the traces.

One last look around the dim studio to make sure nothing was missed or forgotten. Yes, he thought everything was all right. He barely glanced at the thing in the elaborate old chair, its face half in shadow. And then he switched off the light and went out into the night, remembering to slam the main door to engage the lock.

It was a long drive home and it was still raining quite heavily, but Edmund did not mind either of these things. There was not much traffic about, and most of the roads were straightforward dual-carriageways with only an occasional traffic island. He remembered the road quite well, and he did not falter or take any wrong turnings. And with every mile he covered, Ashwood became more and more distant.

He reached his own house midway through the evening, took a hot bath, and put the things he had worn into the washing machine. The thick rain-jacket he had worn and the gloves could be burned; he put them in the potting-shed for a bonfire tomorrow, and then made himself a supper of scrambled eggs with grated cheese. Before going to bed he drank a large whisky and soda, and swallowed a couple of aspirin. He had suffered from quite bad nightmares in his youth, especially after the death of his father. He hoped he would not have a nightmare tonight.

Falling asleep, it was necessary to force his mind away from that last glimpse he had had of Trixie Smith, her eyes destroyed, and the blood drying to a dark crust on her face.

CHAPTER EIGHT

It had been absolutely vital not to think about those dreadful bloodied eye-sockets during the journey to the place called Mowbray Fen. The ambulance would have reached Pedlar's Yard long ago, and if there was anything to be done for the fearsome blinded thing that had groped stumblingly along the darkened hall, then it would have been done by now. There would be a very bad memory of those last moments in the house – of crouching in the dark under-stairs cupboard, not daring to breathe in case the blood-smeared head appeared around the door – and it would be a memory that would last for a very long time, perhaps for years and years. But it could not be allowed to get in the way of leaving London and reaching Mowbray Fen.

And although it was quite scary to be going off into the unknown like this, completely alone, it was not as scary as sleeping in the house in Pedlar's Yard, trying not to hear the stumbling footsteps on the stairs. So I'll cope with the scary feeling and I'll just think about finding that house.

It was not so many years since a child travelling alone would have attracted concerned attention – 'Shouldn't you be with your mother, my dear . . . ?' 'Where are you going on your own . . . ?' But it had been the start of the so-called liberated 1970s:

children went more or less where they liked and did more or less what they wanted, and respecting your elders was uncool, boring, a thing of the past. What's it to you where I'm going, mister?

Mother had always said it was ill-mannered to talk in that way, but at least it meant nobody took much notice of a child travelling alone. And it turned out to be easy to slip into the big anonymous railway station and hide in the lavatories until it was morning and there were enough people milling around not to look twice at a child. It was easy, as well, to carefully study the glass-fronted maps in the railway station, and then buy a train ticket to Peterborough which seemed to be the nearest big town to Mowbray Fen, although it was suddenly heart-bumpingly anxious to sit waiting for the train to come in. What if police come storming in before the train arrives, looking for me? What would I do?

But the train came in, and once on it, once it started away from the station, it was possible to feel safer. I'm going away from Pedlar's Yard, and the farther I go, the safer I am. I am nothing to do with Pedlar's Yard any longer and I am nothing to do with North London any longer. I am a person travelling to Lincolnshire, going to visit my grandmother. The words brought a deep satisfaction. Just as the names of the villages and towns learned from mother had been a litany to blot out the brutality, so now was the phrase 'going to visit my grandmother' a charm that could be recited to inquisitive grown-ups. I am going to visit my grandmother who lives in Mowbray Fen. The wheels of the train sang the names of the stories. Thorney and Witchford and Whissendine. Rockingham Forest and going-to-see-grandmother.

Peterborough was finally reached after lunch, and from there on, buses had to be taken, but this also turned out to be easy. People at bus stations could be politely asked for directions, although once a stout, bossy-looking woman said sharply, 'Shouldn't you be at school?' and there was a breath-snatching moment of panic. But it was easy to point to a well-dressed female on the other side of the square and say there was Mother, and that there had been a dentist's appointment that afternoon.

Seeing the sign that said 'You are entering the County of Lincolnshire' brought a lurch of delighted expectation. Lincoln. Robin Hood and Sherwood Forest. And Pedlar's Yard was a long way behind now, and clearly the money was going to last, which was one huge worry out of the way. It was even possible to be interested in things like newspaper headlines on placards. The Space Race – America and Russia sending up Apollos and Pioneers and probe-ships to Mars. And there were stories about the fairly shocking musical, *Jesus Christ, Superstar*, and about the really shocking films like *Last Tango in Paris*, and *Deep Throat*. People had sniggered about *Deep Throat* at school, but films and musicals had not played any part in the life of Pedlar's Yard. Because there had been no money for them, or because there had been no understanding of how marvellous things like that could be? Yes, but one day I'm going to be grown up and then I'm going to know about films and music and books.

And then at last there was a bus that left Grantham, which rumbled along through all the places with the fairytale names. Thorney and Witchford and Whissendine. Parson Drove and Kings Cliffe and Collyweston . . . There was the feeling of being pulled deeper and deeper into Mother's stories.

And now Mowbray Fen, just the tiniest of tiny villages on the edge of the Lincolnshire Wolds, was only a few miles away, which meant the house in the marshes was only a few miles away as well. And when I get there I'll really have escaped, and I'll have stepped into a different world.

Shall I change my name for that different world? Tear up the birth certificate and be called something entirely new? Would it be safer to do that, so that nobody could ever know about Pedlar's Yard? What could I be called?

The appalling possibility that Mother's whispered stories might not be true could not be considered, not even for a moment. The marsh house must exist and that was all there was to it. It had been dreamed about and yearned for so strongly and for so long, that it could not be simply a fairytale.

But once off the bouncing country bus came the search for signposts that pointed to Mowbray Fen, and a different panic swept in, because supposing there weren't any signposts? Supposing this whole thing was going to turn out to be as elusive as looking for the rainbow's end so that you could claim the pot of gold? Supposing that letter Mother showed me was an old one and the house isn't here any longer? Or supposing I got the journey wrong, and I've ended up miles away from where I should be?

But the panic did not last long, because this was the land of the jack o' lanterns and the will o' the wisps, and there was a strong pure light everywhere – a light that bore no resemblance to London's thick cloggy skies – and if ever will o' the wisps danced in England they would surely dance here, to their own strange wild music, moving across the flat rolling marshlands, in and out of the thick fringings of reeds and rushes. Keep looking. The road will be here somewhere.

The road was there, of course. As if the creatures of the myths were pointing the way, there was the signpost: 'Mowbray Fen, 4 miles.'

Mowbray Fen. Heart's desire and journey's end. I'm nearly there.

Mowbray Fen, when it was finally reached, turned out to be a village with a little straggling street and a big square area of grass at one end, with a stone cross. There were shops – some of them with little roundy windows – and there were houses built out of stone, which was something you hardly ever saw in Pedlar's Yard.

But Pedlar's Yard need never appear again, and it need not be talked about or even remembered. Out here, it was possible to believe this.

Just beyond the main street was a church with a little spire; music came from its half-open door – lovely music, not like anything you had ever heard before, but music that was somehow part of the strangeness of this place and that was all mixed up with the feeling of having escaped.

And there, beyond the church, and behind the green, was a small sign, so weathered it was almost impossible to read. But to the prepared mind it was very clear indeed. 'The Priest's House' it said, and at the sight of it memory stirred all over again.

'It's called the Priest's House,' Mother had said. *'It was built when people could be put to death for believing in the wrong religion, and there are legends that priests hid there before being smuggled out of the country and across to Holland.'*

The house lay at the end of a bumpy, gravelly track. It was not really part of the village at all: it was a mile or two outside the village, and it was much bigger than Mother had described it. Mother had made it sound an enchanted place: a tiny pretty cottage, the walls covered with roses or ivy, and sunlight glinting permanently on the windows. But it was not like that at all; it was built of the same grey stone as the village shops, and it had twisty chimneys and gardens all round it. There was a white gate that swung inwards, and a crunchy path led up to the door. A little lamp hung over the door – it gave out a lovely amber glow that made you feel warm and hopeful – and there was a light on in one of the downstairs windows. And surely, oh surely, the lady who lived here – the lady who had had the handsome young man in love with her all those years ago – would still be here. Because this was the beckoning dream at last: it was the place that had shone like a beacon all your life. I *can't* have come all this way to find she's moved away, or died.

It was the hardest thing yet to reach up to the heavy door knocker, but it had to be done. The knocker rapped smartly down, and the whole world narrowed to this single moment: to the violet dusk and the scents of the garden, and the silence which was not like any silence anywhere else. Light years spun past and whole worlds were born and died, and it began to seem as if Time had become stuck and nothing was going to happen ever again.

And then the door opened and she was there, framed in the doorway, an inquiring look on her face, not particularly worried by an unexpected caller, merely wanting to know what this was about. There was the sound of a radio or a television from one of the rooms, and there was a faint drift of something savoury cooking, all mixed up with the scent of polish and cleanliness.

'Yes?'

She was not quite as Mother's stories had suggested. For one thing she did not seem as old, although there were lines around her eyes and at the corners of her mouth, and her hair was grey. But when she smiled she had the most beautiful smile in the world, and it did not matter if she was seventy or only sixty, or if she was ninety or even a hundred. She had the loveliest voice in the world, as well. In Pedlar's Yard people did not bother over-much about voices; they just said what they had to say, and did not think how it sounded. But from now on, I'll *always* know that voices are important. Not posh accents or anything like that – for a moment Pedlar's Yard surfaced stubbornly, because it was wimpish and stupid to pretend to be posh! – but I'll remember that a voice can be beautiful. Like a midnight sky. Like velvet.

Take a deep breath and then say what you've planned. Say it properly and politely. Here I go, then. 'I'm looking for my grandmother. But I don't know if this is the right house.'

The lady with the voice like a midnight sky and the most beautiful smile in the world, said, 'It could be the right house. What is your grandmother's name?'

'Alice Wilson.'

She did not speak for a moment, and then she said, 'Where have you come from?'

'London. A place called Pedlar's Yard.'

'Oh!' she said, and there was a moment when something seemed to switch on behind her eyes, and there was the feeling of an emotion suddenly springing out of nowhere, and whatever the emotion was, it was so extremely strong that it would not have been surprising to see it leap out and take solid shape in the dusk-lit garden.

Then she said, 'Then this is the right house. I'm Alice Wilson. I know about Pedlar's Yard. But I didn't know I had a grandchild, although I'm very glad to meet you. I think you'd better come inside.'

Come inside . . . The words uttered by all the enchantresses in all the stories . . . Come inside, my dear . . . And sometimes 'inside' was evil and dangerous, and sometimes it was wonderful and magical. And until you actually stepped inside, there was absolutely no way of knowing which it was going to be.

But to do anything other than step into the house was absolutely unthinkable.

Those first days in the Priest's House were filled with bewildering new impressions – so much so that even the aching loss of Mother – the pain that had nagged and gnawed just under the surface all the way here – became nearly bearable.

For some inexplicable reason it had been unthinkable not to tell the whole story of Pedlar's Yard with complete truthfulness. Alice ('You had better call me that – I don't think I can cope with being "grandmother",' she had said) had listened without interrupting that first evening, but at one stage her lips had trembled and she had clutched her hands together so tightly that the knuckles showed white. And – this was the curious thing – the part that had upset her so much had not been where Mother had died; it had been the part where Mother had used the scissors on the man who had brutalized and cowed her for so many years.

But then she had said, 'That was a very dreadful thing for you to see, but the memories will get better after a while. And you'll travel away from the sadness in time. You'll build a bridge away from it and you'll go across that bridge into whatever's waiting for you in the future.'

'I will?'

'Yes. It's how life works. We aren't allowed to be sad all the time.'

'I 'spect you'll have to tell the police about what happened, won't you?'

'Don't look so frightened, you solemn little owl. We're not going to tell the police anything.'

'We're not?'

'No. That house – Pedlar's Yard – is a very long way away from here. And you brought that last letter I sent, didn't you? Well, I know you did.'

'I thought you might need to see it so's you'd know I really was me.'

She smiled. 'I can see you're really you without any letters,' she said. 'Even without the photo you brought, I can see it.' A pause. 'I'm glad you brought that.'

'I wanted to remember Mother as happy. She's happy in the photo, isn't she?'

'Yes.' Alice had looked at the small photo for a very long time, occasionally reaching out a finger to trace the features. Once she said, 'You're more like your mother than your father.'

'I know.'

'Were there any other papers in the house? Anything that might link Pedlar's Yard to this place? Other photographs, perhaps? Old ones?'

'Not really. There wasn't much space for things like that. I only knew about you from the stories. My mother liked telling me stories. She was good at it – she used to make me see the people and the places. Once said she would have liked to be a writer. A proper writer, I mean. Books and things.'

'And – you do remember her as looking happy sometimes? Like she was in this photograph?'

'Oh yes. She once said he – my father – could be very charming.' And for a moment Mother's face was vividly there, half-sad, half-happy, talking about the charming young man she had married and must once have loved very much . . .

'Charming,' said Alice thoughtfully, as if trying out the word. 'Yes, I'm sure that's true.' And again a memory came surging upwards – this time of Mother saying that families were odd things; that if you married someone your family did not like . . .

And then, with a switch of mood to practicality, Alice said, 'Well now, it doesn't sound as if there'd be anything in that house to connect me – or you – with it. And so I think we can count ourselves safe.'

This had to be considered carefully. Then, because it was as well to get things absolutely clear, 'You mean we aren't going to say anything to anyone?'

She took a moment to answer. 'No, I don't believe we are,' she said at last. 'We're going to keep it just between the two of us. I'm glad to know she talked to you about me, though.' She said this half to herself, but there was a flicker of sadness. 'It means that out of all that hatred and violence, I've got you.' The smile showed briefly. 'But now your mother's dead, I think we should make sure we keep her memory as a good one. Keep the photograph carefully, won't you?'

'Yes, of course. Uh – do you mean we're going to keep what she did a secret? In case people think of her as – um – a murderer?' The word came out a bit bumpily, but Alice did not seem to notice.

She said, 'Yes, that's just what I do mean. People love to gossip and to speculate, and they aren't always very kind. You'd grow up with everyone whispering behind your back.' Again there was the pause, as if she was arranging in her mind what to say next. 'And the truth is that your mother was defending herself – and you. Mothers do defend their children – very fiercely at times.' Again there was the flicker of anger and grief all mixed up together.

'Yes, I understand that.'

'Also,' said Alice, 'it's the intention that counts, remember that. I was brought up to be quite religious – most people were when I was young – and I know it's the things in your heart and in your mind that count. That's what God sees and hears and knows about. And I don't believe your mother intended to kill him.'

They looked at one another. Impossible to say, But how can we be sure?

If Alice heard this thought, she did not show it. She said, 'Everything will be perfectly all right. No one will find you here, and no one here will ever connect you with Pedlar's Yard.' This was said with absolute conviction. 'I've lived in this village for a great many years, and I'm very well thought of here.' She paused. 'But I think what we will do is to tell a small lie about you. I don't think you'd better be known as my grandchild, because people are inquisitive. They might say, "Goodness, Alice, a grandchild? We didn't even know you had any children." So I think you'll just be a young relative.' The smile that was so beautiful you wanted it to go on for ever showed. 'But whatever we say, you'll be safe. I won't let anything happen to you, I promise.'

'All right. Thank you.'

'Good.' She stood up. 'So now you are here, you'd better have some supper, hadn't you? If you've been travelling all day you probably haven't had a proper meal. I want to hear all about your journey, and I want to hear all about you. And after you've eaten, we'll see about making up a bed for you. There are a couple of very nice guest rooms upstairs. Would you like to be at the back of the house, overlooking the trees, or would you like to be at the side, overlooking the lane?'

CHAPTER NINE

Incredibly, it had been as unfussed and as straightforward as that. Supper that first night was a delicious chicken casserole with fresh fruit afterwards, and one of the very first lessons to be learned was that eating and cooking meals in this house was friendlier and much more interesting than in Pedlar's Yard.

The evening meal was called supper and the midday meal was lunch. Quite early on, Alice said, 'We'll see about school for you – there's a good one just beyond the village, I believe. During the term you'll have your lunch there, of course, but when you're at home – weekends and holidays – I might not always want to be bothered with breaking off what I'm doing to prepare a meal. Or I might be out – there're various church activities I like to be part of, and charity things. Sometimes I meet one of my friends or a friend comes to lunch here. We shan't want children around while we gossip, and you'd be bored anyway. I'm a selfish lady, my dear, but I've lived on my own for a long time, and I don't think I can change at my time of life. So we'll work round that, and we'll draw up a few house-rules. All right?'

'Yes.' The idea of a set of rules to work to was unexpectedly comforting. It gave the feeling of knowing where you were and what you could and could not do.

'One of the rules,' Alice said, 'will be that if it's half-past twelve or one o'clock and I'm not around, you can sort out some food for yourself. There'll always be soup in the larder that can be heated, and cheese and fruit in the fridge. Have what you want, and wash up afterwards. You can do that, can't you?'

'Oh yes.'

The evening meal was usually eaten together, at the gateleg table in the room overlooking the garden. It might be one of Alice's delicious casseroles, or a chicken or fish cooked in unfamiliar ways.

'I quite enjoy cooking,' Alice said. 'I learned all those years ago when I was a lady's maid. Your mother told you about that, didn't she? About my having been a maid?'

'Yes.'

'Miss Nina – the young lady I was maid to – liked me to cook for her when the family was out.'

This was another of the incomprehensible things about Alice's life. In Pedlar's Yard it had been assumed that all women could cook, and the men had expected to be waited on by their wives and daughters. The concept of a woman who could not cook, and who expected to be waited on, was unfamiliar.

'Couldn't she cook for herself, that Nina?'

'Nowadays you'd think so,' said Alice. 'But this was a very long time ago – the nineteen-twenties – and they were a very rich family. It would never have occurred to Miss Nina to so much as make a cup of tea. It would never have occurred to anyone else that she should even have to do so.'

It was exciting listening to Alice talk about Mother's stories, and to know she was talking from inside them. She *was* the stories. She was the seventeen-year-old girl with whom the handsome young man had fallen in love, but because she had been a servant, they had had to part. It was not quite possible to ask about this – although it might be possible one day – but there seemed no reason not to ask about Vienna.

'You lived there?'

'Yes. It's a beautiful city. You'll go there one day, and you'll love it.'

'Will I?'

'There's no reason why you shouldn't.'

Evenings in the Priest's House, after the supper things had been cleared away and homework diligently dealt with, were best of all. Often they watched television, but sometimes Alice played records – wonderful music by Bach and Schubert and Mozart. 'I like music,' she said. When the real winter came and darkness had enveloped the fens by the middle of the afternoon, the curtains were drawn and the fires glowed in the hearths, and it was a time when other stories could be told.

'Tell about the first time Miss Nina's lover came to the house and saw you.'

'In the exact same words as always?'

It was a joke between them by this time.

'Stories always have to be in the exact same words.'

'Or you might find they've changed when you come to tell them again?'

'Yes. *Yes.*' This was one of the good things about Alice; she understood about stories having to stay absolutely the same, just as Mother had understood.

'What a fussy little owl you are. Well, then—' She leaned back in the rocking-chair with the vivid cushions behind her – rather unexpectedly she liked vivid jewel colours in her house – and began to speak.

And even though it was a wholly unfamiliar world, Alice made it so real that it sometimes felt as if her words were weaving themselves into a magic carpet that could fly back to those long-ago days. The music-filled city of Vienna fifty years ago, and the gaiety and the colour and the dazzling palaces . . . The way the big houses were lit when a grand ball was given, even with lamps hung from the trees lining the carriageways . . . The sound of an orchestra striking up for waltzes and polkas, or of a single musician bringing music rippling and cascading from a piano or a violin . . . The palaces and the coffee houses . . . The swish of silk gowns and the drift of expensive perfume, and the taste of Viennese chocolate and Viennese *sachertorte* . . .

'Miss Nina's parents were important and wealthy,' Alice said, her eyes inward-looking, her head leaning back against the cushions in her chair. 'And she had a great many beaux.'

This was a new word. '"Bow"?'

'No, a French word.' Alice wrote it down, the singular and then the plural. 'In those days it meant suitors. Boyfriends. Young men wanting to marry her – it might have been the money that attracted a lot of them, of course, although she was very pretty. The master held a great many receptions for her; dinners and soirées – that's a musical evening. There was always so much music in Vienna in those days. Famous singers and musicians came to the house to give recitals or concerts.'

'But the night *he* came—? That wasn't a musical night, was it? It was a grand ball, that night, wasn't it?'

'It was a very special night indeed. The ball was to begin at ten, but I helped Miss Nina to dress much earlier. She was wearing white, spangled with hundreds of tiny stars, with a gauze stole around her shoulders—'

'*Gross.*'

'Yes, I know it sounds gross to you, but it was what young ladies wore in those days, and it was very beautiful. Miss Nina looked beautiful that night – at least, at the beginning of the night she did. A little plump thing she was, but with a tiny, tiny waist, and masses of fair fluffy hair. I remember we threaded thin silver strands through her hair, with tiny seed pearls. Real pearls, they were, of course.

'And when she was ready I went to the top of the stairs with her, to watch her go downstairs to help greet the guests. Can you visualize it? There was a great sweeping stairway with gilt banisters on both sides, and banks of flowers in huge tubs everywhere, and a chandelier overhead, all sparkling and glistening. Big double doors at one end, opening on to the ballroom: the musicians were already in there, and they were playing something – Strauss, it was. It was always Strauss in Vienna.' She smiled as if at a private joke. 'And I was only just seventeen, and I had never seen anything like it. I thought I had fallen into fairyland.' For a moment, it was not an ageing lady with silver hair and creases at the corners of her eyes and mouth who sat there; it was a young girl, wide-eyed with awe.

'Miss Nina went down the stairs just as the guests were arriving,' said Alice. 'She was deliberately late, which was naughty of her, because as the daughter of the house she should have been with her parents in time to welcome everyone. But she used to do things like that, to attract people's attention.'

'And you saw all the people coming to the ball.'

'Yes, I saw them all. Richly dressed ladies, and men in formal evening wear. Some army officers – Germans, very smart and correct.' She paused, and for a moment something crept into her voice that was no longer the soft story-spinning tone. 'Members of the Reichstag were there as well, because Miss Nina's father had important government connections.'

'The Reichstag?' The word was unknown but it was an uncomfortable one; it seemed to have brought a sudden fear into the warm comfortable sitting-room. Like when your stomach flutters and you know you're going to be sick. Like when your skin prickles because there's something unpleasant in the room with you – a scuttly spider that you're afraid to rout out . . . (Or like when you lie under the sheets, pretending not to be there, praying not to hear the angry voices downstairs, or the menacing footstep on the stair . . .)

But this word, this *Reichstag*, was something even bigger and more important than that. It was something to do with those old snatches of television newsreels, with the black and white images. Something that happened before I was born . . .

Alice only said, 'The Reichstag was the German equivalent of the English parliament,' but the hardness was still in her voice. 'But also among the guests that night was a young man with dark hair and golden-brown eyes.' The softness came back into her tone so that it was possible to relax again. 'He was wearing a white tie and tails – all the men wore that, in those days; I expect I can find a photograph somewhere to show you what it looked like – and he was the most handsome man I had ever seen. I thought he must be a prince, or a duke at the very least.'

She paused, but it was unthinkable to interrupt at this point, even though this was clearly the young man Mother had talked about: the young man who had not been allowed to marry Alice. Had they clung together and sobbed, like people in films or on TV did? Had they vowed that one day they would find a way to be together? But it did not seem as if they ever had, because Alice lived on her own out here.

Alice said, 'The footman took his cloak and he was about to go into the ballroom with his friends. But then he turned and looked up the stairs. Miss Nina was still only halfway down, and at first I thought he was looking at her.'

'But he wasn't, was he? He was looking at you?'

The smile slid out, slightly mischievous. 'Yes. He was looking at me.'

It was impossible to explain – even to this odd, extraordinarily intuitive child who had become so very dear – how one had felt in that moment, or to describe the mingled emotions of excitement and soaring joy and triumph, because the unknown young man had not even seemed to see the rich, beautiful Nina; he had looked straight at the little servant-girl, the drab-haired, drab-garbed little sparrow who had been standing quietly and rather humbly in the shadows. Alice had been humble in those days, because she had been trained to be.

But the young man with the eyes the colour of the topaz necklace Miss Nina had tossed Alice's way ('I don't care for it any more, Alice – you may have it') had hardly seemed aware of Nina.

Alice leaned back in her chair, her mind going back over the years to that astonishing night. 'He was a famous musician, that young man – although I had never heard of him. He had been intended as Miss Nina's husband – I didn't know that, either – but I found out later that the engagement was to have been announced that very night. That was how people did things in those days, and in those circles. After supper, Miss Nina's papa would have made the announcement, and everyone would have applauded, and champagne would have been served for the guests to drink to the couple's future happiness.'

But none of it had happened, because the young man with topaz eyes had left the ballroom within ten minutes of arriving; he had ignored the claims of his betrothed-to-be and his hosts, and had walked into the servants' hall as bold and as arrogant as a buccaneer. He had found Alice, who fortunately had been on her own, and asked her to come out to supper with him at one of the little coffee places in the middle of Vienna. Yes, he meant tonight, in fact he meant now. He could not bear to spend his evening pretending – he had pretended for too long. And he could not be bothered with being conventional, he said, especially now that he had seen Alice.

He was like no one Alice had ever encountered in her life, and she had gone with him, not bothering to seek permission, simply pulling on her warm woollen cloak and walking out of the house through the little garden door.

They had gone to a restaurant near to St Stephen's Cathedral called the Three Hussars. To Alice it seemed very grand, and full of expensively dressed ladies and gentlemen. She had no idea what she had eaten, because very soon the young man had taken her to his rooms which were in a tall old house in the ancient part of the city, the part that was somehow sinister and where the streets seemed almost to sing with their own dark past, and where anything – *anything!* – might happen to one . . .

Anything might happen . . .

For a little while he had played music to her on the glossy black piano near a window, and although Alice had not known the music or who had written it, while he played, the whole room seemed to thrum with vibrancy. Quite suddenly he had flung away from the piano, and had come to where Alice was seated on a velvet sofa, and had begun to kiss her with such helpless passion and such longing that it was impossible to resist him.

Alice did not resist. She knew, as all good girls knew, that you did not allow young men to kiss you in this way, and nor did you allow them to pull impatiently at the fastenings of your dress so that they could slide their hands inside. On two or three occasions Miss Nina's brother had cornered her in a dark corridor between the dining-room and the servants' hall, and had fumbled with the neck of her frock, and once he had pulled her into the linen room and pressed his body against her. He said it was ridiculous and pretentious for a slut of a serving girl to pretend to virginity, but Alice had been embarrassed by the hard bulge of masculinity against her thighs, and she had pushed him away and scurried back to her own part of the house, thinking that if that was how it felt, it would be easy to remain a good girl and save one's virginity for one's eventual husband.

But no one had told her that a man's hands could feel like this on her skin – soft and sinless and so exciting that it turned you dizzy – and no one had told her how it felt to lie on a soft wide bed with the night-sounds of a city below the window, and to feel the excitement building up and up until, so far from pushing him away, you thought you might die if he did not go on . . .

And although she had known – well, sort of known – what happened in a bed on a marriage night, she had not known that it robbed you of all resistance or that the emotions it brought were so intense and so deeply sweet that you wanted to weep for sheer joy . . .

'I am sorry,' he had said at last, raising his dark head from the pillow. He was not Austrian – Alice did not then know what nationality he was except that he was not English – but he spoke English well. 'My poor little English sparrow,' he said. 'I had not thought you would be a virgin.'

'I'm glad. I'm glad you were the first.' She had wanted to say,

And you'll be the last, but had not quite dared.

'You should go back to the house now. I take you. But we can be together again soon, if you wish that.'

'Yes. Yes, I do wish that.'

'Very good. Then we go now. You will have to walk from the carriageway around the side of the house and go in through the garden door. You can do that? You do not mind that?'

Alice did not say she would have walked through hell's deepest caverns and back again, or that she would have entered the house by way of the sewers or the chimneys if he had asked her to. She said, 'Yes. Yes, I can do all that. I expect it will be quite easy.'

But life is seldom easy, and it is hardly ever predictable.

The house was in an uproar when Alice got back. Most of the guests had left, although a few, more inquisitive than the rest or perhaps simply more insensitive, had remained. To give support, they were all telling one another. Poor little Nina, poor child, jilted on her betrothal night. And betrayed by her own maid, the scheming hussy! Disgraceful. And where *was* the sly creature, that was what they would all like to know! It was to be hoped that the slut would be dealt with suitably when – and if! – she returned to the house!

At the centre of it all was Nina herself, lying on a chaise-longue in the upstairs drawing-room, sobbing and fretfully pushing away all the offers of laudanum or bromide in warm water, her hair in a snarl, and the delicate gloves and silk sandals she had been wearing tossed petulantly to the floor. Her mother sat at one end of the chaise-longue, wringing her hands ineffectually, saying that no one had ever been able to soothe Nina when she got into one of her nervous states, and oh dear, what were they to do, and think of the *scandal* . . . In front of the fireplace her papa and her brother were conversing in low voices.

Alice had hoped to creep unobtrusively to her room, but she was pounced upon, hauled into the drawing-room, and offered to the assembled company to be suitably dealt with. As she looked round, the thought that came uppermost in her mind was not her own plight, but that in Miss Nina's situation she hoped she would have had more self-control than to indulge in a spoilt-child tantrum before everyone.

They fell silent as soon as they saw her; even Miss Nina sat up straight, and forgot about crying. The words *shameful* and *guttersnipe* hissed round the room; Alice had learned a little German by this time – she had, in fact, learned rather more than a little – and she could recognize those words very well indeed.

In the end, it had been Miss Nina's brother who had ordered her from the house, his eyes meeting Alice's in sly triumph. He adopted a prim shocked tone which Alice thought the greatest absurdity of the whole situation, and said she was to go immediately, they could not have such a creature under their roof. And then, possibly mindful of the need to appear considerate before guests, despite the circumstances, amended this to first light. She was to go at first light: she would be allowed to take her belongings with her – they were not thieves in this family, he added righteously. But after tomorrow they did not want ever to see or hear from her again. He glanced at his parents as he said this, and apparently receiving tacit approval, added, in a final burst of spite, that one day he hoped to see her reduced to begging in the streets for what she had done to his sister.

Alice said loudly, 'Well, it is no worse than what you have done to some of your mother's maids,' and saw his face flush with embarrassment. He glanced uneasily at the listening people, and in a burst of bravado Alice added, 'You tried to do it to me as well, but I fought you off.'

This time it was not embarrassment that flooded his face, it was glaring fury, and he took a step towards her, his fists clenched so that she thought he was going to hit her. But then Nina – by now Alice had ceased to think of the pampered little goose as 'Miss' – pettishly threw her shoes across the room at Alice, and followed them with a little cut-glass scent bottle. None of the objects hit Alice, but the scent bottle shattered and spilt its contents all over the polished floor, threatening to tip the scene from tragedy to melodrama, since grand passions do not play well against an overpowering aura of lily-of-the-valley perfume, and the gentlemen of the party had to discreetly cover their mouths and noses with their handkerchiefs.

Alice did not care. She did not care that she was being turned from the house and threatened by Nina's brother; she said defiantly that she would go now, rather than wait until the morning.

She must suit herself about that, they said, and smugly told one another that at least no one could accuse them of turning her out into the night.

Alice whisked from the room, and tumbled her few possessions into the locked box that she had brought with her from England. Carrying it, she set off down the sweeping carriageway to the high road, and embarked on the long walk across the city to the tall old house near St Stephen's Cathedral.

It was a much greater distance than she remembered. By the time she had walked through the sprawling suburbs with the great houses and the parks, and had entered the city proper, Vienna had emerged from its sinister night-persona to become a bustling place of bright daylight, and of workers bound for their daily employment, and milk-carts and street-sweepers, and alleycats foraging for scraps after their night's adventuring. Sunlight trickled over the stones and the walls, and the scents of good coffee and freshly baked croissants drifted from the houses and the cafés. The servants' breakfast would be being served about now; if Alice had not left she would have been in her usual place at the long table. But what's done is done, my girl, and you'll survive a few hours without breakfast. In any case, *he* would give her breakfast. She visualized steaming coffee that he would have brewed himself, and warm rolls stuffed with ham and thin cheese, or buttered eggs. And his eyes regarding her across the small table that had stood in the window of the piano-room . . .

Using the cathedral spire as guide, she entered the maze of little streets and cobbled alleyways surrounding it, and began to look for the tall old house. It was then that the nightmare began.

Last night she had been too far gone in longing to take note of exactly where they were, and she had certainly not looked at street names. But surely she would recognize the place again. She began to walk around the streets, eagerly looking at the houses, craning her neck to find a familiar corbel on a window ledge or a stonework carving above the entrance to an alleyway.

The morning wore on, and the sun began to be high and hot. People came out of their workplaces and bought rolls and paté and fruit to eat in the little squares. Alice began to feel hungry and thirsty; her feet were starting to blister and her arms ached from carrying the box with all her possessions. She had only a few schillings, but there was enough to buy some coffee and a wedge of rye bread with cheese. She ate it sitting on a bench in the cathedral's shadow.

After that she renewed her search. But by late afternoon the shadows were creeping back over Vienna, and the dark underside of the old city was stirring. The lamps were lit in the streets, and when she passed a tavern or a wine cellar laughter and voices and food-scents gusted out. Alice, dizzy with exhaustion, began to have the feeling that she had somehow stumbled into an entirely different city without realizing it. For the first time she began to feel frightened, and for the first time she faced the possibility that she would not find the tall old house.

CHAPTER TEN

Once Lucy had reached her teens she almost forgot about Alraune. There were far more interesting things in life than all that gothic romance stuff about a slightly sinister ghost-child, and in any case who cared about things that had happened all those years ago? demanded Lucy's rebellious fourteen-year-old self. Alraune had never existed. And yet . . .

And yet she never quite shook off the feeling that Alraune was much closer than any of them guessed. She occasionally woke from disturbing dreams – dreams that were half sad but that were also half terrifying, and that had always left her with the feeling that Alraune was not someone she would ever want to meet.

And now Trixie Smith had stirred those dreams up, so that back at her desk after Deb's funeral, determinedly concentrating on Quondam's horror-film presentation, Lucy caught herself thinking about Alraune, and thinking as well that these days all kinds of information was accessible at the flick of a computer key. Births and deaths, and marriages and divorces. Electoral rolls and property tax accounts and census records. Yes, but would Alraune figure in those kind of lists? And if so, under what name, because presumably you would not go through life with a name like that if you could help it. *Mandragora officinarum*. Imagine having that called out in a school register. Imagine giving it as your name if you were applying for a driving licence or making a dentist's appointment or collecting your dry-cleaning. And even if Lucy did find the right name and was inclined to make a search for Alraune, where would she begin? And if Deb had not died so abruptly, could she have talked to her about Alraune? Would she have opened up a bit more? Lucy had sometimes had the feeling that Deb would like to have talked to Lucy about the family, but it had never happened. Was that because Edmund had always been around?

In the house where Lucy had spent her early childhood there had been boxes of stuff about Lucretia and her life; corded trunks and tea-chests full of newspaper articles and photographs and posters, all stored away in attics. Lucy's mother had once said that when Lucretia died, her entire life had been packed into those boxes and those tea-chests. 'After her death no one could face any of it,' she had said. 'Some pasts should die, never forget that.'

'Rot, Mariana, you're simply being melodramatic again,' Aunt Deb had said tartly. 'You love all that stuff about Lucretia, in fact you dine out on it – I've heard you telling your friends all the stories,' she added, and Lucy, who had been hoping for a story about the mysterious Lucretia, had seen something flicker on her mother's face that made her look so unlike her normal self that she had felt suddenly nervous.

'Oh, yes, of course I do,' Mariana had said at once. 'It's all the greatest fun. Dear Lucretia and all the lovers and the scandals. What else is there to do but make capital out of it? But there were other things, weren't there?' She gave an exaggerated shiver, like a child deliberately trying to frighten itself. 'That suggestion that she spied for the Nazis in the war . . .'

Aunt Deb had said, 'Mariana—' but Lucy's mother had not paused, almost as if, Lucy thought, she wanted to stop Aunt Deb from going on.

'. . . but of course the war was over years ago, and we've all forgotten it, and in any case Lucy's too young to understand any of this, aren't you, my lamb?'

But Lucy had understood quite a lot because when she was small people had still talked about Lucretia. Sometimes they called her 'that woman', and used words like 'disgrace' and 'immoral'. Once, in Lucy's hearing, a woman with a pinched-up mouth like Lucy's drawstring gym-bag had said Lucretia had been lucky not to be executed for treason, and she did not care who heard her say so. Lucy thought treason had something to do with people being shut away in the Tower of London, and then being burned alive or having all their insides cut out, which would be pretty gross either way and not something you would want done to your grandmother.

The boxes and the tea-chests had ended up in the attics, which was where Mariana said you put such fusty old things: she did not want them littering up her nice rooms! Oh, nonsense, the attic stairs were not all that narrow; it was simply a matter of manoeuvring the boxes around the little twisty part to the second floor. Perfectly accessible, and also splendid for make-believe games – for Lucy and for Edmund when he came to stay in the holidays. Poorest Edmund, stuck in that house with that dreary old father. The two of them must make a search for old costumes next time; they might organize some games of charades this Christmas, said Mariana.

After Lucy's parents died she had made a private vow never to forget them; to always remember what they looked like and how their voices sounded. But the memories had grown dim and vague with the years – she could remember a lot of laughter, sometimes a bit too shrill, and a lot of vividly dressed people sipping drinks in the evenings and at weekends – but at this distance it all seemed rather unreal and two-dimensional: like watching figures on a stage. It was ironic that the attic memories – the fragments of Lucretia's life – had stayed with her far more vividly than the memories of her parents.

But the greater irony was that if only those stored-away

memories – those crammed-full boxes and those too-heavy-to-move tea-chests – had been available now, Lucy could have plundered them for clues to Alraune. She frowned and pushed this thought away, because the memory of when and how those brittle pages and those stacks of smudgy newsprint had been lost was one of the dangerous memories. One of the bits of the past that should be left to die.

And she thought that even if she had been able to find anything, she would not really have wanted to pass it on to Trixie Smith. She thought she would have wanted to keep Alraune secret. She felt all over again the ache of loss for Aunt Deb, who could have been consulted about this.

Still, whoever you were, said Lucy to Alraune's uneasy legend, and whether you were real or not, you churned up a few nightmares for me, so now that you seem to have been resurrected, so to speak, I think I might like to know a bit more about you. I don't really know very much at all, and I'm not even sure what your place would be in the family tree. And were you really born to Lucretia, or have I simply assumed that because you were named for her film?

So what actual information was there about the dark chimera that was Alraune? Well, Alraune was supposed to have been born at the start of World War II and smuggled into one of the neutral countries when little more than a baby, to lie low in safety until the war ended. The stories of the actual smuggling varied wildly, from quite reasonable, quite credible, accounts of unobtrusive journeys in plain cars across various enemy borders, and then escalated dramatically to French-Revolution-style escapes in baskets of cabbages or mad moonlight flits inside fake coffins with plague crosses on the lids. It was these last tales that made Alraune's existence sound like the purest fantasy. But other than this, there was not a great deal to go on.

Everyone in the family had always shied away from discussing Alraune. Aunt Deb had once said that Alraune's childhood had been bitterly tragic, but she had also said that Alraune was better forgotten. But 'bitterly tragic' could mean anything. If you related it to World War II it could mean an Ann-Frank-style incarceration in a sealed-off attic with Nazi stormtroopers searching the house, but if you took it in a more general sense it might mean an early death from some inexorable disease.

If one was going to look for Alraune, where would one start? Always accepting the old maxim about it being impossible to prove a negative, where could you start, when you were not sure if you had an accurate name, and when you were not even sure of the reality of the person you were trying to find?

As abruptly as a door being slammed back against a wall, the answer was there. What Lucy needed was a link back to that era, and Lucretia herself might provide that link. She had been a luminary of the silver screen – she had been famous and infamous and above all she had been *news*. What today was called a celebrity. Almost everything she had done from the late 1920s to the day of her death had been documented in one form or another. In newspapers, and in the glossy film-star magazines that had become fashionable after the war.

Scouring magazines would be time-consuming, and any accounts Lucy did find might be biased or exaggerated. But Lucretia's life had not just been charted in print; a great deal of it had been captured on film. And Quondam Films had a section devoted entirely to old newsreel footage.

Once the search would have meant meanderings through imperfectly-kept card-indexes or basements crammed with badly-labelled boxes, climbing on to library-steps to reach the higher shelves or crawling on hands and knees to see what was pushed on to the bottom sections. In a way there was a rather faded romance about that kind of search, because it gave you the feeling of thrusting your hands back into the past, and of brushing the tips of your fingers against the cobwebby fragments of history.

But from a practical point of view it was much easier to be able to call up Quondam's archive list on a computer screen, which was what Lucy was doing now, and type in a search request for newsreels between 1940 and 1950 containing anything on Lucretia von Wolff.

Lucy waited while the computer scanned its files – it took a few moments because there was quite a lot of stuff for it to scan. The film and TV news-makers had really got going in those years, and there had been so much going on in the world that they had wanted to record. Quondam had recently acquired some terrific footage of Dunkirk and VE Day and D-Day, and the marketing department were considering assembling the reels into chronological order, with the idea of trying to interest one of the major war museums in them. When Lucy had finished with the horror presentation she might be involved in that, which she would like very much.

The responses to the search request came up, and Lucy leaned forward eagerly. Most of them seemed to deal solely with Lucretia's return to the screen after the war; she had made a couple of films in 1947 and 1948, one with the tempestuous Erich von Stroheim, which had apparently been an explosive pairing, but which had been regarded as a very fine example of *film noir*. There had been a good deal of advance publicity about both films, and from the entry it looked as if some of the footage showed Lucretia arriving at the premières. It would be interesting to see these some time, but at the moment they were not what Lucy was looking for. She scrolled down the screen to see what else there might be.

And there, towards the end, were three entries that sounded as if they focused more directly on Lucretia's private life. Two were from Pathé News, and the other one bore a maker's name that looked to be either German or Dutch. Lucy, aware of a sudden beat of anticipation, requested viewings of all three as soon as possible and sent the request along the inter-office email system.

After this she returned, with slightly diminished enthusiasm, to *The Devil's Sonata*, which had turned out to have telltale amber discolouration, indicating that the cellulose nitrate had started to decompose – probably from storage at the wrong temperature – meaning it would have to be copied all over again. In addition there was a massive flaw halfway through the second reel, which could have been caused by anything, but which meant that the lustfully intentioned and satanically inclined violinist was precipitated straight from the opera house stage (where he had been wearing formal white tie and tails) to the heroine's Left Bank atelier, where he was wearing a velvet jacket and the standard villain issue of cloak and wide-brimmed hat.

Lucy was just wondering if there were any stills that would shunt the plot along, and if so, whether Quondam's technical department could use them to patch over the flaw – this had been done fairly successfully with the famous Frank Capra 1937 *Lost Horizon* – when an email pinged into her inbox to say she could view two of the three newsreels she had requested. The German one, it appeared, was currently the subject of a copyright wrangle, so to all intents and purposes it was verboten at the moment, but she could see the two Pathé reels and welcome. One was nine minutes in length, and one was four and a half, and both were flagged as being in need of restoration, which could mean anything from a few slight hiccups that only a purist would notice, to comprehensive damage by flood, fire or tornado. But that said, a projectionist could be available in the smaller of the two viewing-rooms at half past three, and would Lucy please confirm if this would suit her.

The viewing-room was small and almost completely dark and there was a scent of warm machinery and also of blackcurrant throat lozenges from the projectionist, who had a sore throat and was inclined to be lugubrious as a result.

Lucy waved to him to start the first reel, and sat down. She had no idea what she was about to see, or whether it would tell her anything about Lucretia – and about Alraune – that she did not already know. Almost certainly it would not. Be logical, Lucy. But her heart was thudding, and as the projector began to whirr she clenched her fists so hard that her nails dug little dents into her palms.

The familiar oblong of light appeared on the small screen, and the soundtrack kicked in with the distinctive Pathé music. The commentary began, the commentator speaking in the stilted, pseudo-jolly accents that had been obligatory in the forties and fifties. BBC pronunciation, people used to call it, sometimes meaning it sarcastically, sometimes not.

This one was the longer film of the two, and it seemed to be mostly about Lucretia's arrival at Ashwood Studios, and the plans for shooting the murder mystery – the film that had never been finished because of the real murders. Lucy thought Ashwood had been hoping to rival Alfred Hitchcock and David Lean – hadn't *Rebecca* come out around then? Certainly it had been the heyday of *film noir*: black rainy streets, criminal treachery, victimized anti-heroes and *femmes fatales*. Films like *A Woman's Face* and *Desire Me*, or *Citizen Kane* and the all-time classic, *The Third Man*. Each had had its own sultry intelligent temptress, of course: Joan Crawford, Bette Davis, the luminous Greer Garson. And Lucretia von Wolff.

There was not very much about Lucretia in this newsreel, though, other than some fleeting footage of a sinuous figure emerging from a car. There were one or two blurry shots of the studios; compared to Ealing or Pinewood, Ashwood was quite a small set-up, although it looked busy and people moved around with energy and enthusiasm.

Lucy's interest was briefly caught by a long-distance shot of Leo Dreyer arriving at the studios for some reception or other. She leaned forward, trying to make out his features, but there was little more than an impression of a rather tall man wearing one of the long dark overcoats of the day and a Homburg hat.

The clip came to an end and the projectionist began to wind the second film. There would probably not be anything of use on this one, either. Still, you never knew.

The quality of this reel was poor; the soundtrack was tinny

and there were a number of white zigzags on the surface, indicating scratches or imperfect storage. The commentator was either the same man as on the first reel, or had attended the same elocution classes.

'And now a sight of one of the technological wonders of the age – one of the world's first fully pressurized four-engined airliners – the Boeing Stratoliner 307. And this one is the most famous of them all – it's the "Flying Penthouse", bought by multi-millionaire Howard Hughes to convey him around the world in the style to which we would all like to become accustomed.'

There was a happy pause, presumably for audiences to enjoy the joke, and then the commentator went merrily on. 'The Stratoliner can fly at an astonishing 220 miles an hour, and the pressurized cabin makes it possible to fly at altitudes of 14,000 feet or even higher. That's what they call being above the weather – now there's a good way to escape the English winter!'

The bouncing, isn't-this-a-happy-world, music cut in, and there were shots of what was presumably the Stratoliner taking off and landing, and one of it flying over some unidentifiable country. There were patches of fogginess that might have been the monochrome film, or that might have been the flaws, or that might simply have been the weather that day.

There was nothing about Lucretia, and Lucy was beginning to wonder if the can of film had been wrongly labelled, or if someone had made a mistake in the listings, when the commentator said, 'But here's something that doesn't come as standard with the Stratoliner 307. On this trip, Mr Hughes loaned his plane and a pilot for the transporting of a very decorative piece of cargo – none other than the famous star of the silent screen, Baroness Lucretia von Wolff.'

Lucy's heartbeat punched breath-snatchingly against her ribcage, and she leaned forward, hardly daring to blink in case she missed anything.

'A smooth-as-silk landing for a smooth-as-silk lady,' said the commentator in a rather knowing, nudge-nudge, manner as the huge plane touched down. 'The baroness, on her way to Switzerland, travelled in her usual style, thanks to Mr Hughes' generosity.'

Switzerland, thought Lucy. *Switzerland.*

There was a three-quarters close-up of Lucretia descending the plane's steps, stepping as delicately as a cat on four-inch heels. Even on the scratched foggy film, the mesmeric allure was apparent. Lucy, who had not watched any of Lucretia's films for years, had forgotten how incandescently lovely and how smoulderingly sexy Lucretia had been. No wonder you slayed them in the aisles, grandmamma.

'And,' said the commentator archly, 'for the ladies who are watching, our fashion editors say the baroness is wearing Christian Dior's New Look.'

Behind Lucy, the projectionist sneezed and blew his nose with gusto.

'But something that isn't a fashion accessory is the cuddlesome armful,' went on the commentator. 'On this trip, Madame von Wolff had with her the newest addition to her family – the ten-month-old Mariana, named, so we're given to understand, for the lady in Tennyson's famous gothic poem.'

Lucy felt like sneezing disgustedly herself at this, because gothic Tennysonian poetry and Lucretia von Wolff were not terms you would expect to encounter in the same sentence. Still, Mariana had been her mother, so there was interest in seeing the chubby toddler who was eyeing the camera dubiously.

The commentator made the predictable remark about the baby having her mamma's affinity with a camera, which Lucy thought was stretching it a good deal, and then said, 'Also on this journey, the baroness seems to have brought along another small friend.'

Without any warning, the camera panned down to an older child at Lucretia's side – a child of perhaps seven or eight years. And this time there was no forced jollity about affinity with a camera. Deepset eyes, slightly tilted above high cheekbones, stared suspiciously from under a square fringe; the dark hair was cut short, and for a boy it would have been slightly too long, for a girl slightly short. Which is it? thought Lucy, her eyes fixed on the screen.

There was time to register that the child was wearing a kind of butcher-boy's cap and a buttoned jacket, and then the camera swung back to Lucretia. The commentator gave a few more technical details about the plane, and although there was an almost throwaway reference to Lucretia's plans to make a film at Ashwood Studios next year, it was fairly clear that the point of the newsclip had been the juxtaposition of the eccentric Howard Hughes, the opulent aeroplane, and the infamous Lucretia von Wolff.

The screen flickered and the clip ended, and Lucy sat back, her mind whirling. *Had* that been Alraune? Was there anyone else it could conceivably be? It could not be Deborah, for Deb would have been thirteen or so by this time, and in any case, Deb had never possessed that thatch of dark hair, or those deep eyes. Right up to her death Deb had had a beautifully smooth English-rose complexion, and bright blue eyes.

The date was about right for Alraune, who was supposed to have been born at the outbreak of war – say 1939 or 1940. What was this clip's date? 1947, was it? Yes, October 1947. In 1947, Alraune would have been seven or eight, which meant the dates fitted. The journey to Switzerland might fit as well, because part of Alraune's legend was the exodus to a neutral country. Had that country been Switzerland?.

But, thought Lucy, am I forcing the facts to fit my theory? That child could have been anyone. A friend's child, or the child of one of the air-crew. But she went on staring at the darkened screen. Had she just seen a fragment of the past that everyone had always insisted never existed?

CHAPTER ELEVEN

Francesca Holland thought life must be so much easier for people who did not have a conscience. People without a conscience, for instance, would not have spent a Friday afternoon fighting to get out of London (the M25 was at a standstill *again*!) to a house in the back of beyond.

Most people had thought Fran was mad to be making the trip. Most likely Trixie had simply gone off to interview somebody in connection with her thesis, they said; she was taking it very seriously, that thesis. Anyway, Fran was out of her tree to be dashing off into the wide blue yonder like this.

To all of the protests and reassurances Francesca had said, 'Yes, but the dogs. Trixie would never go off and leave the dogs,' and people had said vaguely, oh well, you could never tell, and had melted away because no one had really wanted to take on the responsibility.

That had been when Francesca had known she would have to take the responsibility herself, because Trixie had been good to her since the day Fran had got home early and found Marcus in their bed with a blonde. Trixie had been the one who had come into the senior staff-room that day and said that if Fran liked, she could have the spare room for a few weeks. Until things got sorted out, she had said, and Francesca had accepted, because there had not seemed to be anything else to do and she could not think where else to go. Walking out on your husband in just the clothes you had on and with only the money you had in your handbag was a deeply satisfying gesture, but it brought a few practical problems – especially when you tried to sneak back later to pack a suitcase and retrieve your credit cards, and discovered your husband had changed all the locks and that his blonde was already firmly in residence.

Fran had tried not to be a nuisance to Trixie, who thought nearly all emotions a waste of time, and she had taken on a share of the household expenses, along with half the cooking and cleaning. She had tried not to mind the smell of the dogmeat that had to be stewed for four hours at weekends and stank out the house for the rest of the week, and she had tried not to mind Trixie's habit of noisily getting up at six a.m. every morning so that the dogs could be exercised on the heath. In her gruff way, Trixie had been very kind. Fran had been in pieces all over the floor about Marcus, and Trixie had been the only one to offer any kind of help, especially after everyone heard how Fran had burst into tears in the middle of taking Middle Year Three for English Literature.

'I dare say,' the Deputy Head had said, interviewing Francesca in some embarrassment, 'that it was the Shakespeare lesson, was it?' Fran had said, yes, that was what it had been, but had not bothered to try explaining how the words of Shakespeare – and come to that, the words of John Donne and Robert Browning and his Elizabeth, and all the rest of that gang – could suddenly come smack-down on a tender spot and send you into floods of stupid tears in Middle Three's English-lit class. The Deputy Head, who taught maths and chemistry, would not have understood, although some of Middle Three might have understood it only too well, providing you discounted the bored and sophisticated fourteen-going-on-twenty-five-year-olds, condom-carrying as a matter of course and imbued with the your-place-or-mine culture.

So in view of Trixie's brusque kindness, Francesca could not simply let her vanish and do nothing about it, and after thinking it over, she decided to begin the search with Lucretia von Wolff's family. Trixie had been in the process of arranging an interview with the surviving daughter – an elderly lady called Deborah Fane. Mrs Fane had died before the interview could take place, although Trixie had driven up to her home all the same, Fran did know that, and she also knew that Deborah Fane's address was in Trixie's address book. It had felt like the worst kind of intrusion to go through this, but Fran had done it because she had needed a starting-point. And there the address had been, in Trixie's firm clear writing.

There had not been a phone number though, and Directory Enquiries did not have anything listed, which was why Fran had decided to drive up there to see if Mrs Fane's family would talk to her. It was a reasonably straightforward journey – a small market town on the edge of Nottinghamshire – not quite Derbyshire, but nearly. A couple of hours' drive? Yes, not much more than that. She would do it, and she would look on it as a small adventure.

The family might still be knocked out by Deborah Fane's death, in which case Fran would retreat with as much tact and politeness as she could manage. But they might remember Trixie's visit, or even know about the research, and they might provide a couple of clues that could be passed to the police. A house where Lucretia von Wolff had lived, perhaps, and where Trixie might have gone, or even an address of someone who had known the baroness or worked with her, and who was worth paying a visit. Fran would have to make it very clear to them that she was not taking up the mantle of Trixie's researches; she was simply trying to track down a mysteriously vanished colleague. It was annoying not to know names or anything; Trixie had merely said that as well as Deborah Fane, there was a granddaughter and some man who was related to Deborah from her husband's side of the family. Edmund Fane, had she said? Yes.

She waited until Friday afternoon, when Middle Three were allowed to finish at two o'clock in order to go about their lawful occasions, God help them; consigned the dogs to their spare-time kennels, threw a few things into a weekend case, topped the car up with petrol, and set off. It felt rather good to be doing something like this on her own, without Marcus pointing out her inadequacies in driving, or sneering if she missed a turning or went wrong at a traffic island.

Deborah Fane's house, when Francesca finally negotiated the narrow lane, turned out to be quite large and also quite old, although Fran, whose tastes ran to the clean uncluttered lines of the later Georgians, thought it rather ugly. It had a lot of character though, and it probably had a lot of history, as well. She wondered how long Lucretia's daughter had lived here.

She was relieved to see lights on in the downstairs rooms, because there had always been the possibility that the house would be empty and shut up. But someone was definitely here, even if it only turned out to be squatters or gypsies or men with a distraint on the furniture. The baroness seemed to have had such a colourful history that Fran was prepared for anything from her descendants.

But the man who opened the door to her was clearly neither a bailiff nor a gypsy. He was thin-faced and he had what Francesca could only think of as a quiet air about him. He asked politely enough if he could help, although he sounded wary.

Francesca had rehearsed what to say on the way here, and it came out more or less all right, although like most rehearsed speeches it sounded a bit stilted.

'I'm sorry to turn up out of the blue like this. I'm Francesca Holland and I'm a colleague of Trixie Smith – the lady who's been researching Lucretia von Wolff's life. And I'm sorry if this sounds melodramatic, but I'm a bit concerned about Trixie, because she seems to have vanished.'

She thought there was a reaction at the mention of Lucretia, which, if this really had been her daughter's house, was understandable. But he appeared to be waiting, quite politely, to see if there was any more, so Francesca went on to the next part. 'I have phoned the police—' That was intended to provide a reference if it was wanted. 'But they're not inclined to crank up the missing-person machinery yet awhile – or not for an adult anyway. So I've driven up from North London to see if I can retrace Trixie's steps and pick up any odd clue that might spur them into action.'

'That sounds quite worrying for you,' said the unknown man. 'But I should explain that I don't actually live here and I'm nothing to do with the family.'

'Oh, I see,' said Francesca rather blankly, and as if realizing that this had not been much of an explanation, he said, 'The lady who lived here left the place to a charity I work for – my name's Michael Sallis, by the way, and the charity's called CHARTH.' This was said in a perfunctory manner, as if he thought he had better offer his own credentials in exchange for Francesca's. 'I've been meeting a surveyor here – he's just gone, and I was getting ready to leave. Did you say you'd driven from London? Well, you'd at least better come inside and have a cup of tea or something. Nobody's cleared the kitchen out yet, and I shouldn't think the odd teabag would be missed.' He stepped back, holding the door open for her.

One of the things you absolutely never did in life was step over the threshold of a remote house, occupied by a lone and unknown man. Lions' dens and wolves' lairs, thought Francesca. Oh, bother it, he looks perfectly all right. In any case, I've just spent five years living with one wolf, so by the law of averages I shouldn't think I'm due to encounter another one for a while.

She said, 'I'd love a cup of tea. Thank you very much.'

And stepped over the threshold.

If Michael Sallis was a wolf, he was a very well-mannered one. There was no milk in the big old-fashioned larder, so he made black coffee, apologizing for the fact that it was instant, and searching the cupboards until he found clean cups.

'We can be civilized and drink it in the sitting-room if you want, but the kitchen's the only place with any heating on.'

'I like kitchens.' Fran accepted the coffee gratefully, and Michael Sallis sat down on the other side of the big scrubbed-top table.

'How unusual is it for your friend to go off without telling anyone?' he said.

'It's not usual at all – she's rather a conscientious sort of person. And she has three dogs who she would never abandon.'

'Have you taken on the dogs as well as the task of tracking her down?'

Fran explained about the kennels, and added, carefully, that she was staying with Trixie after an acrimonious separation from her husband. 'She and I teach at the same school; that's how I know her.'

Michael Sallis studied her for a moment, and then said, 'History or English literature?'

'What—? Oh, I see. English literature. Some grammar as well if I can force it in without the artless little grubs noticing. I help with the drama side a bit, too.' She regarded him over the rim of the cup. 'That was quite perceptive of you.'

'You didn't look like maths or chemistry,' he said, and Francesca grinned, remembering the Deputy Head.

'Why d'you think your friend might be here?'

'I don't think she's actually here,' said Fran. 'But I know she was here a couple of weeks ago, so she might have met some of the family. I wondered if she might have been given some information, something about Lucretia von Wolff, and gone hotfoot after it, and – well, got into difficulties of some kind. The thing is that she hasn't got any family – only an old aunt somewhere in the north – so as I'm still living in her house . . .'

'You've had the task thrust upon you.'

'Yes. I didn't really think it could be passed to the aunt – she's about ninety or something.'

Michael finished his own coffee, and said, 'I wonder if it would be any good to phone Deborah Fane's nephew. He only lives about five miles from here, and he might know something. I've got his number. Would he be of any use, d'you think?'

'Is that Edmund Fane? Trixie did mention him. He'd be worth trying, wouldn't he? Thank you very much.'

'I don't think the phone here is connected, but I've got a mobile if not,' said Michael, reaching into a battered briefcase.

'You're being very kind.'

'That's because this is the classic situation,' said Michael lightly. 'Damsel in distress turning up out of the blue and requesting help. How could I refuse? Although to be correct you should have waited until a blizzard was raging, or at the very least a thunderstorm – you said you taught drama: where's your sense of theatre, Ms Holland?' He smiled and suddenly he no longer looked quiet or scholarly; he looked mischievous and as if he might be rather fun if you could get through the outer layers of reserve.

The phone call was brief but productive. 'Your friend did talk to Edmund Fane,' said Michael, putting the phone down. 'And he somehow managed to arrange for her to get into Ashwood Studios.' He saw Fran's reaction, and said, 'Didn't you think of checking Ashwood? It'd be the first place most people would think of in connection with Lucretia. And if you live in North London it isn't very far, is it?'

Francesca thought it was not very far at all. She thought Trixie could have got there and back in an afternoon. 'But she didn't believe she could get access, so I haven't really thought about it.'

'Edmund Fane got access for her. He tracked down a solicitor who holds the keys. And,' said Michael, looking at her very intently, 'he met your friend there on Monday afternoon.'

'Monday afternoon would fit,' said Francesca, thinking back. 'I didn't actually miss Trixie until Tuesday night. I had a parents' evening on Monday, and some of us went out for supper afterwards. I got back quite late and went straight to bed. Mornings can be a bit of a scramble, so it was Tuesday evening before I realized properly that she wasn't around.'

'Would she have gone out to Ashwood without telling you?'

'There was no particular reason for her to tell me. I'm only a sort of lodger. She'd probably have talked about it afterwards though, because she liked talking about her thesis, and she'd have been pleased with herself for getting into the studios.' This sounded rather nastily critical of Trixie, so Fran said, 'But we're midway between East Barnet and Enfield, so it's not far.'

'Edmund Fane said he left her at the studios at about five,' said Michael. 'She wanted to prowl around a bit and draw some plans of the layout, so he left her to it. Fane says he drove home and as far as he recalls, got back about half past seven.'

For some reason – perhaps something in Michael's voice – Francesca did not much like the sound of Edmund Fane. She said, 'Why did he have to go all the way there? Couldn't Trixie go on her own?'

Michael considered and then said, 'Yes, *I* think she could have done, but Fane is very meticulous and a bit fussy. He probably thought it was the correct thing to do. Or maybe he was asked to go along to verify your friend's genuineness. Solicitor to solicitor, or something.'

'Oh, I see. That doesn't give us any leads though, does it?' said Francesca. 'Unless Trixie crashed her car driving back.'

'A crashed car would have been found and reported by now, I should think.'

'But if it happened on a lonely stretch of road—'

'Nowhere's that lonely these days.'

But Francesca had had a sudden vivid image of Trixie lying dead in a ditch somewhere, being rained on and investigated by weasels, and because this was not an image she wanted to get stuck with, she said firmly, 'What I think I'd better do is get in touch with this Ashwood solicitor.'

'All right. Fane gave me his number. His name's Liam Devlin. D'you want to borrow my phone?'

Liam Devlin, reached by Michael's phone, said he would be

perfectly happy to meet Miss – Mrs? – Holland at Ashwood. Yes, he would bring the keys out later today if she wanted, although she had better come clad as if for tempest, fire and flood, on account of the entire Ashwood site sinking into a mire after days of rain.

Francesca promised to arrive suitably garbed, hung up, and accepted Michael's offer of a quick wash-and-brush-up in the rather antiquated cloakroom off the hall. She was a bit tousled and pale from the long journey, and her mouth looked too wide for her face in the way it always did when she was tired or anxious. She brushed her hair, which she had had cut very short after leaving Marcus – it made her look like Joan of Arc after a night on the tiles, but it had represented a very satisfactory two-finger gesture to his simpering blonde and her gleaming shoulder-length hair – and went back to the kitchen to thank Michael for his help.

It was infuriating, having got all the polite thank-yous and interesting-to-have-met-yous, and all the conventional safe-journey farewells out of the way, to encounter a completely unresponsive engine when she turned on the ignition. Absolutely dead. Not a spark.

Fran swore and tried it again, and this time a faint, slightly sinister, smell of petrol came into the car's interior. Petrol-flooded or waterlogged or something. Third time lucky? She turned the key again, and this time, in addition to the ominous silence, the warning light for over-heating the engine glowed balefully at her from the dashboard. Hell's teeth. Now there was nothing for it but to go back into the house and find the number of a local garage. The trouble was that it was Friday afternoon and the odds were that no one would be able to come out until tomorrow at the earliest. Which meant she would have to phone Liam Devlin and put off their meeting at Ashwood, and that, in turn, would most likely mean Monday morning before she could get into the place. Bloody, *bloody* internal combustion engine!

A shaft of light showed from the open door of the house, and

Michael's voice said, 'It looks as if you'd better come back inside, doesn't it?'

'Wretched thing,' said Fran crossly. 'I don't suppose you'd know how to fix it?'

'You suppose right. What time were you meeting Liam Devlin?'

'Six o'clock.'

He looked at the car, and Francesca had the sudden impression that he was holding a brief, silent argument with himself. But he only said, 'You do the damsel in distress role very thoroughly, don't you?'

'I didn't mean to get stranded,' said Francesca, and heard with annoyance the note of apology in her voice that had always infuriated Marcus.

'I'm going back to London this afternoon,' said Michael. 'So I could drive you to Ashwood – at least, I could if you know the way. And I could wait for you while you take a look round, and then drop you at your house afterwards.'

So this was what the inner argument had been about. His sense of chivalry had been nudging him to make the offer but he had not really wanted to do it, so he had been trying to think of a polite way out. Perfectly understandable. Francesca said, very firmly, 'Certainly not. I couldn't possibly put you to so much trouble. I can easily phone Liam Devlin and arrange another meeting.'

'But if your friend's been missing since Monday, perhaps you shouldn't delay matters. Give me ten minutes to lock everything up, and I'll be with you.' The smile that made him look unexpectedly mischievous showed again. 'Chalk it up half to chivalry and half to curiosity. If nothing else, it'll be nice to have some company on the journey.'

The second thing you absolutely never did in life was to get into an unknown man's car and embark on an unfamiliar journey with him.

But for the moment Francesca was more concerned with

wondering how to tactfully reimburse Michael Sallis for the extra miles he would have to cover, than with speculating whether he was planning to carry her off to a serial-killer's lair or a bordello in some steamy Eastern port. She supposed if she offered to pay for petrol he would refuse. Perhaps she could suggest a meal or a snack on the road somewhere, and pay for that. Or would it look like a come-on? When you had been married for five years you got out of training for this kind of thing. Would it be better to send a note of thanks to him c/o CHARTH's offices, enclosing a book token or a Thresher's voucher, or something of that kind? Oh, for goodness' sake! said her mind crossly. Surely he's not going to interpret a cup of coffee and a sandwich at a Little Chef as an invitation to unbridled passion!

These doubts having been put firmly in their place, she opened a road map to find Ashwood, and scribbled down directions on the back of her cheque-book. It would not hurt to appear efficient and organized, even if you were neither of these things. Fran made careful notes, and then, hoping she had got all the roads and traffic islands properly identified, said, 'Tell me a bit about CHARTH. It sounds quite an unusual charity. Shall you actually use that house for your homeless teenagers?'

He took his eyes off the road for just long enough to look at her, as if he might be trying to decide if this was a genuine request, or if she was just being polite. Francesca had the feeling that he probably found small-talk boring. He had nice eyes, though: very clear grey and fringed with black lashes.

'A lot depends on the surveyor's report and builders' estimates,' he said. 'We'd need to add extra bathrooms and probably a second kitchen. The attics are quite large, though, so we might make use of them. I'd like to think we could actually use the house rather than sell it and invest the money – I think that's what Mrs Fane really wanted us to do.'

He paused, as if weighing up whether to say any more, but Francesca, who was interested, said, 'Go on. How would you use the house?'

'Most of the teenagers we deal with come from the real bottom of the heap – they're often homeless through no fault of their own. Some of them were born into squats and doss-houses, or abandoned by a mother who went off with the newest man and left them to fend for themselves. Some ran away from abusive parents at incredibly young ages – seven, eight years old – and lived rough.'

'How about reading and writing?'

'Trust a teacher to go for the literacy side,' said Michael. 'But you're quite right: a good many of them can't read, or even count to ten, or tell the time. We try to get them on training programmes or into adult literacy classes so that they're at least semi-equipped for life. We aren't a particularly aggressive set-up – we don't force anything on anyone, but a surprising number of youngsters do get referred to us by probation officers and child-care specialists and organizations like Centrepoint or the Samaritans.'

'Do you actually deal with the training?' He looked as if he would be more at home in an Oxford common-room than trying to teach under-privileged teenagers how to cope with today's world.

'My side of it's a bit more basic. I arrange for them to learn the real nuts and bolts of life: the things that you and I don't think about twice, but that they don't understand because they've never had them.'

'What kinds of things? I'm not just being polite – I'm liking hearing about this.'

'Well, for instance, if you've always lived in a derelict house with no gas or electricity or running water you won't know much about cooking a meal and eating it at a table with knives and forks. You've probably had takeaway food all the time, or eaten straight out of tins of baked beans and soup. So you don't know how to use a cooker or how to shop for food.' When he talked about his work the reserve melted a bit, and his whole face looked different. 'Or even simpler things than that,' he said. 'Like how to switch on an immersion heater to heat water for a bath, or change a light bulb. So we have halfway houses where we put a group of them for two or three months, and try to teach them. It's better to use fairly remote places for that – some of them can be a bit undisciplined. But if that goes all right, we promote them to a bedsit if we can find one, and from there to acquiring employment skills. I do think Deborah Fane's house would make a good halfway house.'

'It's an unusual line of work,' said Fran thoughtfully. 'Do you deal with any of the asylum seekers? Some of them are quite young, aren't they?'

'We'll probably have to in time. At the moment we're leaving them to the government organizations, though.' He gave her another of the sideways glances. 'When it's successful, it's rewarding work,' he said, and Francesca had the feeling that he had considered first whether or not to say this, in case it gave away too much of his inner self.

'It must be very rewarding indeed.'

'There's a high percentage of failures. Some of them inevitably revert to type. Sleeping rough, dealing in drugs.'

'We get the drug problem at my school sometimes – I don't suppose there are many schools that escape that, though. And we get the usual quota of difficult teenagers, of course. It's not always easy to know how best to cope with them. They're so defensive.'

'Everybody's defensive sometimes,' said Michael, and Francesca felt, as if it was a tangible presence, the barrier of reserve click back into place.

CHAPTER TWELVE

Liam Devlin's office in Ashwood was on the first floor of a beautiful old building that might once have been the town house of an Elizabethan merchant. His room was disgracefully untidy, but Francesca thought it was the kind of untidiness you would rather enjoy working amidst. She glanced at Michael and had the impression that he thought so, as well. There were masses of books and documents, and ancient Ordnance Survey maps, and several nice old prints on the walls. The jutting bow window apparently overlooked the main street, but it was difficult to see out of it because a large black cat composedly occupied most of it.

'You do realize,' said Liam, having let them in and introduced himself, 'that this appointment is wholly out of character for a man of the legal profession. It's six o'clock on a Friday evening, and everyone else has gone home. In fact the conventions require me to have left the place about three and headed for a golf course, or the local Conservative Club, or a mistress's bed.'

He did not look as if he ever did anything as conventional as play golf, and the only political organizations he might be likely to support would be ones with romantic or rebellious aims, on the lines of restoring an exiled monarch or fighting for downtrodden serfs. On the other hand, Francesca could easily believe in the mistress's bed. She said, 'It's very good of you to meet us so late.'

'It is, isn't it? Sit down while I get the keys – the chairs are cleaner than they look.'

The chairs were perfectly clean, although it was necessary to remove various files from two of them before they could be sat on. The desk was just as littered, but it was still possible to see that it was at least a hundred years old and that it had a master craftsman's graceful lines. Fran glanced at Michael, who was inspecting two framed caricatures of legal scenes which hung near the door.

'Hogarth originals?' he said when Liam returned with the keys.

'Yes. How did you know?'

'Something in the quality.'

'I like having the real thing,' said Liam carelessly. 'You never know when you might need to sell something to stave off the creditors. Shall we go? We'll take my car, if you like. It's not very far, but since I know the way—'

'All right.'

'So now,' said Liam, as they set off, 'we're looking for the elusive Ms Smith, is that right?'

'Well, we're trying to find clues as to her whereabouts,' said Francesca from the back seat, which was strewn with cassettes and files and two or three battered paperbacks. The cassettes were a mixture of Gregorian plainchant, Bach cantata, and what Fran, from daily exposure to classrooms of teenagers, recognized as very goth, very aggressive, hard rock. The paperbacks were *Mansfield Park*, Kazuo Ishiguro's *The Remains of the Day*, and the latest *Harry Potter*.

'She was certainly a memorable lady,' said Liam, driving too fast along Ashwood's main street, and turning on to an open stretch of road. 'So I shouldn't think you'd have much trouble in picking up her trail. Is she given to disappearing for several days, do you know?'

'I don't think so.'

'Ah well, life's full of these surprises that jump out at you, flexing claws and teeth, and people are full of surprises as well.' He swung the car into a narrow rutted lane with overgrown hedges on each side. 'This is the lane leading to Ashwood's site. Shockingly overgrown, isn't it? But one day it'll be bought by a rich consortium, I expect, and they'll bulldoze it to the ground and build neat little boxes for people to live in, and there'll be a proper road here instead of a tanglewood lane that might lead to a sleeping-beauty castle, complete with moss and bats. And once that's happened,' said Mr Devlin, who appeared to possess his fair share of Irish eloquence, 'the von Wolff legend will dissolve like a cobweb over a candle-flame and be lost for ever. And that'd be a pity, wouldn't you agree, Mrs Holland?'

'I would. Uh – it's Francesca, by the way. Or Fran, for speed.'

'Well then, Francesca, I hope you've got weatherproof shoes on, because once we get to the gates and I've found a bit of terra firma to park on, we have to get out and walk.'

'Will we be able to see anything?' asked Michael.

'Not very much, for it's as dark as a—' The car's headlights cut through the darkness as Liam swung round to park, and the analogy, whatever it might have been, was never uttered. Fran said, sharply, 'What is it? What's wrong?'

'Over there,' said Liam, and his voice was so different to his previous offhand tones that Fran felt a stab of fear. Something's wrong. And then she saw where Liam was indicating, and the fear came surging up more strongly.

Parked a few yards away, just inside the car's headlights, was a rain-splattered estate car, and it did not need a second look to know it must have been parked in that same spot for a long time, because the wheels were half-sunk in the wet mud.

Trixie's car. The weatherbeaten, seldom-cleaned vehicle she had driven ever since Fran had known her, because it was reliable and there was room for the dogs in the back. Absolutely unmistakable.

After what felt like a very long time, Michael said, 'I suppose I'm reading this situation right, am I? That's her car, is it?'

'Yes,' said Francesca. 'Yes, it is.'

'In that case, Devlin, it's as well you brought the keys, because I think we'll have to take a look inside this studio. Francesca, will you stay in the car?'

But Fran was not going to stay out here alone in the unfriendly evening which already seemed to be filling up with shadows and whisperings. 'I'll come with you,' she said firmly, and got out of the car before either of them could argue the point.

But neither of them did. Michael passed her her scarf, which had fallen on to the floor of the car, and Liam switched off the car's engine and said, 'I think there's a torch somewhere on the back seat.'

The light from Liam's torch played thinly over the ground as they walked cautiously forward, several times disturbing little clouds of darting insects that rose up.

'Like will o' the wisps,' said Liam.

'*Ignis fatuus*,' said Michael, softly. 'The foolish fire. Odd how the old English folklore stays around, isn't it?'

'In Ireland they'll tell you that will o' the wisps meddle with none but the guilty,' said Liam. He paused, and then said, 'None but the murderers and the cheaters of widows and children,' and this time there was something in his voice that made Francesca turn her head to look at him.

'I think,' said Michael, 'that we've got quite enough to worry about, without encountering creatures from ancient myths.'

But Fran thought he glanced uneasily over his shoulder as he said this, as if he suspected someone might be following them, and this was such a disturbing idea that she said, 'Is that the studio over there?'

'It is. Studio Twelve.' Liam's voice had regained its lightness. 'The one your friend asked to see, Francesca. I'll spare you the ghost stories: I suppose you both know what happened here, but it was a long time ago, and as somebody once said, it was in another country—'

'And besides, the wench is dead.' Francesca completed the quote almost on a reflex, and then wished she had not.

'Exactly,' said Liam rather dryly. 'Can one of you hold the torch, while I unlock the door. Thanks.'

It had not been possible to live in the same house as Trixie without picking up quite a lot about this place; Fran had rather liked hearing about it, although after a while she had found it vaguely troubling, and she had wanted to say, 'Please leave this whole thing alone! Can't you see that you're prising open a fragment of the past, and don't you know that there are some pasts that ought never to be disturbed?' The same impulse had seized her now, and she found herself wanting to stop Liam unlocking the door. But of course they must unlock the door. This was not about ghosts, it was about Trixie; it was about discovering what had happened to her.

As Liam pushed the door inwards Francesca had the sudden impression that Ashwood's history and its memories – all the quarrels and rivalries and all the jealousies and adulteries – had been piled in a jumbled heap against the inside of the door, and that opening the door had brought them tumbling out to lie in an untidy tangle on the ground. But as Liam led the way across a big square hall and into the main part of the studio, she saw that so far from the place being peopled by the ghosts of old romances and faded renunciations, it was simply a sad dusty warehouse, covered in the dust and dirt of years. There was a sense of scuttling black beetles and cockroaches, but there was nothing very menacing about it. (Or is there? said a voice inside her mind. Are you sure about that?)

'There's an appalling smell of damp,' said Michael, hesitating in the doorway. 'Or cats. Or something. Are you sure the place is weathertight, Devlin?'

'No.'

'We'll have to look round, won't we?' said Fran, and heard with irritation that her voice sounded a bit uncertain. 'Properly, I mean?'

'I'm afraid so. But there's a light switch just inside the door and it'll be a whole lot better if we can see what we're doing. Wait now till I find it—'

There was a click, and a solitary light flared overhead. 'That's better,' said Liam. 'Francesca, shall you stay here by the door, while Sallis and I explore?'

'I'll explore with you.' Just as Fran had not liked the silent twilight outside, she was not liking this vast place with the huge dust-sheeted shapes under which anything might be crouching, and she was not liking, either, the sense that eyes were watching from the pools of thick darkness beyond the single pallid light. Perfectly ridiculous, of course. And yet . . .

And yet, walking between and around the mounds of stored furniture and scenery was an eerie experience. Fran could not rid herself of the feeling that they were brushing against sealed-away sections of Ashwood's history, or tiptoeing past invisible doors behind which might lie all the make-believe worlds that had been spun here. Worlds where cities were made of canvas and plywood – where walls flew apart and where people flew into love and into tempers. Over there was an elaborate chaise-longue that might have graced Cleopatra's barge, or a Turkish seraglio, or Elizabeth Barratt's sickroom. And the remnant of stonework propped against it was clearly only plasterboard and paint, but once it might have formed a battlement on a Norman castle, or a wishing-well, or a raven-infested midnight tower . . .

Or, said a small voice Fran had not known she possessed, the lid of Alraune's grave, wherever that might be . . .

And of all thoughts to have, this was surely the most outrageously ridiculous of them all, although if you could not spin a few ghostly fantasies in a place such as this – a place where people had sacked cities and seduced lovers and killed enemies all on the same afternoon! – then where could you spin them? Yes, but it was disturbing the way her mind had thrown up that reference to Alraune . . .

('*A ghost-child.*' Trixie had said. '*That's what most people believe now . . .'* she had said. *'Alraune's name was surrounded with myths and moonshine but I'm convinced that once there was a real child . . .'*)

Once there was a real child . . . Francesca pulled her mind back to the present. Liam was moving ahead, shining the torch into the corners, occasionally making a comment about, Jesus God, would you look at the state of this place, but Michael was silent and Fran had the impression that he was disliking this very strongly indeed. She felt guilty at having more or less dragged him into the whole situation, because none of it was his concern.

Whoever had covered up the old furniture and the tag-ends of scenery had not done so very thoroughly or very neatly. Here and there bits of a table or a chair showed under the edges of the dust-sheets, or a spray of marlin-spikes or a fake tree lay untidily across the floor. Perhaps, when Ashwood was silent and dark, the abandoned film props crawled out to reassemble in the groupings they had known when Ashwood was alive and filled with people and lights and life. Like the ghost stories where toys came to life and moved around a nursery while the children were sleeping. Perhaps the entrance of Francesca and the two men had taken the props by surprise so that they had not had enough time to scuttle back under cover.

Fran shivered and wrapped her scarf more securely around her shoulders, tucking a fold across her mouth, because the stench in here was making her feel slightly sick. Damp, Michael had said. Or cats.

One of the chairs seemed to have got itself completely out of its dust-sheet, and it was standing by itself, half in and half out of a pool of deep shadow. Like the last reel of a werewolf film where the wolf is caught in mid-metamorphosis just as the silver bullet hits it. It had once been a rather elaborate chair: you could still see the carvings along the wooden arms and the remains of beading on the edges of the seat.

Someone had thrown a length of dark brown fabric over this half-and-half chair – perhaps an old curtain – and had flung down some shoes as well. The uncertain light striated the fabric so that if you looked at it for long enough, it began to seem like a pair of corduroy trousers . . .

A cold horror closed over Francesca, and words started to dance dizzily through her mind: words that repeated themselves maddeningly in her brain, saying over and over, that something dreadful had happened here – you do understand that, don't you, Fran? It's something that's all part of the stench that's been making you feel sick, except that you're not going to be sick, you're absolutely *not* . . . But you do understand that someone has done a terrible thing in this place? And then there was her own inner voice was saying weakly that, yes, she did know that, of course she did . . . A terrible thing . . .

But her mind was somehow stuck, like a car with the gears jammed, and she was unable to move beyond these conventional words and phrases. Something dreadful had happened. An outrage. In a moment she would be able to identify what it was, this outrage, this thing that was so very dreadful, and then she would know what should be done about it.

She was aware that Michael had taken her arm as if to move her away from the outrage, and as if from a distance she thought how odd that she should know it was Michael without needing to turn her head to look at him. But she could not spare any attention for this, because she was still trying to unglue her mind from the stuck-in-one-gear state.

But she was seeing now that somebody was sitting in the elaborate upright chair. Yes, that was what she was seeing, and that was one of the things that was so very wrong, because nobody would sit here in the dark like this. And there was something hideously wrong about the head of the person in the chair, although it seemed to have the face of a person Fran knew. Was it the eyes that were wrong? There seemed to be thick dark ribbons hanging down from the eyes: ribbons that were plastered flat against the cheeks . . .

The eyes.

The frozen paralysis began to dissolve and Francesca's mind started to move again, jerkily and painfully, but enough for her to recall some of the grislier things Trixie had said about Ashwood, and some of the old newspaper headlines she had shown to Fran. They were all flickering on to Fran's mind like vagrant images on a scarred screen in an old movie theatre . . . *'Von Wolff's victims both mutilated and left for dead . . .' 'Macabre and vicious injuries . . .' 'The eyes, the EYES . . .'*

She drew in a deep shuddering breath, and her mind snapped properly free so that she knew and understood what she was seeing. The flung-down fabric really was a pair of corduroy trousers – it was a pair exactly like the ones Trixie often wore – and the shoes that were lying higgledy-piggledy under the chair were Trixie's shoes. Sensible flat-heeled shoes they were, with good leather uppers: Trixie always said she could not be doing with fancy flimsy shoes.

Trixie. Dear God, it was *Trixie* who was sitting grotesquely upright in the chair, her hands lying submissively along the wooden arms. Brusque, kind Trixie, who had been piecing together an old scandal so that she could eventually put the letters MA after her name, and be able to teach at a higher level than the present sullen fourteen- and fifteen-year-olds. Trixie, who had doggedly tracked down people who might provide links back to that tragic old scandal – and who had probably annoyed several of them in the process, because she often did manage to annoy people, poor old Trixie, poor old thing.

Her head with the dreadful dark tracks beneath each eye was turned towards the door, as if watching for someone to come in and find her. But she could not be watching for anything because she was dead, and even if she had not been dead, she could not have seen anything, because—

Because someone had re-created Ashwood's brutal legend exactly. Some time between Monday night and today, someone had stabbed Trixie through the eyes, first the right and then the left, using a skewer. Francesca knew this, because she could see the skewer that Trixie's murderer had used, sticking out of the left eye.

The entire studio began to blur, and Fran backed away, banging into the sheeted mounds, making stupid ineffectual movements with her hands as if to push away the sight of the terrible thing sitting in the chair.

'For Jesus Christ's sake get her out,' said Liam's voice angrily, and Fran heard her own voice saying she was all right, but she had better have some air—

And then, blessedly, she was outside, with the night coldness on her face, and Michael was telling her to take slow deep breaths, and his arm was around her, which was a good thing really, because Fran thought she might have fallen over otherwise.

'I'm sorry – didn't mean to make a scene. I really will be perfectly all right in a minute—'

'I know you will. Devlin's phoning police and ambulances, and in a minute I'll get you somewhere where you can have a drop of brandy or something.' He paused. 'Francesca, I'm so sorry you had to see that.'

Fran managed to straighten up at last, and discovered that the world had at least stopped spinning. 'Michael, she – she was dead, wasn't she?'

He understood at once. 'Yes,' he said quietly. 'Yes, she was dead.'

But neither of them said there was no means of knowing whether Trixie had still been alive when her murderer left her here, or how long it might have taken her to die in the dark and lonely studio.

CHAPTER THIRTEEN

Edmund thought it could be assumed that somebody somewhere would miss Trixie Smith reasonably soon, and that inquiries would be put in hand. He wondered how long it would take for people to work backwards to the visit to Ashwood Studios. A week, perhaps? Yes, a week seemed a reasonable length of time. On this basis, he set himself to expect a call by the weekend, and he thought it would be interesting to see if his psychology had been sound and if the crime was put down to someone with a fixation on that old case.

But whatever the police decided, once they had found Trixie, they would presumably want to talk to Edmund himself. His fingerprints would be on the main door of Studio Twelve, of course, and the forensic people might find one or two of his hairs – you had only to read a detective novel nowadays or watch a television police drama to know all about that particular tripwire! But that would be perfectly in order because he had openly been inside the place. He went over everything he had done, and he knew he had not left any evidence at Ashwood that might damn him.

He had not left any evidence in Deborah Fane's house that might damn him either, but he was not going to take any chances on that count. It was a big old house and it had belonged to the family for a good many years, and Edmund could not be absolutely sure that there were no dangerous fragments of the past still tucked into any of its corners. After the funeral he had cleared out all of the cupboards and desks, conscientiously labelling everything as he went. The missing share certificates and title deeds had finally turned up, and he had placed them in a folder which he had taken to the bank.

But despite his care there could still be unexpected notes or photographs in chimney nooks or crannies – or old letters folded up to wedge rattling windows, or newspaper cuttings lining kitchen drawers ... So early on Friday morning he dictated several lengthy reports to his secretary to keep her busy for the rest of the day (you could not trust these girls not to sneak off to the hairdresser or spend hours gossiping on the phone to friends), and drove out to the house to make one final check before probate was granted and the keys irretrievably handed to CHARTH.

As he went methodically through the rooms, paying careful attention to the backs of drawers and little tucked-away cubbyholes, he wondered if Michael Sallis's charity would sell the house and invest the proceeds, or whether they would let their yobs actually live in it. Well, it was nothing to do with Edmund what they did with the place, and he would not want to live here himself – there were too many memories. But even though it was a bit remote for some people's tastes – right at the end of that bumpy unmade lane – it was a good big house with good big gardens and when Edmund thought about the price it might have realized, he could not find it in his heart to regret putting Deborah Fane out of the way.

He ended up in the main bedroom at the front of the house. It was very quiet everywhere and the soft autumn sunshine came gently in through the deep bay window, lying across the slightly worn carpet. There were fade marks on the old-fashioned mahogany wardrobe where the sun had touched it every day for goodness-knew how many years. Deborah Fane's clothes were folded in boxes and a couple of suitcases, ready for a local charity to collect, but Edmund went through the boxes, feeling inside coat pockets and linings and examining the zipped compartments of the handbags. Nothing. He straightened up and crossed to the deep bay window for one last check of the tallboy and the dressing-table. And there, lying flat on the bottom of a small shallow drawer at the dressing-table's centre – the filigree key so flimsy it could be snapped off with a fingernail – was the long brown envelope.

It was so faded that it was almost indistinguishable from its background, and it was not really surprising that Edmund had not noticed it earlier. It was probably nothing of much importance, but . . .

But as he lifted the envelope out, he was aware of his skin starting to prickle with nervous tension. It'll be nothing, he thought. It's an old envelope, but it'll contain an ancient seed catalogue or a forgotten bank statement or something of the kind. But his hands were shaking and he knew that whatever was inside the envelope was very important indeed. He took several deep breaths and then, moving with extreme care, he slid the contents out.

The quiet bedroom began to disintegrate into splinters of whirling, too-bright sunlight like a fragmented looking-glass, and Edmund reached out blindly to the dressing-table's edge to stop himself from falling headlong into the tumbling maelstrom of light and dancing dust-motes. He had no idea how long he sat like that, clutching on to the solid wood, waiting for the room to stop spinning – it was as if time had slipped its moorings or as if Edmund himself had stepped completely outside of time – but when finally he was able to release his grip he was trembling and out of breath as if he had been running too fast, and he had to wipe sweat from his forehead with his handkerchief.

He stared down at the single sheet of paper in his hand and felt cold and sick at how he had so nearly missed this.

The surface of the paper was faintly yellow and the edges were splitting, and it was sad, it was so infinitely sad to be looking at this tiny, fragile shred of the past . . . Edmund ran his fingers lightly over the brittle surface of the paper, which was brown-spotted with age, the ink so faded that the writing was almost indecipherable.

But it was not so faded that he could not read almost all of it. The headings were in German, but it was easy enough to translate.

Certificate of Birth, said the heading in black ornate lettering. And underneath: *Date of birth: 10th December, 1940. Place of Birth, Poland. Mother, Lucretia von Wolff. Father, unknown.*

Beneath that again were the words: *Child's name: Alraune.*

Alraune.

So you really did exist, said Edmund to the thin sheet of paper. The legends were all true, and you really did exist, and after all Lucretia really was your mother. But he had known ever since the day inside Studio Twelve that Alraune existed. Even if Trixie Smith had not said, 'A child listed as "Allie" was there that day,' Edmund would have known, because he had felt Alraune's presence in the deserted studio, and he had been aware of Alraune's hand taking his, and he had heard Alraune's childish voice whispering to him.

You don't need to believe in me, Alraune had said that day. *All you need to believe in, Edmund, is the practice of* morthor – mord . . .

Returning to the office was unthinkable; Edmund could not have concentrated on ordinary routine work if his life had depended on it.

He locked the damning sheet of paper in his briefcase, and drove back to his own house. Once inside he carried the briefcase and its explosive contents through to the sitting-room, where a small fire was laid ready for lighting. He liked to have a fire in the evenings at this time of year – people said it made a lot of work and what about polluting the environment, but

Edmund did not consider the environment to be his responsibility, and most of the work fell on his cleaning lady who came in three times a week from the nearby village and had instructions to rake out the ashes and re-lay the fire ready for the next day. The room was at the back of the house and no one could possibly see in, but Edmund drew the curtains before opening the briefcase.

He carried the certificate to the fireplace, holding it flat on his upturned palms (Like a sacrifice? Don't be ridiculous!), and placed it in the exact centre of the hearth. Then he lit a match and set it to a twist of newspaper. It caught at once, and the flames licked across the brittle sheet with its spider-faded writing. Edmund watched the sad dryness curl in on itself, and the tiny charred flakes shrivel into powdery ash.

And now you're really gone, Alraune. Even if you ever existed, there's no longer anything left to prove it. I've put an end to you once and for all.

Are you so sure about that? said the sly scratchy voice deep within his mind.

Yes, I am. In fact I still question whether you did exist. That certificate could have been a fake. Part of the legend they created about you.

Oh Edmund, said Alraune's voice reproachfully. *We shared a killing . . . We shared* mord, *Edmund . . .*

We shared a killing . . . But I'm perfectly safe on that score, thought Edmund. They'll never trace it to me. And I've burned the birth certificate, and I've severed all the links to the past.

But, said Alraune's voice inside Edmund's mind, *can the past – particularly that past – particularly MY past – ever really die, Edmund . . . ?*

Some pasts might never die, and most pasts could not really be rewritten, but it was gratifying to find that when it came to the present, Edmund had got it right.

Early on Saturday morning, just as he was eating his leisurely weekend breakfast and scanning the papers, a young but perfectly polite voice telephoned from Ashwood police station, apologized for disturbing Mr Fane, and explained that the body of a Miss Trixie Smith had been found at the derelict Ashwood Studios site.

'Dead?' said Edmund in a shocked voice. 'Trixie Smith? You *did* say dead?' He paused, and the polite voice said, yes, certainly dead, and the body had been found early on Friday evening.

'Good God,' said Edmund. 'What exactly happened?'

The voice said that a colleague of Miss Smith's had found the body – a Mrs Francesca Holland. A clear case of murder it was, and a very nasty business, as well. Inquiries were already in hand, but the reason for this call was to arrange for Mr Fane to give a statement. Their understanding was that Mr Fane had been at the studios with the lady earlier in the week, was that right?

'Yes, it is,' said Edmund, switching from shock to concern. Nice helpful Mr Fane, distressed by what had happened, eager to assist the police in any way he could. Certainly he would make a statement, he said. Of course he would. A terrible thing to have happened. A wicked world we live in, don't we?

Well, yes, he might manage to come to Ashwood for his interview, if they preferred that, he said. When exactly might that be? Oh, within the next forty-eight hours. That was extremely short notice, but of course he understood that with a murder inquiry time was of the essence. Very well, he would see what he could arrange.

'We could send a police car for you if transport's a problem, sir,' said the polite voice. 'Or if it's a question of expense, we do have a small budget for this kind of thing. If you wanted to submit a note of the cost – along with receipts – we can reimburse you for petrol or train tickets.'

But Edmund was not going to have a police car with its gaudy paintwork roaring up to his well-mannered house for all and sundry to see and speculate about, and he was not going to let anyone think he could not afford a piffling little tank of petrol either.

He said, coldly, that he would make his own way there, thank you very much. Would mid-afternoon today suit them? Very well, he would be there as near to half past three as possible.

He rang off thoughtfully. The family would have to be told what had happened, and it might be as well for Edmund to get his version in first. He made a few notes so that he could present the information in the way he wanted to present it, jotted down possible answers to potential questions, and then dialled the number of Lucy's flat. It rang for quite a long time before Lucy answered, sounding a bit out of breath.

'Hi, this is Lucy Trent, and whoever you are, sorry to have taken so long but I was washing my hair and— Oh, it's you, Edmund – hold on a minute while I get a towel— OK, I'm with you now.'

Edmund had a sudden mental picture of Lucy curled into the deep armchair of her flat in the rackety old house, wearing a bathrobe, her wet hair tumbling around her face, turning her into a mermaid or a naiad. To dispel this somewhat disturbing image, he said in his briskest voice that he was phoning with some rather unexpected news. No, he was perfectly all right, and so far as he knew everyone in the family was perfectly all right as well. But something rather – well, rather disturbing had happened, and he was letting her know before the wretched tabloids got their paws on the thing.

'I suppose it's something to do with Lucretia, is it?' said Lucy.

'It is, as a matter of fact,' said Edmund. 'How did you know?'

'The words "tabloids" and "unexpected news" were the clue,' said Lucy. 'In this family they nearly always add up to something to do with Lucretia. What's emerged about her this time?'

Using his notes Edmund explained about Trixie Smith, and about how her body had been found inside Studio Twelve at Ashwood.

Lucy's distress reached him strongly, even over the phone. 'Oh no! Edmund, that's dreadful. Oh God, that poor woman. Do they know who did it?'

'I shouldn't think so,' said Edmund. 'It's barely twenty-four hours since they found her.'

'Oh, I see. Yes, of course. Who *did* find her?'

'Some woman who was staying with her, apparently. I don't know any details, but they want me at Ashwood this afternoon.'

'Why on earth?'

'To make a statement. I seem to be the last person who saw her alive.'

'If we were in the pages of a whodunnit that would be rather sinister,' said Lucy, and Edmund replied coldly that he did not find it a subject for facetious remarks.

'Sorry, I didn't mean to be flippant. Nervous reaction.'

'Understandable,' said Edmund. 'But I'd better go now, Lucy, because if I've got to get to Ashwood Police Station for three-thirty, I'll have to leave fairly soon. It's a two-hour drive.'

He paused rather deliberately, and Lucy said, 'Will you let me know what happens at the police station?'

'I suppose I could call on you,' said Edmund, as if this had just occurred to him. 'It wouldn't be much further to drive. Assuming you'd be in, of course. Saturday night, and all that—'

'I'll be in, Saturday night or not,' said Lucy rather dryly. 'If you recall I'm entirely footloose and fancy-free at the moment.'

'Oh yes, I remember now.' Lucy had recently parted company from some man whom Aunt Deborah had said was not worthy of her, although Aunt Deborah had never thought anyone worthy of Lucy. Edmund knew this perfectly well, of course, just as he always had known the precise timing of Lucy's entanglements. (Had those men seen her with rippling wet hair and bare shoulders . . . ?)

'I'm not sure what time it will be when I get to you, though. Somewhere between six and seven, I should think.'

'That's OK. Uh – will you be wanting something to eat?'

'Oh, I think so,' said Edmund, who had assumed that Lucy would make this offer. Family was family and there were certain obligations. 'Then I could drive back later. I'd have had a break, you see, and it would be less tiring.'

'Yes, of course.'

'Don't go to a lot of trouble, though. I don't want to eat a heavy meal with the drive home ahead of me. Just something light and nourishing.'

Dry-as-dust Cousin Edmund, with his delicate digestion and his old-maidish insistence on regular meals. Edmund could hear Lucy thinking it and he smiled. But she said she would have some food ready, and to just turn up when he could.

CHAPTER FOURTEEN

Edmund took to the Ashwood police interview neatly prepared notes of conversations and phone calls, and dates of meetings with Trixie Smith. Correct, precise Mr Fane, efficiently prepared for whatever questions might be asked.

Still, it was slightly disconcerting to find that the interview was to be conducted by a woman – Detective Inspector Jennie Fletcher. No doubt it was rather old-fashioned of him, but Edmund would have thought it more suitable for a man to be in charge of this kind of case. But he shook Inspector Fletcher's hand, and nodded pleasantly to the very young sergeant who was with her. He was offered and accepted a cup of tea, and while it was being brought took his own notes from his briefcase, so that he could refer to them.

He explained about Trixie Smith's approach to his aunt, careful to keep solely to the facts, and when he had finished, Inspector Fletcher said, 'That seems quite clear. Let's talk about your own involvement, Mr Fane.'

'Certainly,' said Edmund, who had not been expecting the police to regard him as involved in this at all.

'First of all, was there any particular reason why you went to Ashwood Studios that day? Or were you just along for the ride?'

A slight edge to the voice there, which Edmund did not care for.

But he explained that he had driven down to meet Miss Smith from what one might call a sense of responsibility. Of courtesy. 'My aunt had died before she could provide the promised information to Miss Smith – a rather sudden death, that was – and so I thought the least I could do was help by getting access to the studios for her.'

'I'm sorry to hear about your aunt's death,' said Fletcher conventionally. 'Presumably you met Miss Smith at the site that day—'

'I met both Miss Smith and Mr Devlin there,' corrected Edmund, who was not going to have that disreputable Liam Devlin overlooked.

'Ah yes, Mr Devlin. You had contacted him direct, I think you said?'

'I phoned the local council to find out who looked after the place,' said Edmund. 'And Devlin agreed to give Miss Smith access. He may have checked that with the owners, or he may have just used his own discretion. I didn't ask him who the owners were,' said Edmund. 'Because of client confidentiality. But I had the impression it was some property developer.'

'Yes, we know about that. Mr Devlin's letting us have the address of the owner, although it sounds as if it's changed hands a few times over the years. It's probably been a case of small property developers wanting to build on the site, but encountering problems and selling again as quickly as possible.'

'Fly-by-night profiteers, I expect,' said Edmund disapprovingly. 'Buying land cheaply in the misguided belief that there's easy money to be made from building ugly little dolls' houses on it.'

'Perhaps. Although the Ashwood site is quite near to Green Belt, so there might have been difficulties about planning consent.' She looked at him thoughtfully. 'You went to considerable trouble on Miss Smith's behalf.'

'Not especially. I've already told you I felt a degree of responsibility on my aunt's behalf,' said Edmund, and then, in case this had sounded defensive, spread his hands in a deprecatory gesture

– Crispin's gesture – charming and frank. 'I was curious about the place, Detective Inspector,' he said. 'All the tales, all the ghosts in my aunt's family. The disreputable Lucretia von Wolff and Conrad Kline and so on.'

'Family ghosts,' said Fletcher expressionlessly, making a note. 'So you drove to Ashwood on Monday afternoon. What time did you arrive?'

'About four,' said Edmund, disliking Fletcher's tone even less this time. 'I can't be precise, although I remember it was already getting dark. Miss Smith had arrived ahead of me, and so had Devlin. He might know the exact time if it's important. Was he there when the body was found? I suppose he'd have to be, because of unlocking the place.'

'Mr Devlin was certainly there,' said DI Fletcher. 'But Mrs Holland was accompanied by a Mr Michael Sallis.' She looked up. 'Do you know Mr Sallis?'

'As a matter of fact I do,' said Edmund shortly, angry that he had apparently displayed a reaction and that Fletcher had spotted it. 'He works for an organization called CHARTH.' That sounded better; it put Michael Sallis in his place, and it also made it sound as if Edmund himself was associated with charity work.

DI Fletcher did not comment on this and she did not explain Michael Sallis's involvement. She said, 'You got to Ashwood around four. And you went into Studio Twelve with Miss Smith.'

Edmund gave another of the rueful smiles. 'Yes. I told you – I was curious. I thought I'd take the opportunity to see where Lucretia's legend had ended.'

'And so having taking the opportunity, and having communed with the ghosts and the legends, you left?'

'Yes. Miss Smith stayed on, though; she wanted to sketch some layout plans, and also to soak up the atmosphere – her expression, not mine. She was going to slam the door shut when she left. It's a Yale lock, and she was the kind of person who could be trusted to slam it properly. I drove home; I got back about half-past seven as far as I recall.'

'So,' said Inspector Fletcher, eyeing him thoughtfully, 'You didn't actually see Miss Smith leave Studio Twelve?'

'No,' said Edmund. 'No, I didn't see that.'

It was well after five when Edmund finally left the little police station, and he drove back through Ashwood's main street, curious about the place, slowing down to take a look at Liam Devlin's offices when he spotted them. They seemed to take up most of a large old house near to Ashwood's centre, and Edmund grudgingly acknowledged that the building itself was attractive with its bow windows and wavy glass, although everywhere could have done with a lick of paint. He remembered with satisfied pleasure his own immaculately restored house at home, and the neat offices where he worked.

It was annoying to see Devlin himself coming out of the building – Edmund certainly would not have been in his office on a Saturday afternoon – and it was even more annoying that Devlin should see Edmund and put up a hand in greeting. Clearly, it would be the height of rudeness to simply drive off, so Edmund wound the car window down, and prepared to be politely friendly.

Liam asked had the police hauled Edmund in for questioning about the murder.

'Just a few questions to establish times and background and so on,' said Edmund repressively.

'Ah, isn't that always the way of it with the law. And they'll go for the alibi every time, of course. Not that any of us will have one. I certainly didn't.'

'They questioned you, I suppose?'

'Grilled me for hours,' agreed Liam cheerfully. 'I daresay they did you, as well. But you'll be used to police stations.'

Edmund took this as an assumption that he handled criminal work, and said his practice was mostly conveyancing and probate with a few boundary disputes.

'I do a fair bit of criminal work,' said Liam. 'I enjoy it. They're good company, the villains. Many a burglar I've restored to his friends and relations. Are you driving straight home, or will we have a drink together along at the wine bar?'

But Edmund had no intention of drinking in some sleazy bar with Liam Devlin, and certainly not at this time of day, for goodness' sake, so he said thank you, but he had an appointment in London, and drove on.

Lucy's flat, when he reached it, was warm and welcoming, and although Edmund would have preferred a more conventional set-up himself, he acknowledged that the disreputable charm of the place suited her.

They ate at the table by the window – Lucy did not draw the curtains, which Edmund thought peculiar, but Lucy said she liked looking down on the lit streets. She liked it best when they were shiny with rain, and you could see the reflections of street lights and cars.

She had prepared a fluffy fish pie for him, which Edmund found very acceptable, and there was a bowl of crisp salad.

'And Edmund, if you don't tell me exactly what this is all about – Trixie Smith and you being at Ashwood and everything – I'll explode from sheer curiosity. What on earth were you doing at Ashwood in the first place?'

Edmund explained about meeting Trixie, and about leaving her in the studio to make her notes and sketch plans.

'And it seems that when she didn't turn up after three or four days, some colleague worked back to her visit to Ashwood and went along there to check. That's when they found the body. The police contacted me because I was the one who arranged for the access to the studios.' He looked up. 'That surprises you?'

'Yes, it does. I'd have thought,' said Lucy, speaking as if she was choosing her words very carefully, 'that Ashwood and Studio Twelve would be the very last place you'd want to visit.'

'Why?'

She looked back at him, and this time Edmund was aware of

a flicker of apprehension. What's she going to say? What might she know that I wasn't expecting?

Lucy said, 'Well, because of Crispin.'

Crispin. Silence came down between them. In a moment I'll be able to say something, thought Edmund. Something quite ordinary, so that she won't think I'm at all thrown by this. But alarm bells were sounding in his mind, because Lucy had used Crispin's name so lightly and so familiarly. As if she knew all about Crispin. Did she? But how much could she know – really, actually know . . . ?

He resumed eating, and said offhandedly, 'Oh. Yes, I see what you mean. Crispin. Did you say there was pudding, Lucy?'

'What? Oh yes, sorry.'

The pudding was some kind of pastry concoction with honey and nuts in it.

'It's Greek baklava,' said Lucy, when Edmund expressed his appreciation. 'And before you ask, no, I didn't make it myself, I bought it from the delicatessen on the corner. I've tried to get the recipe out of them, but they won't tell anyone; it's a family secret, or something.'

A family secret. The words set the alarm notes jingling in his head all over again. Family secrets . . . And some things must be kept secret, at all costs.

Lucy was saying, a bit hesitantly, 'Edmund, while you were there, did you actually go inside Studio Twelve?'

'What? Oh, yes, I did. Just for a short time.'

She had stopped eating, and she was fixing him with a wide-eyed stare. 'What was it like?'

It was peopled with ghosts who watch while you commit murder, only the ghosts at Ashwood don't call it murder, they call it mord *. . . And what would you say, Lucy, my dear, if I told you that I think one of those ghosts was Alraune . . .*

Edmund said, 'It was dark and dismal and the whole place was in a disgraceful state, in fact it was little more than a few muddy fields with most of the buildings falling down where they stood.'

'How sad,' said Lucy softly. 'I rather wish I hadn't asked you, now. All those years of films and people, and all the friendships and romances and quarrels and feuds there must have been inside the studios— All those years of spinning dreams and now it's just a clump of ruined bricks and mud.'

Go on, said Crispin's voice in Edmund's mind. There's your cue. And she's always attracted you, hasn't she, *hasn't she* . . . ?

'Oh, Lucy,' said Edmund softly, 'you're such a romantic under that tough façade.'

Lucy, disconcerted, looked sharply up and met Edmund's eyes. 'Am I?'

'I've always thought so,' said Edmund very deliberately. 'Didn't you know?'

'No,' said Lucy, still staring at him. Silence hung over the table for a moment, and then, with what was clearly an effort to return the conversation to a more ordinary level, she said, 'But Edmund, you have to admit Ashwood is romantic. All the ghosts of the past—'

'Oh, I'm not very keen on ghosts,' said Edmund.

'I know you're not.'

'I'd rather have the living than the dead.' He put his hand out to take hers. Good! said Crispin in his mind. Go for it, dear boy! But as Edmund's fingers closed around Lucy's, she gave a start, and then pulled her hand free.

'What's wrong?'

'I could be wrong, but for a moment I thought you were trying to hold hands with me.'

'I dare say there are worse ideas,' said Edmund, offhandedly. He finished the last spoonful of the Greek pudding, and looked at his watch. 'It's nearly nine o'clock. Did you say we'd have coffee? I usually have a cup after my evening meal, but I don't want to be too late getting home.'

He followed her out to the kitchen, putting the dishes in the sink, and then standing behind her as she spooned coffee into the percolator. When she turned round, he put his arms round her and pulled her hard against him. Her body felt slender and supple, and there was a scent of clean hair and clean skin.

This time there was no doubt about her reaction; she flinched from him as if his touch had burned her, and put up a hand as if to defend herself.

'Edmund, what on earth are you doing?'

'I've had an extremely upsetting day,' said Edmund. 'Police statements and that wretched Trixie Smith's murder. Poor woman,' he added conscientiously. 'And so I just thought a little human warmth might— And you said you were footloose and fancy-free.' This came out in a slightly injured-sounding voice.

'Yes, but we're cousins!' said Lucy, backing away from him. 'I can't— I mean, not with you I can't! It's – it's very nearly creepy!'

Creepy. She would pay for that one day, the bitch. Edmund turned away as if he had lost interest, but he was having to beat down a strong desire to grab her and force her against him. And then? Back into the sitting-room, to that deep comfortable sofa before the fire? Or into her bedroom, which he had never seen . . . ? An image of Lucy, her hair rippling against white sheets, rose up tauntingly, but he only said, in an offhand voice, 'We're quite distant cousins as a matter of fact. William Fane was my real uncle – he was my father's brother – and Deborah only became my aunt when she and William were married. So you and I aren't actually related at all, Lucy. But we'll forget it. It was only an idea I had for a moment.' Your loss, my dear, said his tone. 'I hope there's semi-skimmed milk to go with that coffee,' said Edmund. 'I only ever drink semi-skimmed milk these days.'

After Edmund had gone, Lucy washed up the dishes, her mind churning.

That had been a very odd encounter. But she must surely have jumped to a wrong conclusion. 'Oh, Lucy, you're such a romantic under that tough façade,' Edmund had said, and his tone had been that of someone deliberately injecting a caress into his voice. A *seductive* caress. And then, in the kitchen, he had forced that embrace, and that had been the most un-Edmund thing of all, in fact Lucy had found it slightly sinister.

But there was nothing sinister about Edmund, just as there was nothing come-hitherish about him. She must have misread the whole thing. And he had spent most of his afternoon tussling with the police about being at Ashwood with Trixie Smith – yes, he had said something about wanting some human warmth after an upsetting day. He had probably been agonizing about Lucretia being splashed all over the Sunday newspapers because of this murder, as well; Edmund, of all the family, had always hated anything to do with Lucretia. Poor old Edmund, thought Lucy determinedly.

But it was still odd that he had so readily driven all the way to Ashwood that day to meet Trixie Smith. Not because of the distance, or because of the disruption it must have made to his carefully ordered life . . .

Because of Crispin.

It was rather a pity that Lucy had not responded to his approach, although there might be other opportunities. As Edmund drove out of London, he smiled in the driving mirror as he considered this possibility. And at least it had knocked her away from talking or thinking about Crispin, which had been the real aim. (Or had it? Be honest, Edmund. Yes, of course, it had!)

Once clear of London, the motorways were fairly light on traffic, and his mind wound back to before dinner at Lucy's flat, and replayed the police interview. He was inclined to think that had gone quite well, and he was as sure as he could be that DI Fletcher had not suspected anything, although there had been one or two sharp-edged comments that he had not cared for. Sarcastic bitch.

One thing had lodged in his mind from the interview, though, and that was the brief reference to Ashwood's ownership. Ought he to look into that? But if it had changed hands several times, any links to the past were likely to have become long since buried beneath land registrations and transfers. Company secretaries might have said disinterestedly, Haunted, is it? But they would have gone on to say, Well, so long as it doesn't affect the value. We're not scheduled to develop for two years anyway. And then some finance wizard somewhere would have decided that it was not a viable proposition after all, and the site would have been off-loaded as quickly as possible.

Still, it would not hurt to request an official search of the Land Registry, although the land would not necessarily be registered – it depended on how recently it had changed hands. But Edmund could certainly make application. If necessary he could say he had a client who might be interested in the place. Yes, he would do that first thing on Monday.

CHAPTER FIFTEEN

There had been no anticipation of what lay ahead when Alice reached the streets surrounding St Stephen's Cathedral in Vienna.

They were badly lit, these streets, and seen by night, seen when you were utterly alone and almost penniless, they were sinister and imbued with a menace that Alice had never before encountered or even dreamed existed.

'People talk about Vienna's beauty, and how its streets smell of good coffee and croissants, and how the very pavements thrum with music,' she said to the absorbed child curled into the chimney corner, firelight painting shadows in the dark rebellious hair. 'And that is certainly one side of it. But the Vienna I stumbled into on the night after Miss Nina's parents ordered me from the house was cold and unfriendly, and the people were bedraggled and impoverished. There were narrow cobbled streets and alleys with stone arches overhead, and unexpected little flights of stairs leading down to cellars . . . It was still Vienna, but it was so different from the Vienna I had known that I began to think I had fallen into a completely new world.'

'Oh, I can understand that. Because—'

'Yes? Whatever it was, you can say it. You can say anything to me.'

'I know. I was going to say that when I came here it felt like coming into another world. Not just because it's different to Pedlar's Yard, although it is. It's more than that. To start with I thought it was this house, only now that I've lived here for a bit I don't think it is. I think it's you. But I don't really understand why.'

This was the most intimate speech ever made since coming here, and there was a sudden stab of anxiety. What if Alice doesn't like me saying that? What if she doesn't understand?

But of course she understood, just as she always did understand. She said, slowly, 'I think it might be because the whole world believes me to be dead. And,' she said, 'the whole world must continue to believe that.'

It was amazingly easy to call up the memories for this unusual child and to paint the word-pictures, although it was necessary to be selective; to employ a little censorship. The word made Alice smile rather wryly.

On that first night and on several nights afterwards, she had slept in a doorway in one of those very alleyways in the cathedral's shadow. There had been others there with her; others who were homeless and hopeless. They had not exactly welcomed her, but there had been a curious comradeship. They were the dregs and remnants of humanity, and the rejected and the unwanted, but Alice had felt oddly comfortable with them. Because I, too, am rejected and unwanted.

But even with the casual fellowship of the homeless, it had taken a good deal of fortitude to get through those days. She had continued doggedly to search for the tall narrow house, because surely he would help her, surely he would not let her become one of the lost and nameless ones – the beggars and the paupers and the street musicians who wove their own melodies into the city streets. But she had known by the end of the second day that she was not going to find it. Vienna was too big, too bewildering, too intricately threaded with mazes of streets and unexpected courtyards.

By the end of a week, when her tiny savings were used up, she had gone with some of the other homeless people to stand near to the cathedral entrance, to wait for the rich visitors who came to sight-see. Begging. Am I reduced to this? Has *he* reduced me to this, that man with the golden-brown eyes? But by that time she had discovered that when you are sick and dizzy from hunger, and when your stomach knots into cramp-pains with emptiness, you no longer care. You would steal if you thought you could get away with it. You would do other things, as well as steal . . .

The sumptuous Grand Tours of the last century were no longer *de rigueur* for the sons of the wealthy, but enough of them still travelled around Europe as part of their education, and a great many came to Vienna. When one or two of them stopped their carriages and walked across to her to make their sly suggestions, Alice had at first shaken her head and backed away. But later, she had shrugged and had gone with them to their hotel rooms. It meant a certain amount of bravado; it meant braving the rich plush reception halls and the stony stares of the hotel staff – some of them disapproving, some smilingly knowing. But it also meant she could eat for several days, and after the first few times she acquired the trick of donning an air of disdain, and of walking arrogantly through the hotels. Accepting a few more offers of the same kind meant she could take a room in the poorest lodging-house.

Most of the men were well-off travellers from other countries, but a few were the smart, sharp German army officers who were so often to be seen in Vienna nowadays. Alice discovered that almost all the men liked to talk about themselves – about their lives and their families and their work if they had any work – but that the German officers did not. They were courteous enough and most of them were fairly considerate, but there was a rigid silence about their army duties and their regiments. Almost as if they counted themselves as part of a secret service.

But it did not matter who the men were or what they looked like, because Alice already knew that was something that would never matter again. Unless the man in bed with you had golden-brown eyes and a quick eager way of talking . . . Unless he could make music so beautiful it would melt your bones and make you want to cry when it stopped . . .

'Somehow I survived,' she said, staring into the fire, no longer fully aware of the comfortable English sitting-room or the listening child. 'Somehow I lived through those bad days and I emerged from them stronger. Remember that – enduring bad times in your life, which is something everyone has to do – makes you stronger. What happened to you in Pedlar's Yard will make you very strong indeed.'

It was not quite possible to believe this yet, but there was a vague feeling that it might one day be possible. For the moment, the important thing was Alice's story.

'So you got through the bad times. And then—'

The smile came again. 'And then,' she said in a much lighter voice so that it was almost as if a different person sat there, 'and then, my dear, there came a day when I knew I must leave behind that poor beaten thing who had loved and lost and been hurt. I knew I must find a way of shaking off the darkness. I had a little money stored up by then: not very much, but a little.' A pause.

'There's a bit there you aren't telling, isn't there? Is it about how you got the money?'

'Yes, there's a bit there I'm not telling, and yes, it is about how I got the money. But one day I will tell you. When you're a bit older.'

'OK. Don't stop the story though.'

'By that time,' said Alice, 'there was no one to know or care where I went or what I did. So I vowed that I would become an entirely different person.' The slanting smile came again.

'I also vowed,' said Alice softly, 'that if I could become another person, it would be someone who would make people sit up and take notice. A person who would make a stir in the world.'

A stir in the world. The idea had been exciting and frightening – can I do it? How can I do it? What could I become?

Her parents had been so pleased when Alice had gone into what they called good service, although they had been anxious when, later on, the family had asked Alice to go with them to that foreign place. They were nervous of Abroad, although Alice's father had been in France during the Great War – Alice had only been a child at the time, of course – and once they had gone on a day trip to Ostend, which they had not much cared for.

But it would be all right for Alice to travel Abroad in this way because she would be with the family, and the family would look after her. Alice's mother had been a parlourmaid in the house of a titled gentleman; her father had been his lordship's valet. They had got married late in their lives, doing so timidly and unobtrusively, and Alice had been born a good many years afterwards, taking them by surprise since they had ceased to hope the good Lord would send them a child.

But altogether they had been in service for forty years, they said proudly, and they knew that the upper classes looked after their servants. Why, only look at how his lordship had given them something called an annuity when they had reached the end of their working lives. They did not rightly understand how it worked, but what it meant was that they were given a sum of money every week for as long as they lived. Oh no, it was not a large amount, but the rent of this little house was very cheap, and if necessary, Alice's mother could always do a little plain sewing for the ladies who lived on the Park; her father could take on a bit of carpentering. They were very grateful to his lordship for taking care of them.

They were gentle and unworldly and unambitious and trusting, and Alice was torn between exasperation and love for them.

Respectable service. Honourable work. What was so honourable about one human being waiting on another? What was respectable about fetching and carrying for the aristocracy who thought themselves too grand even to dress themselves? And at the end of it all, being grateful for a few miserable shillings every week in your old age, and even then having to take in sewing? All that when you had worked for more than forty years, every day from six in the morning until midnight! For goodness' sake, hadn't that kind of humility and gratitude been blown away by the war, by feminism, by women gaining the vote?

Whatever else I may do in the future, vowed Alice during those days in Vienna, outside of illness or old age I will never again wait on another human, and I will never expect another human being to wait on me!

In the small room she had rented in the Old Quarter, just off a cobbled alley, rather sinisterly named the *Blutgasse* – Blood Alley – she considered how difficult it would be to throw off the quiet lady's maid and replace her with a completely new person. It was exciting and terrifying, but if she did it, it might mean she would no longer have to submit to the prodding hands and insistent bodies of all those nameless men in anonymous hotel rooms.

I could be anything and anyone I wanted, thought Alice with a little thrill of excitement.

What she had not been prepared for was how much fun it was to plan a whole new identity. All it needed was a little money, and a little resolve. Not much more.

Alice Wilson, that nice, well-behaved girl, had always looked exactly what she was. An English girl of the servant class, respectable, quietly dressed, her complexion as God had made it, save for a light dusting of rice powder on her nose when it was her day off, because only females of a certain type – which meant tarts and actresses – painted their faces. Well, all right, and bright young things who danced to jazz, and painted their mouths and showed their ankles.

Alice considered her appearance. She had unremarkable eyes, somewhere between grey and green, and slightly fluffy mid-brown hair. Pretty hair, people had sometimes said, indulgently. A pretty girl. Yes, but I don't want to be pretty any longer. Prettiness is for good girls. For nicely brought-up girls who would not dream of going to men's rooms, and doing with them the thing that should not be done until after marriage . . . (No man will ever respect you if you don't remain pure, Alice's mother had said. No man will ever want to marry you.)

There were other things that nicely brought-up girls did not do, as well. They would not, for instance, dream of dyeing their hair. But Alice dyed hers that day, buying the preparation from a tiny shop, trying not to feel guilty. The process of darkening her hair to a shiny raven-black was complex and messy, but after it was done and her hair had dried in the warm afternoon sunlight streaming through the windows of the little room, she brushed it smooth so that it fell in glossy wings on each side of her cheeks. And then she stared at herself in the small oblong of mirror which hung over the weatherbeaten dressing-table.

The transformation was startling. It was beyond her wildest hopes. She was almost a different person. But was 'almost' enough? She must be unrecognizable to everyone who had ever known her. All right, what else could she do? How about cosmetics? Greatly daring, she tried the effects of outlining her eyes with kohl and of darkening her lashes with mascara. At once the nothing-coloured eyes became mysterious and slanting. *Good.* Now for the lips. She applied a dark, mulberry-hued lipstick, getting it crooked the first couple of times, and having to wipe it off and start again. It felt dreadfully sinful but it also felt exciting, and at the third or fourth attempt she got it right. This time, when she considered her reflection in the mirror, she was aware of a little thrill of delight, tinged with fear. Is that really me? And dare I go into the streets looking like this? Yes, said the rebellious little voice in her mind, yes, you dare, and yes you will.

So now, what about clothes? As Miss Nina's maid she had worn a neat black frock with a crisp apron – plain for daytime, frilled muslin for evening. On her day off she had worn her good navy serge in winter, with a cloche hat, and for summer there was a brown linen costume, with a straw boater. When she had tied an orange ribbon around the boater's brim the master's butler had said, My word, Alice, that looks very dashing, but the housekeeper who oversaw the female servants had tutted and thought it a bit fast, and said Alice was not to wear it to church this Sunday.

But the person Alice intended to become would not wear brown linen (even with the orange ribbon on her bonnet), and she certainly would not wear navy serge either. She counted her money out again, nodded to herself, and bundling her hair under the navy hat so that no one would see the halfway stage of her transformation, went out to one of the little backstreet clothes shops.

She knew about these shops that existed in any city and that bought and sold the cast-offs given to maids by the rich, bored ladies they served. She had, in fact, entered one or two of them herself after Miss Nina had rather pettishly given her gowns. 'I'm bored with this thing, Alice, and the colour is ugly. You might as well have it.' Never once wondering where a maid would have the opportunity to wear a silk dance frock or a velvet tea-gown. In England Alice had done what most maids did; she had accepted the cast-offs politely, and then sold them. Now she would enter the second-hand shops in Vienna, but this time she would be buying, not selling.

She spent her dwindling store of money carefully, but she was fortunate in her purchases. A damson silk gown that clung to her thighs when she walked and swished across the ground with careless elegance, and an evening frock in jade green that made you think of unprincipled temptresses reclining on satin-sheeted beds. The labels – Schiaparelli and Madeleine Viennet – were pristine. 'Neither garment has been worn more than twice,' insisted the proprietress of the little shop, and then, having surveyed Alice's appearance with a professionally critical eye for a moment, she darted into the back of the shop once more and brought out a black velvet cloak, ruched and lined with sable. The fräulein should buy this as well, she said. So great a pity not to have it; it might have been made to go with both gowns. A very modest price was all she asked – almost she would be making a loss. But it would add the finishing touch. Cunningly she draped it around Alice's shoulders and led Alice to the mirror again.

Alice stared longingly at her reflection. The velvet was soft and sensuous, and the black fur was like a lover's caress against her neck. If ever there was a Cinderella-setting-off-for-the-ball cloak . . .

No. She could not afford it. But even after she had laid it back on the counter she went on looking at it, making a swift mental inventory of her resources. Could she perhaps manage it after all? If she bought it, she would have just enough money to pay for her room until the end of the week. What about food? She could buy rye bread and slivers of cheese to eat, that was cheap enough. She might as well be hanged for a sheep as for a lamb, and she might as well end up destitute for three costly outfits as for two. She bought the cloak.

Alice Wilson, that well brought-up girl, had never in her life gambled on anything, but now she gambled everything on one single night. She chose the famous Vienna Opera House for the birth of her new self, buying the ticket from a small booth, doing so humbly and politely, letting it be thought she was buying the seat for her mistress. She had never been in the Opera House in her life, but Miss Nina's family – no! *Nina's* family! – had often made up parties for a concert or an opera. Supposing some of them were present tonight? Would they recognize her? What about the brother who had fumbled under her skirts and been pushed away, and had later caused her to be thrown out of the house? Might he be there?

As she carried her parcels and the ticket back to the lodging house her mind was working furiously, planning and calculating. What if this huge gamble failed? If she did not attract people's attention at the Opera House – if she was not approached by men and women who might open up a different life for her – then she would have wasted all her sordidly acquired money and she would end up back on the streets. But she must not fail.

That night she outlined her lips with the sinful dark red lipstick and her eyes with the black kohl. She brushed her hair into its new smooth shape, and then put on the damson gown. It was completely backless, as was the fashion, and above it her skin was creamy white. It felt depraved to be exposing so much of her body, but it also felt exciting.

There were long silken gloves to wear with the gown; Alice drew them on over her bare arms. They reached to above her elbows, and if the gown had been striking before, the contrast between the rich magenta silk and her bare alabaster shoulders and upper arms made it seem quite immodest. It also, thought Alice, caught between delight and panic, made her look extremely sexy. She contemplated this last word, and the crimson lips curved into a smile in the mirror. She had never thought of herself as sexy before. But she was, she was. If only the man with golden-brown eyes could see her like this— No. Don't think about him.

She pushed down the ache of loss, swirled the sable-lined cloak around her shoulders, and went out into the badly lit streets. It was a long walk and it was probably quite dangerous to walk through these streets dressed so richly, but she could not afford to do anything else. Once in the prosperous part of the city, where carriages rumbled along the wide streets, and where there were brightly lit windows of restaurants and coffee houses she felt safer, although her mind and her stomach were turning over and over. I'm clad in extravagant striking clothes, and I'm wearing paint on my face and I have dyed my hair. I look absolutely nothing like I have looked for the last eighteen years, and I think this is a night when anything – *anything*! – might happen to me.

As she walked up the steps and entered the Opera House she had the feeling that she was crossing over some kind of line. This is it, she thought. This is the moment when I'm going to step out of one world and into another. Rubicons and Rivers of Jordan, and valleys of decision and destiny . . .

She took a deep breath and went inside.

* * *

At first the sheer vastness of the Opera House, and the heat and the brilliance, were bewildering, and she felt as if she was walking into a solid wall of light and noise and movement. But she forced herself to appear cool and detached, and after a moment she was aware that several heads had turned to look at her. With curiosity? With disapproval? I don't mind about the disapproval, thought Alice. I'd mind more if they didn't notice me.

But they were noticing her. There was a look in the men's eyes that suggested they were intrigued, and in the women's that suggested they were annoyed at this stranger for stealing the attention. Alice felt a spurt of delighted triumph. I'm across that invisible threshold and I'm into this new world, and there's no turning back.

Turning back was the last thing she intended. She remained where she was, looking about her, listening and watching and surreptitiously absorbing it all. This is the time when you must appear very sure of yourself, said her mind, and when you must seem rather disdainful, because you are used to all this, remember. You are used to glittering crowds of people – you even find them a little boring, and perhaps also slightly absurd – and you are used to opulent rooms lit by hundreds of candles. Most of all you are used to the soft perfumed aura of wealth, because you are extremely wealthy yourself. So far so good.

But don't do anything yet, said this little voice, and above all, don't go looking for your seat or peering anxiously at your ticket. Wait for someone to approach you to conduct you there. Someone will definitely do so – if you believe that strongly enough it will happen, because if you believe anything strongly enough it will happen.

And above all, pray to that God whom you used to know in the English churches that no one will recognize you and that no one will challenge you and demand that you are thrown out . . .

'But no one did recognize you, did they? No one did demand that you were thrown out?'

The fire had burned low in the hearth, and the shadows had stolen across the English garden outside, but somehow the two people in the room had been transported to another country and another time. They had gone back to a long-ago night when a dark-haired female in a silk gown and sable-lined cloak had walked into the glittering Vienna Opera House and surveyed the assembly with cool indifference.

The smile that was so incongruous on the ageing English lady came again.

'No. No one recognized me. Three of the Opera House staff came up to me and two of them escorted me to my seat. There were stairs to descend – I had no idea where we were going, of course – but I went down that staircase so extremely slowly that it caused a hold-up for everyone else. People murmured in annoyance at that, but I pretended not to hear. I looked neither to right nor left as I walked, but I could feel them all watching me.' Her eyes narrowed with remembered amusement. 'But you know all this. You know a little of what comes next in the story as well.'

'Yes, but tell the story anyway.' Because it was like the pronouncing of a spell to hear her say it; it was like an incantation that would set a particular magic working – a magic that would unlock the doors of that long-ago enchanted world and bring the people and the adventures all tumbling out. It was a spell that would conjure up that other person that Alice had been all those years ago – the mysterious beautiful lady.

With an air of entering into the game, and of pronouncing the spell, Alice said, 'On that night, late in 1928, a young English lady's maid called Alice Vera Wilson left a sparse lodging in the Old Quarter of Vienna . . .

'And the Baroness Lucretia von Wolff walked into the famous Opera House and took the seat that had cost her her last few schillings in all the world.'

CHAPTER SIXTEEN

Alice had not paid much attention to the poster displaying the evening's concert, or to the printed ticket she had bought. She had been concentrating her whole mind on being Lucretia: on being this imperious, disdainful baroness she had so carefully created; this lady whose nationality might be anything at all, who spoke with a sultry accent, and who was sexily beautiful and expensively garbed. She had supposed vaguely that there would be a programme of Mozart or Schubert – it was nearly always Mozart or Schubert, or perhaps Strauss – and she had assumed she would listen to it with about a tenth of her mind, because she would be waiting for the intervals so that she could mingle with the people.

But the programme was not Mozart or Schubert. It was a concert by a man called Conrad Kline. And the instant he stepped on to the stage and took his seat at the great gleaming concert grand, Alice recognized him and from then on she heard almost nothing of the marvellous music he poured into the brightly lit auditorium.

Conrad Kline. The man with golden-brown eyes.

He had recognized her almost straight away, and when the concert ended he had swept her back to the tall old house that she had thought never to see again. 'You ruined the slow movement of the Tchaikovsky,' he had said with a kind of loving severity. 'For that was when I looked up and saw you. After that I was aware of no one else.'

The slow movement of the Tchaikovsky had not been ruined at all, of course, and he had certainly been aware of every other person there. His performance had been greeted with deafening applause and cheering, and he had responded to the shouts of 'Encore' by promptly sitting down again to play something that Alice had not recognized, but that was exciting and intense and full of rippling cascades of beautiful sound. 'The Appassionata,' he said, lying next to her on the silken-sheeted bed. 'Beethoven. And I play it entirely for you, because although you are a small English sparrow, also you are passionate and beautiful.'

Even then, dizzy with delight and love, caught in the sheer sexual glamour that he seemed almost to wear like a cloak, Alice had known perfectly well that he had not played the Beethoven piece entirely for her; he had played it because the audience had wanted him to, and because he loved all his audiences with an intensity that transcended everything else. She suspected he had planned beforehand what he would play for the encore; a long time afterwards she found that she had been right. Conrad unfailingly planned his encores and spent hours practising them.

When he said, 'I think I am in love with you,' Alice had regarded him thoughtfully, and said, 'What about Nina?'

'Oh, pouf, Nina.' He made a gesture as if to sweep aside some small inconvenience. 'It was a matter of business. An arrangement her father wanted to make, and that I agreed to in a moment of absent-mindedness. Also,' said Conrad with one of his disconcerting bursts of candour, 'I had not, then, met you.'

He was entranced by what he called Alice's masquerade, and wove dozens of stories about the fictional baroness. Most of his stories were wildly improbable and quite a lot of them were scandalous, and one or two were just about credible.

The Baroness von Wolff should be Hungarian, said Conrad,

weighing the possibilities with serious eyes. Or perhaps Russian would be better. Yes – Russian. Revolutions and *russalkas* and hypnotic Siberian monks. And she should be mysterious and exotic, just as Alice had already made her, but also there could be a hint of something shocking in her ancestry – that was a good idea, yes? An idea to develop, although it would be necessary to be subtle over the details. Subtlety was a fine thing, declared Conrad, who was flamboyant and extravagant and adored grand gestures, and who had never been subtle in his life.

Vienna in the twenties and thirties might have been created solely as a frame for a beautiful baroness with an intriguingly mysterious past. Alice sometimes thought that Lucretia could not have existed in any other time or in any other city. It was the time of *la belle époque*, the beautiful era, and life had been filled with excitement and beckoning promise, and with gaiety and music.

Music. Until now it had been something for other people. In London you might occasionally have an outing to a music-hall, and in the servants' hall some of the other maids might sing the songs of the day while polishing the silver. The war songs were still much enjoyed – 'Tipperary' and 'The Only Girl in the World', but American jazz and what was called blues were starting to be popular. 'Bye Bye Blackbird' and 'Tea for Two', which everyone agreed was wonderful for learning the cha-cha, although the housekeeper had been very shocked to catch Alice and one of the parlourmaids trying out the steps in the scullery one night.

Now, under Conrad's aegis, Alice listened to, and learned to appreciate the music of, Stravinsky and Hindemith and Schönberg, and danced to the melodies of Ivor Novello and Irving Berlin and Franz Lehár. On New Year's Eve she and Conrad attended the famous Vienna Opera House Ball, and danced together beneath the glittering chandeliers. Whirling around the ballroom in Conrad's arms, Alice thought: if only I could take hold of this moment and keep it – lay it away in lavender and tissue paper, so that in years to come I can unwrap it and relive it, and think: yes, of course! That was the night when I was happier than at any other time in my life.

The exotic baroness was invited everywhere – often with Conrad, but frequently on her own. The damson gown alternated with the jade green, but after wearing the jade one a couple of times Alice managed to sell it back to the second-hand shop and bought in its place a very plain, much cheaper, black two-piece. To this she added several velvet and beaded scarves and stoles: rich reds and glowing ambers and one in sapphire blue silk, shot with kingfisher green. It was remarkable how a different scarf changed a plain black outfit.

Conrad wanted to take her to the great fashion houses, so that she could be robed in silks and velvets and furs. She must always wear black or dark red gowns, he said: the colours of wine and heliotrope and wood-violets. Perhaps jade green was also acceptable at a pinch. As to the cost, oh, that was of no matter; no one ever paid a dressmaker's bill, in fact most people considered it slightly vulgar even to consider doing so. Alice was starting to feel extremely close to Lucretia as a person and she was starting to know her very well indeed, but she did not think she could be close to someone who did not pay bills, purely because some people considered it vulgar.

As well as that, she was starting to be aware of a strong vein of independence. I've survived by my own wits and without help this far, and I'd like to keep it that way! So she said, coolly, that she could buy her own gowns, thank you, although she might at times ask Conrad's opinion of a colour or a style.

At this he called her stubborn, and said she was a cold, too-proud English spinster and a sexless feminist, but Alice saw at once that he had expected her to accept his offer and display suitable gratitude – despite his unconventional ways he was rather old-fashioned in many things. She also saw that her refusal had intrigued him, and that so far from finding it sexless, he found it very sexually alluring indeed. Very well then, if this kind of feminism intrigued him, he should go on being intrigued and he should certainly go on being sexually allured.

The hair dye lasted for about six weeks and then it was necessary to shut herself away and go through the complicated procedure all over again. The powder and lipstick lasted a lot longer because she only wore them in public.

At first she only wore Lucretia's identity in public as well, but gradually Lucretia became stronger and more clearly defined. It was not precisely that she began to gain the upper hand: it was more that Alice, like the polite obedient girl she was, gave way to the more dominant personality. Oh, do you want the limelight? she seemed to be saying to Lucretia with a touch of ladylike surprise that anyone should actually want such a thing. Then of course you may have it: it would not become either of us to quarrel over such a thing.

But once or twice she had the uneasy suspicion that there might be things Lucretia would want to do that Alice would flinch from. It was already clear that the baroness could be very self-willed.

It had probably been inevitable that at that time, in that city, mingling with Conrad's musician friends, Lucretia would attract the attention of people within the rapidly evolving world of film-making. It was still the era of the silent film but the technicalities of sound were starting to be enthusiastically explored. One day – and that day might be soon – the movies would be known as the talkies and people would not only be able to watch an unfolding story, but would also be able to listen to it. One day it might even be possible to make films in colour – now there was a dream to aim for!

But in the meantime it was the dark-haired, pale-complexioned females who best suited the monochrome images; they were striking and vivid and memorable.

Dark-haired, pale-complexioned females . . . Just as the Vienna of the day might have been created as a frame for Lucretia von Wolff, so, too, might Lucretia von Wolff have been created specifically for the film-makers.

It happened because of Conrad – Alice thought that everything in her life of any real importance happened because of Conrad – who was approached by a well-known German studio to write background music for two films. Music was important for setting a mood, for creating an atmosphere, they explained, as seriously as if Conrad would not know this. Someone at the studios had attended Conrad's last concert, and had said why should they not secure the gifts of this rising young composer. Why not indeed?

Conrad was delighted to be approached, although he would not admit it. He told Alice that he was being offered an entirely contemptible sum for his beautiful compositions: did these plebeians, these groundlings, believe him to be a machine to churn out beautiful music at a button-press?

'Press of a switch,' said Alice, more or less automatically. 'Will you do it?' she asked, and Conrad hunched a shoulder and looked at her from the corners of his eyes like a mischievous child who knows it is being clever, and said he might as well. But the money was still an insult to an artist, he said, although to Alice, still juggling the damson frock with the black, the money seemed a very large amount indeed.

He shut himself away for several weeks, but when he emerged (a little thinner from not always bothering to eat, smudgy shadows around his eyes from fatigue and concentration), he was perfectly right about the music being superb. The film-makers were delighted with it, and they were delighted, as well, with the sultry baroness who appeared to be the composer's frequent companion – it was best, perhaps, not to inquire too deeply into the precise nature of this companionship. They were all men of the world, yes?

They beamed at Alice across a table at the Café Sacher, which was where Conrad took them to celebrate, but which Alice, managing not to blink at the menu, thought might cost him most of the film-makers' fee. (She had worn the damson gown for the occasion, and had added a narrow black velvet throat-band which was a new idea, and already being copied.)

The film-makers studied Lucretia, at first covertly and then, since she appeared not to notice their regard, more openly. There was the dark hair that was so much admired these days, and the smooth magnolia complexion. Very alluring. And would the baroness perhaps find it entertaining to see the inside of their studios? A very short journey – a car would of course be sent. And – perhaps while she was there, she might agree to a test for the screen? An experiment, an hour or so of amusement for her, probably nothing more.

This was unexpected. Alice thought: Do I want to do their screen-test? I don't suppose anything will come of it, but I think I'd better agree, because those two frocks won't last for much longer, and there're other things to be bought. Underwear, shoes, food . . . And I won't ask Conrad for money; I'll hate it and it'll put me under an obligation to be grateful to him, and I won't do it.

And so Lucretia took the screen test, staring with seductive insolence into the camera lens, and the results were pronounced to be dazzling.

A film called *Alraune* – the story of a girl born in macabre circumstances, growing up with the burden of a dark legacy, growing up to be a wanton – went into production.

In the village where Alice had been a child, they had sometimes played games of Let's Pretend. Let's dress up and pretend to be somebody else for a while. I'll be the queen or the empress, and you can be the servant, and for a few hours we'll believe it's real. Like that old poem, 'When I was a King in Babylon, and you were a Christian slave . . . '

Making films was a little like a grown-up version of the game. Let's pretend to be a girl called Alraune; a creature consumed by bitterness and surrounded by dark sexuality . . .

Alice knew, with the logical, sensible part of her mind, that Alraune was not real. She knew that Alraune was a being forged from dark dreams and subterranean myths; and that she had been born out of a writer's macabre fantasies.

'But I don't think,' she said to Conrad, 'that I should like to meet that man, that Hanns Heinz Ewers who created Alraune's story. I suppose he's long since dead; the original book was written years ago, wasn't it? In 1911 or 1912.'

'He is not dead, and I think he still writes a little,' said Conrad. 'Most of his work is as dark and as – as uncomfortable as *Alraune*.' He paused, and then said, 'I think he has campaigned quite strongly for the German cause, and I believe he is a supporter of the Nazi Party and Herr Hitler.'

'There's nothing wrong with that, though, is there?'

'No,' said Conrad slowly. 'No, of course not.'

CHAPTER SEVENTEEN

The irony was that while the film-makers' money solved one set of problems, it set up a whole new set of difficulties of its own. Alice Wilson, that sheltered English girl, had never in her life seen a bank cheque, and when the first one was given to her, at first she had no idea how to deal with it. Her parents had said banks were not for such as them; servants were paid their wages on each Quarter Day in the year, as was right and proper, and their own tiny pension was brought to them on the first of each month by his lordship's agent, who counted it out on the kitchen table and then made them sign a piece of paper. Alice's mother had always maintained that it was not for women to know about money; Alice had found this slightly exasperating at the time, but looking back she found it rather sad.

In Miss Nina's employment she had been paid the princely sum of £40 a year, ten shining sovereigns on each Quarter Day, together with a Christmas gift of two dress lengths of cloth, one of wool, one of muslin, and a stout pair of leather shoes. This was all that any servant, fed and housed and wanting for nothing, could possibly need or expect. But now Alice would have to deal with banks whether she wanted to or not, because the film people assumed she had a bank account into which she would pay their cheques. They also expected her to sign what Alice uneasily suspected to be legal documents – contracts and agreements requiring her to act in a specific number of films for them over the next two years. This was gratifying, but it was also worrying. She could not possibly sign her real name to the contracts, but she was afraid that signing her false name might constitute the committing of a crime.

In the end she took the problem to Conrad, who said, Pouf, it was a matter easily dealt with. He took her to the offices of a discreet Viennese lawyer who drew up something called a Deed Poll that made her new name legal. She could be called anything she liked, said the lawyer, and once the appropriate documents were signed and witnessed, all would be entirely legal and proper.

When Alice said, But what about the title? the lawyer had said, Zut, what, after all, was a title? Nothing but what someone created for you, or that you created for yourself. Sign here, Madame Baroness, and you have created it. Alice had thought: yes, creating it is exactly what I have done. I have created a person out of dreams and fears and shadows and hopes, and now that person is real. I really am a King – I mean a Queen – in Babylon.

The accent that most people found so fascinating had needed no legal documents. Alice's mind was quick and inquiring, and she had acquired a good smattering of German since she had been in Austria with Nina's family. The housekeeper had marvelled at how she could get her tongue round the heathenish foreign words: would you just listen to that Alice Wilson gibbering and gabbering away – better than a music hall turn, it is! Now, living among German-speaking people, Alice was daily more fluent. She spoke the language with an accent, and she did not make any attempt to smooth it out. Viennese society adored it and thought it seductive.

It was Conrad who said that the illusion required an occasional display of temper in public; it would be expected of her. All great artists succumbed to temperament. Nonsense, of course she could do it.

But while the baroness's occasional displays of fiery anger became legendary, what also became legendary was her unfailing habit of afterwards making some lavish, generous gesture of reparation towards those who had suffered the most. A gift of wine or perfume, or a dress-length of expensive silk. Cuban cigars or supper at one of Vienna's sumptuously expensive restaurants. Who minded the scenes when they were followed by such prodigality? And one had to remember all that Romanian passion. Oh – was the baroness not Romanian? Well, Hungarian then, or Russian. Or something. Who cared.

The première of *Alraune* was a glittering occasion.

Alice wore a Chinese silk gown in a rich dark wine colour. It turned her shoulders and arms the colour of polished ivory, and clung sinuously to her figure. Black jewellery to set it off – could she manage that? Yes, she could. Ebony and jet earrings and a long rope of black pearls twisted negligently around her neck.

'Pearls for Madame von Wolff?' the jeweller had said, beaming. 'But of course. A very great pleasure, and here are some exceptionally fine stones . . . Ah yes, they are quite superb worn like that . . . The cost? Oh, zut, the cost will be arranged to please all parties.'

The black pearls were stunning and exotic. Alice had studied them longingly, thinking, Of course I can't possibly afford them. And then – oh, be blowed to the cost. She had left the shop with them coiled in a plush velvet-covered box.

On her hands she wore two large rings of ebony. She enamelled her nails to match the wine silk gown and painted her lips the same colour. Over the dark red gown she draped a cloak of mink edged with sable tails dyed a glowing crimson to match the gown. ('Four times she returned it to be re-dyed!' the designer had said, weeping hysterically. '*Four times!*') The cloak was slightly too long for her – the edges would trail on the ground when she walked, which pleased her greatly. I am so rich, you see, that I do not give a second thought to the hem of my furs becoming draggled in the gutter. The practical side observed that luckily it was a fine, dry night, with no rain-puddles anywhere.

Conrad was at her side, dressed in exceedingly well-cut evening clothes, his eyes bright with delight and expectation. He was overjoyed to see his little English sparrow tasting this success. Pouf! who were this Clara Bow and this Marlene Dietrich! Alice would show all of Austria and all of Germany – all of the world! – that she could out-act every one of them!

He had written the music for tonight, of course – Alice did not think he would have allowed any other composer to do so – and he was pleased with the results. His music would make a fitting background to Alice's fine performance, he said. There would, of course, be a gramophone recording of it later.

There were posters and photographs outside the film theatre near to Vienna's famous Opera House. '*Lucretia von Wolff as the mysterious, sinister* Alraune,' they said. And, '*The Baroness von Wolff IS Hanns Heinz Ewers' astonishing creation of soulless evil . . .*' '*Von Wolff is the definitive child of the mandragora root . . .*'

There were illustrations of mandragora – the plant said to grow in the shadow of the gallows – and there were brief descriptions of the legend.

'All to do with the fable of the hanged man,' Conrad had said, when Alice cautiously broached this subject once, wanting clarification, not wanting to appear naïve before the film-makers or her fellow actors. 'It is told that mandrake root – mandragora – grows beneath the gallows because of the seed spilled by the men hanged there.'

'And – does it?'

'Who knows?' He had smiled at her. 'There is a lewd old belief that when a man is hanged, semen is forced from him by the death spasms he endures. So to the legend of the half-mythical mandrake root growing where the seed spills—'

'And so,' Alice had said thoughtfully, 'to Herr Ewers' book, and Alraune's conception. Yes, I see. It'll be interesting to see how they deal with that aspect for the film's publicity, won't it?'

But in fact the posters merely said, quite decorously, that mandragora was said to possess powers to enhance men's prowess as lovers, and mentioned, as a chaste afterthought, that the roots were said to shriek when torn from the earth.

'A model of restraint and purity,' said Alice drily, reading this as the taxi drew up before the theatre and the driver leapt to open the doors.

She took a deep breath, and, remembering to let the sables trail negligently on the ground, swept into the auditorium on Conrad's arm.

She had seen rushes of the film, but tonight, for the first time, she saw the finished article flickering across the screen in its proper sequence; edited and trimmed and polished. It was astonishing and shocking but it was also utterly compelling.

The opening scenes were of Alraune's macabre conception in the shadow of the gibbet. The gibbet itself dominated the first few frames: it was black and forbidding and it cast its unmistakable outline on to the patch of scrubland, and on to the figure of the unstable brilliant scientist as he scrabbled in the earth for the phallus-shaped mandrake roots.

Mandragora officinarum, thought Alice, who had managed to read up on some of the legends by this time. Sorcerer's root. Devil's candle. And mandrakes live in the dark places of the earth – they drink the seed spilled by dying men in their last jerking agonies, and they eat the flesh of murderers. Myths and old wives' tales, of course, but still . . .

Now came the furtive meeting between the scientist and the prostitute and the prostitute's unmistakable greed as he offered her money. She tucked the money into her bodice in the age-old courtesan's gesture, glanced about her as if making sure there were no watchers, and then lay on the ground, her arms automatically held welcomingly out, but her eyes weary and bored. The camera moved away at that point – the censor would not have permitted anything explicit – but the director had focused on the uprooted mandragora roots, subtly suggesting movement from them, and this was so strongly symbolic, Alice wondered if the censor had missed the significance altogether.

It had been hoped to indicate a resemblance between Alice and the actress playing the prostitute, and Alice thought this had been reasonably successful, although the woman looked blowsy and over-painted on the screen. What Alice's mother might have called laced mutton, although whatever you called it, it was to be hoped that Alice herself did not look the same in a few years' time. I'll cut down the kohl on my eyes when I'm thirty-five, promised Alice. I really will. Or could I stretch that to forty? But I think I'd rather become a plump grey-haired grandmother-figure than look so tawdry.

The audience stirred expectantly at the baroness's first appearance, which was the grown-up Alraune being incarcerated inside a convent so that the scientist could study her as she grew up. Do they like me? thought Alice glancing round the theatre. Or are they simply curious?

Here was the brief scene with the music-master, with whom Alraune had her first real taste of passion. There had been some anxious moments about the timing of this, and Conrad had threatened to walk angrily out of the theatre if his music did not synchronize perfectly with the actor's simulated playing of a violin, but Alice knew he would not do so, because he would not spoil her night.

But it was all right. The music – beckoning and faintly sinister – came in exactly on cue, and the scene moved from the music room to the bedroom, the bed discreetly veiled in gauze drapings, again in deference to the censor. It was a sumptuous setting, and Alice was still surprised that no one had seen anything bizarre about having such a sensual scene inside a convent.

The story spun itself on to the discovery by Alraune of her own heredity, and to the first unfolding of the black and bitter hatred. Alice remembered that scene very vividly indeed; she had found it almost impossible to imagine how a girl of sixteen or so would react on learning she had been conceived in such circumstances. The pain and the self-loathing all looked convincing on the screen though; in fact they looked frighteningly real, and Alice was again aware of a sense of deep unease. Where did I get those emotions from? Supposing such feelings don't always come out of the past or the present? Supposing they sometimes come from the future . . . ?

The writers had added a scene in the fourth reel, in which Alraune, now eighteen, destroyed the damning evidence of that grotesque conception. Alice watched critically as the camera moved to the tall old house where the prostitute lived. In an upstairs room, stuffed into an old bureau, were the letters exchanged between the scientist and the prostitute, clearly testifying to their dark pact. A good scene, the writers had said, pleased. A shocking and dramatic scene. Herr Ewers had been consulted, partly as a courtesy, but mostly because of copyright, and he had approved the scene. Entirely in character for Alraune to do that, he had apparently said. Very good indeed.

As the cloaked and hooded outline that was Alraune crept up the stairs of the house, casting its own distorted shadow on the wall, Conrad's music began to trickle in again. At first it was so fragile it was barely audible – no more than a wraith of sound, tapping gently against your mind. But then it began to take on strength and substance, becoming rhythmic and menacing. The beating of a hating heart . . .

As the fire, ignited to burn the letters, blazed up, the camera panned outwards to take in the whole house front, and there, at one of the windows, surrounded by the leaping flames, was the terrified figure of the prostitute. Alraune's mother. Trapped in the burning building, her hair already alight and blazing, her mouth wide open in a silent cry for help . . . *Get-me-out . . . Get me out before I burn alive . . .*

There was a brief shot of Alraune standing in front of the house, her eyes on the trapped figure of her mother, her eyes huge with terror, thrusting her fist into her mouth to force back her own screams. And then the music spiralled upwards, shrieking out panic-notes like sirens, throbbing like the boiling blood in a burning woman's veins . . . The flames blazed into the night sky – a matchwood house frontage had been built for the scene and then set alight, and the prostitute was a dummy-figure, manipulated on the end of a long steel rod. Everyone had been a bit worried about how it would look, but Alice thought it looked convincing.

And now, at last, here was the room that Alraune had prepared for the scientist: the room with the velvet hangings and the trailing greenery framing the silken couch . . . The film slid seamlessly into the second of the scenes written in – that of the darkened and altered climax to Ewers' book. Despite herself, Alice felt again the sick apprehension at the sight of Alraune approaching the prepared death-chamber, the glittering stiletto in her hand. Take it slowly, they had said to her when they shot that. Go catlike and menacingly towards the door. There won't be any sound, of course, but let people *feel* your footsteps. *Pad-pad, I'm-going-to-kill* . . . Hold the stiletto up as you go along, let's see it catch the light, let's signal to the audiences that you're intent on murder.

Alice leaned forward, gripping the sides of her seat, knowing she was being absurd, but a tiny ridiculous part of her hoping that in some undreamed-of way it might come right after all, that Alraune might not commit that last appalling act . . .

It did not come right, of course. Conrad's music was filling up the auditorium, echoing the thrumming of a mind embittered and corroded by the need for revenge, and the sound of Alraune's footsteps were inside the cadences. *Pad-pad-I'm-going-to-kill* . . . And for the second time tonight Alice had the curious impression of scudding emotions pouring down from the future . . .

As Alraune raised the stiletto, and as the once-mesmeric figure of the scientist turned his head and widened his eyes in horror, the stiletto came flashing down on to his face . . . Once . . . Twice . . .

The screaming music reached its impossible heights, and the

final frame came up: shocking, pitiable. As the music began to fade in a long and terrible moan, the man who had created Alraune pawed in helpless agony at the dark bloodied holes where once his eyes had been . . .

Alraune watched for a moment, and then took the man's hand and led him solicitously to a high-backed chair. While he thrashed in his death throes, as if in macabre echo of her years in the convent she lit votive candles which she placed on each side of him. A sacrifice. A libation. The dark flames burned up, casting unearthly shadows on the dying man.

Alraune studied the effect, and adjusted one of the candles. Then she sat on the ground at the feet of her creator, and watched him die.

It was not until the lights were turned back up in the auditorium that Alice became aware again of the packed theatre, and the looks being sent in her direction, half-admiring, half envious. A very dark film, people were saying to one another. Very dark indeed, and far more shocking than the version done by Brigitte Helm a few years ago. Very disturbing. That final scene . . . Ah, that had *not* been in the original book? *Most* explicit it had been, one felt quite upset. And were they to understand that the scientist had died from Alraune's attack on him or not? Oh, left to the imagination of the audience, was it? Very modern. Er – was it correct that champagne was to be served in the foyer now? Ah, it was correct. And a little supper as well? Caviare and smoked salmon? Well, that would be very acceptable indeed.

It was necessary, as it always was, to remain cool and distant; to appear unmoved by the attention and the curious looks. But actually, thought Alice, sipping her champagne, actually I'm loving every moment of it, although I mustn't let anyone guess that. And yet at the deepest level of all was still the thread of anxiety that seldom left her, because it would be so easy for this to suddenly end. If I were to be recognized – if I were to be confronted with a visitor to the house where I was a maid, or even a man from those shameful, shaming nights near to St Stephen's Cathedral . . .

I could be anywhere, in any company, she thought, and someone might suddenly fling out an accusing finger, and say, But this isn't a real baroness at all. This is only some drab little servant girl, brought up in an English village, aping her betters, pretending to be grand and rich and beautiful, drinking champagne as if she's used to it, wearing expensive clothes instead of the ones suitable to her rightful station . . . What would I do if that happened? thought Alice.

She would not contemplate it. She would keep Lucretia's mask firmly in place, and she would make sure that no one ever connected the dazzling baroness with a little brown-haired lady's maid who, once upon a time, rather than face starvation, had sold her body in Vienna's streets.

CHAPTER EIGHTEEN

It was rather odd the way that word, *secret*, had kept cropping up while Edmund was having that meal in Lucy's flat. Edmund had always thought that Crispin was the only one who knew about the secrets in this family, but after that evening he had several times caught himself wondering. *'I'd have thought Ashwood would be the last place you'd want to visit . . .'* Lucy had said. And when Edmund had asked why, she had said, *'Well, because of Crispin . . .'*

How much might Lucy know about Crispin? About the secrets?

They had played a game called Secrets on that night all those years ago when Lucy's parents died. Edmund had been invited for the weekend; Lucy's mother, bright, butterfly creature that she was, loved filling the house with people and she had said that of course Edmund must come, wasn't it his autumn half-term from Bristol, or something? Nonsense, of course he could be there; all work and no play, remember the old warning, Edmund.

Mariana Trent's party-game that weekend was a hybrid: a mixture of the old-fashioned Murder and Sardines, all to do with hiding in the dark (which would be pleasantly flirtatious, said Mariana), and with trying to elude the designated murderer (which should be deliciously spooky). It was Mariana's own invention: a super game and it was called Secret Murder, and everyone would hugely enjoy it.

The party had had a 1920s theme, which meant the females could dress up like mad in fringed outfits, and Mariana could wear a jewelled headband and a feather boa, while the men were persuaded fretfully into dinner jackets. There would be a nice supper, and Bruce would see to the drinks; he mixed a *lethal* Sidecar and they would have White Ladies or Manhattans with the food.

'She's trying to re-create Lucretia,' said Deborah, on hearing Mariana planning all this. 'She's always doing it and I wish she wouldn't, because no one ever will re-create Lucretia. You'd think Bruce would get tired of it, wouldn't you, but he's nearly as bad as she is. I suppose that's why they married. Kindred spirits. She'll be nicknaming people Bunty or Hugo next, and telling Lucy to call her mumsie-darling. Like something out of Somerset Maugham or a Noel Coward play.'

Lucy, who was only eight, would go to bed as usual; her room was at the top of the house, so she would be far enough away from the party not to be disturbed. They would look in on her from time to time, said Mariana, but she would sleep through it all, the lamb.

Everyone was very complimentary about the 1920s theme, saying wasn't it fun to dress up like this, and imagine playing a Murder game before supper, what a hoot, and it would be just like an Agatha Christie book. And look at this – Mariana had set out little displays of '20s and '30s photographs and theatre programmes and things, how clever of her, where on earth had she found all that?

'Oh, I just ferreted around a bit,' said Mariana, delightedly. 'There's oceans of stuff in the attics, all packed away in trunks, in fact no one's thrown anything away for the last hundred years; we're all absolute magpies, you could write a whole family saga from the stuff if you wanted to. Eat your heart out, Mr Galsworthy.'

The game of Secret Murder required everyone to imagine the

house to be in the middle of nowhere. There had been a power cut, and it had just been discovered that there was a mad killer among the house-guests . . .

'It's not Agatha Christie at all, it's a remake of *The Cat and the Canary*,' said somebody disagreeably and was told to hush.

'And,' said Mariana, with mock-severity, 'you'll all be given a folded-up card, which will assign you a role at the house-party. There's a shady lady and a sinister foreigner and a colonel and so on – oh, and a butler, of course. And whoever gets the card marked with a cross is the murderer.'

Bruce, chiming in good-humouredly, explained that everyone's identity must be kept secret, but the object of the game was for the guests to keep out of the murderer's reach until the lights came on again. They could all go anywhere in the house, well, anywhere except Lucy's bedroom, which was on the little second floor, and the killer had to find as many people as possible in the dark and murder them.

'How?' demanded the person who had said this was *The Cat and the Canary*.

'Well, by tapping the victim on the shoulder and saying "You're dead".'

'How extremely polite and refined. If I get the murderer's card I'll do a bit more than tap shoulders, I promise you.'

This was greeted by several, slightly nervous, female giggles.

Bruce was on light-switching duty, said Mariana, and the lights would go off exactly ten minutes after the printed cards had been drawn, and remain off for half an hour. Then they would all gather in the big sitting-room for the interrogation.

Edmund had joined in, agreeing that it was marvellously spooky. A terrific game. He had been enjoying the party; there were one or two younger girls to whom he had been introduced, and everyone was friendly. Just before the lights went out, he heard one of the older female guests asking Mariana who *was* that nice-looking boy, and he paused, pleased to hear himself described as nice-looking and wanting to hear the reply.

'Oh, that's Edmund Fane,' said Mariana. 'He's a relation of Deb's husband. He's reading law – it's only his first year, but they say he's so clever. Yes, he is nice-looking, isn't he? But he has such a bleak time of it, poor Edmund, with the most frightful father, you wouldn't believe how awful – well, yes, it *is* a medical condition, melancholia or something, and we're all so sorry about it. That's why I said to Bruce, let's for goodness' sake give the poor boy some *fun* for once, prime some of the girls to flirt with him a bit . . . I said to Bruce, it's only *kind* . . . '

The bitch. The all-time, gilt-edged, venom-tongued bitch. Edmund stood very still, the noise and the laughter of the party going on all round him, but coldly and angrily detached from it all. As if a glass panel had come down between him and the guests.

They were sorry for him. Mariana and Bruce Trent were sorry for him because of his father – that was why he had been invited. *'He has such a bleak time of it, poor Edmund . . . '*

He heard, as if from a long distance, an amiable response from Bruce, saying something about it being open house here, everyone welcome, but how about getting on with the game. Nearly time for the murders, ha-ha, hope everyone's enjoying themselves, let's have some more drinks before the lights go out, shall we . . . ?

The drinks were duly distributed, and the cards were given out, and the lights went off on schedule. There was a good deal of scuffling and giggling and muffled squeaks as people trod on other people's feet, and anxious questionings about what on earth one was supposed to *do* for goodness' sake, and shrill-voiced girls saying, Oh, Henry, wherever are you? and, Do hold my hand.

The darkness seemed to rush at Edmund, and it was a thick smothering darkness, full of hateful whisperings . . . *'He has such a bleak time of it, poor Edmund . . .' 'That frightful father . . .' 'Give him a bit of fun for once . . . '*

Edmund shivered, despite the well-heated house, and wondered if he would ever get Mariana's words out of his mind. He could feel them trickling through his brain like acid.

And he had forgotten how alive the darkness inside a house

could be, and how it could fill up with sly whisperings and scalding emotions. His father, retreating more and more into a terrible inner darkness of his own, sometimes talked about it, and although nowadays the old man was as near mad as made no difference, lately Edmund had found himself understanding. Once or twice during these holidays, his father had taken to mumbling about his own past, dredging up memories.

Memories. As Edmund crossed the hall, the photographs and the faces that Mariana Trent had thought interesting enough and fun enough for her display swam out of the shadows. Memories. Lucretia von Wolff and those long-ago glittering glamorous years. Mariana loved them; she adored her mother's legend, and she was always trying to revive it, exactly as Deborah said.

It would teach Mariana a lesson if all those memories were destroyed tonight. If every snippet and every tag-end – all the cuttings and photographs and scrapbooks about Lucretia – were to be irretrievably lost, and it would serve the smug bitch right for pitying Edmund . . . *'Prime some of the girls to flirt with him a bit . . . I said to Bruce, it's only kind . . .'*

His heart beating furiously, the uncertain light casting his shadow before him, Edmund began to climb the stairs to the attic floor.

Lucy had gone obediently to bed just after eight o'clock and had lain awake listening to the party sounds, which were all mixed up with the sounds of the rain outside.

She liked lying in bed hearing rain pattering down on the windows and the roofs; it made you feel warm and cosy and safe. Mother usually complained if it rained when she was giving a party because she liked people to wander into the garden with their drinks, but tonight she had been pleased about the rain; she said it would add atmosphere to a game they would be playing later on.

The party was being pretty noisy. There was a lot of shrieking and laughing going on. Lucy hoped her father would not sing the extremely rude song he sometimes sang at parties after he had drunk too much and which made everyone helpless with laughter, but which always made Mum say, Oh, *Bruce*, half embarrassed, half laughing with the rest.

But whether Dad sang the song or not, it did not seem as if Lucy was going to be able to sleep through the noise. It did not much matter, because tomorrow was Saturday and not a school day, but she was starting to be very bored with just lying here doing nothing. She might read a bit of her book and hope to fall asleep over it, or she might get out her drawing-book which she could prop up on her knees, and the coloured pencils, or . . .

Or she might take this really good chance to explore the attics, which was something she absolutely loved, but that Mum and Dad did not really like on account of there not being any electricity in the attics. Lucy might trip over something in the dark, Mum said, and what about those twisty stairs which she might easily fall down.

But tonight no one would know if she went up there, and so she got out of bed, put on her dressing-gown and slippers, and padded along the landing, careful to be extra-quiet. It might be a bit spooky in the attics at this time of night, but if so she would come back to her bedroom. Lucy went through the little door, remembering to duck her head because of the sagging bit of oak on the other side which smacked you in the forehead if you were not careful, and then she was there.

It was not spooky at all. It was exactly the way it always was: the exciting feeling of stored-away secrets, and the scents of the old timbers and the bits of furniture that long ago had been polished with the kind of polish you did not have nowadays. Lucy loved it. She loved the feeling that there were little pieces of the past scattered around up here, so that if you looked hard enough you might find them – maybe inside the old cupboard that stood in a corner, or locked up in one of the tea-chests, or folded inside the sewing-table with the green silk pouch under the top, or tucked away under the slopy bit of roof at the far end.

Usually she brought her birthday-present torch with her so that she could look at the photographs in the albums, or read bits from the old magazines. Sometimes there were things about her grandmother, which was very intriguing indeed, because there were big mysteries about Lucy's grandmother. But she had not brought it tonight, so it was very dark and quiet. The rest of the house seemed suddenly to have grown very quiet, as well. It would have been nice to think this was because she had slipped through one of those magic chinks that take you into other worlds, but it would not be that at all; it would be everyone playing Mother's game, whatever it was.

Lucy found the oil lamp which they used in power cuts, or if plumbers came up here to do something called lag-the-pipes, and which would give pretty good light. There were matches at the lamp's base, fastened there with a rubber band – she was not really supposed to use matches but she knew how the oil lamp worked and she would be careful. She struck a match, and set it to the part of the lamp that was called the wick. There was a glass funnel thing that you had to slide down over the flame so that it would not burn anything.

The lamp made splashy yellow puddles of light, which Lucy liked. She set it against one wall, and thought she would see what was stored under the slopy bit of roof at the far end. She was just crawling across to a boxful of old photographs – old photographs were the best things of all up here – when there was a sound from beyond the attic door. Lucy looked round, because it sounded exactly as if someone had come up the twisty stairs, and was creeping very quietly across the tiny landing outside. It might be part of Mum's game, although Mum had said nobody would come up to the second floor – there was only Lucy's bedroom there, and the rest of the house was plenty big enough for the guests. They would put a little notice up at the foot of the second-floor stairs saying not to go up there, so Lucy could feel quite safe in going off to sleep as usual.

Probably whoever was out there was just somebody who had

not seen the notice. Or perhaps the notice had fallen off. Lucy was not exactly frightened, but this was starting to feel a bit scary. The oil lamp was still burning, but she had closed the attic door, and she thought whoever was out there would not see it.

And then her heart bumped with fear, because the door was being pushed slowly inwards and a shadow had fallen across the dusty floorboards. Lucy could not see who it was; she could only see the shadow, which was huge and oddly-shaped because of the flickering oil lamp. She had thought it would turn out to be Mum or Dad, who had found her room empty and come up to look for her, but neither of them would creep scarily around like this; they would just come inside, calling out to know where she was.

The shadow did not come inside and it did not call out. It just stood there, as if it might be peering around. Lucy stayed absolutely still, praying that she could not be seen, clenching her fists so that the nails dug into the palms of her hands. The big black shadow might be a burglar; you heard about burglars creeping into houses when people were having parties. But burglars did not bother with attics, did they? Attics were just places where people stored rubbish. Lucy was trying to decide if this made her feel better or worse, when the shadow suddenly ducked its head and stepped into the attic. And Lucy saw who it was.

Edmund. Her cousin, Edmund Fane, who was here for the weekend, on account of his father being mad or dying or something. Edmund, with whom she had shared those really good holidays at Aunt Deb's house, because Aunt Deb loved having them both there; she kept bicycles for them to ride around the village, and there were picnics and nature rambles. Sometimes in the evenings Aunt Deb told Lucy stories about her own youth which Lucy loved, although Edmund always pretended to find them boring.

Why had Edmund come up here in the middle of the party? And why was he looking round the attics and smiling to himself, as if something was pleasing him very much? Lucy began not to like the way Edmund was smiling – it made him look completely different. And then he turned his head and saw her and for a moment the scary, un-Edmund-smile stayed on his face as if it had frozen there. But when he spoke, his voice was quite ordinary.

'Lucy?' he said. 'What on earth are you doing here?'

He did not sound especially angry and he looked entirely ordinary again, so Lucy scrambled out from under the roof slope and explained about not being able to sleep, and about liking to come up here and look at the old photographs and things. There did not seem any reason to pretend about that, and it was always better to tell the truth. 'Only I'm not really s'posed to be here on my own, so it'd be good if you didn't tell anyone.'

'It'll be our secret,' said Edmund. 'I understand about secrets, you know,' and for a really dreadful moment the other Edmund came back and looked at Lucy out of Edmund's eyes. But he only said, 'I see you've lit the oil lamp. That's a bit silly – you might have started a fire up here.'

The really odd thing was that when Edmund said this about the lamp, Lucy had the feeling that he was not annoyed, but actually very pleased. She mumbled that she had been careful to blow out the match and put the glass funnel in place.

'So you have. But I'll turn it out now,' he said. 'And then we'd better go back downstairs.' His hand – a long big-knuckled hand, made bigger and longer because of the flickering light – came out to the lamp. Lucy saw his fingers slide the funnel up so that the little flame was unguarded.

Between one heartbeat and the next – so quickly that Lucy could not see quite how it happened – the lamp tipped over, and a sizzling line of flames ran along the dry floor timbers of the attics, and with a little whoosh of sound a stack of old newspapers, tied with twine, caught fire and blazed up.

Edmund said, 'Go downstairs at once, Lucy. *Now*! Tell them what's happened – tell them to bring buckets of water up. It's all right,' he said, as Lucy stared in horror at the tongues of greedy fire.

'It's really all right – it'll be out in minutes. But go and tell people now, while I start stamping this out.' He grabbed at a pile of old curtains, and moved forward to fling them over the flames.

'Buckets of water,' repeated Lucy obediently.

'Yes. We can form a chain from the bathroom – we'll pass the buckets up the stair. Hurry up, but tell everyone there's no need to panic. It's only a tiny fire.'

People were starting to reassemble downstairs for the next phase of the Murder game. They were coming cautiously out of various hiding places and laughing and swapping experiences, and asking what happened next. The interrogation, wasn't it? And then supper? Oh yes, look, Mariana was just going across to the kitchen. This was all being rather fun. There was an atmosphere of slightly tipsy friendliness and one or two people might well have been a bit more than merely friendly while hiding in the dark from the murderer, but no one was roaring drunk or making embarrassing accusations of unwanted groping.

There was a bit of a delay about switching the lights on – Bruce Trent was supposed to be doing that, wasn't he, although he was nowhere to be seen – Oh, one of the *victims*, was he? Well, wouldn't you know he would get himself bumped off, silly sod, good old Brucie.

One of the men found the under-stairs cupboard with the mains switch, and there were cries of 'Ah' as light flooded the house once again. People started arguing about how many victims there were, and somebody began to talk bossily about *habeas corpus* and was told to hush because that meant something different.

'No, it doesn't, it's in Magna Carta.'

'Oh, bugger Magna Carta, let's *habeas* some more gin before we start searching for the *corpus*.'

'Well, Bruce is one of the corpuses, we already know that.'

'Not very good manners to murder your host, though.'

'No, but in the dark you wouldn't necessarily know who you were murdering.'

'That has to rank as one of the most bizarre remarks in the history of— Hold on a minute—'

'What's the matter?'

'I think – in fact I'm sure – I can smell smoke.'

'It'll be from the kitchen – Mariana's going to serve chicken curry and rice at half past ten—'

'No, it *is* smoke,' said another voice. 'And it's coming from upstairs—'

It was at this point that Lucy came tumbling down into the hall and gasped out what had happened, and that they were all to fill buckets of water and pass them up to the attics – and *please* to do it fast, because even though Edmund had said it was only a tiny fire, it was burning up quite dreadfully . . .

CHAPTER NINETEEN

Only a tiny fire.

To begin with everyone accepted Edmund Fane's message that there was no particular need for urgency over this tiny fire, and several of the guests ran outside to find the garden hose and connect it up to the bathroom tap. Somebody asked if they ought to phone the fire brigade, and if so, had anyone done it? Oh, somebody had, oh, well done.

And even though it was just a tiny fire it had to be dealt with quickly, and it was a good thing Edmund Fane was here because Bruce Trent, when he was finally found, was three-quarters sloshed, and Mariana had never been any use in a crisis, in fact she was running around flapping her hands distractedly, and saying, Somebody *do* something; and, Oh, Bruce, why must you drink too much tonight of all nights?

It seemed to be falling to Edmund to organize people into filling buckets and plastic washbowls, and Lucy was taken firmly into one of the downstairs rooms where she could be out of the way of the panic. People formed a chain up the stairs, passing the buckets and bowls of water, but it was a big old house and the stairs were very steep, so that passing the full buckets up took a surprisingly long time.

Lucy tried not to be scared and she tried not to get in anyone's way. The guests were all running around, and it was all a bit confusing. She lost sight of her parents, but she saw Edmund go back up the stairs towards the attics. It was not a raging inferno up there, and everyone was saying the fire was not likely to spread much in the next few minutes, but it was still very brave of him.

Lucy tried to concentrate on how brave Edmund was being, and she tried not to think how she was the one who had caused the fire by lighting the oil lamp. Would Edmund tell people about that? But the lamp had been perfectly safe until he had turned it out – Lucy was sure it had been perfectly safe. Or had it? whispered a horrid little voice inside her head. Mightn't you have fixed the funnel a bit crookedly? Or put the lamp on a bumpy bit of floor so that it overturned? Did I? But even if I did, it'll be all right. They'll put the fire out and there won't really be any harm done. Make it be all right, she said in her head. *Please* make it be all right.

It seemed that the fire was getting a bit more of a hold – all those old, dry roof joists, and all that stored-away junk in the attics! – but the fire brigade would soon be here and they would douse the flames.

There was a kind of soft explosion from the attics, and Edmund cried out and came tumbling down the narrow stairs, half running, half falling, his hands blistered, his face and hair black with smoke.

'Get out!' he shouted. 'The whole top floor's alight! For God's sake, everybody get out of the house *now*!'

Somebody grabbed Lucy and half carried her outside to the big lawn at the back of the house. It was cold and the rain was still coming down, but flames and smoke were shooting up into the night sky, tinting it crimson. Lucy stared at it in new horror, because it was exactly as if the house was bleeding into the darkness. She began to shiver, but she still tried not to cry and be a nuisance.

People were saying this was all absolutely dreadful, but the fire brigade was on its way and the fire would soon be under control, and Bruce and Mariana would probably be able to have the place reroofed on the insurance. In fact where *were* Bruce and Mariana? Had anyone seen them?

Between one breathspace and the next, a situation that had been quite serious, but in control, spiralled shockingly out of control. A man who had found the garden hose and had been connecting it to the water tap at the side of the house suddenly looked up and pointed at the tiny skylight window at the very top of the house. One of the women screamed and then clapped a hand over her mouth.

'What is it? What's happening?'

'There's somebody still inside the house!'

'Where? Oh God, *where*?'

'Up there. The attic window.'

And then Lucy saw the flash of colour at the skylight window in the attics. Bright jade green. The distinctive outfit her mother had worn for the party. Green silk and the jade earrings she often wore in the evenings, because she loved vivid colours. She saw that her father was there as well, standing next to her mother, and quite suddenly she could feel her father's arms around her, and she could smell the nice scents of him – soap and clean cotton shirts, and the disreputable old jacket he wore for gardening – and she wanted him to be down here on the wet grass with her more than she had ever wanted anything in her entire life.

'Shout to them to make a dash for it!' cried one of the men. 'They might just do it – if they run straight through the flames.'

'Handkerchiefs over their mouths so they don't breathe in the smoke,' said a woman. 'That's what you do. Or sleeves – anything. Shout to them to do that!'

'They'll never make it!' said Edmund. 'Both stairways are in flames.' He was staring up at the attic window, his face sheet-white, oblivious of his own burned hands. Lucy looked at Edmund's burned hands. My fault. I lit the oil lamp and it overturned . . . My fault that my parents are trapped up there . . .

'If they smash the window—' said the man who had thought they could make a dash for it. 'Yes, listen, if they smash the window, they could just about squeeze through – they could jump down—'

'They'd break their legs,' said somebody. 'They're thirty feet from the ground. More, probably.'

'Better to have broken legs than burn alive,' said the first man angrily.

Bruce Trent's hands were beating uselessly on the tiny window – the window that was never opened because hardly anybody went up into the attics, and that certainly would not open now – and in the livid light of the fire Lucy could see her mother's face stretched in a silent scream of fear and entreaty. *Get me out . . . We're trapped . . .* The little pulse of panic and horror redoubled. *They're-trapped, they're-trapped . . . And it's my-fault, my-fault, my-fault . . .*

'Jesus Christ, can't somebody do something!' demanded one of the men. 'Where's the fire brigade? They *have* been called, haven't they?'

'Yes, I phoned them and they're on their way.'

'They're going to be too late! We've got to do something—'

'No, it's all right,' said the woman who had said about handkerchiefs. They've managed to smash the window. Look, Bruce is knocking all the shards of glass out—'

'The window's too small,' said the man who had phoned the fire brigade. 'They'll never do it.'

'They will. Bruce is helping Mariana to climb out—'

Mariana Trent was trying to get through the tiny window, crying out to the people below to help her. It was appalling to see her like this, the silk skirt rucked up above her knees, her legs cut and bleeding from the jagged window-frame, and her face crimson and shiny from the heat. There was a terrible moment when Lucy thought her mother's head looked exactly like a giant baked apple in the oven – just at the moment when the apple-skin had turned scarlet with the heat and was starting to split, and all the juices were running out. She tried to shut this picture out and to think of the figure as her mother but the dreadful image stayed stubbornly on her mind. A thin figure with a giant baked-apple head trying to climb through a window . . .

It was screaming, that grotesque figure; its mouth was open. It was halfway through the tiny window when the flames reached the frame, and there was a burst of flame as its hair caught light and a shower of sparks, and the thing that Lucy could no longer think of as her mother flailed wildly with its hands, trying to beat out the flames. But the flames caught at one of the hands and ran up the arm, and the figure fell helplessly back into the burning-up attics.

Lucy could not bear it. She sank on to the rain-drenched grass, wrapping both arms around herself because she was shaking so badly she thought she might break apart, and she was dreadfully cold as well, which was stupid with the heat of the fire and everything.

The garden hose was spurting water on to the fire, but every time it got close enough to do any good the rubber began to melt from the intense heat. There was smoke everywhere – huge black clouds of it, and lumps of burning timber and charred wood were falling on to the garden. In the distance Lucy heard the wail of the fire engine, and looked up hopefully because perhaps it would all be all right after all. But the fire station was miles away – it was on the other side of the town, and when Lucy remembered this she did not think the firemen would get here in time.

Through the steam and the smoke she could see the bare roof timbers now, like the bones of a skeleton sticking out through a dead body. There were two of the nightmare roasting-apple heads at the window now, and the screaming was going on and on, all mixed up with the crackling fire and the spluttering hosepipe and the dreadful bones of the house, and the really terrible part was that it was starting to become annoying, that screaming, so that Lucy wanted to shout to it to shut up . . .

She sobbed and began to run towards the house, but somebody caught her and held her back. Edmund. Lucy struggled to get away from him but he held her tightly, putting his hands over her ears to stop her hearing the screaming, but Lucy heard it anyway. She heard, as well, Edmund's voice saying in a horrified whisper, 'I'm so sorry, Lucy. Oh, Lucy, I'm so sorry.'

The fire engine came clanging along the lane, the sirens shrieking, so that if either Mariana or Bruce Trent were still screaming from within the flames, no one could hear them. The firemen ran about, unhooking ladders, and connecting steel hoses to taps, and huge powerful jets of water rained down on the house and clouds of steam rose up. The flames hissed angrily for a few moments, and then died down.

A little night wind had started up, and it blew the billowing smoke straight into Lucy's face. It was dark heavy smoke and it was laden with something greasy and too-sweet . . . As the terrible rich scent reached Lucy's stomach, she pushed Edmund away and was violently sick on to the rain-sodden ground. People came to help her – putting their arms around her, telling her everything would be all right, please not to cry, oh the poor darling child—

Everything would not be all right, of course, because nothing would ever be all right again in the entire world. The world would forever consist of two helpless figures with nightmare heads, screaming as they burned up. Lucy was sick on the grass again, and somebody sponged her face, and somebody else wrapped blankets round her. She tried to stop shaking but could not, and she tried not to look at the house.

And all the while, the night-rain beat ceaselessly down on the burning house and on what lay inside it.

There had to be an enquiry, of course, and there had to be an inquest. Sympathy was extended to Lucy and the rest of the family, and a verdict of accidental death was recorded. It was a terrible tragedy, but it was nobody's fault, said people. It had been a freak accident – a bizarre sequence of events that could not possibly have been predicted. Perhaps a spark from a faulty bit of electrical wiring had started the fire, or, more probably, someone had carelessly thrown a cigarette down somewhere. It was not very likely that anyone would ever admit to that, however.

One or two people murmured that if only Mariana had not gone running up to the attics and if Bruce had not then chased up there after her, they might still be alive. The top part of the house would still have burned, and anything in the attics would have been lost, but for goodness' sake, what were some bricks and timber and a few bits of jumble against two people burned alive!

Edmund had told his father what had happened, of course, even though he was not sure if his father entirely understood – you could not always tell these days. Severe clinical depression, the GP had said a few months earlier, summoning Edmund from Bristol University because he had not wanted to have a patient sinking irretrievably into the twilit world of melancholia without somebody in the family being aware of it. He added that the condition had probably been present for years under the surface, although you could never be certain about these things. Oh no, it was nothing anyone could have spotted, Edmund must not blame himself for any of it. Who knew what went on in the minds of even the closest of friends or family? Well, yes, he would have to say that the psychiatric consultant he had called in did think this particular case was progressive, but *nil desperandum*, because there were treatments and drugs that could help. An institution? Oh dear goodness, they did not need to think about that kind of thing for a long time yet, he said.

The best thing for Edmund to do was to keep his father as much in the ordinary world as possible – there seemed to be this strong tendency to look back on the past, had Edmund noticed that? Ah, he had. Well, anyway, cheerfulness, that was the watchword. Edmund should try to keep his father's mind focused on pleasant things: bits of family news, his own studies, light-hearted events in the world – not that there were many of those these days, eh?

It was difficult to tell if the news of the fire and the deaths of Mariana and Bruce Trent distressed Edmund's father or not.

'Everything was burned?' he kept asking Edmund. 'In the fire?'

'Yes. The top floors of the house were ruined.'

There was a long silence, and Edmund could almost feel his father trying to clutch at the rags of his own sanity. It was a relief when he asked a perfectly sane question about Lucy. 'What will happen to her? Where will she live?'

'With Bruce Trent's family, I think.'

'Not with Deborah?'

'No. Deborah suggested it, but I think everyone agreed Lucy would be better with her father's family. I should think she'll spend holidays with Deborah, though.'

'Ah. Yes, of course.' For a moment Edmund thought his father had sunk back into the dreadful darkness and he was just preparing to leave when his father suddenly said, 'Deborah would have liked having Lucy with her. Pity about that. But bring Lucy to visit me one day, will you?'

'Yes, of course,' said Edmund surprised.

'I'd like that. Will she grow up to be like her grandmother, d'you think?'

'I've no idea,' said Edmund.

Just before the inquest Edmund said to Lucy that it would be better not to tell anyone about the oil lamp.

Lucy had regarded him with solemn eyes, a little too large for her small face. 'Not ever?'

'No,' said Edmund. 'Not ever.'

She frowned, and Edmund realized that she was going to say something about it having been Edmund himself who had overturned the lamp – he could feel the thoughts forming in Lucy's bewildered mind. So, not giving her time to frame the words, he said, 'Lucy, listen. People might not understand about – about you being up there that night.' A pause. 'They might even decide the fire was your fault.'

It was rather dreadful to see the child's expression change, but it could not be helped. Lucy was a truthful, intelligent child, and anything she said might be believed. No matter how badly Edmund's plan to be revenged on that condescending bitch Mariana Trent had gone wrong – no matter how appalled he might be at what had happened – he had to cover his tracks.

'Might I be punished?' said Lucy after a moment.

'No. No. I don't really think anyone would do that,' said Edmund, making it sound as if he was not absolutely sure. 'But just in case, it would be better never to tell anyone about being in the attics.'

'Yes, I see. I won't ever say anything,' said Lucy. 'I promise.'

'Good girl.'

'But I thought,' said Lucy, speaking very carefully as if she was determined not to cry, 'that the rain would put the fire out. Didn't you think that, Edmund?'

'Yes. Yes, I did.'

'I used to like night rain,' said Lucy wistfully. 'Didn't you? It makes you feel all safe and cosy. And then in the morning everything's all clean and sparkly and fresh. But I don't like it now.'

'I don't like night rain at all,' said Edmund.

CHAPTER TWENTY

There was night rain when Edmund's father died a few weeks later – a ceaseless downpour that spattered against the windowpanes like bony fingers tapping to get in.

Edmund had spent his early childhood in this house, and he would have said he knew all its moods. He thought he knew the pace at which Time moved through the rooms, although he was already aware that when you were nineteen Time moved at a difference pace than when you were nine. But it would not matter if he lived to be ninety, or a hundred and ninety, the night on which his father died would always be the longest night in the world.

Since the fire his father had slipped further and further away from the normal world. 'Well, we knew the condition was likely to worsen,' said the GP when Edmund tentatively pointed this out. 'And now he's picked up this bronchial infection, probably because of his low physical state. We're having a bit of trouble shifting that, in fact I suspect that he's not taking the antibiotics I've prescribed. In view of his mental condition that's very likely.'

'Shouldn't he be in hospital?'

But hospitals, it seemed, were full to brimming with people who were about to die, or who needed urgent operations.

Edmund's father was a comparatively young man – barely past his middle fifties – and he did not need to be carted off to hospital just for a chest infection. But because of the – well, the other problem, he needed to have someone with him, just for the next few days, said the GP. Just to make sure he took his pills, and stayed in bed. It would not be a problem for Edmund to do that?

'No,' said Edmund, wondering how many lectures he would miss, and whether he would eventually manage to catch up.

'Isn't there anyone you could ask to stay with you to share things a bit? Family, perhaps. Or there are these medical organizations who supply nurses.'

But Edmund did not want any of the family there. Aunt Deborah would certainly come rushing over to help, but Edmund did not want her hearing his father's wild ramblings, seeing the run-down state of the house, seeing the run-down state of his father. He did not want some gossipy busybody of a nurse there, either. So he said there was no one and that he could manage quite well by himself.

'All right. Try to get the antibiotics down him – one tablet every four hours – and keep him warm,' said the GP, preparing to leave. 'And give him whatever fluids you can. Sweet tea, glucose drinks, fruit juice, anything. He's quite dehydrated. Oh, and don't leave him alone, will you?'

'He's not violent, is he?'

'No, but I think his mental state is deteriorating, although that's not my field. We might need to call one of the on-duty psychiatrists in if he doesn't improve.'

'Might he have to be taken to a – a mental hospital?'

'Let's not look that far ahead.' But the GP frowned, as if reassessing Edmund's comparative youth, and said, 'Are you sure there's no one you could contact?'

'I don't need anyone. I can cope perfectly well on my own.'

He made up a bed in his old room, and he tried to persuade his father to take the pills left by the GP, and to eat and drink. He was horrified at how much his father had changed in the last few weeks, and how the once tall, once well-built figure had become shrunken and wasted. He's given up, thought Edmund. He's given up the fight to remain in the sane world, and I don't think there's any way of bringing him back. He realized with sudden surprise that his father was tired of fighting, and that he was grateful to the darkness that was at last pulling him into its deep oblivion.

Edmund only left the bedroom on two or three brief occasions during the evening – once to heat some soup for his father and once to make a glucose drink, both of which his father refused, turning his head away on the pillow. Each time he returned to the room he did so with a beat of apprehension, more than half-expecting to find his father dead. Could you die, purely by wishing it?

Towards midnight the house slid down into a cold and haunted state that no longer seemed to be in the real world but in some desperately lonely wilderness. Was this the place his father had inhabited during all those appalling attacks of melancholia? This silent desolation? Edmund went round the house, turning up all the heating and switching on all the lights, but it did not seem to make much difference. The rooms began to smell of despair and ghosts.

Ghosts . . .

Shortly before one a.m. his father began the fearful head-turning that Edmund found so eerie. He constantly turned his head this way and that, as if he could sense the presence of something invisible creeping across the room, and as if he was trying to find it, not with his sight, but with his instincts.

'What's wrong?' Edmund had been half dozing in a chair near the window.

'Did you hear something?' His father had pushed himself up on the pillows, and there was a feverish colour across his thin cheekbones. Edmund heard with a chill that his father's voice sounded different. It sounded *old.* The two antibiotic pills he had managed to get him to swallow had had no effect; his breathing was like the slow creaking of a lump of thick yellowed leather.

'It's raining like fury outside,' said Edmund. 'I expect that's what you heard. Try to go back to sleep. Or if I make a cup of tea could you drink it?'

His father shook his head impatiently and dismissively. 'Listen,' he said. 'Can't you hear? It sounds like someone creeping up the stairs.'

'I can't hear anything—' He's hallucinating, thought Edmund. But despite himself he crossed to the partly open bedroom door and looked into the deep well of the stairs. Nothing. He came back and sat on the side of the bed, and his father's hands reached for him with the sudden frightening strength he sometimes displayed. 'You imagined it,' said Edmund. 'There's no one here except us.'

'I'm not imagining it. I'm going to die tonight, Edmund. And *they* know I am. That's why they're here now. That's what I'm hearing.'

An icy finger traced its way down Edmund's spine, but he said, '*They*?'

'The murdered ones. They walk, Edmund – that old belief's perfectly true. The murdered ones really do walk. That's why I've never been able to forget.'

'Ashwood,' said Edmund, softly. 'That's what you mean, isn't it? You were there that day, weren't you?'

'Yes.' The voice was no longer old and sick; it was younger, more vigorous. He's going back, thought Edmund. In his mind he's going back to those years.

'I never forgot what happened that day,' said this eerily younger voice. 'That's the trouble, you see. You think that in time you'll be able to put it from you, but you can't. All the time, for all the rest of your life, you have to watch everything you do and you have to measure everything you say, in case someone finds out . . .' He broke off, and Edmund waited, not speaking. 'I was articled to a firm just outside Ashwood village – you never knew that, did you?'

'No,' said Edmund obediently.

'I've never talked about it. Or have I?' A look of puzzlement crossed the thin face. 'Have I talked about it, Edmund?'

'No,' said Edmund again. No point in saying Deborah had talked about it to him and to Lucy; that she had liked remembering those meetings at Ashwood, which had led to her marriage to the older brother, William Fane.

'The firm I was articled to did a lot of work for the studios. Contracts for the actors, details on the leasing of the land. It was quite interesting. I used to be taken to Ashwood quite often, to take notes, to gain experience.'

Edmund could feel the memories crowding in, and he could see his father as he must have been in those days: young, charming, eager, his hair the colour of honey with the sun in it, his eyes vividly blue . . .

'Lucretia had come to live in England after the war,' said the voice that was no longer his father's. 'I think she had bought a house near to Ashwood – Essex or Sussex, somewhere like that. The first time I saw her I thought I had never seen anyone so beautiful. She was perfect, Edmund – skin like porcelain or ivory, and that black hair like polished silk. And a shining quality, as if she was perpetually surrounded by light. You didn't actually see it, but you felt it. She could light up a room just by walking into it. But she was mischievous as well. Come to bed, she said, and I went. It was like being under a spell – I sometimes thought she was a witch, but I would have done anything for her.'

He paused again, his mind still deep in the past. 'A long time afterwards I married your mother – an old childhood friend, someone I had known all my life. A marriage based on friendship it was, and I thought it might help me to forget. It didn't, of course. After Lucretia, no other woman could ever—' Sanity flared in his face, faded away, and then struggled pallidly back, like an electrical current flickering on and off in a thunderstorm. Edmund wanted to tell him not to speak, to try to forget, but his father's memories were winding their tendrils around his own mind now, pulling him into that same past.

'That day,' said his father, 'that day at Ashwood, I believe I stepped over some kind of invisible line. I crossed a Rubicon or I forded a river somewhere, but whether it was the Jordan river or Charon's Styx or the measureless sacred Alph, I never knew. But once you're over that line, Edmund, you can never get back.' A spasm of coughing wracked him.

'Try to sleep,' said Edmund rather helplessly. 'Everything's all right.' But of course it was not all right, because the final strings of sanity were unravelling fast, and his father's mind was moving beyond anyone's reach.

'Sleep, yes, sleep. To sleep perchance to dream, that's the worry though, that's always been the worry . . . And supposing death is only the prince's hag-ridden sleep, after all . . . ? Aye, there would be the rub, wouldn't it? What punishment do they keep in hell for murderers, I wonder? Do you know, Edmund?'

'You aren't a murderer,' said Edmund after a moment. 'Lucretia von Wolff killed those two men. Afterwards she stabbed herself rather than face the gallows. She was – she was bad. Cruel.'

'Was she?'

'Murder is cruel and bad.'

'Oh Edmund,' said the unfamiliar voice from the pillow. 'I know all about murder.' A pause. 'I'm a murderer,' he said. 'I was the one who murdered Conrad Kline that day at Ashwood.'

The silence that closed down was so complete that for a moment Edmund almost believed his father had died and pulled him down into death with him.

After what might have been moments or hours, he said, 'Dad, listen. Lucretia von Wolff killed Conrad Kline.'

'Lucretia didn't kill Kline.' The strength came back into the weak voice. 'Listen to me, Edmund. I was nineteen when it all happened, and she was – I don't know how old she was. Thirty-eight. Forty, perhaps. It didn't matter. It was my first time with a woman – they'd laugh at that today, wouldn't they: nineteen and a virgin, but it's quite true. And I was clumsy and fumbling and mad with excitement, but I thought I had found the heaven that the religious talk about.'

I'm hating this more than I can ever remember hating anything in my entire life, thought Edmund. I don't want to hear any of this.

'It went on for three weeks. I would have died for her, killed for her. And then, that last day, Kline caught us together. He stood in the doorway of her dressing-room – I can see him now, standing there, insolent devil that he was. He said, "Oh, Lucretia, are you at that game again?" And he sounded so – so indulgent. So loving. As if he was reproving a wayward child. I said, "It's not a game – we love one another," and he laughed. He took me into some other room – a wardrobe store, it was – and he said, "You ridiculous boy, she'll ruin your life. Let her go. Find some nice English girl instead. Someone of your own age."'

He broke off, struggling for breath, and Edmund said, 'You don't need to tell me this—'

'I told him she loved me,' said the harsh voice. 'But he said, "She doesn't love you. It's a diversion for her." I snatched up a knife or a dagger – something they had used on the film set earlier – and I attacked him. I just kept on stabbing him – I had to wipe out the words, you see. "She doesn't love you," he had said, and I had to get rid of those words, so I brought the knife down on his face – on his mouth – over and over again. There was so much blood – you can't imagine how much blood there is when you stab someone, Edmund. And it smells – it fills up a whole room within seconds, and it's like the taste of tin in your mouth.

'I ran away then. Kline's blood was everywhere, it was all over me, and I didn't know what to do next. But I knew I had got to save myself. They would have hanged me, Edmund, they really would—' Once again the hands came out, clutching, seeking reassurance. 'I ran out of Ashwood as if the Four Furies were chasing me, and I ran until I reached the road and somehow – I don't remember it all – but somehow I got back to the house where I was living in Ashwood village. I locked myself in, and later I pretended I knew nothing about the murders; I pretended I had left Ashwood an hour before it all happened.'

He pulled Edmund closer. 'But all these years I've wondered if someone did know and if someone had seen. I could never be sure, that was the thing.' He turned his head away. 'I was mad that day, and I think I've been mad ever since, Edmund. But if I'm really mad, I shouldn't still be hurting, should I, not after all this time, thirty years since she died . . .' His voice became fainter, not physically, but somehow spiritually, as if he was moving further away from the world.

Edmund had no idea what he should say. He kept hold of the thin hands. The echoes swirled and eddied all around the room.

Then his father said, very softly, 'I think I'm going to die very soon, Edmund.'

'No—'

'Yes, I think so. I shall go down into oblivion and peace. Or will it be down into a tempestuous darkness, where hell's demons dwell? People don't know until they get there. But I'll know quite soon, because I'm going to die tonight, aren't I?'

Edmund stared down at the bed, watching the sanity come and go in the thin face, conscious of a dreadful pity. He could just remember the bright-haired, bright-minded man of his early childhood, and he could remember his father's lively intelligence and imaginative mind, and the feeling of security he had given Edmund. When Edmund's mother had died when he was tiny, his father had said, 'I'll always be with you, Edmund. You won't need anyone else, because whatever you do and wherever you go, I'll be there.'

'You won't tell anyone about this, will you?' his father was saying. 'You won't ever tell anyone.'

'No,' said Edmund slowly. 'No, I won't tell anyone. No one outside this room will ever know that you're a murderer.'

The shadows seemed to creep closer, and to reach out to claw the words and take them into their darkness, and then return them.

You're-a-murderer . . . You're-a-murderer . . .

'You'll be quite safe,' said Edmund in the same soft voice, and it was only then that the clutching hands loosened their grip, and Crispin Fane fell back on the pillows, exhausted.

Shortly after midnight Crispin seemed to slip into an uneasy slumber, and after a few moments Edmund went out of the room. He had not eaten or drunk anything since midday; he would make himself a sandwich and a cup of coffee.

There was hardly any food in the house, so whatever the doctor had said, he would have to go out tomorrow. He was just grating some rather stale cheese when the floorboards creaked overhead, and he went back out to the stairs. He was halfway up when he saw his father's outline, pitifully frail in the thin pyjamas, making a slow, fumbling way across the landing. There was a moment when the overhead light turned Crispin Fane's hair to the shining red-gold it had been in Edmund's childhood. He waited, and saw his father go into the bathroom at the far end, and close the door.

Nothing wrong with that, said Edmund's mind. If he feels well enough to walk to the loo on his own, that's perfectly all right. He went back down to the kitchen, and heard the taps running in the old-fashioned bathroom that his father had never bothered to modernize. After a few moments the tank began to refill. The pipes were slow, clanking things, and the tank always took quite a long time to fill up; when Edmund was very small he used to lie awake listening to it, wondering how the water knew when it had reached the top and had to stop. Sometimes the rushing of the water seemed to go on and on.

It went on and on tonight, almost drowning the single chime from the old carriage clock that had belonged to Edmund's mother. One a.m. The smallest of the small hours. The murdered walk, his father had said. If that was true, this was surely the hour when they would do so. Who would they be, those murdered ones? The long-ago Conrad Kline, killed by a jealous boy . . . ? Mariana Trent and Bruce, screaming as the flames burned their flesh, with the appalling stench of burning human flesh, like meat cooking in an oven filling up the night . . . But I never meant that to happen, cried Edmund in silent anguish. Yes, but it happened all the same. It was your fault. And that makes you a murderer . . .

Crispin had been a murderer, as well. He had killed Conrad Kline. But what about the other man – Leo Dreyer? Who had killed him? Had it been Lucretia after all?

The slopping water filling up the tank had died away, and in the silence the ticking of the carriage clock seemed unnaturally loud. *Tick-tick . . . The murdered walk . . .* Crispin had said that, as well. *Tick-tick . . . They walk, they walk . . . Burned alive or stabbed in the face, they always walk . . .*

He carried his sandwich and the mug of coffee upstairs. His father's room was still empty, the bedclothes pushed back. Edmund set down the plate and the mug, and went along the landing.

The bathroom door was not locked, but when he called out to know if his father was all right, there was no response. I don't want to go any further with this, thought Edmund. I truly don't. But I'll have to. I've called out to him – that's a reasonable thing to do, isn't it? He took a deep breath, and opened the door.

The bathroom was full of pale thick vapour, as it always was if someone took a long hot bath and forgot to open the window, and for a moment Edmund could only make out the shapes of the washbasin and the deep old bath and the cloudiness of the misted mirrors. But here and there the mists were tinged with red, like clouds reflecting a vivid sunset.

It was a large bathroom by modern standards: the house had been built at a time when space was not at a premium, and one of the bedrooms had been converted some time before Edmund was born. For a moment he could not see any sign of his father, but then the mistiness cleared a little as the cooler air from the open door began to disperse it. The pulsing fear that had been beating inside him changed key, and began to drum against his temples.

Because there was someone lying in the bath.

There was someone lying absolutely still in the bath, the head turned to the door as if watching for someone or something it would never see again. For the space of six heartbeats the lisping trickle of water still dribbling into the tank whispered all round the room, seeming to mock the confused panic in Edmund's mind. *S-s-someone lying in the bath . . . S-someone with blood-dabbled hands, and blood-smeared che-s-s-t, and someone who's grinning through gaping bloodied lips-s-s . . .*

Someone who had deliberately run a hot bath, and then had got into it and was grinning with macabre triumph at having cheated the world. The tiles around the bath were splattered with blood, and there was blood on the damp tiled floor. The razor lay on the tiles.

How am I supposed to interpret what I'm seeing? thought Edmund. I must concentrate, I must work out exactly what I'm looking at, because they'll want to know – police and doctors, they'll all want to know. So what am I seeing? I'm seeing that he's smiling – that's the first thing. But his mouth's in the wrong place.

His mind finally snapped out of the frozen paralysis, so that he could think logically again. His father was not smiling, of course. His lips had a blueish tinge and they were slightly open. They were expressionless, giving nothing away. It was the other lips directly underneath, the lips of the deep, gaping wound across his throat that curved into that dreadful grin, and that glistened wetly with blood . . .

He's cut his throat, thought Edmund. That's what's happened. He found the old-fashioned razor and then he got into a hot bath, and he slashed the razor across his throat. That's what I'm seeing. I'm seeing someone who no longer wanted to live.

A dozen different emotions were scalding his entire body, but at last he walked across the damp tiles. The hot tap was still dribbling into the bath; moving like an automaton he turned it off, and then reached into the still-warm water for one of the flaccid hands, feeling for a pulse. Nothing. And Crispin's skin was unmistakably lifeless. Dead meat. But I've got to make sure, thought Edmund. How about a heartbeat? It was unexpectedly distasteful to reach into the warm water to touch the bloodied chest, but it was necessary. Don't think, said his mind, just do it. You've got to make certain beyond all doubt that he's dead. If you phone an ambulance now, that's what they'll tell you to do. The flat of your hand against the left side of his chest. A bit higher. That's about right. And if there's the least sign of anything beating—

But there was nothing at all, and at last Edmund stepped back from the bath, suddenly realizing that he was shaking violently, and that despite the warm damp bathroom he was icily cold. He leaned back against the wall, wrapping his arms around his body as if it might bring back some warmth, staring down at the thing that had been his father. For several moments he fought to remain in control, because he must not give way to nerves or confusion, he must *not* . . . And looked at logically, there was nothing in here that could possible hurt him or threaten him.

Or was there?

The trembling had stopped and he was just gathering himself together to go downstairs to the phone, to summon ambulances or doctors, or whoever else might need to come out to deal with a dead man in the middle of the night. It was then that he caught a flicker of movement on the rim of his vision, and he spun round at once, his heart leaping up into his throat. Someone here? Someone hiding in the tiny bathroom, standing in the pale mistiness watching him? He remembered what his father had said earlier. 'Listen,' he had said. 'It sounds like someone creeping up the stairs.' Edmund felt the blood start to pulsate inside his head again.

And then he realized that what he had seen was his own reflection in the big oak-framed mirror above the washbasin. A small nervous laugh escaped his lips, releasing some of the throbbing tension. Only his own reflection.

Or was it? He peered through the wisps of vapour. The surface of the mirror was still patchily misted, but wasn't it a subtly different Edmund who stood there; an Edmund who was somehow more definite, more vivid? An Edmund whose hair seemed almost to catch an unseen shaft of light, so that it gleamed faintly red . . .

Edmund moved one hand experimentally, and the other Edmund moved his hand also, but not quite in synchronization, more as if he was sketching a half mocking, half amused salute from the depths of the glass.

I'll always be with you, Edmund . . .

The memory made Edmund's lips twist in a brief acknowledgement that was almost a smile. At once the image in the mirror gave the same near-smile as well, and this time there was no doubt about it; this time the smile was definitely not his own. It was the smile of a young man who once upon a time had possessed sufficient charm to attract a wicked, mischievous lady – a lady with skin like porcelain and hair like polished silk . . . A young man who had killed and escaped the consequences of killing . . . A young man with hair the colour of honey with the sun in it, and a smile filled with charm . . .

Crispin. Crispin standing in the mirror's smoky depths, looking out at him. Speaking to Edmund inside his mind.

I'll always be with you, said Crispin's voice, just as it had done when Edmund was very small. *Remember that, Edmund . . . You won't need anyone else, because whatever you do and wherever you go, I'll always be there to help you . . .*

After a long, long time Edmund remembered that there was still a world beyond the house, and things that must be done, and somehow he got to the phone to dial the GP's night service. An impersonal voice answered and Edmund said, in a perfectly calm tone, that his father had just died, and that he was on his own and he had no idea what he should do but he thought he had better start with his father's doctor.

Yes, he was quite sure that life was extinct, he said. No, there was no possibility of survival whatsoever. So could the doctor – or one of his partners – come out as quickly as possible? Yes, he understood that it might take a little time to locate whoever was on call. No, of course he would not leave the house in the meantime. He wondered if the owner of the voice suspected him of preparing to zap off into the night to whoop it up somewhere while rigor mortis set in on his father's corpse.

But he listened to the explanation about calling 999, and then said coldly that in view of the fact that his father was undoubtedly dead there did not seem much point in summoning the emergency services who might be better employed elsewhere, to say nothing of waking the entire neighbourhood with sirens and flashing lights. What he needed, he said, was a doctor and an undertaker, and he did not mind in which order. The voice appeared to find this an inappropriate remark, and said primly that an on-call doctor would be there as soon as possible.

Edmund had to wait three hours for a very young, very rumpled-looking duty doctor to arrive. He spent the hours sitting on the landing floor, with the bathroom door propped open, watching his father's body, trying not to wonder what he would do if that the dreadful head with the two sets of gaping lips – one pallid, the other blood-caked – suddenly turned towards the door.

While he waited the carriage clock downstairs ticked away the minutes and then the hours. *Tick-tick . . . Always-be-with-you-Edmund . . . Tick-tick . . . The-murdered-ones-walk-Edmund . . .*

The murdered ones. Conrad Kline. Leo Dreyer. Mariana and Bruce Trent.

Edmund listened to the ticking rhythmic voices for a long time, and very slowly he began to understand that Crispin – the real Crispin who had been young and good-looking and full of confidence – was filling him up, and he knew that Crispin would stay with him no matter what he, Edmund, did. He could hear Crispin's voice inside the ticking clock, and inside the goblin-chuckling of the rain as it ran down the gutters. *We're both murderers, Edmund . . . We've both killed someone . . . So I'll stay with you, Edmund . . . I'll make sure you're safe . . .*

Shortly before dawn Crispin's body finally began to stiffen, slipping down in the cold water so that it washed against the sides of the bath, adding its slopping voice to that of the ticking clock. *The murdered walk, Edmund . . . I'll always be with you, Edmund . . . Always be with you . . . Whatever you do and wherever you go, I'll always be there to help you . . .*

After the fire Lucy had not minded living with her father's family, who were kind and generous, and who made her part of them. There were holidays with Aunt Deborah, who talked to Lucy about Mariana, which Lucy liked. Looking back, she thought she had eventually managed to have a reasonably happy childhood, although she had been glad when she was old enough to leave home and work in London and have her own flat.

But the trouble with memories was that even though you fought them as hard as you could, they were sometimes too strong for you; they could lie quietly in a corner of your mind – sometimes for years and years – and then pounce on you. Lucy knew very well that there were some memories that were dangerous and painful, and that must be kept out at all costs.

CHAPTER TWENTY-ONE

Alice had always known that the past was something that might be dangerous, and she had always known, as well, that the ghosts of that past might one day be responsible for destroying the careful, false edifice she had built up. It would only take one wrong move, or one unexpected moment of recognition, and the baroness's career would be over.

But what Alice had not known was that there were other ghosts in the world who might destroy far more than a fake identity. Ghosts who were eagle-talon cruel and who stalked nations and haunted entire generations, and ghosts who bore as their device an ancient, once-religious image, which they had arrogantly reversed in the service of an implacable regime . . .

It was not until after *Alraune* became a success (Brigitte Helm was reported to be furious at this impudent annexing of her most-famous role) that Alice began to have the feeling that Viennese society was changing; that the gaiety was a little too hectic to be quite natural, and that the lights were burning a little too brightly. Afterwards she was to wonder if those days had held a touchstone moment – if there had been an hour or a day or a night when those faint scribblings on the air had formed into the patterns of augury, like the tea-leaves in old women's cups, or the misted surface of a scryer's glass . . .

But surely she was not the only one who had sensed that the dangerous sinister ghosts were regrouping their forces and preparing to enter the world once again? For every major event in the world there were always people ready to nod wisely, and say, Oh, yes, we knew there was something wrong . . . We said so at the time . . . We had a feeling . . . Had those Cassandras sensed that a grisly chapter of history was being revived and mobilized so that it could march forward once more . . . ? Had some of them glanced uneasily over the years to a time when the lights of an entire continent had gone out and when they had stayed out for four long years . . . ?

But everyone agreed that no government would allow another war to happen, and that after the Great War there would be no more conflict. Alice had only been eight years old on that November day in 1918; at the time she had not really understood the cheering and the celebrations, and the word 'Armistice' had meant nothing to her except that people had been shouting it joyfully in the streets. But she understood it now; she understood that the war to end all wars had come and gone, and that since that time the world had become safe.

So forget this unease. Dress up in something startling, go to an outrageous party – better still, *give* an outrageous party! Order pink champagne, commission an extravagant gown from Schiaperelli, a flagon of perfume from Chanel . . .

And close your ears to the tales of injustice and oppression said to be rife under that ridiculous, vulgar little man in Germany, and remember that Vienna is a self-governing state, self-contained, perfectly safe even if the rest of Europe runs mad. Ignore the stories about the suppression of free speech, about the censorship of letters, about the burning of books thought to preach anti-Nazi propaganda – yes, and ignore the alarmists who warn that people who burn books may end in burning men, and who whisper dreadful things about Göering's labour camps . . . Above all, close your ears to the accounts of the spies who prowl the streets, seeking out people with Jewish blood . . .

Jewish blood. Conrad. For a moment the two things interlocked grimly in her mind, and as if the interlocking was a yeast ingredient that had been quietly fermenting in wine or bread, the danger and the darkness suddenly felt much closer.

Conrad had not been faithful to Alice, of course; probably he was congenitally incapable of being faithful to any woman. He was handsome and charismatic, and possessed of enough charm and sexual energy to lure an abbess into bed and then take on the rest of the convent afterwards.

The first time Alice discovered that he had spent a weekend with a little Russian singer, she had hurled herself on to the bed and sobbed all night. This did nothing but give her a pounding headache and a swollen face next morning.

The second time (a wickedly *gamine* Parisienne mannequin), she had not hurled herself on to the bed; instead she had hurled crockery, aiming most of it at Conrad, and then stormed out of his rooms. This time he had followed her, and there had been a grand reconciliation. He had put a gramophone record of Wagner's *Tannhäuser* on – he adored making love to music – and they had spent a delirious afternoon in bed, staying there until the summer evening sunshine streamed into the bedroom, both of them wine-flown by then, both riotously trying to time orgasms to the swelling crescendos of the music.

So, Alice thought afterwards, tears and vapours get you nowhere. Tantrums and smashed crockery do. So much for polite behaviour and ladylike restraint.

It was a gratifying discovery, but what was even more gratifying was finding that it was perfectly possible to embark on the occasional bedroom adventure on one's own account, and to return to Conrad afterwards. These escapades were fun, but what was even more fun was that they always made Conrad violently jealous. Alice took care to make sure he always knew where she had been on those occasions, although not who she had been with, not after the time he had challenged the other man to a duel. ('I will meet you in the village of Klosterneuberg overlooking the city,' hissed Conrad, with gleeful relish at such drama. 'Be there at the break of dawn, and I will kill you and throw your body into the Vienna Woods for the bears to eat.')

I believe, thought Alice, stepping in to prevent the duel, that I've turned into a vamp. Imagine that. One day my children – if I have any – might hear about all this, and perhaps they will enjoy the drama of it, as Conrad does, or perhaps they will sigh and say that Mamma was really too outrageous for words when she was young.

Children . . .

She had not intended that there should be any children at all, but a daughter was born just over six years after that amazing night at the State Opera House. Conrad's, of course, people said, smiling a little slyly, and the baroness had smiled back, apparently unruffled.

One or two people wondered whether the outrageous couple might now marry – a child ought to have a proper father, after all – and one or two of them asked the question openly. Lucretia simply laughed at such a preposterous idea – boringly conventional! – and did so loudly enough to cover the fact that she would have dearly liked to be married to Conrad.

But marriage or not, Conrad was completely charmed with his small daughter. He had been immersed in ancient music at the time, and he had suggested naming the child Deborah after the Old Testament prophetess who had stirred up Barak to march against Sisera. Alice liked the name, and she liked Conrad's description of Deborah's song, which had been sung on the occasion of Israel's victory, and which he said was one of the oldest Hebrew compositions. 'But one day I shall compose a new variation of it,' he announced, with that blend of arrogance and naïve enthusiasm that was attractive and infuriating by turns. 'When I have finished writing music for films, I shall compose a piece of music that will be called *Deborah's Song*, and everyone will know it is for my beautiful daughter. And a little,' he added, 'for her even more beautiful mamma.'

Alice wondered if Deborah would grow up hearing the stories about her wanton mother and be shocked. She supposed her grandchildren – if ever she had any – would hear the stories of their grandmother's wild and tempestuous youth, and regard her with disbelieving fascination.

Grandchildren. I shall *never* be old enough to have grandchildren! I shall stay like this, caught in this marvellous world of films and music and lovers – of money and good clothes and jewellery and adulation – and if I do grow old, I shall not let the world see it.

But if one day I do have to be old, I shall make sure it is a dazzling oldness, and I shall make sure it is a disgraceful and scandalous oldness as well!

By the time Deborah was born, Alice had made three films, and she had seen the acting of the real stars of the screen – people such as John Barrymore and Erich von Stroheim; Conrad Veidt and Marlene Dietrich. She knew perfectly well that despite the adulation she received she was not in their league, and she was certainly not in the same league as Dietrich, with her smouldering eyes and her remarkable ice-over-fire quality. But Alice thought that Lucretia looked all right on the screen and she thought she could convey most of the emotions, although she knew, deep down, that she was relying on personality and on her own legend rather than on acting ability.

She always gave of her best on film sets; that was her early training, of course, the training that had instilled into her that if you were paid for a service – whether it was sewing a torn hem or scrubbing a sink, or playing a part in a film – you gave your employer what he had paid for. For being ravished by a sheikh, for dying bravely and aristocratically on the scaffold, for heading armies and sacking cities and defying tyrants. For being a King in Babylon, and making profane and forbidden love to a Christian slave . . .

And really, thought Alice, for a jumped-up parlourmaid with a false name, I'm doing rather well.

Conrad, who adored his small daughter, had written the promised music for her, but it was not until an early summer night in 1938, with Deborah three years old, that the first public performance took place. It would be a glittering occasion, said Conrad happily. People from several continents would flock to hear his music, and he would have a spectacular success, and it would all be because of his enchanting daughter. Lucretia would occupy the stage-box for the occasion, and she would be wearing something dazzlingly beautiful.

'I shall be dazzlingly bankrupt at this rate,' said Alice, but made expeditions to the couture houses of Lanvin and Worth.

On the night of the concert it felt wrong to leave the sturdy, bright-eyed toddler in the care of the nurse. Alice, who had returned to filming when Deborah was six months old, and who was perfectly accustomed to long absences from the baby and had not considered herself particularly maternal anyway, found herself snatching the child up in her arms and covering the small flower-like face with kisses.

'This ought to be your night, Deborah,' said Alice to the child. 'It's your very own piece of music that's going to be played, and you should be there, listening to it, dressed up in a silk frock with ribbons in your hair. One day your papa will play for you in a concert hall, though, I promise you he will.'

'She'll be perfectly all right with me, madame,' said the nurse, a rather stolid Dutchwoman.

'Yes, I know she will.'

Alice had commissioned a backless evening gown of jade green for the concert, and over it she draped a huge black-and-jade-striped silk shawl, which enveloped her almost to the ankles. Her hair was threaded with strands of jet studded with tiny glowing emeralds, and on her feet were green satin shoes with delicate four-inch heels. They were impossibly impractical, but she would not need to walk far in them. Cab to theatre foyer, foyer to stage-box, perhaps a sip or two of champagne in the crush bar at the interval, supper somewhere afterwards with Conrad and a dozen or so guests. And then a cab home. It did not, therefore, much matter if she was wearing four-inch heels, or five-inch heels, or shoes made of paper, or if she was wearing no shoes at all. She had enamelled her toenails silver to match her fingernails, and fastened a silk chain around one ankle.

At a time when most women were starting to wear their hair in rolls and elaborate swirls, and gilt hairnets for the evening, Alice had retained her smooth sleek blackbird's-wing style. It was cut for her by a glossily fashionable French hairdresser on the Ringstrasse, but she dealt with the colouring of it by herself and in private – imagine if a story got out that Lucretia von Wolff, the infamous sable-haired temptress, actually dyed her hair! And it was rather amusing to don a drab disguise – to become a ladies' maid again – and go into the small anonymous shops on Vienna's outskirts to buy the hair-dye.

The concert hall was filled with glitteringly dressed people, and there was a pleasant buzz of expectation in the air. The baroness was escorted to the stage-box, which was sufficiently near to the platform for most of the audience to see her, and which faced the gleaming Bechstein. ('I shall not look up at you during the performance,' Conrad had explained seriously. 'Because once I begin to play, I shall not know about my surroundings at all.')

But he blew her a kiss when he came on to the platform, and Lucretia gave him the now-famous cat-smile and watched him sit down at the piano, flinging the tails of his evening coat impatiently behind him. He removed the heavy gold cufflinks he wore and the onyx signet ring, and laid them on the side of the keyboard. He looked handsome and patrician, and the sharp formality of the white tie and tails suited him.

The audience were silent now, waiting. Some of them would

be here purely because it was an Occasion and one must be seen at such things, but a good number would have come because they were genuinely interested in music and because they admired Conrad Kline and wanted to hear his new piano concerto.

Conrad was allowing the anticipation to stretch out, adjusting the music stand which did not need adjusting, flexing his fingers which were more supple than saplings anyway, frowning at an imagined speck of dust on the Bechstein's gleaming surface. He would judge the moment absolutely precisely, of course, because he would know the exact second to signal to the conductor that he was ready, and then he would bring his hands down on the keys, and his marvellous music would flood the auditorium. Alice, who had shared a very small part of Conrad's agonies throughout the composing of *Deborah's Song*, and who found it beautiful and moving, prayed that the audience would find it so. Conrad would be like a hurt child if they were less than wildly enthusiastic.

He lifted his eyes from the keyboard, and met the waiting eyes of the conductor. And then into the charged silence, into the thrumming expectant atmosphere, explosively and frighteningly came the sounds of the outer doors being flung open, and of booted feet marching across the foyer.

Impassive-faced men, wearing the sharply efficient uniform of Göering's Staatspolizei, erupted into the auditorium and ranged themselves along the walls. As the audience rose bewilderedly to its feet, and as women began to cry out in fear and clutch their escorts' arms, four of the men mounted the platform and surrounded Conrad. He leapt to his feet at once, and Alice heard him say, 'This is an outrage! How dare you—' and then one of the uniformed men who seemed to be the leader said, in machine-gun German, 'We dare anything we wish, Herr Kline. The soldiers of the Schutzstaffeln have today marched into your city. Vienna is no longer a congress, and from today, you are all part of Germany.' A gasp stirred the audience, and Alice felt, as if it was a solid thing, the fear start to fill up the auditorium.

The conductor was staring at the soldiers, and even from here

Alice could see the horror in his face. He said, 'Vienna part of Germany—'

Alice did not wait to hear the reply. She was already out of the stage box, running along the corridors that would bring her to the ground floor and the main part of the theatre, cursing the ridiculous shoes that had been so elegantly flattering but that now felt like stilts. She reached the head of the stairs and paused, impatiently tearing the shoes off, and then running on in her stockinged feet, heedless of the uncarpeted floors, because even if she tore her feet to shreds she must get to Conrad.

She had just started down the last curve of the stair, and she could see the deserted foyer below. But as she hesitated, the auditorium doors were pushed open and the SS soldiers appeared with Conrad, forcing him towards the street. The auditorium doors closed again, and Alice understood that the other officers were still guarding the audience and the orchestra. Until Conrad was out of the way?

The soldiers were holding Conrad firmly, but he was fighting them every inch of the way. His eyes were blazing and his black hair had become dishevelled in the struggle so that it fell over his forehead in the way it did when he was working. He automatically tried to put up a hand to brush it back in the familiar impatient gesture, but the soldiers snatched his arms and pinioned them to his sides. The pettiness of this sent rage slicing through Alice's entire body and her hands clenched involuntarily into fists. She would have liked to tear out the men's throats with her enamelled nails, but she stayed where she was, listening intently, but pressing back against the wall so as not to be seen.

Conrad said angrily, 'Where are you taking me? What is this about?'

'You are listed as an enemy of Germany, Herr Kline.' This time Alice caught a faint note of contempt under the steely voice.

'That is ridiculous! I have no interest in your politics!'

The man who Alice had thought was the leader regarded Conrad for a moment. 'You are half Russian,' he said, at last. 'You do not deny that?'

'Certainly I do not deny it. My father was Russian,' said Conrad haughtily, and even at such a confused and desperate moment he managed to conjure up old imperialism. 'And my mother was from Salzburg.'

'Your father was a Russian Jew,' said the man coldly. 'Therefore you are half a Jew. And you write and perform the music of the Jewish people.'

A cold fear began to close around Alice. The music of the Jewish people. *Deborah's Song*! That's what he means. But surely music isn't something that the Nazi Party would care about? Surely they would not arrest a man for writing music? Yes, but they burn books believed to spread anti-German sentiments, said her mind. They confiscate property and listen in to telephone calls.

'We are pledged to the Führer's vow that the security of Germany will be guaranteed,' the man was saying. 'And we are pledged, as well, to ensure that never again will the Jewish-Bolshevistic revolution of subhumans be kindled from the interior or through emissaries from outside.'

'You're mad,' said Conrad angrily. 'I'm not a revolutionary. This is the most fantastical nonsense I have ever heard.'

'We are not mad. We obey orders, and we are sworn to be a merciless sword of justice to all those forces who threaten the heart of Europe and who threaten Germany,' said the man, and Alice had the impression that he was repeating something learned by rote. 'Jew,' he said, and this time he made the word an insult. Alice saw him lean forward and spit in Conrad's face.

Conrad flinched, but he glared at the man in fury. 'You are all madmen,' he said. 'And your Führer is a postulating, prancing lunatic!'

The man's lips thinned and his eyes resembled chippings of flint. He said in a cold rasping tone, 'Herr Kline, you will regret ever having said that.'

'I will not. And I will not go with you tonight.'

'You will. We are taking you to one of Herr Göering's camps,' said the SS man.

'On whose orders? I demand you tell me that!'

'You are not in a position to demand anything. But since you are insistent, I can tell you that it is the Kreisleiter for this area who has sent the order.'

Conrad said, coldly, 'And who is he, this *Kreisleiter*?'

As Alice took a cautious step on to a lower stair, from the street door a voice said, '*I* am the Kreisleiter for this part of the City, Herr Kline, and it was I who gave the order for your arrest.' And this time the horror engulfed her entire body.

The voice was the voice of a man she would never forget. A man who, all those years ago, had caused her to be thrown out of his parents' house into the street.

Leo Dreyer. Miss Nina's brother.

Alice pressed back into the shadowy curve of the stair at once. She was shaking uncontrollably, and she was more frightened than she had ever been in her entire life.

Conrad recognized Leo, of course. In a startled voice, he said, 'Dreyer? What the devil is all this? For God's sake tell these men they've made a mistake.'

'No mistake has been made, Herr Kline.' The voice was no longer that of the young man in the Vienna house; it was colder, more authoritative, and Alice recognized that it was laced with rancour. Was Dreyer still bitter against Conrad for abandoning his sister, and was it possible that he was using his position in the Nazi Party to mete out a punishment he thought due? Hardly daring to breathe, Alice edged a little way out of the shadows and peered down into the foyer. Yes, it was Dreyer all right.

'You are to be taken to a place where you will be kept with other Jews,' said Leo Dreyer. 'We are seeking them all out, and we shall find them, Herr Kline, be very sure that we shall find them.' A pause. 'We shall also find their families, and those they consort with,' he said, and Alice felt a fresh wave of fear. Their families, and those they consort with . . .

At Dreyer's signal, the soldiers pushed Conrad through the

main doors and out into the street. There was the sound of several car engines being revved, and then the cars snarled away into the darkness. By the time Alice, still barefoot, had tumbled down the remaining stairs and reached the pavement outside, the cars were out of sight and there was nothing except the swirling exhaust fumes tainting the sweet-scented spring night.

CHAPTER TWENTY-TWO

The spacious apartment rooms that Alice had furnished with such delight no longer provided the haven they once had done.

We are seeking them all out, the Schutzstaffeln man had said. We are seeking out all the Jews, and their families and those they consort with . . .

Their families. Alice was not especially concerned for herself, but there was Deborah, sweet, helpless, trustful Deborah, who was known to be Conrad's daughter. But surely they would not harm children, not even those steel-eyed, rat-trapped SS men would do that, not even Leo Dreyer with the bitter hatred burning in his face.

And yet . . .

And yet she found herself whisking around the apartment as if the Furies were driving her, flinging clothes into suitcases, calculating and planning as she did so, and rapping out orders to Deborah's nurse, who only partly understood what was going on, but who had heard the marching soldiers in the streets earlier on and had grasped that this was not just one of Madame's tantrums. She dragged out suitcases under her mistress's directions, stammering fearful questions. Where were they going? How were they to travel? Alice stopped in the middle of her bedroom for a moment, her mind working.

'England,' she said, very positively. And then, seeing the woman's surprise, said, 'It's perfectly possible if you keep your head and do exactly what I tell you. You have your passport here, haven't you?'

'Yes, from when I first came to you from Eindhoven, madame, but—'

'Good.' Alice spared a moment to thank whatever gods might be most appropriate that when she engaged a nurse she had chosen a Dutch girl who had at least travelled a little and who possessed a passport. 'Then listen carefully. What you must do is to take Deborah now – tonight—'

Yes, tonight, said her mind, because at any moment we might hear the marching feet outside, because if Leo Dreyer can order them to take someone as innocent as Conrad, he can order them to take Conrad's family as well.

'You can get a cab downstairs to the railway station,' she said. 'It's barely ten o'clock, and there'll be plenty still around – oh, wait, though, you'll need money—' She snatched folded rolls of bills from her dressing-case and thrust them into the woman's hands. 'And you had better have something to sell if the money runs out, or you can't change it for English currency. Here – and here—' Shining tumbles of gold and silver went haphazardly into a velvet bag, to be thrust into the side pocket of a suitcase. Most of the baroness's jewellery had been gifts from Conrad and a lot of it had been bought to mark special occasions – their first meeting, the première of *Alraune*, Deborah's birth. Each one held a memory, but Alice would sell every stone and every carat of the jewellery and her entire wardrobe of clothes as well, if it would ensure Deborah's safety.

'Sell everything if you have to,' she said, 'but go to small, anonymous jewellers, and only sell one piece at a time because that will be less noticeable.'

'Yes. I understand. But where am I to go—?'

'I would like to tell you to get on the first train that comes in and get as far away from Vienna as you can,' said Alice. 'But that might be a train that would take you nearer to Germany, and because of what is happening here Germany had better be avoided. So if you can, go down to Salzburg – if anyone questions you, say Deborah is your daughter and you're taking her to your family there. Can you do that? Can you lie convincingly?'

'I dislike lies, madame, but in this case I will lie very convincingly indeed.'

'Good. In Salzburg station get on a train for Switzerland. Or if there are no suitable trains, hire a car and a driver if need be. The expense does not matter, you understand that?'

'Yes.'

'Your papers are all in order, and you should have no problem in crossing the borders,' said Alice. 'From Switzerland you go into France. Again, by train if you can, but by car if not. Have your passport always ready and do not seem to be trying to hide anything. Most big railway stations have hotels attached; book into them overnight when you have to – it's probably better not to seem in a hurry with the journey. Keep Deborah with you at all times, of course. Once you are in France it should be easy enough to take the ferry to England.'

'Yes. I'll do my very best.'

'Once in England, go to Mr and Mrs John Wilson,' said Alice. 'I'll write the address down for you. You'll have to ask people for help for that part of the journey, but there will be police stations, railway officials— And your English is very good.'

'Who are Mr and Mrs Wilson?'

'It does not matter. But you can trust them absolutely, and so can I.' Her parents would disapprove of Deborah's existence – a child born out of wedlock, they would say, shocked – but they would look after her, Alice knew this. She said, 'I'll write a letter for you to give them, explaining what has happened.'

'But aren't you coming as well? Madame, if there's danger, you must come with us.'

'I'm not coming,' said Alice. 'I can't. I must stay here until I find out where Conrad is. One of the labour camps, the SS man said. If that's true, I must find a way of getting him out.'

It had torn Alice apart to send Deborah away, but it had had to be done. And once the nurse had taken her, and Alice, leaning out of the windows, had seen them get into a passing cab, she experienced a huge bolt of relief. They would be all right. They would almost certainly get to safety.

She moved swiftly about the rooms, flinging things into a suitcase, listening all the time for the sounds of heavy SS vehicles in the street below. Would Leo Dreyer come after her? Would he do so tonight? But don't think about that. Think about getting out of this apartment, leaving no trace behind, and concentrate on vanishing, on becoming anonymous. This last was so nearly absurd that Alice could have laughed aloud. Lucretia von Wolff, anonymous! The infamous baroness with her strings of lovers and her exotic gowns to vanish into obscurity! Yes, but I came from obscurity, let's never forget that. And now I can go back to it.

She had given Deborah's nurse most of the money, but she counted what was left and thought there was sufficient to keep her for a while if she lived carefully. She was just searching the bureau for her passport when she became aware that the humming of the traffic outside had changed. She listened intently. Was she imagining it, or had she heard the staccato sounds of marching? Yes, she could hear the ring of boots on the cobbled street and the shouting of crisp orders. Some kind of heavy vehicle was lumbering along, and there was the growling purr of motorbikes. She darted to the light switches, plunging the apartment into darkness, and peered cautiously out of the windows.

The panic came in a huge breath-snatching wave because the soldiers really were here, they were halfway along the street, going systematically from house to house, hammering on doors, peering through windows. With them was one of the Nazis' large distinctive army-type vehicles, flanked with six outriders on motorbikes. If that really is for me, I'm getting the full honours, thought

Alice, beating down the fear. Six motorbikes, no less. And at least twenty soldiers.

A thin dispiriting drizzle was falling, turning the helmets of the soldiers and the leather capes of the motorbike riders shiny black, like the carapaces of scuttling insects. Clouds of vapour came from the lorry's exhaust and at intervals its powerful engine revved, turning it into a snarling surreal monster, its bulbous headlights searching the darkness for victims. I can't fight that, thought Alice in horror. I can't fight monsters, and I can't outwit all those shiny-armoured men. But in the next instant she knew she must try, and she took several deep breaths and held on to the window-ledge as tightly as she could, forcing the narrow edge of the sill into her palms. The small pain helped clear her head, enabling her to think clearly again.

She stared down into the street. The rain had turned everything into a grainy monochrome painting: black and grey and bleak, a landscape from a nightmare, or a madman's distorted ravings. Almost like a scene from one of my own films. But if I'm going to play the heroine in this one, I don't think I'd better stay here long enough to risk any dramatic encounters, in fact I'd better vanish before the villain reaches me.

The villain. Alice could not see Leo Dreyer among the soldiers but she thought he would be there. She had no idea yet if he knew her real identity, but he had said they were seeking out the families and the associates of Jewish people, and he would certainly relish capturing the infamous baroness . . .

But they aren't going to capture me, she thought determinedly, and stepping back from the window she snatched a long dark raincoat from the wardrobe, stuffing the money and the few remaining strands of jewellery into the pockets and thrusting her passport into an inner pocket. She grabbed the suitcase, trying not to gasp at its weight, and went out on to the communal landing, closing the apartment door as softly as possible. But already there was the sound of the gilded-cage lift clanking up from below, and with her heart pounding Alice ran along the landing and through the door that led to the back stairs. She skidded down the stairs, praying not to miss her footing, and reached the bottom safely. As she went out through the side door into the narrow alley that ran alongside the building, she heard the angry shouts of the SS men from above.

Not daring even to glance over her shoulder, she half-ran into the maze of streets beyond.

The frightened lady's maid of all those years earlier would probably have spent the night huddled miserably in a doorway somewhere, hoping to avoid the soldiers. Lucretia von Wolff, of course, would have sailed imperiously into the largest, plushest hotel she could find, and demanded a suite.

Alice did neither. She walked as far as she could, occasionally putting the suitcase down to rest her arms, and eventually came to a slightly run-down district on the eastern side of the city. The houses had peeling façades, and some of them looked a bit seedy, but several had signs in the windows offering rooms for rent. This was what she had been looking for. After a careful appraisal she chose the one that looked the cleanest, but before approaching it she took from her case a silk headsquare which she tied over her hair. She would not be able to entirely obliterate the baroness, but she could at least quench her a bit.

Once inside the small room, the incurious owner given a week's rent, she felt safer, although the panic was still clutching her stomach and she was again aware of agonized fear for Deborah. Was I right to send her away like that? Should I have gone with her?

And abandon Conrad? said her mind at once.

When Alice thought of it like that, she knew she could not have acted in any other way.

Several times in the weeks that followed she considered taking people into her confidence – perhaps one of her friends from the film days, perhaps the lawyer who had drawn up the change of name documents – but she dared not trust anyone. Nazi rule was tightening around Vienna and people were eyeing one another uneasily. There were curfews for Jewish people in the city, and tales of ordinary men and women spying for the SS were rife.

Alice altered her appearance as much as she could. It was impossible to get rid of the baroness's distinctive black hair – she would have to wait for the last lot of hair-dye to grow out – but she dressed unobtrusively and tied her hair beneath a headscarf when she went out. She changed her lodgings twice, each time going to a different part of the city, each time making casual acquaintances in shops and coffee houses, listening to all they had to say.

But the summer wore stiflingly on, and although she talked to more and more people, and although she hired cabs which took her into the Vienna Woods on the east and almost to the German border on the west, she did not pick up any clue as to where Conrad might be.

There were more soldiers on the streets now – the sharp-eyed men of Göering's Gestapo – and people scuttled along without looking to right or left. It grew colder; the leaves turned golden brown. Alice usually loved autumn, but now she found it hateful.

And then, just after October had slid down into November and there was a bite of coldness in the nights, a carefully casual remark to a chance acquaintance in a shop brought forth an inquiring look, and then the question: 'You have a friend who was taken by the SS?'

'A friend of a friend,' said Alice, who by this time had worked out a reasonably safe system of questions and answers.

'Jewish men and women from this area are being taken to Dachau,' said the woman. 'Your friend will perhaps be there.'

'Dachau?' Alice had never heard of the place.

'A village in Germany. Fifteen or twenty kilometres outside Munich.'

'That is a long way from here,' said Alice thoughtfully.

'Oh yes. Several hours' journey. Four or five hundred kilometres certainly.' A sideways look. 'But your friend may not be kept there – we hear stories of prisoners being moved around.'

'Why would prisoners be moved? Where would they be moved to?'

This time the pause, the sideways look were more pronounced. Then there was a shrug. 'Who knows how the minds of Nazis work? Who knows what will happen to any of us next?'

Alice, not daring to appear too curious, said, 'Who indeed?' and left it at that.

And indeed, who could have guessed that the next thing would be for the intricate spider-web of intrigue and spying to pick up that fragmentary conversation? And who could have guessed it would be painstakingly traced all the way back to the quietly dressed, quietly living lady so recently moved into a small apartment on Vienna's outskirts? Had that chance acquaintance been one of the spies after all? Or had the scrappy conversation been overheard?

Alice was never to know. Two days later, eating a modest and solitary supper in one of the little coffee-houses near to her lodgings, she was aware of the sounds of some kind of tumult from the direction of the inner city. People were looking towards the sounds, and pointing, and Alice saw that the sky had a curious dull reddish tinge.

'Fire,' people were saying. 'Lots of fires.'

'And shouting,' said another. 'Like people rioting.'

'Listen,' said one of them suddenly.

It was then that Alice heard the heavy menacing growl of the SS vehicles, and the wolf-snarl of the motorbikes they used as outriders roaring down the narrow street towards them.

CHAPTER TWENTY-THREE

This time there were no convenient back stairs or alleyways into which a fugitive could flee and achieve invisibility.

The jeeps screeched to a halt outside the coffee-house, and the soldiers spilled out and came running in. They were fast and efficient and they came straight across to where Alice was sitting, snatching her from her chair before she could do anything about it. She heard the fearful murmurs of 'Jew' from some of the other diners, but no one moved to help her.

She fought to get free, kicking out at the soldiers and clawing at their faces, but they pinioned her arms behind her back and one of them hit her face with the flat of his hand. Alice gasped, her eyes smarting with the sudden sharp pain. 'Bitch,' said the soldier unemotionally, and they dragged her outside and pushed her into the back of a canvas-covered jeep, nodding to the driver. The vehicle moved off at once, the outriders on the motorbikes surrounding it closely so that even if Alice had dared jump from the moving vehicle she would have been caught by them instantly.

'Baroness,' said a hated voice from the jeep's shadowy interior. 'Or shall I dispense with the pretence you have spun for so long and simply call you Wilson?'

Alice had been staring through the flap of the canvas, trying to see in which direction they were going, and she had barely registered that there was someone in the jeep. She turned sharply, but even before she had tensed her muscles to hit out, strong hard hands came out to snake around her wrists.

'What a hellcat you are,' said Leo Dreyer, keeping her hands tightly imprisoned in his. 'Didn't you expect to encounter me?'

Alice had expected it at some stage but she still felt as if she had received a blow across the eyes. She glared at him. In the closeness of the jeep's interior he was thinner and more severe than the young man she had known, and he was wearing a monocle with a thin black cord on it. It ought to have made him slightly ridiculous – foppish and effete – but it did not.

She said in Lucretia's disdainful voice, 'So you know who I am?'

'Of course. Ever since *Alraune*.'

So it had been *Alraune* who had betrayed her and led to Conrad's capture. Alice gestured to the motorbikes and the soldiers. 'All this seems somewhat excessive. Have you really sent your soldiers scouring the streets for me, purely because Conrad preferred me to your sister all those years ago?'

Dreyer's eyes were still on her, the left monocled eye hugely distorted, and Alice tried to look away, but could not. He said softly, 'My dear, I would have scoured far wider places than Vienna to find you for what you did that night.'

The truck had gathered speed, and he loosened his tight grip on her wrists and leaned back against the vehicle's sides. But Alice could feel the coiled tension within him, and she knew that if she made the smallest move to escape he would pounce.

'After you left my father's house that night . . .'

'After you threw me out of your father's house,' said Alice at once.

'. . . Nina became ill,' said Dreyer, as if she had not spoken. 'She cried for all of that night and all of the next day. She made herself sick with crying, and then she became hysterical. We began to fear for her sanity, and we called a doctor to her – he gave her bromide but for days she was overwrought to an impossible degree. She was always highly-strung, of course. She lived on her nerves.'

Alice, who had always considered Nina Dreyer a spoiled, self-willed show-off, thought this sounded more like the tantrum of a child demanding attention, but did not say so.

'At first she seemed to recover,' said Dreyer. 'But then we discovered that she was becoming reliant on the sedatives. She took more and more of them, and then, after a few months, she began to take cocaine – it was considered fashionable to do so in the set she moved in; it was considered modern and chic.'

Alice, who knew about the fashion for cocaine among rich young things and about the so-called Snow Set, but who had never taken cocaine herself, remained silent. They were travelling very fast now, but several times she caught the glare of what looked to be bonfires in the streets, and the sounds of people crying or shouting, and of running feet. She would have liked to peer out through the canvas to see what was happening – certainly to see where the jeep was heading – but she would not give Dreyer even this small satisfaction.

'Eventually, of course, the cocaine ruined her,' said Dreyer, apparently oblivious to what was happening outside. 'She began sleeping with men who would get the stuff for her; later she stole – jewellery from her friends, to start with. Twice she faced criminal charges – we thought that might pull her out of the habit, but it did not. After that she forged my father's name on cheques. Little by little she turned into a desperate and haggard harpy.' He glanced at her. 'And the worse she became, the more I hated you,' he said.

There was a bad moment when Alice was back in the days of the Vienna household, remembering that this was the master's son, and that she should remember her place and be respectful and obedient. But Lucretia, with imperious annoyance, said, Rubbish! This is a bully and a brute, and I owe him nothing and I refuse to be cowed by him.

So when she finally spoke, it was the baroness who said, 'This is all utter nonsense, Leo.' Yes, call him Leo, remind him that you're equals these days. 'You're behaving as if we're living inside a Victorian melodrama,' said Lucretia. 'All this absurd talk about having your revenge on the woman who wronged your sister— It's like something out of *East Lynne*.' This sounded satisfyingly disdainful, but inside she was panic-stricken. I'm cooped up with a powerful man who hates me and who's almost certainly taking me to some miserable prison camp, and I'm telling him he's behaving like a Victorian villain! I wonder if I'm entirely sane at the moment?

'I'm extremely sorry for what happened to Nina,' she said. 'But it isn't my fault that she became a drug addict. I didn't steal Conrad from her, in fact I had no idea your father had intended him to marry her.' A pause. 'I will admit that I behaved less than well that night, but plenty of girls lose a lover and survive. Nina had looks and money and position. And a doting family.' She leaned back in the jeep and studied him. 'Back then I told a roomful of people that you had tried to seduce me and that I refused to be seduced. Surely you aren't still resentful of that, Leo? Such a small event, wasn't it? Or perhaps it wasn't a small event to you. Perhaps it was important to you.'

His eyes snapped with anger, but he mastered it almost at once – it was rather frightening to see the iron self-control clamping down. In a tight, clipped voice he said, 'I am entirely within my rights to take you to a labour camp. Himmler has ordered that all Jews be segregated.'

'I'm not a Jew,' said Lucretia at once.

'Among so many, that will never be noticed. And you have the colouring.' Incredibly, one hand came out to touch her hair. As she flinched, he smiled. 'And,' said Leo Dreyer, 'if you try to protest against wrongful incarceration, among so many that will not be noticed either. In any case you have consorted with a Jew all these years. You gave birth to his bastard.'

'One day, you will pay for that remark,' said Lucretia, sounding bored. She peered through the jeep's sides again, and in a sharper voice, said, 'Something's happening out there, isn't it? All those people shouting – the soldiers everywhere— Whatever it is, you've used it as your cover to get at me—'

'Yes, something is happening,' he said. 'Last night the German government unleashed a pogrom against the Jews—' He stopped, watching her reaction. 'I see you know what the word means.'

'Mass killing,' said Lucretia, a completely new horror crawling over her skin. 'Organized mass murder.'

'Yes. An interesting derivation – Russian, originally. Used, of course, when the Jews in Russia were massacred in the early years of the century.' For a moment he leaned forward, moving the jeep's canvas covering to peer out at the streets.

'We are burning the synagogues,' he said. 'Throughout the cities of Germany and Austria we are destroying everything Jewish – all the Jew-owned shops and businesses, all the Torah scrolls we can find, all the prayer-books. Can you see how the sky is lit up with the flames? Over there to the west?' He was looking out into the streets, his attention momentarily away from his prisoner. Was this the moment to make a lunge forward and jump out? No. The helmeted and visored soldiers were still riding level with the jeep. She would not get five yards.

As Dreyer let fall the canvas flap, she said, 'Where are you taking me?' And please say Dachau, you evil bully, for at least that would mean Conrad and I would be together, and perhaps there would be a way to get out of Germany with him . . .

'You are being taken to a place near to Weimar,' said Dreyer. 'It is a very charming part of Eastern Germany, fairly near to the Czechoslovakian border. Miniature castles overlooking the river, and pine forests and traces of the ancient Kingdom of Thuringia.'

'Ah yes,' said Lucretia, coldly polite. 'Bavaria and Bohemia. Home of the cruellest of the fairytales. Woodcutters changing into prowling wolves when there's a full moon, and princesses shut in doorless towers. Madmen slaughtering the innocents through an entire night and arrogantly attempting to destroy a religion.'

Dreyer smiled slightly. 'You always had a romantic side,' he said. 'But also, you always had claws just beneath the surface.'

'If I had claws I would use them to scratch out your eyes, believe me, Leo.'

'Would you, Alraune?' he said, very softly. 'Don't stare at me like that. You know quite well what I mean. The final scene. Alraune stalking the man who made her. Gouging out his eyes and then offering him up as a sacrifice. You would like to play Alraune to my Professor, wouldn't you? You would like to sink your talons into my eyes. You won't get the chance, of course.'

'Don't count on it,' said Lucretia acidly. 'What is this place you're taking me to? Wherever it is, I shan't be there for ever.'

'No. But you'll like Weimar. And it has a good many cultural associations. Goethe lived there for a time; also Franz Liszt and Bach. Unfortunately, however, you won't see much of the town.'

'Aren't you forgetting that I'm very well known in Vienna? People will search for me—' But even as she said it, Alice knew that she had already burnt her boats on that score. If people had been going to search for Lucretia von Wolff they would have done it weeks ago. Even so, she said, 'Questions will be asked. You really can't expect to get away with this.'

'I can get away with it,' he said. 'Tonight we are the masters. Tonight, baroness, I can do anything I wish.'

They looked at one another, and as the silence stretched out between them, Alice was suddenly aware of a stir of emotion that no longer had anything to do with fear or hatred. It vanished almost as soon as it formed, but it left an indelible, shameful, print on her mind, and she knew she would not be able to forget it. This is the man who imprisoned Conrad and who threatened Deborah, and I felt that wrench of sexual attraction for him! Had he sensed it?

She said, 'You're taking me to a labour camp?'

'Yes. What did you expect? You are going,' said Dreyer, 'to the place of the beechwood forest.'

And, as Alice stared at him, he said, 'Konzentrationslager Buchenwald.'

The journey to Buchenwald was the most appalling experience Alice had ever known.

The SS truck drew up at a small station – Alice had long since lost all sense of direction, and she had no idea whether they were still in Vienna, or even whether they were still in Austria – and along with what seemed to be two or three hundred others, she was herded into a train.

It was a long, jolting, sick-making ride. The carriages were sparse and uncomfortable; some were roofless, little better than cattle trucks, and the prisoners were packed in haphazardly, forty and fifty to a coach.

Alice still had on the clothes she had been wearing when Leo Dreyer found her – the long dark raincoat and the plain dark skirt and jumper which she had hoped would render her unnoticeable – but many of the other prisoners had on loose shirt-like garments with the yellow Star of David either sewn or painted on the fronts. She had no idea if this was intended as a brand or simply as some kind of identification, because the prisoners all seemed to wear it in numb obedience. Some of the women were crying in a miserable, beaten way, but most of them seemed sunk in a dreadful patient acceptance. Most of them had lost their homes to the Nazis in what Alice had already heard called *Kristallnacht* – the Night of Broken Glass, named from the smashing of glass fronts of so many hundreds of Jewish shops. A great many of them had lost their families as well. The few women present held on to their children with frightened desperation, but other than that they seemed to be beyond caring what came next, and they did what they were told by the armed SS guards, cringing if the machine-guns were raised threateningly.

Had Conrad been treated like this? Forced to wear the yellow insignia, beaten into this shambling, cringing servility? Agony squeezed round Alice's heart at the thought of it.

Somewhere during the nightmare train journey all the colour and all the light seemed to drain from the world. I'm back in one of my own films, Alice thought, drifting in and out of an uneasy half-slumber, occasionally waking to massage her cramped limbs. Everything's gradually becoming black and gloomy and filled with shadows. And there certainly isn't going to be a romantic rescue in the final frame, in fact I'm not at all sure if there's even going to be a final frame. No, I won't think that. There'll be a way to escape. Perhaps when we get into a station . . . ? Yes, I'll wait until then.

But when they reached Buchenwald's small railway station the Schutzstaffeln were everywhere, and almost all of them were armed with sub-machine-guns, so that only a lunatic would have tried to run away.

The exhausted prisoners were tumbled out of the hot, evil-smelling carriages, and into the waiting lorries. As they drove through the town a heavy dusk was starting to close down, but it was possible to see that Buchenwald was, as Leo Dreyer had so tauntingly said, a picturesque little place, with little doll's houses for the people to live in, and a minuscule church and an inn.

Wood-carving and violin-making, thought Alice. Wine festivals and toy-making and miniature castles overlooking the rivers. Yes, there was Ettersburg Castle on a ridge of the hillside, with its pepperpot turrets and toy drawbridge. This was a place where you might come for a holiday, just as Goethe had done, and just as Liszt and Schiller had done. You would enjoy the quaintness and the fairytale atmosphere of the place, and if you were so minded you might write your music or pen your luminous essays. But most fairytales had a dark side, and now that they had driven out of the little town, the road was already starting to feel lonely and sinister. Like the feeling you got in a dream where safe, familiar things became suddenly imbued with menace, so that the dream slid down into a nightmare.

It was dark inside the truck, but she could see that they had left the town and that the road was fringed with the characteristic pine trees. Was it dark enough to jump from the back of the truck and trust to luck that she could reach the forest's shelter before the soldiers fired on her? She was just trying to decide this when the truck rumbled around a curve in the road, and there ahead of them were immense iron gates – massive heavy structures, like the gates guarding a giant's castle.

Konzentrationslager Buchenwald. The darkness at the heart of the nightmare.

At the sight of it the men and women in the lorry drew instinctively closer to one another for comfort, and even from the lorry, Alice could see the high fences surrounding the entire compound, with, beyond them, serried rows of barrack-like buildings. Guard towers jutted up from the fences at intervals, with massive black-snouted machine-guns mounted in each one. A terrible bleak loneliness closed around her. No one knows where I am. Conrad doesn't know, and Deborah doesn't know. There's absolutely no means of anyone reaching me here.

The gates swung slowly and silently open, as if some invisible machinery were being operated, and the lorries drove through. Alice glanced back and saw the gates close. Shutting her into the nightmare.

CHAPTER TWENTY-FOUR

Lucy had almost finished the horror-film presentation for the satellite TV companies, and she was quite pleased with it. Her idea of setting it all in a tongue-in-cheek horror framework seemed to have worked quite well. Quondam's technical department had dubbed part of Tartini's *The Devil's Trill* to use as background for *The Devil's Sonata*, and although there had been a bit of a royalties tussle with the record company who had included it in a recent compilation of semi- and quasi-religious string music, Lucy thought the tussle had been worth it because the music gave terrific atmosphere to the film.

She was putting together a final set of visual and audio effects – she had unearthed some beautifully menacing out-takes from an ancient Tod Slaughter version of *Dracula*, which could be blown up and possibly tinted with suitably blood-hued crimson or even back-projected on to a screen – and she had spent two hilarious afternoons in the sound department, helping them to fake creepy footsteps and creaking doors.

But since finding the old newsreel of Lucretia on Howard Hughes' Stratoliner, the unreadable face of the dark-eyed child who had been at Lucretia's side kept coming between Lucy and the grainy black-and-white images she was working on. With it came the familiar nagging curiosity from her own childhood: the need to know the truth about Alraune and to know whether Alraune had really existed. Who were you? said Lucy to the ghost-child on the film. And what were you? Did you exist, and if you did, what happened to you? But I daresay that even if I could trace you, I'd find that you were only on that newsreel because you were the son or daughter of one of the cabin crew, or a friend's child that Lucretia was chaperoning to or from some Swiss resort.

If Aunt Deb had still been alive Lucy would have let her see the newsreel; Aunt Deb would have loved it, and she would probably have known the exact circumstances of Lucretia's journey to or from Switzerland – she might have recalled some tantalizing fragment of scandal about Lucretia and Howard Hughes, and she might even have been persuaded to say whether the child in the newsreel could actually have been Alraune. Lucy felt all over again the ache of loss for Aunt Deb who had spun all those stories, and she remembered how she had always believed that Deb had known far more about Alraune than she had ever told.

Was there was anyone else she could talk to about the newsreel? How about Edmund? Edmund, finicky and pedantic as he was, disapproving of Lucretia as he always had been, had always been deeply interested in Deborah Fane's side of the family. And he did not have to have Alraune explained to him, because he had more or less grown up with all the stories and the rumours and the speculation, just as Lucy had. He was, in fact, the obvious person, but Lucy hesitated. 'Oh, Lucy, you're such a romantic under that tough façade,' Edmund had said that evening, and there had been the sudden urgent thrust of his body against hers as they made the coffee. Or is my memory making it a bit more sexually charged than it actually was? thought Lucy. Even so, she felt awkward about phoning Edmund at the moment, although he would certainly like to know about this fragment of the past that she had uncovered. She was just trying to decide whether to ring him when a call came in from a Detective Inspector Jennie Fletcher.

'We haven't met,' said DI Fletcher, brusquely polite. 'But I know who you are, of course, and I expect you know that I'm heading the investigation into Trixie Smith's murder.'

'Yes, of course,' said Lucy, assuming the inspector wanted to know about that original meeting with Trixie.

'I've got a favour to ask,' said DI Fletcher.

'A favour?' This was unexpected. 'What kind of favour?'

'I want to know about Alraune.'

'Oh,' said Lucy a bit blankly. 'The film or the child?'

'The film. What exactly is it? I mean – what's it about?'

Lucy had the feeling that DI Fletcher knew quite a lot about Alraune already – the fictional one and also the real one – but the mental exercise of rolling up the plot into a couple of sentences was unexpectedly calming. She said, 'Well, I've never read the original story, but I do know it's a pretty freaky one.'

'So I understand.'

'It's sort of *Frankenstein* re-told, only the "creature" is female: a girl who's conceived in the shadow of a gallows-tree as an experiment, and named Alraune after the mandrake root that's supposed to grow beneath the gibbet, due to – well, perhaps you know the hoary old myth about hanging, do you?'

'Spontaneous ejaculation because of the spasming? Yes, I do know.'

Lucy thought that on balance this was a nicely polite and suitably clinical way of putting it. She said, 'Alraune's conceived from the mandrake's – um – potency I suppose is the term. She's beautiful but evil and she ends in destroying both herself and the tormented genius who created her. Maybe it's *Frankenstein* meets *Svengali*.'

'Silent films used to evoke a remarkable atmosphere, didn't they?' said Inspector Fletcher. 'As much because of the silence I've always thought.'

'That's true. The film versions of *Alraune* are all based to a lesser or greater extent on a book written around 1910 or 1912 by a German author called Hanns Heinz Ewers. At least three or four films were made of it – some silent, some with sound, all mostly in the 1920s and early 1930s, although Eric von Stroheim did a rather cheesy re-make in 1951 or 1952.' Lucy thought it was not necessary to mention that von Stroheim was credited with having been one of Lucretia's lovers.

Inspector Fletcher appeared to be making notes of all this. After a moment, she said, 'What else?'

'The early versions were considered rather shockingly erotic for their day,' said Lucy, hoping she did not sound as if she was giving a lecture. 'But the film my grandmother made is generally accepted as the darkest and most dramatic version of them all – in fact before the Ashwood murders it was regarded as one of the great examples of early *film noir*.'

'But not any longer?'

'After Lucretia died the cranks and the weirdos latched on to it,' said Lucy. 'And it achieved a sort of underground near-cult status. Unfortunately it's got all tangled up with the legend – Conrad Kline and Leo Dreyer butchered at Ashwood, and Lucretia committing that spectacular suicide – so nobody's very objective about it any more. That's a great shame, because it really was a remarkable film. Very innovative and quite daring in parts. And the director achieved some terrific effects.'

'You've seen it?'

'Yes, I saw it when I was at university.'

'Is it ever shown publicly now? On TV for instance?'

'I don't think so. It sometimes gets trotted out at film festivals, or rented by the more *avant-garde* film clubs – that was where I saw it.' It had been fashionable, in her second term at Durham, to admire *film noir* and the gloomier epics of German Expressionism – she was always vaguely irritated that the loss of her virginity would forever be associated in her mind with Orson Welles and the zither music of *The Third Man*. To Inspector Fletcher, she said, 'It's probably a bit heavy for modern tastes, so it isn't usually seen— Oh, no, wait, one of the satellite TV companies showed it a few years ago. They offered it to viewers as a curio. A stormy petrel, or the *Macbeth* of the silent film era, the announcer called it.'

The inspector appeared to absorb this, and then said, 'There are still copies of the film in existence, then?'

'Yes, certainly,' said Lucy, feeling on slightly safer ground. 'Not too many, and what there are are a bit weather-beaten by now – it was 1928 or 1930, which means it's the old cellulose nitrate composition, and that sometimes decomposes beyond recall. The layers of film actually weld together.' She paused, and then said, 'But it's still around. D'you want to see it?'

'Yes, I do. Could it be arranged?'

'I think Quondam have got it, but if not I can probably track it down with one of our rivals,' said Lucy, who knew perfectly well that Quondam had got it, because she had looked for it within a week of joining the company. 'How about my grandfather's backing music? Conrad Kline, I mean. He tends to get a bit overshadowed by Lucretia, but he was a gifted composer in his day. D'you want that as well?'

'Well, if it's to hand, yes. But it's the film I really want.' A pause. Lucy waited, hoping to find out what might be behind all this, but Fletcher only said, 'We don't know yet if there's any connection between the old murder case and Trixie Smith's death, but we want to consider every angle.'

'Starting with a look at *Alraune*,' said Lucy.

'Yes.'

'The murderer more or less copied the last scene of *Alraune*, didn't he?'

'It sounds as if you've been reading the tabloids, Miss Trent. Very unwise. How soon could you let me know about viewing the film?'

'I'll do it at once,' said Lucy. 'And I'll phone you back. If I hit any problems, you can invoke the might of the British constabulary.'

'What about actually running it? We're fairly high-tech in the police, but I don't know if we'd be equal to a seventy-year-old reel of – what did you say it was made of?'

'Cellulose nitrate. Actually, a lot of the early stuff is being fairly successfully transferred to DVD these days. I don't think that's happened to *Alraune* though, so you'd probably need the old projectors. But that needn't be a problem: I expect I can set up a viewing for you. We've got a couple of viewing rooms here, and the larger one will seat about ten people. Would that be enough?'

'Yes, I think so. Thank you very much. I'll wait to hear from you.'

'The viewing's on,' said Fletcher to her sergeant after Lucy had called back to say that as she had thought, Quondam did possess a copy of the film, although it had not gone through any kind of restoration process. 'But I still want you to work through that list of the film clubs. If anyone's recently hired the von Wolff *Alraune*, I want to know about it.'

Sergeant Trendle said there was nothing to report from the film clubs yet, and asked why they needed to view the film.

'I want to see exactly how closely our man did copy this famous final scene,' said Fletcher. 'If it looks as though he knows the film in real detail, that might give us a lead – there can't be all that many people who've seen the thing; not these days. And you've got the list of satellite TV companies as well, haven't you? Lucy Trent said one of them put it out a few years ago. If it was eight or ten years back, it probably isn't relevant, but if it was only a couple of years, we might have to start getting lists of satellite TV subscribers. Yes, I know it's tedious, but think of it as an armchair version of door-to-door inquiries.' She frowned, and then said, 'I think we'll fix this viewing for Saturday afternoon if Quondam will agree.'

Trendle, who viewed the prospect of *Alraune* with dismay (it had been made before *sound* even, could you credit it!), asked who was to be at the viewing. Just their own people, was it?

'No,' said Jennie. 'I want to watch one or two reactions while it's being played. Lucy Trent will have to be there, of course.

Partly courtesy, because she works at Quondam, but I'm not forgetting she's Lucretia von Wolff's granddaughter. She knows the film, as well – she saw it when she was at university.'

'We aren't suspecting her, though, are we?'

'We're suspecting everybody at this stage. But I don't really think she's a contender. But listen now, the ones I do want to be there – and don't make any mistakes or hand me any excuses, sergeant – are those three who found Trixie Smith's body. Francesca Holland, Michael Sallis, and that insolent Irishman.'

'The solicitor?'

'The solicitor,' said Jennie Fletcher. 'He's an irreverent devil, although I'd have to say he's an efficient irreverent devil. As a matter of fact he's got rather a good reputation when it comes to criminal law – the ACC thinks very highly of him – and he's a tiger in the magistrates' court, I've seen him in action. That's the silver-tongued Irish, of course.'

Sergeant Trendle, who had been checking the list of Ashwood's previous owners, said it looked as if Liam Devlin had given them genuine information about the land.

'It's mostly been owned by small-time entrepreneurs, who thought they were getting a bargain, and then couldn't get rid of the place quickly enough when they realized it wasn't a bargain at all.'

'Which is what we thought. I think Devlin's all right, but we'll still have him in for this film experiment, although we'd better have a pinch of salt with us when we're talking to him. Do you ever read Shakespeare, Trendle?'

Trendle, who liked a bit of a laugh on his days off, said he did not.

'There's a line in one of the plays – "First thing we'll do, let's kill all the laywers,"' said the inspector. 'Remember that. Always watch a lawyer, Trendle.'

Sergeant Trendle, who could not cope with the inspector when she was in this mood, suggested that if they were speaking of lawyers, what about the other one?

'Edmund Fane?' said Fletcher, softly. 'Oh, yes, I want him there as well.'

'You don't like him?'

'I don't trust him, Trendle. So I don't care if you have to invoke Magna Carta or the European Human Rights Law, just make sure he's there.'

Edmund was not best pleased to be telephoned by Sergeant Trendle and politely requested to come to Quondam Films' premises on Saturday afternoon for the purpose of viewing the infamous von Wolff *Alraune*.

He thought it a preposterous idea to screen the film – in fact he had thought the thing had been lost years ago. It had not been lost? It never had been lost? Oh well, Edmund had never bothered overmuch about all those old-fashioned films or books. Still, he would come along if the police really insisted.

He was, in fact, rather pleased at the thought of seeing Lucy again, and it might be intriguing to see her in her professional setting, so to speak. Would she wear a sharp, dark office suit? And would it be possible to have supper with her afterwards? Perhaps she would invite him to her flat again. His mind flew ahead, seeing the two of them seated at the little table in the deep bay window, and then moving across to that deep sofa before the fire . . . And then . . . ? There was a sudden strong pleasure in remembering how his father had gone to bed with Lucy's grandmother all those years ago, and in wondering if, on Saturday night, Edmund might go to bed with Lucy herself. There was a symmetry about it which pleased him. I'm not re-creating what you did, he said to Crispin's image in his mind; I'm really not. No? said Crispin's voice, mockingly. Whatever you're doing, the symmetry of it sounds slightly skewed to me. But let's go for it anyway, dear boy. Lucretia's granddaughter . . . Oh yes, Edmund, oh *yes*, let's go for it . . .

Edmund phoned Lucy there and then, explaining about Sergeant Trendle's call. He was not going to drive up, he said –

all that traffic, and parking in London on a Saturday. He would get the twelve thirty train; it got in just before two, and he could have his lunch on the train.

'But I'm not sure what to do afterwards. Perhaps we could have a meal together. The last train back is at ten, so there would be plenty of time.'

'Oh, what a shame,' said Lucy at once. 'I'm going out later on. But you could easily get the six fifteen back after the viewing, couldn't you?'

'I suppose so,' said Edmund, annoyed. 'It'll mean getting home rather late, and not eating until at least half past eight. Still, it can't be helped.'

Lucy felt guilty at having lied to Edmund about going out, but relieved to have sidestepped any idea of spending the evening with him. He would probably annoy everyone all afternoon by making pointed remarks about his delicate digestion, and how he had only had a British Rail sandwich for his lunch and how he would not get home for his supper until late. Oh, blast Edmund, thought Lucy, crossly. I refuse to feel guilty about him. He can perfectly well have something to eat before getting the train back; Quondam's smack in the middle of Soho, for pity's sake – eating-places every ten steps!

And at least there would not be any embarrassingly unfamiliar seduction techniques to contend with, or pounces over the coffee percolator to ward off. Lucy was not sure if she could cope with Edmund being amorous and seeing Lucretia as Alraune all on the same day.

CHAPTER TWENTY-FIVE

'Jesus God Almighty,' said Liam Devlin, eyeing Quondam's projector for the running of *Alraune*. 'Are you sure you actually need electricity to power that thing? If you told me it relied on the magic lantern principle, it wouldn't be a surprise.'

Devlin had arrived late for the viewing, which Edmund thought just went to show what kind of feckless person he was; his black hair looked more than ever as if it needed combing, never mind cutting, and he was wearing cord trousers, a ramshackle pullover and a long raincoat that looked as if it had been dragged on in the dark. It was annoying to see Michael Sallis shake hands with him in a very friendly way – from what Edmund remembered of Sallis at Deborah Fane's funeral, he could not have very much in common with the disreputable Devlin. He noticed, as well, that the females present all sat up a little straighter at Devlin's entrance – including Lucy. This annoyed Edmund so much that he pointed out with some acerbity that Devlin's arrival was a good twenty minutes after the arranged time.

'Yes, I'm late,' agreed Liam. 'And I'm sorry for it, what with punctuality supposedly being the politeness of kings, although I shouldn't think the particular king who said that had ever tried getting across London on a Saturday afternoon – it's nearly as treacherous as negotiating the waters of the Styx, in fact the Styx would be preferable because you could bribe the ferryman to queue-jump— Will I sit down now I am here?'

'Sit where you like,' said Inspector Fletcher, and Liam considered the room for a moment and then took a seat next to Lucy.

'You're the wicked baroness's granddaughter,' he said, which Edmund felt to be an ill-chosen remark but which Lucy did not seem to mind. 'So if this film is very highbrow and esoteric you can explain it to me as we go along. I've never actually seen Lucretia von Wolff on film, in fact I've never seen a silent film at all now I come to think about it. Although I have,' he added unexpectedly, 'heard Conrad Kline's music somewhere or other, and it's extraordinarily good.' He regarded Lucy for a moment, and then said, 'He would be your grandfather?'

'It was never proved, but we're pretty sure he was,' said Lucy tranquilly, and Edmund sucked his teeth at the indelicacy of this. She glanced at the inspector. 'I've got the backing music Conrad wrote for *Alraune*. It's an old vinyl recording and it'll be pretty scratchy because it's nearly as old as the film – it was recorded quite soon after the première – but I've played it and it's reasonable. I know you said it wasn't vital to have it, but since it was available I thought I'd bring it. We can put it on the turntable when the film starts and with a bit of luck it'll be in synch with the action.'

'I'd like to hear it,' said Liam at once. 'If Inspector Fletcher doesn't mind.'

'So would I.' This was Michael Sallis.

'By all means let's have it,' said Fletcher, and nodded to the projectionist, who had been earnestly explaining to Sergeant Trendle about intermittent motion and toothed sprockets and escapements.

The lights were turned down, although it was not as dark as a conventional cinema would be – Edmund presumed this was because Quondam's staff would need to make notes when they watched a film in here. A rather sparse set-up it was though; just a few chairs grouped around a couple of tables, although one of the tables had a computer terminal on it. There were no windows, of course, and the screen took up three-quarters of the far wall. Still, Lucy had arranged for a pot of coffee and a pot of tea to be brought in, which Edmund supposed was something.

A few scratchy clicks came through the loudspeakers as the old gramophone record was set on the turntable, and the heavy whirring of the old projector began. There was a crackle of light, and then an oblong of fly-blown whiteness appeared on the small screen, immediately followed by the German studio's symbol.

Lucy had thought she would be able to face watching this film perfectly calmly, but as soon as Conrad Kline's music swept in, her heartbeat punched painfully against her ribs, and she was aware all over again that a tiny fragment of a long-ago world was about to be prised open. And there are some pasts that should be left alone, she thought. There are some pasts that should be allowed to die and I think this is one of them.

The opening sequences of the film were darker and more menacing than she remembered, or perhaps she had simply been too young to pick up the darkness. She was able to pick it up now, though, and she found it disturbing. And how much of the film's present impact was down to what had come afterwards, to the inevitable parallel between Alraune's mad scientist creator and the Nazis' macabre attempts at altering the blueprint of human life – the experiments on Jews and on twins . . . ? Astonishing to remember that the film predated that by at least ten years, thought Lucy.

The actual conception of Alraune in the gallows' shadows was rather tame compared with some of the stuff you saw on film today, but it was still extraordinarily evocative, and the music held a strong undercurrent of sexuality at this point. There was a faint rhythmic pattern that, at the romantic end of the spectrum, might have been a lover's heart beating but that, at the comic end of the spectrum, might have been a bedspring twangingly bouncing. And then listen to it again, and it could equally well be the sound of a gibbet, creaking and swaying with the weight of a strangled murderer . . . I do wish I'd known you, said Lucy to Conrad Kline's ghost. You've got a bit overshadowed by Lucretia as far as the family's concerned, but I think I'd have liked you very much.

The scenes slid into one another – to one accustomed to twentieth- and twenty-first-century technology they were not entirely seamless, but the links were smooth enough not to be distracting. Lucy spared a thought to wonder if Inspector Fletcher's own experiment, whatever it might be, was working. She glanced round the room. Michael Sallis's face was partly in shadow; he had not said a great deal since arriving, but he had seemed pleased to see Lucy again, and he appeared interested in the film. He was sitting with Francesca Holland, Trixie Smith's colleague, who had raised the alarm when Trixie vanished. Lucy thought Francesca was not exactly pretty but she had the kind of face you would want to keep looking at. She was watching the film closely, and as the prostitute who was Alraune's mother harangued the scientist, Lucy saw her exchange a brief appreciative grin with Michael, as if they had both recognized some allusion or allegory in the scene.

On Lucy's left, Edmund had donned a pair of spectacles and was looking over the tops of the lenses with scarcely veiled disapproval.

Liam Devlin, on Lucy's right, was watching the film as well and with unexpected absorption. But as if becoming aware of Lucy's covert regard, he half turned his head to look at her and sent her a slightly quizzical grin. He had the mobile mouth of many Irish people, and very bright, very intelligent eyes. Lucy blinked, and turned hastily back to the screen, where the scientist, by now realizing the evil results of his gallows-tree experiment, was carrying his sulky and soulless child through the night to place her in the keeping of the cloisters. The music went with him, a faint element of menace creeping in now, like a heart knocking against uneasy bones. There was a nicely brooding shot of the convent for which they were bound, standing wreathed in mist in some unidentifiable forest remoteness.

And then without any preliminaries, she was there. The young Lucretia von Wolff, her face flickering and erratic and her movements slightly jerky because of the hand-cranked camera of the day. But smoulderingly charismatic and chockfull of sex appeal. Lucy realized afresh how incandescently sexy her grandmother had been.

When Inspector Fletcher suddenly leaned forward and said, 'Could we just freeze that frame?' several people jumped.

'Certainly,' said the projectionist, and there was a loud click. Lucretia, reclining Cleopatra-like on a sumptuous, absurdly unmonastic chaise-longue, preparing to be seduced by the convent's music-master, regarded the world from insolent slanting eyes, half predatory, half passionate. Her curtain of dark hair swung silkily around her face, and the actor playing the music-master knelt adoringly at her feet.

'Oh, Grandmamma,' murmured Lucy, 'why couldn't you crochet sweaters and join ladies' luncheon clubs, or take up gardening like other people's grandmothers?'

'It's a perfectly respectable scene, though,' said Liam, his eyes still on the screen. 'Your man's still got one foot on the floor.'

'The old censor's law,' said Lucy, amused.

'Of course. You can't get up to much if you've got to leave one foot on the floor.'

Edmund frowned, as if he thought this to be another remark in questionable taste, but the others grinned.

'She was a stunning-looking lady,' said Liam thoughtfully. 'I didn't realize what a knock-out she was. In fact—'

'Yes?'

He frowned. 'Oh, I was only thinking that the reputation's suddenly very understandable. Wasn't she supposed to have had a fling with von Ribbentrop shortly before the outbreak of World War II? Or is that another of the rumours?'

'Nothing would surprise me,' said Lucy. 'Ribbentrop was a

champagne salesman before World War II, wasn't he? And Lucretia was never especially discriminating, and she did have a taste for champagne.' Sorry, Grandmamma, but you did bring this kind of conversation on yourself. Fairness made her add, 'The spying rumours were never proved, of course.'

'I don't know about spying, but with looks like that I wouldn't be surprised if she took the entire Third Reich to bed on the same night,' remarked Liam.

Edmund made a *tsk* sound of impatience, and the inspector glanced over her shoulder to where the projectionist was waiting. 'Thanks, we can go on now if you would. I just wanted to check the faces.'

As the film rolled on again, Lucy saw Edmund set his coffee cup down and lean back in his chair with an air of bored resignation.

Edmund was bored and resigned in about equal measures. He had not been in the least apprehensive about this afternoon's outlandish experiment, because he knew he had nothing to worry about; there was nothing anywhere to link him to Trixie's death, and it was patently clear that this female, this Detective Inspector Jennie Fletcher, was simply casting around in the dark. Looking for clues within the film – which she would not find, because there were none there. He would be glad when the charade was over and he could catch his train home, although it was a pity that he would not be having that cosy alluring meal with Lucy.

But as for this film, this apparently acclaimed piece of early cinema, Edmund simply could not see the point of it. If you asked him, *Alraune* was nothing but a dismal dreariness, the story incomprehensible, the behaviour of the actors meaningless and overdone. He sneaked a quick look at his watch, and saw that they had about another half hour to sit through. To while away the time he looked surreptitiously at the others. They all seemed to be watching with interest – Lucy was clearly enthralled, which annoyed Edmund.

Francesca Holland looked enthralled as well. Edmund considered her for a moment, remembering that she had been staying with Trixie Smith, wondering whether the two of them had talked about Trixie's research for the thesis. Presumably you did not share a house with somebody without referring to your work. What shall we have for supper tonight, oh, and by the way, I've found out who really killed Conrad Kline . . . Or: Your turn to pick up the dry-cleaning, and did I tell you that Lucretia von Wolff had an affair with a young man called Crispin Fane . . . Now Edmund came to think about it, he could see that this was exactly the kind of thing that might have been said. Was there any real danger here? He thought probably not. Still, Francesca Holland might need to be watched.

Michael Sallis was seated at the end of the small row of chairs, leaning back slightly, one arm resting on the arm of his chair. Edmund was about to look back at the screen, when Sallis half-turned his head to say something to Francesca. His profile caught the faint glow of the overhead light, and Edmund stared at him, the juddering screen images and the other people in the room momentarily forgotten. Deep inside his mind something was starting to thrum and he thought: I know that profile. Those eyes, that slightly too-wide mouth – I've seen them somewhere. But where? And then: why am I so concerned? he thought. So Michael Sallis resembles a client or someone on TV or the man who services the photocopier in the office. So what?

But as he turned back to the screen, the throbbing unease was increasing. His mind darted back and forth, trying to pin down the resemblance. There's something to be wary of here. Something I need to identify. Some*one* I need to identify. A nervous sweat had formed on his forehead; he blotted it with his handkerchief, doing so discreetly, pretending to dab his nose as if he had a slight cold, and keeping his eyes fixed on the screen. In a moment he would look back at Sallis, doing so quickly, as people did when they could not read someone's handwriting and tried the trick of taking it by surprise. He would take Michael Sallis by surprise, and hope his mind would make the identification ahead of his eyes.

He watched the screen for a few moments – something about

Lucretia and the scientist outside a burning house. It was all very flimsy and childlike: anyone could see the actual house had been constructed out of cardboard and plywood.

And now Lucretia was in the centre of the action, flinging herself about with over-emphatic melodrama, covering her mouth with the back of her hand in the classic gesture of shock and fear, and then suddenly facing the camera in close-up, her eyes narrowed and glittering, her lips curving in a smile of evil calculation. She was plastered with make-up; Edmund thought it very unbecoming. All that eye-black, and some sort of dark shiny lipstick. He dared say it had been all very fashionable and daring in Lucretia's heyday, but it was not his idea of what was attractive.

On the outer rim of his vision he saw Michael Sallis turn his head again, and this time he looked directly across at Sallis. And with a shock so deep that he felt as if a fist had slammed into his stomach, he knew exactly who Sallis reminded him of.

The film wound to the final reel, and the doomed scientist was lured to his fate against a background of claustrophobic skies and what Edmund considered some rather showy music. But he was only dimly aware of it, although he did look with attention at the climax, when Lucretia von Wolff, as Alraune, brought her creator to his grisly end.

(*The eyes, Edmund,* the ghost-child Alraune had said in Ashwood that day. *There is no other way . . . Remember the eyes, Edmund, remember* mord . . .)

It made several people jump when Inspector Fletcher said, in her cool detached voice, 'Can we have a replay of that scene again, please?' but Edmund had no real interest in Fletcher now, and he no longer had any energy to spare for Alraune. His entire attention was focused on Michael Sallis. He knew, with an unshakeable conviction, who Sallis was.

What he did not yet know was what he was going to do about it.

* * *

'Did you get what you wanted out of that?' asked Lucy of Inspector Fletcher, as they all dispersed. 'Or shouldn't I ask?'

'You shouldn't ask,' said Liam Devlin, overhearing this.

Fletcher regarded Lucy for a moment, and then said, 'I did get something, Miss Trent. Not quite what I was expecting, but something very interesting indeed. I can't tell you any more than that.'

'I didn't expect you could,' said Lucy. 'I'm glad it wasn't a waste of time though.'

'It wasn't a waste of time as far as I was concerned, Miss Trent,' said Liam, and Lucy glanced at him in surprise because this was the first time she had heard him speak seriously. 'Thank you very much for arranging it.' He sent Lucy another of the quizzical smiles, and went out.

The inspector said, 'It wasn't a waste of time for me, either.'

It was dark by the time Edmund reached home, and he went all round his house, closing curtains and switching on lights. Then he poured himself a drink and sat down at the little desk in the sitting-room, reaching for the phone.

But he hesitated for a moment before dialling. The spider-strands of the plan that had formed throughout the homeward journey were still strong and good; Edmund had tested each one as the train sped away from London and he knew they formed a sound plan. But dare he carry that plan out?

Of course you dare, said Crispin's voice in his mind. *Trust your instinct . . . And if you can't do that, then trust mine . . . When did I ever let you down . . . ?*

There had been times lately when the two voices – the silky assured voice that was Crispin, and the sly childlike voice that was Alraune – had fused in Edmund's mind so that it was not always easy to tell which of them was speaking. Like a radio when it was slightly off the station, so that you got two sets of voices warring with one another. Once or twice Edmund had been a little confused by these blurred-together voices, although he always sorted them out after a moment or two.

But now, as he dialled Michael Sallis's number, there was no doubt about who had the upper hand. This was unmistakably Crispin, and when Michael answered, it was Crispin at his most charming who said, 'Sallis? Oh good. I hoped I had the right number. It's Edmund Fane.'

'What can I do for you?' Sallis sounded polite but not especially friendly.

'It's about my aunt's house,' said Edmund. 'As you know, although your company gets the actual building and gardens, the contents come to me.'

'Yes, I do know.'

'The auction firm's coming out next week to pack everything and take it to the sale-rooms,' said Edmund. 'I'm keeping one or two bits for my own house—' No need to mention that the one or two bits included an eighteenth-century writing table and a set of Sheraton dining chairs. 'I thought,' he said, 'that if you will be using the house for these homeless youngsters, you might like some of the more basic furniture. Wardrobes or tables. The fridge is only a couple of years old, as well. And there's quite a good set of gardening tools in the potting shed.'

Sallis said slowly, 'Yes, I believe we might like them very much. Are you offering to give them, or can we negotiate a figure?'

'Oh,' said Edmund offhandedly, 'I don't want anything for them. I'm happy to let you have them if they can be of some use.'

'Thank you very much.'

'Is there a day you could come up here and see which of the things you'd like?' said Edmund. 'It would need to be some time in the next week, because the auction people are coming next Friday. I need to know what to let them take, and what to tell them to leave in place.'

'I could probably make it on Tuesday,' said Sallis. 'Would that be all right?'

Edmund pretended to consult a diary, and then said that Tuesday would be convenient. He had no appointments that day.

'Shall you be staying overnight? It's a hellishly long drive to do in one day. I could book you into the White Hart – you stayed there last time, didn't you? Or you could camp out at the house itself – the electricity's still on.'

He felt the other man's hesitation. Then, 'I'd rather not stay overnight,' said Michael. 'If I set off early enough I can get to you around mid-morning. That would give me a good three or four hours at the house.'

Not ideal, of course; Edmund wanted Sallis there all night. But the essence of a good plan was to adapt as you went along, so he said, 'All right. I've still got a bit of clearing out to do, so I'll be there from ten o'clock onwards.'

'If there's any heavy lifting or anything massive to shift, maybe I can give you a hand.'

'That would be kind. I'm afraid it's a dismal business sorting out the possessions of someone who's just died,' said Edmund.

CHAPTER TWENTY-SIX

It's a dismal business sorting out the possessions of someone who has just died, and when that someone has been brutally murdered, the task is a hundred times worse. But when DI Fletcher's men had finished their search of the house, Francesca discovered that there was no one else to take it on.

She rather diffidently suggested to the Deputy Head that perhaps the school should assume responsibility for packing away Trixie's things, but the Deputy Head instantly said, 'Oh, I don't think we could interfere in anything like that.'

'But she hasn't got any real family, you know,' said Fran.

'I know. It's very difficult. Of course, you having lived in the same house for the last few weeks—'

So much for paternalism. Fran supposed she had better get on with it. The police seemed to have been looking particularly for a will, but there had not appeared to be one – or if there was it was as well hidden as if this was a Victorian melodrama with a final chapter involving secret marriages and unknown heirs, which were all unthinkable in connection with Trixie.

Bank statements and bills had all been in order, and the only money owing was a couple of hundred pounds on a credit card, from Trixie's purchase of new dog kennels last month. It also turned out that Trixie had owned the house outright, which rather surprised Fran, who had assumed there would be a mortgage. But perhaps Trixie had inherited money or even the house itself from her parents: Fran did know they had died when Trixie was quite young. As well as the house there was a modest building society savings account and a couple of insurance policies, both timed to mature in just over fifteen years' time.

'I suppose she was planning on retiring early,' said DI Fletcher, preparing to leave Fran to her dismal task. 'She was almost forty, wasn't she?'

Fran said she had not actually known Trixie's age; it was not something that had ever come up. She asked if the police really thought anyone would commit that nightmare murder for a house in North London and a few thousand pounds?

'At the moment, Mrs Holland, we're prepared to believe anything of anyone. But I'd have to say I don't see this as being linked to sordid coinage. We haven't been able to trace any family, by the way. Except for the elderly aunt – great-aunt, I should say – and even the wildest stretch of imagination couldn't cast her as first murderer.'

'I do know Trixie used to visit that aunt in the holidays,' said Francesca thoughtfully. 'But I believe she's at least ninety. I shouldn't think she could even manage the journey to Ashwood, let alone anything else.'

'I shouldn't think so, either.'

And so, taking it all in all, it looked as if there was no one prepared to shoulder the responsibility for Trixie's things. Fran thought she would make a start on Friday afternoon, go along to Quondam Films on Saturday as requested, and finish the sorting out on Sunday. It would be a bit of a nuisance to have to break off midway through the weekend, although she was intrigued by the prospect of seeing *Alraune*.

She had consigned the dogs to the care of the RSPCA with stern instructions that they must be found a good home, and the home must be for all three of them together. Trixie would never forgive Fran if her beloved dogs were split up, and Fran thought there was enough to contend with as it was, without risking being haunted by a peevish and accusatory ghost, purely because the ghost's dogs had not been found sufficiently luxurious homes.

The actual sorting out was not as time-consuming as she had feared, and by Sunday lunchtime she was more than halfway through. As she worked, she thought about yesterday's viewing of *Alraune*. She had found it disturbing but rather moving.

Trixie had not been very tidy, but at least she had not been a magpie keeping bundles of old letters or postcards, or even photographs. There were a few photographs though, mostly pushed haphazardly into a couple of large manilla envelopes on top of a wardrobe. Fran, who rather liked old photos, even when they were of other people's families or friends, put these to one side thinking she would look through them later, although it was rather sad if Trixie had had so few stored-away memories of her life. On the whole it was probably better not to surround yourself with sentimental fragments, but it meant a lot of the romance of the past got lost. It was not so many years since you could practically piece together entire lives from faded letters, or construct long-ago love affairs from theatre programmes and dance programmes or scratched gramophone records.

But she could not see today's teenagers squirrelling away posters from pop concerts or print-outs of text messages. This strengthened her resolve to destroy everything from that disastrous marriage: Marcus's letters and some theatre tickets, and the hotel bill from where they had spent their first romantic weekend, when they had not got out of bed until it was time to go home. Some romance, thought Fran cynically, and with the idea of forcing Marcus and his perfidy out of her mind, she worked doggedly on, making an inventory of furniture and the contents of drawers and cupboards. If you had no family, did you simply become just a typed list of saucepans and crockery and cretonne-covered chairs?

By mid-afternoon she had finished, and she stood in Trixie's bedroom, conscious of aching back and neck muscles, and feeling unpleasantly grubby, and also very hungry. People deserted by cheating husbands were supposed to lose their appetites and dwindle to mere shadows of their former selves, but Fran was not a die-away Victorian heroine or a twenty-first-century stick-thin model, and she was not going to stop eating just because she was getting divorced. And she had been carting boxes and books and clothes back and forth ever since breakfast and she had missed lunch.

She tipped the contents of some tinned soup into a saucepan to heat, and switched on the grill to make toast to go with it. While the grill was heating up, she looked through the photographs she had brought downstairs, trying to allot relationships to the faces. The slightly countrified woman standing in front of a nice old stone cottage might be Trixie's mother, and the little group with 1950s hairstyles could be aunts. Were the dates right? Yes, near enough. There were one or two shots of a sturdy, somewhat belligerent-looking child whom Fran recognized after a moment as being Trixie herself. These had mostly been taken in gardens or on what looked like holidays on the coast.

But other than this there was not very much of interest. Fran turned over the last photograph in the envelope, thinking she would just label the whole thing as 'Photographs' and include it in the inventory for the unknown elderly aunt.

The last photograph was a postcard-size black-and-white shot taken against the background of some unidentifiable city. It showed a three-quarters view of a child around eight or nine years old, wearing a corduroy jacket. The child had deepset eyes and dark hair that flopped forward and there was something about the eyes that Francesca found slightly chilling. I wouldn't like to meet you in a dark alley on a moonless night, thought Fran, and then took in the writing on the white strip along the bottom and instantly felt as if a giant, invisible hand had slammed into her stomach.

On the bottom of the photograph was written a single name and a date.

Alraune. 1949.

* * *

Francesca sat at the kitchen table for a long time, staring at the enigmatic face of the dark-eyed child, occasionally putting out a hand to touch the photograph's surface, as if she could somehow absorb the past through her fingertips, or as if buried within the images might be a key that would unlock the past.

Eventually she took a square of glass from a framed print Trixie had had of a Tyrolean snow-scene, and laid it carefully over the photograph. At this point the smell of burning reminded her that the grill was still switched on and was blasting toast-flavoured heat into the kitchen, and she hastily switched it off. She was no longer in the least bit hungry, which was ridiculous, because Alraune – the child, the ghost, the legend – could have nothing whatsoever to do with her. You don't affect me in the least, said Fran silently to Alraune's enigmatic stare.

But the kitchen suddenly seemed cold and unfriendly, and Fran repressed a shiver and glanced uneasily towards the garden door. The top half was glass, so that she could see the outline of the thick laurel hedge between this house and the neighbour's, and also the tubs of winter pansies that Trixie had planted because they made a nice splash of colour when everything else had died down and the dogs did not try to bury bones under them.

It had started to rain, and the thick old laurel hedge that Trixie had never got round to trimming this autumn was tapping gently against the window. Fran got up to draw the curtains across the darkening afternoon and flipped the blind down over the upper part of the garden door. The kitchen immediately felt friendlier and safer. But you don't feel at all friendly or safe, she said to Alraune's photograph. And where on earth did Trixie get you, I wonder? Were you just part of her research into Ashwood? Or did you instigate the entire project? Meeting the child's uncompromising stare, Francesca was inclined to think the latter might be more likely, because if ever a face would print itself on your mind . . .

It was already almost six o'clock, and although she had never felt less like food, if she ate something it might stop her from thinking about ghosts and imagining them peering in through the windows. She was about to turn the gas up to heat the soup when she heard something outside that was certainly not the rain or the wayward laurel hedge and that was too substantial for a ghost. Footsteps. Footsteps coming down the gravel drive, moving slowly, as if the owner either was not sure of his or her welcome, or did not want to be heard.

Fran stood in the middle of the kitchen, staring out into the half-lit hall and the old-fashioned Victorian stained-glass panels of the door. Silence. No one there after all. And then a dark shape – unmistakably that of a man – stepped into the porch and a hand came up to lift the door-knocker.

This time Fran's heart leapt into her throat, even though logic was already pointing out that it was most likely someone from school wanting to know if there was any news about Trixie's killer, poor old Trixie, or even the Deputy Head inquiring how the packing up of Trixie's things was going. But before she went out to answer the knock, some instinct made Fran snatch up a teatowel and drop it over Alraune's photograph.

'I could have thought up an excuse about you having left something at Quondam yesterday and that I was returning it,' said the man standing on the step. 'But I won't bother with that. The truth is that I wanted to see you again.'

His coat collar was turned up against the cold and his hair was lightly misted with the rain. But his eyes were the same: grey and clear and fringed with black lashes, and the smile was the same as well; outwardly reserved but with that faint promise of something that was not reserved at all.

'Hello, Michael,' said Francesca. 'Come in.'

It was as easy to be with him as it had been at Deborah Fane's house, or at Quondam's offices yesterday. There was no awkwardness; it was like meeting up with an old and trusted friend; one with whom you were always on the same wavelength even when you had not met for years. Francesca thought this was probably something to do with that appalling experience inside Ashwood, and then she glanced at Michael again and thought it was nothing to do with that.

He sat at the kitchen table while Fran made coffee, and talked a bit about yesterday's film, and asked how she had coped with the police interviews.

'Reasonably well. The police were more courteous than I expected. I had to make a statement and give them as much information as I could about Trixie. Which wasn't so very much when it came down to it. You?'

'Much the same. Questions about when and where and how, and can anyone verify that, sir. In the main, nobody could verify anything about my movements,' said Michael. 'I live on my own.'

So he was not married or, from the sound of it, linked up to anyone. Francesca found this slightly surprising. With his looks he must have had opportunities, to say the very least. Yes, but there was that reserve; that would make it quite difficult to get close to him. She suddenly wanted to find out if she could do so. This would be nothing more than curiosity, though.

The kitchen was rather old-fashioned – Trixie had thought it a waste of good money to spend out on streamlined appliances when the old ones were still perfectly serviceable, and could not see the point of papering walls or painting doors every five minutes when the dogs scratched things to shreds as soon as your back was turned – but in an odd way the outdated background suited Michael. Fran, studying him covertly over her coffee mug, thought he did not entirely belong in the hard-edged world of high technology or fast foods or computer-generated music in supermarkets. She remembered that her original impression had been of someone whose spiritual home was an Oxford common-room, but seeing him again she revised this and set him instead against the background of an old house – not an especially quaint or inglenook-picturesque place, just a fairly old house with a good many books that had been well read, and perhaps a nice untidiness of music and old programmes of plays or exhibitions seen and enjoyed, and maybe notes for a book he would never get round to writing . . .

And then she remembered that his work took him into the world of homeless teenagers and concrete-block skyscraper flats, and into the twilit realms of drugs and crime and sullen or violent adolescents, and her opinion of him received another shake, like a child's kaleidoscope rearranging the colours and the patterns, although she was not sure precisely how the colours and patterns would fall.

She was just wondering how he would take it if she offered to make an omelette for them to share – it was coming up to seven o'clock – when Michael said, 'You've probably already got some kind of commitment for tonight – I know teachers are always having to attend parent meetings and things – but if not, I noticed an Italian restaurant just along the road. It looked quite good. If you can eat pasta and feel like some company for a couple of hours—'

It was nicely done. He had made the suggestion in a casual way, at the same time presenting her with a polite get-out which would not make either of them feel awkward. Fran said at once that she loved pasta. 'And the only thing I was going to do this evening was pack away some more of Trixie's things.'

'Do I need to ring up to book a table?'

'I shouldn't think so. They get quite busy during the week because the food's good, but Sunday evenings are usually fairly quiet. How about if I just rinse these coffee cups and then dash upstairs for a quick wash.' She could scramble into something a bit more respectable than the ancient jeans and dust-streaked shirt she was wearing, although there was no need to say this.

'All right.'

He carried his cup to the sink, and Fran turned on the taps and without thinking reached for the teatowel covering the photograph.

Michael saw the photograph at once, and he saw the slanting writing under it, and he flinched visibly as if someone had suddenly shone a too-bright light into his face, or as if he had received a blow. Francesca, still holding the teatowel, turned to stare at him. When he finally spoke, his voice was strained and harsh and so different from his normal voice that it was as if a stranger had taken his place.

'Where did you get that?'

Fran said carefully, 'It was among Trixie's things. I found it this afternoon. I'm not sure what to do with it – I'm not even sure if I ought to do anything with it at all.' When he did not speak, she said, 'Trixie talked quite a bit about Lucretia von Wolff and Alraune while she was putting together her research, so I got very familiar with the stories. But I thought a lot of them were journalists' exaggeration. Until I saw that photo I never really thought Alraune existed.'

Michael said very softly, 'Alraune did exist.' His eyes were still on the photograph.

Fran had no idea what to say. But because he was still looking shaken, and because clearly they could not pretend that nothing had happened, she said, 'I don't know why it was in Trixie's things. I don't think it's anything to do with her family.'

'No.'

The frozen look had not gone from his face, and Fran suddenly wanted to reach out to take his hand in hers. To dispel such a ridiculous idea she said, 'I suppose it's something of a find, isn't it? I mean – to anyone interested in Lucretia von Wolff's life it would probably be worth quite a lot.'

'Oh yes.'

Fran had no idea what was behind all this, but clearly something was behind it, and so by way of edging nearer to the heart of the matter she said, 'Uh – Michael, I'm not sure how much you know about Lucretia von Wolff—'

'Quite a lot,' he said. 'I know quite a lot about Lucretia.' He paused and then, almost as if he was bracing himself to plunge neck-deep into icy water, he said, 'Lucretia von Wolff was my grandmother. I knew her very well indeed.'

The kaleidoscope received another shake, and this time the coloured patterns fell in entirely different, wholly incredible shapes. His grandmother, thought Fran. That can't possibly be true. He can't expect me to believe that.

She said, 'But – you can't have known Lucretia. She died fifty-odd years ago. She died at Ashwood – she killed herself to escape being charged with the double murder. That's the legend – it's one of the famous murders of its time.'

'Lucretia didn't die at Ashwood that day,' said Michael. 'And when I was eight years old I ran away to her house and lived with her for the next ten years.'

CHAPTER TWENTY-SEVEN

Francesca ended up making the omelettes after all, since Michael's astonishing revelation seemed effectively to put an end to any idea of going out and attempting to eat anything even approaching a normal civilized meal.

But when he said, rather ruefully, 'Sorry, Francesca, I didn't mean to explode a bombshell – there's no reason why we can't still go out to eat,' Fran said at once that of course they could not go out; if Michael thought she was going to discuss Lucretia von Wolff and Alraune with waiters and other diners eavesdropping on their conversation, he had better think again.

'Are we going to discuss Lucretia and Alraune?'

'Well, not if you'd hate it and not anything that's private, of course. Can you eat omelettes?'

He made a brief gesture, half defeat, half acceptance, and said, 'Yes, of course I can eat omelettes.' And then, as Fran reached into the fridge for eggs and cheese, he said, 'Where d'you keep the plates and cutlery? I'll lay the table.'

'In that drawer. Thanks. D'you mind eating in here? The dining-room's a bit gloomy.'

'Not at all,' said Michael, setting out knives and forks on the table. 'But telling your life story is the ultimate in ego-trips. Like telling your dreams.'

'You're forgetting I've lived with Lucretia's life story – and with Alraune – ever since Trixie started her thesis,' said Fran. Clearly he could not be asked about the running away part, but it should be acceptable to ask about Lucretia and about the years with her. Lucretia . . . Am I believing him, I wonder? More to the point, am I trusting him, because after all, I don't really know anything about him. I suppose I could phone CHARTH tomorrow and verify that he works for them, but that wouldn't tell me anything about his childhood. Surely he *can't* have lived with Lucretia. She died years ago. If this is some kind of hoax, it's a very elaborate one, though – unless he's mad, of course, I suppose that's a possibility. But she glanced at him again, and knew it was not even a remote possibility. He was unmistakably sane. And so when you have eliminated the impossible, my dear Watson, whatever remains, however improbable, must be the truth.

She discovered that he was looking at her. 'You're finding it difficult to accept,' he said.

'Well, yes. Did you really live with her? With Lucretia?'

'I did. For ten years. In a nice old house on the edge of the Lincolnshire fens, on the outskirts of a little market town, where she lived a perfectly conventional life. Women's Guild and shopping and library reading groups. She did quite a lot of charity work – that's how I got involved in CHARTH – and she had a good many friends locally, although I'll swear that not one of them had the smallest suspicion of who she really was. Which was how she wanted it. Oh, and she loved music.'

'Conrad's influence,' said Fran, remembering the film music yesterday at Quondam, and feeling that she was reaching back to grasp a handful of the past.

'Yes, I think so. She used to take me to concerts in Lincoln and Norwich or Cambridge – and gorgeous choral stuff in Ely Cathedral at Christmas and Easter. I had never heard music or singing like that before and it knocked me for six – in fact at one stage it nearly swept me into a religious vocation.'

He glanced at her as if expecting a reaction. Fran said, 'But – it didn't?'

'I found out I had a fairly unspiritual side,' he said gravely. Fran grinned, and saw that he had relaxed for the first time since he had seen Alraune's photograph. But then he said, 'Shall I grate the cheese?' and she felt the barriers go back into place.

Even so, it was friendly to have him sharing the small task of making the omelettes. Marcus's forays into the kitchen had been rare, and had usually involved cooking an impossibly elaborate dish, the preparation of which necessitated using every saucepan they possessed and apparently absolved him from washing up afterwards. Michael simply reached for the cheese and got on with it.

'Lucretia had no patience with men who expected to be waited on,' he said, apparently picking some of this up. 'She was quite domesticated as a matter of fact. And she made sure I knew how to cook a reasonable meal. I'll make you my five-star gourmet Hungarian goulash some evening if you'd like that.'

Francesca had a sudden image of Michael's flat or his house, which would be warm and comfortable and safe-feeling, and of the two of them eating goulash and drinking wine at a small dining-table. She discovered she was smiling at the prospect, so in case he got the wrong idea, she said, 'I'd have to say that the words domesticated and Lucretia von Wolff don't seem to belong in the same sentence.'

He smiled properly this time. 'Her real name was Alice Wilson, and she had been a servant in a big house in Vienna until the late nineteen-twenties.'

Francesca finished beating the eggs and poured them into the omelette pan. 'Not kidnapped Russian royalty or the heiress to a Carpathian castle, after all?'

'Nowhere near. A perfectly ordinary background in fact.' He passed the little heap of grated cheese to her. 'Would you like me to open that bottle of wine?'

'Yes, please.' She handed him the corkscrew and reached for two wine-glasses. They might as well use the expensive ones Trixie had brought back from one of her walking holidays; perhaps Bohemian crystal would lend an air of grandeur to the very ordinary meal and the even more ordinary bottle of supermarket plonk. This discussion of resurrected legends and ghost-children ought to be given at least a smidgeon of ceremony and be dignified by a touch of class. And Michael Sallis was somehow a person with whom you associated more than just a touch of class.

She tipped the grated cheese on to the just-setting eggs, and said, 'It's a remarkable thing, but ever since I heard about the Ashwood murders from Trixie, one thing seems to have overshadowed all the rest.'

He paused, and then said, very softly, 'Alraune.'

'Yes.' Fran determinedly avoided looking towards the curtained windows which hid the dark whispering night. 'Alraune seems to overshadow everything.'

'That,' said Michael, looking at her very intently, 'is exactly what Alice said to me on the night before my seventeenth birthday. The night when she finally told me the truth about Alraune.'

*

One of the things Michael had loved about growing up in the Lincolnshire house had been listening to Alice's stories about her past.

She had unfolded the stories bit by bit, as if she understood that he wanted to absorb the details gradually, and she told a story as his mother used to; making it vivid and exciting and real. Most of the time she had talked to him as if he were already grown-up, although he had always known there were parts of her life she had not told, and that she might never tell.

But on the night before his seventeenth birthday – the night she talked to him about Alraune – she did not make a story of it; she talked plainly and rather flatly, and several times Michael thought she was going to stop partway through and not go on. *And if she does that, I'll never know.*

'Alraune's birth seemed to overshadow everything else that had ever happened to me,' she had said in the firelit room that night, seated in her usual chair, Michael in his familiar inglenook seat.

Alraune . . . The name whispered around the warm safe room like a cold sighing voice. Like something sobbing inside a bitter night-wind, or like brittle goblin-fingers scratching out childish letters on a window-pane in the dark . . .

'Alraune was bad,' Alice said. 'I don't just mean dishonest or selfish or bad-tempered. I mean truly bad. Cruel. It's as if – oh, as if Nature occasionally gets things a bit twisted and lets loose something wicked on the world.'

Something wicked . . . Michael shivered, and edged nearer to the fire.

At once Alice said, 'You should remember, though, that it's nearly always possible to spot the world's bad people very easily. And once you have spotted them you're perfectly safe, because you can give them a wide berth.'

'It's as simple as that, is it?'

'Most of the time. Don't be cynical, Michael, you're still too young to be cynical.'

'Sorry. Tell me about Alraune. You never have done, not properly. Tonight tell me properly.'

She studied him for a moment. 'What a heart-breaker you're turning into,' she said unexpectedly. 'I pity the girls you meet. And don't grin at me like that, I'm quite well aware of what goes on in the world of teenagers. But I don't know how much I can tell you about Alraune. Alraune never seemed quite real to me.'

Her eyes had the sad look that Michael hated, and her face, with the framing of white hair, suddenly looked older. Once upon a time her hair had been a deep shiny black, and once upon a time her skin had been smooth and pale, like cream velvet. When she was younger. When she was Lucretia. One day I'll see if I can find a photo of her as Lucretia, thought Michael. And one day I might be able to find one of the films she made and watch it. Would that be possible? Would she mind?

He said, carefully, 'Alraune was part of a nightmare – that's right, isn't it? You lived inside a nightmare.'

'That's sharp of you. Yes, I did.'

'I know about living nightmares – well, a bit about them.'

'I know you do. And you shouldn't have to, not at your age.'

'It's all right. I've forgotten most of that. So listen, start with the beginning – that was Buchenwald, wasn't it? – and go on from there. That's what you always tell me to do with difficult things.'

'How sharper than a serpent's tooth it is . . .' began Alice.

'. . . to have a thankless child. Yes, I know. But I'm not thankless.'

'You're disgustingly precocious. I'm starting to wonder if I've brought you up all wrong.'

'No, you haven't.'

'Well, how many other seventeen-year-olds would quote *King Lear*? Why aren't you staying out late and getting illegally drunk and listening to too-loud pop music like the rest of your generation?' She smiled at him.

'I don't know. I don't care. I do stay out late sometimes, though.'

'I'm aware of it,' she said, dryly.

'Tell me about Buchenwald. Didn't you try to escape? I would have done.'

'At first I thought I would,' said Alice. 'I even thought it would be easy. All through that train journey I planned what I would do and how I would get away.'

'To find Conrad and Deborah.' This was entirely understandable. 'So there you were on the train trying to plan an escape.'

'Not just precocious, persistent as well,' said Alice. 'But yes, I was on the train, and I thought about escaping all through the hours and hours of jolting and the biting cold, with people being sick on the wooden floors from terror, or relieving their bladders in front of everyone simply because there was nowhere else to do it. Captivity isn't romantic or noble, Michael, not like it is in stories. It isn't the Prisoner of Zenda, or the rightful heir to a kingdom being shut in a stone cell by a usurper and then rescued in a swashbuckling fight. The reality's squalid and horrible and dehumanizing – the Nazis loved the dehumanizing part, of course; it fitted very neatly with their propaganda and their murderous schemes against the Jews. Even so, all through that journey I clung on to how I would find a way to fool them and outwit the SS, and how I would cheat Leo Dreyer and get away—'

'But you didn't?'

'No. There were escapes from the camps, of course, and quite a lot of them were from Buchenwald. Towards the end of the war there was an underground resistance network that smuggled people out. But in those early months it was a very difficult camp to escape from.'

'What made it so difficult?'

Alice paused, as if arranging the memories in her mind. 'All the concentration camps were dreadful places,' she said. 'You can't believe how dreadful they were. Most of them were death camps – "*Rückkehr unerwünscht*" they were labelled. That means, "Return not desired". Death camps, you see. Buchenwald wasn't that; but it was "*Vernichtung durch arbeit*". Extermination by work.'

Again the pause. Then, 'Originally it was intended for political prisoners,' she said. 'So groups of people were taken into nearby factories or quarries in Weimar and Erfurt, and made to work there, sometimes for twelve hours at a time.'

'Did you have to do that?'

'Yes, for a while. I hoped I could escape that way, but the guards were with us all the time, and it was impossible. There were roll calls twice a day – sometimes three times – and the SS patrols were everywhere. Anyone caught trying to escape was shot at once.' She paused again, and then said, 'To me – to all of us – Buchenwald was an outpost of hell.'

Once the initial shock and the exhaustion of the gruelling journey had worn off a little, the days inside Buchenwald had begun to blur into a sick bleak misery that seemed to have no end. Alice had found this almost more terrifying than anything she had yet experienced, because once you were caught in it you began to lose count of the days, and you stopped caring which day or which month it was anyway. But earlier on she vowed to keep careful count of the days, and she scratched a rough chart on the edge of her wooden-framed bunk so that she could cross off each day and know how much time had passed.

Some of the women with whom she shared the hut – Hut 24 it had been – believed themselves to have died, and to have gone to hell. This was the real hell of the preachers and the rabbis and the priests, they said with fearful eyes. This was the place where you paid for your sins and who knew how long that might take? Alice thought this a naïve outlook, but once or twice she found herself wondering whether there was some form of retribution at work. Supposing this is the reckoning, she thought – the payment for those enchanted ten years? For having Conrad and Deborah, and for all the extravagances and the fun and the admiration.

Supposing that like Faust, I sold my soul to the devil during those nights in Vienna's Old Quarter, or on any one of the nights since? And supposing the devil has been stalking me ever since, watching his chance to settle the account . . . ? Aha, there's Alice Wilson, he might have said. I think it's time to call in the debt on that one. Quite a lot of self-indulgence went on, I see. A great deal of money spent on personal adornment – a good deal of fornication as well – oh, and a bastard child: dear me, she's had a very good run indeed, this one. A very extravagant ten years. It's certainly time for the arrogant little sinner to settle my account.

There were forty-five women in Hut 24, all of them sleeping and eating and living in the cramped barrack-like room with the single lavatory and washbasin, and the flimsy wooden-structured bunks for sleeping. As far as Alice could make out, most of them were innocent of any crime other than the crime of being Jewish, although there were one or two whom she would not have cared to meet in a lonely dark alley. Best not forget that Buchenwald, whatever else it might be, had originally been intended for political prisoners. Best, as well, to keep the baroness firmly in the background, and simply be Alice Wilson for the moment. In any case, very few people would have recognized the svelte sleek Lucretia von Wolff in the raggle-taggle creature living in Hut 24 and working in the munitions factory in Weimar each day.

They left for Weimar every morning after the 4 a.m. roll-call, and after the meagre breakfast apportionment of a slice of bread and a tin mug of coffee. Alice hated the dry bread and the watery milkless coffee, but she hated, even more, the factory where they sat at wooden benches, mostly sewing coarse uniform cloth for the German armies.

But surely there would be a way to escape, and surely she would find it and get out, either as Lucretia, or more likely as plain ordinary Alice Wilson, who had been used to hard work and subservience, and to an unobtrusive, unremarkable appearance. Yes, if she got out of here, it would have to be as Alice.

When the prisoners went to Weimar they marched in step, the guards walking alongside the little group. At times, to vary the monotony, Alice thought how Conrad might write music to fit the marching steps of them all. It would be thin, metallic music. Staccato. Clip-clop, tap-tap . . . Death-by-work . . . Death-by-work . . .

Conrad. Was he being forced to work in the same way? Was he allowed music? If they were denying him music – even the tinniest of instruments – he would never survive, for music was his life and his breath and his food, and without it he would succumb to the blackest of black despairs.

He had once said to her that he was a pagan. 'I worship life and laughter and good wine,' he had said. 'And love,' he had added, his eyes slanting with mischief. 'I worship love, of course. "Some toward Mecca turn to pray, but I toward thy bed, Yasmin." You are my Yasmin, Alice.'

'Rot,' Alice had said, after she had got over the extravagant romanticism of this sufficiently to remember Conrad's most recent entanglement with a red-haired Florentine actress from the *commedia dell'arte*. 'Utter rubbish. If you worship anything at all, you worship music.'

And so Conrad, who worshipped music, might die if they took that away from him. Alice wondered how she would bear it, and then she wondered whether it would be worse simply to lose him without knowing what his fate had been.

After a few weeks the staccato music of the prisoners' weary footsteps and the grinding pain of working for twelve hours at a stretch, and being constantly, achingly hungry and thirsty, changed. Now the music drummed out a different rhythm. I-must-get-out . . . I-will-do-anything . . .

I will do anything to get out, thought Alice. There is nothing I will not do.

CHAPTER TWENTY-EIGHT

There is nothing I will not do to get out . . .

But it gradually became clear that escape was impossible; the prisoners were closely guarded, and in the first two weeks of her imprisonment, two young men – Russian Jews – were shot for trying to climb over the electrified fence by night.

Nightmare visions of Conrad, hungry and beaten or lying dead in some wretched unknown grave, haunted her, and to quench them she began to look for SS men who might be open to seduction; when you have been living in hell you will take the devil himself to bed, and although Alice had temporarily abandoned the idea of escape she thought she would not flinch from one or two sessions in the guards' quarters if it would improve her lot, and that of her companions. Hot water for washing. Better food – or at least more substantial food. Clean clothes occasionally.

I'd do it if I could, she thought. Yes, but how can I exert any kind of seduction technique with my hair chopped short, and the smell of sweat on my skin, and wearing this shapeless half-shirt, half-dress they give the prisoners? But she was prepared to try, even though she was already recognizing the black irony of her situation. Not so long ago my most pressing concerns were whether to enamel my nails silver or scarlet, or the problem of obtaining eyelash-black. Now I'm contemplating going to bed with men who are sadists and torturers and murderers, just to get a few extra slices of bread.

From time to time, news from the outside world reached Buchenwald. Germany was being mobilized for war, although it was being said that Herr Hitler did not really expect to have to fight any kind of war at all. Against this was the fact that Hermann Göering, always the evil genius of the Nazi Party, had lately announced a fivefold extension of the Luftwaffe.

'The Third Reich seems somewhat divided,' observed Alice rather caustically to the others in Hut 24. 'Or does Göering intend to fight on his own?'

'I heard there were rumours that Herr Hitler means to annexe Czechoslovakia in the way he annexed Austria,' said one of the women – Mirka – who was from a village just outside Prague, and who had been raped and beaten on *Kristallnacht*, before being brought to Buchenwald. 'But if he does, he will not find it easy. Slovakian people are strong and fearless, and they will defy the Reich armies. They will fight. And our good friends in France will come to our aid,' said Mirka confidently. 'You will see.'

The spring buds were just starting to unfurl when the information reached Buchenwald, via a new consignment of prisoners, that Hitler's armies had marched into Bohemia and Moravia, and that France had done nothing to prevent them. Mirka had sobbed with angry despair that night, muffling the sounds in her pillow, and Alice sat on the side of her bed, trying to comfort her. The two of them had talked softly until dawn, exchanging memories, and Alice thought they had both drawn strength from one another.

Several days afterwards some Czech women were brought to Buchenwald, and they told how the Czechoslovakians had indeed fought the German armies.

'They fought and they are still defiant,' said one of them, who had been assigned to Hut 24, and Mirka nodded at this as if she would have expected nothing less. 'But they are defeated, for all that,' said the woman. 'My village was burned to the ground and my family all died.' Her eyes flashed. 'I would take on Hitler's entire army single-handed for what they did,' she said.

It was shortly after the arrival of the Czech prisoners that Alice's name was called at the evening roll-call. 'Prisoner 98907, Wilson, Hut 24?'

'Here,' said Alice, managing to speak calmly although her heart had started to race. What have I done? she thought frantically. What do they want me for? But she stepped two paces forward as was the rule, and waited.

'Come with us,' said one of them, taking her arm and pulling her across the concrete quadrangle where roll-call always took place.

Alice was extremely frightened, but she said, coldly, 'I prefer to walk,' and brushed off their hands. 'Where are you taking me?'

'To the commandant's office.'

'Why?'

'Those are our orders.'

The rain-sodden concrete yard and the rows of people blurred, and there was the feeling of something huge and oppressive pressing down on the top of her head, making the blood pound painfully against her eyes. Satan, leather-winged and cloven-hoofed, finally fastening his arms around her? Time for the reckoning, my dear . . . Don't be ridiculous!

Inside the commandant's office the SS guards gave the sharp, heel-clicking German salute, and then went out, leaving Alice alone. The sound of the door closing brought a panic-filled claustrophobia, but she was determined to show no fear. Remember the Let's Pretend game, Alice . . . ? Remember how you fooled everyone by being Lucretia, and remember how you invoked the old game for the film-makers. *When I was a King in Babylon and you were a Christian slave* . . . And now I'm a Christian in a Jewish concentration camp, but the burden of the song's the same. Fool them, Alice. Play the pretend-game. All right, here I go.

On this note she raised her eyes and looked about her. The

office was warm and well-lit, and there was a carpet on the floor and books on the walls. Books, warmth, comfort. Oh God, what wouldn't I give to have such things back in my life! But one day I'll be back in the real world and I'll have them again.

Through a partly open door was a small, rather sparsely furnished bedroom, where the commandant sometimes slept if a new batch of prisoners was due in the early morning, or if there was to be a visit of inspection by some Reich official or important Party member and he wanted to be on hand. Alice could see the bed and a washbasin with soap and towels. Hot water. Scented soap. I'm not bearing this, she thought. I'm exhausted and I'm permanently hungry and I'm bone-cold all the time. I'm wearing this appalling sacking garment and my hair has been shorn to keep it free of lice, and for the past six months the only washing facilities I've had are cold water in a stone trough, and a bar of lye soap shared with twenty others.

I will do anything to get out of here . . . There is nothing I would not do . . .

The words sang through her mind like a litany, like a prayer or a curse, and at last she looked properly at the man standing by the desk. Buchenwald's commandant, SS Colonel Karl Koch. He had mean little eyes, set deep into a rather coarse-grained face, and his neck was too thick for the sharply-cut SS uniform.

The little squinty eyes inspected Alice, and after a moment, Karl Koch said, 'First I should tell you that I know who you really are.' His voice was discordant and unpleasant, but Alice did not detect any especial mockery.

She said, non-committally, 'Do you, indeed?'

'I have seen two of your films, baroness,' he said. He used the title as if he believed it perfectly genuine. 'For me it was a great pleasure.'

'Thank you.'

'So, I think that for you, life inside Buchenwald must be harsh.'

'Yes, it is a hard and cruel place, this,' said Alice after a moment. Her mind was working at a furious rate. He knew about Lucretia.

More to the point, he *believed* in Lucretia. Was this something she could turn to her advantage?

'Well, some things are unavoidable, I fear,' said Koch. 'I think it is six months now since you were brought here, yes?'

'Yes.'

'So. I have been thinking that there could be a way to soften things for you, and I have a small proposition to make.' He moved from behind the desk and came to stand nearer to her. Alice could smell the garlic on his breath and she remembered that he was believed to enjoy rich food and good-looking women.

She said warily, 'A proposition?'

'I want you to listen to the talk of the other inmates,' said Koch. 'I have watched you, and although you pose as an Englishwoman – Alice Wilson, yes? – still they are attracted to you. You are a very fascinating woman, baroness; even stripped of your rank, it is still so. And you have many admirers in Buchenwald, of both sexes.'

'I have always had admirers,' said Alice offhandedly. 'That is beside the point. Herr Koch – I would have preferred my – my name and title to remain unknown in this place.'

'It can do so. It can be just between us.' Koch's eyes were on her neck and her breasts. Repulsive. But don't let him see you think that.

'Because of this attraction you have for people,' said Koch, 'you will be welcomed into many discussions; people will talk to you. I want you to listen to these discussions very carefully, and then to bring to me any – ah – information you think might interest me. Anything that might be of value to the Third Reich.'

'Spying,' said Alice thoughtfully. 'That's what you mean, isn't it? You want me to spy for you?'

He smiled, pleased at her understanding. 'There are signs that an underground movement is starting up inside Buchenwald – an organization intending to arrange escapes, or rebellions. It is necessary that I identify the ringleaders and deal with them before they can cause any trouble.'

'You think I might be able to find out about this organization?'

'It would be a service that could be well rewarded. You understand me?'

'Yes.' Alice studied him for a moment, her expression deliberately blank. But her mind was working at top speed, thinking, considering, planning. She said, slowly, 'You referred to advantages? To a reward?'

'There are a number of things we could do to make your life more comfortable.' He had visibly relaxed now. 'You must miss such things as good food and hot water for washing. Clean bed-linen on a regular basis. I could arrange for you to have most of those things.'

'But not my freedom? You couldn't arrange my freedom?'

He hesitated, and then, as if thinking it over, said, 'If you provide us with what we need, it might be possible. It could appear to be an escape; I could pretend to transfer you to another camp. Perhaps to Dachau, which is not so very far from here. An escape might occur on the journey. In that circumstance you would be given money and papers to aid you.'

Dachau. Money and papers. *Dachau*. Conrad. The ache that Alice had tried to suppress all these months returned a hundredfold. I don't trust Karl Koch, though, thought Alice. I don't think he entirely trusts me either, but that may be a good thing.

'Very well,' she said at last, looking him straight in the eyes. 'I will do what you wish.'

*

'I cheated him, of course,' said Alice, her eyes full of memories that seemed to be spilling out into the warm safe room, like ghosts from old black and white newsreels.

'How did you dare?' said Michael, coming up out of this sinister world where tanks drove arrogantly through city streets, and people were shut away behind barbed wire and threatened by black-snouted machine-guns. But even as he said it, he knew that of course she had dared; she would have dared anything.

'It was not as dangerous as it sounds,' said Alice. 'There was indeed an underground organization being formed in Buchenwald – the commandant had been right about that, although it was so new and so tentative it was as insubstantial as a spider-web. But it was a web that was being spun very determinedly indeed, and even a hint of its existence alerted the SS sufficiently to recruit spies on their own account.'

'And they thought you would be one of the spies?'

'Yes. They had assumed, you see, that I would do anything for food and warmth and all the other things. They thought they were dealing with Lucretia von Wolff, who was luxury-loving and pampered, and that was their mistake. They didn't know that Lucretia was just a smokescreen, or that I was far better equipped to cope with the harsh regime than they could imagine. I had started life as a kitchenmaid in the big house in England – I had been used to getting up at half past five in the depths of a freezing winter and raking out fires and kitchen ranges, and pumping cold water from a well in the yard. And when I was promoted to be Nina Dreyer's maid, there was still all the fetching and carrying, and sitting up until three or four in the morning to help her undress after a party or a ball.' She paused, and then said, 'Also there had been those months of living rough in Vienna's back streets. I believed that if I could survive that, I could survive practically anything.'

'But to deceive the *Nazis*. The *Gestapo*—' The words had been coined long before Michael was born, but they still carried their own dread. Iron armies reaching out their iron talons to victims, inflicting such damage and such suffering on those victims that they would never forget, not for an instant . . .

'When it came to it, they were easily deceived,' Alice said. 'I enlisted two or three of the other women – people I could trust – and between us we concocted various stories that we thought the Nazis would swallow. The discovery of a planned break-out from one hut or another. False papers being prepared somewhere else. At careful intervals I carried these stories to the commandant, and he believed them. He was a stupid man, Karl Koch.

Much of the time he was drunk or gambling, so that made him easy to hoodwink.'

'Didn't he find out you were feeding him false information?'

'Not for a long time. We were very careful not to put anyone in danger with the information we gave him, but we managed to keep attention away from the real plotters.'

'Tell me about the real plotters.' Again, Alice had evoked the people of the stories, so that it was easy to see the little groups of ragged women huddling together in wooden huts, planning and whispering, their thin faces intent and serious.

'They were the ones who really were getting people out to freedom. It was all kept very simple though – mostly prisoners being smuggled out in laundry baskets or disguised as workmen. We didn't build aeroplanes out of matchsticks like the officers in Colditz Castle, or dig tunnels under stoves or dress up as German officers. And not all of the ones who escaped from Buchenwald made it to safety. But some did. Some reached Switzerland or England. Our successes were pitifully few, but the fact that we had successes at all gave us hope. They gave us something to work for.'

'Why didn't you go with them, those people who escaped?'

She took a moment to reply to this. 'Karl Koch and his men watched me,' she said. 'So did the higher-ranking Nazi officials who visited Buchenwald. They used to question me very closely. And twice while I was there Hermann Göering came, although I did not speak to him. But he knew about me – he knew I had been enlisted as a spy. And so I had to play the part of a greedy selfish little gold-digger. As far as the Nazis were concerned, I was Lucretia, you see. Someone prepared to sell her companions for the sake of food and clothes. Once, I remember, I had dinner in the commandant's rooms with Karl Koch and two of Hitler's chief of staff.' She grinned and the mischievous baroness was suddenly and vividly there in the room. 'For all their posturing and pretence at style and at being part of *la belle époque*, the wine was dreadful and the food mediocre. And the company was boring. I remember von Ribbentrop was there that night.'

'I know about him. He killed himself rather than be executed after the war.'

'He did. He was an unpleasant little weasel,' said Alice. 'Nothing more than a jumped-up wine salesman.' For a moment the baroness's arrogance surfaced. 'But I pretended to relish it. I was such a hypocrite, Michael, you can't imagine what a hypocrite I was. But I gave the performances of my life inside Buchenwald and it worked. The Nazis were so delighted with their scheme to use prisoners as spies in return for better conditions – there was even a suggestion that Hitler knew and approved the arrangement, and the SS officers would have climbed mountains and swum oceans to get Hitler's approval. But that meant they all kept very firm tabs on me.'

'Did you get the better food and all the other things?'

'Yes,' she said. 'Yes, there were improvements. And I was permitted to send a letter to my parents in England, and later on to receive two letters from them. That at least gave me news of Deborah, who was living with them by that time – they had taken her and the nurse in, of course, as I had known they would.'

Michael said, 'But in the end the Nazis found out that you were cheating them? That you weren't really spying at all?'

Alice paused for so long that Michael thought she was not going to answer. But finally she said, 'Yes, they found out. And they sent me to another camp.'

'As a punishment?'

'Yes. The camp was in a little Polish town in the middle of swamplands. It had originally been a barrack and there was some kind of abandoned factory there as well, but when I was taken there it had just been enlarged and part of the swamps had been drained. But it was still surrounded by huge stagnant ponds, and it was like a stark lonely world, forgotten by the rest of mankind. It stank of human misery.' She looked across at him. 'It was known as Auschwitz,' she said.

Auschwitz . . . The name hung on the air between them, and Michael felt an icy shiver on the back of his neck. Auschwitz was the deep dark core of all the evil, he knew that, and his mother had known it as well. 'A bad place,' she had said, her eyes unreadable. But when the much-smaller Michael had pressed for stories about this place, she had shaken her head and refused to talk of it. 'It isn't a place to make stories about,' she had said. 'It's one of the world's dark places, and I don't want you to ever know about that kind of darkness, Michael, darling. You and I will only ever make up stories about happy things.'

But the seventeen-year-old Michael knew that Auschwitz was the iron prison of all the nightmares, hemmed in by swamps, surrounded by spiked fences that would tear spitefully into people's flesh if they tried to get out. And once upon a time inside that iron prison . . .

He took a deep breath, and said, 'Is it true that Alraune was born inside Auschwitz?'

This time the silence seemed to descend on them like a thick stifling curtain, and with it came a feeling that somewhere beyond the warm safe house something might be listening, and biding its time . . .

Michael shivered again and waited, and at last, as if she was coming back from a long way away, Alice said softly, 'Yes. Alraune was born inside Auschwitz.'

CHAPTER TWENTY-NINE

If Buchenwald had been hell's outpost, Auschwitz was its deepest cavern, and the minute Alice entered it she knew that all the stories about hellfire were wrong. Hell did not burn: it froze, with a deep, despairing bone-coldness.

It was night when the armed escort drove through the gates, and the camp was shrouded in a pouring violet dusk. Discs of harsh white light from the watch-towers moved constantly to and fro; they shone on the rows of barrack huts and the concrete exercise yards, and then swung round to the east, to silhouette several massively tall chimneys jutting up from a cluster of brick buildings on the camp's far side. Alice stared at these buildings for a moment, and then the searchlights moved again, this time catching the glint of black iron on the ground – parallel lines of railway sleepers. There were several open-topped railway trucks nearby. So Auschwitz had its own private railway line. To bring prisoners in? To take them out?

She got down from the armoured truck, and stood for a moment feeling the place's atmosphere sink its bony fingers into her mind and her heart. For a moment there was nothing in the world save this coldness, and this utter and complete hopelessness. Dreadful. I survived Buchenwald, but I don't think I can survive this. Or can I? How about Deborah and Conrad? Yes, for them, I think can survive it.

She clutched the small bundle of belongings she had been allowed to bring out of Buchenwald – shoes, some threadbare underclothes, that precious letter from her parents telling her Deborah had reached them safely – and as the gates closed behind the truck, the guards took her through the compound, towards one of the barrack huts. The door was unlocked, Alice was pushed unceremoniously inside, and the lock clicked home once more. Shut in. But with what? And with whom?

It was not completely dark in the hut, but only thin threads of light trickled through the cracks in the window-shutters. Alice could make out only vague shapes – narrow beds with people on them, most of them sitting up and looking questioningly towards her. But she barely took this in, because as soon as the door had closed she had had to fight not to retch from the smell. It was like a solid wall, assaulting her whole being – stale human sweat and other human exudences best not identified too precisely. But she stood still, forcing her body not to rebel and waiting for her eyes to adjust to the dimness. Presently she was able to look about her, and she saw that several of the hut's occupants had padded across the floor and were standing quite close to her. They're inspecting me, thought Alice. They're sizing me up.

She was more exhausted than she could ever remember being in her entire life – the journey from Buchenwald had taken over ten hours – but she summoned up her last shreds of energy, and said in German, 'Good evening to you all. I'm sorry about the abrupt entrance. I'm a – a new prisoner.' Hateful word. 'Is there – have you any means of making a light so that I can see you and you can see me?'

There was a pause, and then the thin scrape of a match or perhaps a tinder. Three or four tiny candle flames burned up, and half a dozen or so faces swam through the darkness, lit from below to hollow disembodied life.

'What's your name?' said one, and Alice realized for the first time that they were all women. So at least there was still a semblance of segregation in this place.

'Whoever you are, you must be important to be brought here as a single prisoner,' said a second voice. 'The guards usually bring people in by the dozen.'

'I've been brought here from Buchenwald,' said Alice. 'I don't know why I'm here on my own, though.' She paused, aware of them studying her, trying to decide whether to give them her real name. Would the Buchenwald officials have sent her here as Lucretia von Wolff or as Alice Wilson?

Then the one who had spoken first, said suddenly, 'I know who you are. You're that rich baroness – von Wolff, that's your name. Lucretia von Wolff. You make films – I've seen you on them.'

Well, at least that decision's made for me, thought Alice.

'In that case,' said the voice who had asked where she was from, 'we know all about you. You're a *spy*, Madame von Wolff.' She spat the word out as if it was poison. 'You spied inside Buchenwald for the Nazis – we heard all about you.'

'We have our own ways of hearing what goes on in the other camps,' said a third voice, and there was a murmur of assent, threaded with hostility.

'We have our own ways of dealing with spies, as well.'

Alice flinched at the angry hatred in their voices, and took an instinctive step backwards before remembering that the door was locked.

'Are you here to spy on us?' said a new voice, hard and accusing.

'I'm not here to spy. I never have spied. I was working against the Germans in Buchenwald—'

'Oh yes, of course you were,' said a younger voice sarcastically. 'Don't you know all spies say that? "I did it for my own country . . . I was a double spy, working for Poland, or Czechoslovakia or the Ukraine." That's a load of shit, baroness. You had a very profitable little game going on in Buchenwald – we heard about your cosy dinners with Karl Koch and your sherry parties with von Ribbentrop.'

'And now,' said the first one, 'you're here to spy out our secrets and then go running to the Gestapo with them.'

Fighting to speak calmly, Alice said, 'You've got it all wrong. What can I do – what can I say – to convince you?' But even if she had not been recognized, her instincts were warning her not to disclose her real identity. She might one day be very glad to have Alice Wilson's identity to escape into. 'Truly, I never worked for the Nazis,' she said.

By now the small flames had burned up a little and she could see the hut more clearly. The narrow beds were arranged in rows along both walls, and at one end was a squat iron stove with a metal cup carefully placed on its surface as if some liquid was being warmed. Several of the dimly seen figures seemed to be huddled around the stove, their thin hands held out to it. Alice, trying to take in as much as she could through the sick waves of exhaustion, had the fleeting impression of some kind of organized grouping, as if turns might be taken to sit around the stove for warmth.

'I'm here because I cheated the Gestapo,' she said.

'How? What did you do to cheat?'

The voice was still hard and uncompromising, as if its owner was prepared to dismiss as lies any kind of answer given, but Alice said as levelly as possible, 'I supplied false information about escapes from the camp. Several of us did so – we fooled the commandant and made it possible for others to get out.'

'I say she's lying,' said a woman from the stove, who had not spoken yet. 'Leave her to her own devices. That's what we do with jackals who snoop for the Gestapo, don't we?'

There was another murmur of assent, and they turned away, leaving Alice standing helplessly inside the door. Panic swept in again, this time at the prospect of being an outcast in this place. Shunned by the prisoners, and certainly the focus of the guards' enmity, since they would know what she had done at Buchenwald.

The thought had barely formed when there was the sound of footsteps outside. The hut door was unlocked and the violet dusklight slanted in, showing up the bare floorboards and the sparse furnishings. But even before that happened, the tiny comforting candle-flames had been quenched and the accusing faces had melted into the darkness.

Four men stood in the doorway, all of them in the dark uniform of the Gestapo. The tallest of them stepped across the threshold, his lips thinning into a fastidious line as the smell of unwashed bodies reached him. A thin scar puckered the skin of his face from the cheekbone to the corner of his mouth. Sabre scar, thought Alice, as the searchlights fell across the man's face. The duelling scar that was once a mark of honour among German officers. It gave his mouth a twisted, snarling look, so that just for a moment it was as if a wolf had donned a human mask, and as if the mask had slipped a little.

His eyes rested on her, and then in a terse clipped voice he said, 'Baroness?' It was not quite a question; it was more as if he was identifying her to himself, but Alice lifted her chin challengingly, and said, 'Yes.'

'I am Rudolf Mildner, chief of Gestapo at Kattowicz and head of the political department at Auschwitz. You are to come with us.' He nodded to the men with him, and two of them grabbed Alice's arms, so that she was forced to let go of her small bundle of belongings.

'Where are you taking her?' demanded the woman who had seemed to be the leader of the hut's occupants, and this time there was an unmistakable note of protest in her voice. Alice could see now that she was younger than the others, and that she had the distinctive high cheekbones of an Eastern European.

'She will be punished for her behaviour and her deceit,' said Mildner. 'She is an arrogant bitch who attempted to make fools of the Third Reich.'

'It was not very difficult to do so,' said Alice softly, and this time there was a definite wave of warmth from several of the women.

But Mildner's eyes snapped with fury and he came closer, his thin lips twisting into the wolf-snarl again. 'Tonight, baroness,' he said, 'you will be taught a lesson. It will be a lesson you will not forget, and from it you will learn that those caught trying to deceive the Führer receive no mercy.'

Alice was never to know exactly where in the camp the Gestapo took her that night. Auschwitz was too alien for her to work out its layout, and too big. In any case, the world had shrunk to a hopeless misery where time had ceased to exist or even to matter, and where all paths looked the same.

The months inside Buchenwald had taught her that to struggle against the SS or the Gestapo was useless, but she did struggle, although it was a hopeless sobbing struggle and she knew she would not escape.

Mildner's men took her to a low brick building and pushed her into a long room that looked as if it might be some kind of officers' mess. There were tables and chairs, and the semblance of a bar at one end with drinks and glasses set out. The curtains were drawn against the night, and an iron stove stood in one corner, roaring its iron-smelling heat into the room. Four Gestapo officers were seated at a table; they turned as Alice was pushed through the door, inspecting her with their eyes.

With a fair assumption of anger, she said to Mildner, 'Why have you brought me here?'

He gave the smile that only lifted half of his mouth. 'I told you that you were to be taught a lesson, baroness,' he said. 'And so you are. For my men it will be a very pleasurable lesson.' He paused, and two of the men laughed in a horrid jeering way. Alice hated them.

And then a figure seated in one of the deep, high-backed chairs stood up and walked towards her. The light from the iron stove fell across his face, and there was a moment when one eye caught the red glow, and seemed to swell and to grow to monstrous proportions. Alice stared at him, a wholly different horror rushing at her.

Leo Dreyer. Leo Dreyer here in Auschwitz, as cool and as in command as ever. He was again wearing a monocle, the black silk string lying across his face like a sleeping insect, and even through her fear Alice could feel the authority that radiated from him.

'So,' he said, softly, 'you thought you would escape the realities of Buchenwald by making that devil's bargain with the fool Karl Koch, did you, baroness?'

'It took you a long time to realize how much of a fool he was,' retorted Alice.

'It does not matter. He is being suitably dealt with,' said Dreyer. 'You were more the fool to think you could double-cross us. But you, also, will be dealt with.'

'How, precisely? And what is your idea of suitable? I ask out of a sense of involvement rather than vulgar curiosity,' said Alice, and thought: well, that came out more or less all right, although there was a hint of a tremor towards the end. Damn.

If Dreyer had heard the tremor he gave no sign. He said, 'Tonight, my dear, you are going to pay for your naïve arrogance at Buchenwald. Tonight Mildner's men are going to draw lots for you.'

At these words the men moved forwards, and while two of them held her arms behind her back, two more undressed her. They took their time, laughing when she aimed a kick at them, laying each item of clothing on a chair, considering her body at every stage.

'A bit too thin for my taste,' said one of them, and the other said, dismissively, 'But that's the camps. They always look half-starved.'

They carried her to a long deep sofa, and one of them stood guard while the others grouped themselves around the table and took it in turns to cut a pack of playing cards set out by the youngest of the officers.

'Highest to go first,' said one of them, glancing at Mildner, who nodded carelessly. The men paused to refill their glasses: Alice thought they were drinking schnapps or perhaps kümmel. Some of them were clearly becoming a bit intoxicated, but none of them seemed incapable. Neither Dreyer nor Mildner took part in the card-cutting, and when it was done Mildner moved detachedly to the door, as if to stand guard, but Leo Dreyer remained where he was, one arm resting lightly on the high narrow mantel over the stove.

'Try not to impregnate the bitch,' he said offhandedly, and for the first time Alice saw a flicker of embarrassment on some of the faces and understood that while most of them felt no particular awkwardness or guilt about raping this traitor, they were uncomfortable at the idea of doing it in front of one another.

During the hour that followed Leo Dreyer scarcely took his eyes from Alice. He stood facing the deep old sofa, one hand leaning negligently on the high mantel over the stove, unobtrusively sipping his drink – except that there could never be anything in the least unobtrusive about him. Once he gestured to the young officer to refill his glass, but other than this he hardly moved. The light from the stove washed over him, and Alice knew that when the worst of tonight's memories had faded a little (and please God they would fade), this was the image that would have burned itself indelibly into her mind. Leo Dreyer standing watching her, the hideously magnified eye behind the monocle washed to living fire by the stove's light.

But what you don't know, you vicious cruel creature, she said to this hateful image, is that after you threw me out of your house I lived among Vienna's back streets and alleyways, and I survived by selling my body. And if I could cope then with being fucked by half a dozen men in one night, I can cope with it now.

The small private obscenity helped to steady her, and it brought the defiance flooding back. I can't escape this, but I can try to disconcert these animals. How? Well, perhaps by reminding them who I am and what I have been. Leo Dreyer knew the truth about her, but for reasons Alice had not yet fathomed, he seemed to be letting the legend stand. So to these German officers she was still the infamous baroness – the decadent aristocrat whose lovers were said to be legion, and whose private entertainments were whispered to be Bacchanalian in the extreme. Lucretia von Wolff, rumoured to have committed every sin in the calendar, and whose sexual proclivities had been unfavourably compared to those of Messalina . . .

As the first man approached her, Alice smiled at him and held out her arms.

The small unexpected act did not stop them, of course – Alice had known it would not – but it certainly gave them pause. They glanced furtively at one another as if each of them needed to check his colleagues' reactions before doing anything on his own account, and this brought Alice a small shred of courage and self-esteem. You see? she said silently to Leo Dreyer. You thought I would be beaten and humiliated but I'm neither of those things and I never will be!

Even so, what followed was an appalling ordeal. The men were all relatively clean, and most of them had clearly bathed or showered in the last forty-eight hours – Alice knew from those long-ago black days that this was something for which to be grateful. But the enforced and brutal intimacy inflicted a mental uncleanness on her mind that she feared might never wash away.

Only one of the men displayed any degree of sensitivity, and that was the very young officer who had poured out drinks. He was fourth in line, and as he approached her he avoided meeting her eyes as if he found the whole business shameful. But his excitement was stronger and more frenzied than the others, and when he finally shuddered in climax Alice cried out in pain from the uncontrolled thrusting. As he withdrew he put out his hand to touch her face as if in apology, and their eyes met. But then he seemed to recollect his surroundings and he got up quickly, turning away, embarrassedly fastening his trousers.

The lower half of her body felt as if it was one massive bruise, and she thought she was bleeding as well, although it was impossible to be sure because the sofa on which she was lying was a wet squalid mess from the men. 'Try not to impregnate the bitch,' Leo Dreyer had said, and most of them had withdrawn before reaching orgasm. One – a heavy, fat-jowled man – faltered after a time, and Alice felt him slide flaccidly out of her. But he reached a hand down, guiltily and furtively, and fumbled frantically between his legs until there was the sudden wash of hot stickiness on her stomach. A wave of nausea engulfed her. Dreadful! This man is a Nazi murderer – he probably took part in the massacre of *Kristallnacht* – and he's masturbating on to me!

She had expected Mildner to take his turn, but he did not; he remained near the door, the wolf-snarl strongly evident, and when the men had all finished, he rapped out a terse order and went out with them, closing the door behind him.

Leaving Alice alone with Leo Dreyer.

She had thought he had not been physically aroused by the rape, and she had thought that like Mildner he had obtained his satisfaction simply by watching.

But he walked slowly to the sofa, and looked down at her, and said, 'And now it is my turn, baroness.'

The pain was threatening to swamp Alice's whole body by now, but from out of its clawing depths, she said, 'Why do you still call me that? Why did you maintain that identity with Mildner and the others?'

'Because tonight I am settling an account with the arrogant creature who double-crossed the Führer,' said Dreyer. 'It was Lucretia von Wolff who played her arrogant game inside Buchenwald so tonight it is Lucretia von Wolff I am punishing.' As he unbuttoned his trousers and lowered himself on to her, Alice realized that far from being unaroused, either the sight of his officers raping her or his own burning hatred – or perhaps both of these – had brought him to an almost unbearable pitch of hungering excitement. And that he was about to slake that hunger.

* * *

He was far more brutal than the others had been, and he was vicious and pitiless.

Alice, already in more pain than she could have believed possible, finally slid into a semi-conscious state, where she was no longer fully aware of her surroundings but where the pain was still a monstrous black and crimson swelling tide hammering with rhythmic insistence against her body. On and on and on, until you wanted to die . . . On and on and on, until at last you knew you were dying, and you welcomed it, because once dead you would feel nothing . . .

And then swimming back to the surface for a moment and to realization again – oh God, yes, I'm in this dreadful place, and I'm being raped . . . Oh, for pity's sake, reach your horrid climax – for the love of all the saints in the world, just *come* and let me fall back down into this uncaring darkness . . .

There was a final unbelievable wrench of agony, and she heard herself cry out, and then the darkness closed over her.

A slightly harsh, but vaguely familiar voice, somewhere beyond the darkness, said, 'I think she's coming round now,' and another voice, also vaguely recognizable, said, 'If only we had a drop of brandy – or proper bandages.'

'No, she's all right. She'll recover. She's a very tough lady.'

Alice opened her eyes to the thick-smelling atmosphere of the hut, and the concerned faces of the women who, a few hours earlier, had denounced her as a spy. She was lying on a narrow bed; two of the women were sponging her face, and there was a thick comforting pad of something between her thighs. Someone had wrapped blankets around her – they were thin and not very clean and the surface was scratchy, but Alice did not care.

'You're still bleeding a bit,' said the woman with the slanting cheekbones. 'But we've cleaned you up as well as we can, and we don't think you're in any danger.'

Alice sat up and her head swam. She started to ask a question, and then said, 'I'm sorry, but I think I'm going to be sick—' and at once the woman put a tin basin under her mouth.

'Thank you,' gasped Alice when the spasms had stopped. 'I'm sorry – this is disgusting for you.'

'Not in the least. My father was a doctor, and my brother was training with him. If the Nazis had not come to my village I would have studied medicine as well. My name is Ilena,' said the woman. 'Do we call you baroness, or my lady, or what?'

And again there was that flare of warning that came not from within but from without. Don't give away any more than you have to. On the crest of this flare, Alice said, 'Lucretia. Just Lu, if you like. It's quicker.'

'And it doesn't have the Borgia ring to it,' said Ilena, and Alice caught the dry irony of this, and suddenly liked Ilena very much.

'We've managed to brew some coffee,' said one of the others, carefully carrying a tin cup from the stove. 'It isn't very good, but it's hot.'

Alice said, gratefully, 'I don't care what it is. Thank you.' She sipped the coffee gratefully, and then said, 'You're being very kind to me.'

'We look after our own,' said Ilena, and the others nodded.

CHAPTER THIRTY

We look after our own . . .

With the women's help Alice recovered from the physical effects of the rape, and was pulled down into the grinding routine of Auschwitz.

'Terrible,' Ilena said. 'Inhuman. When the history of these years is written, it will be Auschwitz that will bear most of the shame.'

Alice stored the few belongings she had been able to bring with her beneath the narrow bed in the hut which was already becoming familiar. This, then, was her home. No worse than Buchenwald, really. I shall bear it.

Her bed was directly beneath one of the windows, and each night the outside shutters were firmly fastened, keeping the prisoners in, and keeping the world out.

But the shutters over Alice's bed had a chink on to that lost world. There was a small split at one corner where the wood had warped slightly, and through this Alice could see a little part of the night sky. She could watch the moon wane and become a thin paring of silver, and she could see it swell and grow plump again. Sometimes its light seemed to be unrolling a silver path along which you could walk freely, if only you knew how to reach it. One day I will reach it though.

As the weeks slid past, and as she watched the moon's inexorable path, she could think how odd it was that even in this enlightened century, and even in this soulless place, the moon and its phases still ruled a female's blood. And that there were times when it did not rule it . . . How many days was it now since that night with Dreyer and the other men? It was difficult to keep track of time in here. But how many weeks had it been?

Two moons went by with no response from her body. Many explanations for that, though. The poor diet in here, the desolation. Oh, please let it just be that. And keep remembering what Dreyer said to those men. 'Try not to impregnate the bitch,' he had said, his eye on fire from the stove's light. 'Try not to impregnate . . .'

The third moon brought a bout of sickness – several bouts of sickness, and always in the early morning – and also a perceptible swelling and tenderness of her breasts.

'We'll get you through it, Lu,' said Ilena, when Alice finally asked for help. 'I told you, we look after our own in here.'

'The doctors—'

But Ilena made a face expressive of disgust and loathing at mention of Auschwitz's doctors. Everyone knew about them, she said derisively, and everyone gave them as wide a berth as possible. You did not have to be in here very long to learn about the infirmary block, and the experiments that were carried out there. The sterilization of men and women. The endurance tests where prisoners were force-fed with salt water and immersed in ice-barrels for six and eight hours at a stretch, in order to simulate conditions that German pilots might have to face in battle.

Alice asked hesitantly whether someone – the guards? – might not insist that she receive some kind of medical care. Would they perhaps even enforce an abortion? You could not hide a pregnancy, said Alice, and Ilena laughed.

'We can hide anything if we plan it carefully enough. But we do not need to do so. No one will care if you are pregnant. Children are born here sometimes.'

Alice thought she would sooner trust Ilena's half-knowledge of medicine, and the collective knowledge of the other women, several of whom had had children of their own, than trust the doctors in Auschwitz's infirmary blocks. She thought, and hated herself for thinking, that hampered by pregnancy and later by a baby she would have no chance of escaping. But this war could not go on for ever. Auschwitz could not go on for ever. Yes, but what if the Nazis won the war? What then?

The birth, when it came, came at night and was far worse than she had expected. The months of unremitting toil in the camp, and the sparse, poor-quality food, had taken their toll. There were hours and hours of grinding agony, and alongside the physical pain was the mental anguish of the child's conception. I will never be able to look on this child with any love, thought Alice. And even if it survives, it will never forgive me for bringing it into this dark joyless place.

Some of the women had managed to secrete a little store of things for the birth. A few teaspoons of brandy, stolen from one of the guards; cotton wool and antiseptic taken from the infirmary during a cleaning session; a bundle of clean cotton rags. Deborah had been born in a Viennese nursing home with every possible luxury to hand, and a distinguished surgeon in attendance. Conrad had shipped in flowers by the cartload and champagne by the bucket, and later he had written that marvellous music for his daughter – *Deborah's Song* . . . And now Deborah's half-brother or sister would be born on a pile of straw and rags, with no one except a clutch of women in attendance. But this child had been conceived in fear and pain, and now it was being born into a hating world.

When finally it lay between her thighs, Alice could feel, even before she saw it, that it was small and shrivelled.

'But alive,' said Ilena. 'Breathing well.'

They wrapped the child in a square of blanket, and then Alice felt the small flailing hand against her breasts, and saw the little mouth opening and closing like a bird's beak.

'You have hardly any milk,' said Ilena presently.

'That was to be expected.' To Alice's horror the thought formed that if the child were to die she would be free to plan an escape, and there would be nothing to remind her of what Leo Dreyer and those others had done to her that night. There was a brief and rather terrible glimpse of herself watching the child grow up, searching its features in the years ahead, praying that it would not resemble the features of the man who had stood by the stove's glow, watching her being raped. And then had raped her himself . . .

And then the child let out a thin mewling cry, and something of the old defiance stirred. Alice was suddenly aware of a fierce protectiveness. She would force this child to survive, she would see it as a symbol of hope. Forgive me, little one, I didn't mean it about letting you die.

But her breasts were empty and barren, and the tiny daily allowance of milk for the hut would not be anything like sufficient for such a weakling. Alice looked at Ilena, who was still seated on the edge of the bed.

'Help me,' she said. 'There must be something—'

Ilena said slowly, 'I think there is one thing you could do. Something I have seen animals do in my village. Not pleasant, but an immediate and immense form of nourishment – it would mean you could feed the child properly. My grandmother used to point it out to us when animals were born. You see how Nature always provides, she used to say.'

Alice stared at her for a moment, and then quite suddenly her own country upbringing asserted itself, and she understood. Nature provides.

After a moment she reached down between her thighs, feeling in the bloodied straw that Ilena had spread on the bed. Almost at once her hand closed about the still-warm afterbirth.

The child would live, even inside a place such as this. Alice would make very sure of it.

* * *

'I don't know it all,' said Michael, seated opposite to Fran in Trixie's kitchen, the three-quarters-empty wine bottle still between them. 'That's mostly because I don't think she wanted to tell it all. But over the years I managed to fill in a good many of the gaps. One of the things I do know, though, is that Alraune was born in Auschwitz and that the birth was the result of Lucretia being raped by several Gestapo officers.'

'Dear God,' said Fran softly, and without thinking put out a hand to him. His hand closed about her fingers, and at once something passed between them. Like an electrical spark, thought Fran. Or like being in the shower when the water suddenly catches a glint of sunshine so that for a couple of seconds you stand inside a rainbow. She withdrew her hand, but the brightness of that moment stayed on the air.

The dishes were stacked in the sink: Fran supposed they would get washed up at some stage, but for the moment there were more important things to consider. Alraune's photograph was on the table where they had left it and she put out a tentative hand to touch the glass covering it. 'Michael, that *is* Alraune, isn't it? I mean – there isn't likely to be a mistake? The name written on someone else's photo by mistake or anything like that?'

'No. It's unquestionably Alraune.' He had taken an apple from the dish of fruit Fran had put on the table, and was quartering it rather abstractedly. Fran waited and after a moment he said, 'Alraune was smuggled out of Auschwitz some time during 1943 or 1944. Lucretia fixed that, although I'm not sure how, and after the war she brought Alraune back to England. Later on Alraune got married, although it wasn't a very happy marriage.'

Francesca glanced at him, but his eyes had the shuttered look again, so with the air of one concentrating on the nuts and bolts of the situation, she said, 'If Alraune lived in Austria Trixie could have found the photograph this summer. She used to go on walking holidays in the long summer holidays, and this year she went to the Austrian Tyrol.'

Trixie had in fact suggested that Fran went along with her. 'Good fresh air and lots of brisk, hearty exercise, that's what you want. It'll stop you brooding and moping over that rat, Marcus,' she had said, but Fran had still been in the stage of wanting to brood and mope, and the thought of tramping briskly and heartily all round Austria in Trixie's undiluted company had been so daunting that she had stayed at home.

Michael said, 'Where exactly did Trixie go, d'you know?'

'Not in any detail. But when she got back she talked about staying for a week or two in a place called Klosterneuberg. It's one of those tiny villages in the Vienna Woods, apparently. There's a minature monastery and vines are hung over the doors of inns for the wine festivals, and all the villagers get sloshed on the new harvest. Trixie got to know some of the locals while she was there – she taught modern languages so her German was fluent. She mentioned being invited to some of the local houses for supper.'

'You think she might have come across the photograph then?'

'I think it's more likely that it came from a bookshop somewhere. Trixie liked foraging in second-hand bookshops – she used to look for stuff that might be useful as translation projects for some of her classes. Boxes of old books and leaflets, or even theatre programmes and playscripts – something a bit out of the normal run of textbooks. She liked old prints and maps as well – she sometimes bought those jumbled-up boxes of stuff at sales on the grounds that ninety-nine per cent would be rubbish, but that there was always that unpredictable one per cent.'

'The wild card,' said Michael thoughtfully.

'Yes. Alraune's photograph might have been tucked into one of those boxes – or perhaps in a silver frame that was being sold.' Francesca looked at the photo again. 'It's a face that stays with you, isn't it? And juxtaposed with the name—'

'Would the name have meant anything to Trixie?'

'It might have done. She might have known about the original book. She might even have chosen her thesis subject because of that photograph,' said Fran. 'Put all the elements together, and you've got quite a good mix. The whole psychology of what happened at Ashwood Studios – Lucretia and Alraune, and the war and Ewers' book—' And the reasons for Lucretia killing two men, said her mind. Oh God, no, I can't think about that one, not yet.

Michael said, 'You didn't find anything else relating to Lucretia among Trixie's things?'

'No.' Fran drained her wine glass and set it down. 'But I didn't actually open envelopes or read letters. This was just in a pack of old photographs – it didn't seem especially private.' She hesitated and then said, 'Michael – earlier tonight you said that after Alraune came to England there was a marriage.'

'Yes, but it was a very unhappy marriage,' said Michael. 'I lived with Alraune until I was eight.'

Francesca looked at him. 'Alraune was your mother,' she said carefully. 'That's right, isn't it? Lucretia von Wolff was your grandmother, and Alraune was her daughter. So Alraune must have been your mother.'

For a moment she thought he was not going to answer and the silence stretched out and threatened to become embarrassing.

Then he reached for his jacket, which was on the back of the chair, took out his wallet, and opened it to show Fran a small, and quite old, photograph tucked into the front. A man of about twenty-eight, and a woman a little younger. The woman had Michael's eyes, and she looked as if she was trying not to laugh while the photograph was taken. Her dark hair was slightly windblown, and she was leaning happily against the man who had his arm around her shoulders.

Fran stared at the photograph, and then looked back at Michael. 'But that's—'

Michael said very quietly, 'It's a photograph of Alraune. But Alraune wasn't Lucretia's daughter, Francesca. Alraune was Lucretia's son. Alraune was my father.'

*

'Arranging for the baby to be baptized as Alraune was Leo Dreyer's cruellest jibe,' Alice had said on the night she told Michael about Auschwitz. 'I hadn't especially thought about baptism or any kind of christening – I was too caught up with making sure the baby survived and that I survived with it.'

Michael registered that she referred to the child as 'it'.

'But a week or so after the birth, one of the camp commandants came into our hut, and took the child away to be baptized. There was some diatribe about Jews with the order, of course – they were still trying to maintain the myth that I was Jewish at that time, and one of the subtler tortures they had devised around then was to force Christian baptism on all new-born Jewish children. To a real Jew that would have been torment, of course. But I had no feelings about it.'

'So the baby was given Christian baptism.'

'Yes. And on Leo Dreyer's instructions – he was Colonel Dreyer by that time – the name given was Alraune.'

There was no need for Michael to suddenly shiver and to glance uneasily over his shoulder to the partly open door, but he could not help it. At once, Alice said, 'It's perfectly all right, Michael, you're completely safe here.'

'I know. It's OK. Go on about – about him.'

About Alraune, said his mind. Alraune. *Mandragora officinarum*. The strange plant called by the Arabs 'Satan's Apple' considered by the ancients to be a soporofic, but also to excite delirium and madness. Anathema to demons, said to shriek when uprooted. But attributed with aphrodisiacal qualities. When he was fourteen Michael had looked up the word *alraune* in the local library, and although he had not understood all the references, he had understood enough. At fourteen he had certainly understood about aphrodisiacs.

'I loathed the name, of course,' said Alice. 'I knew quite well it was Dreyer's way of branding the baby – because of the film and because of the stigma attached to the name. Alraune, the evil soulless child born from a bizarre sexual experiment . . . But when they gave me the birth certificate I just shrugged and looked bored.'

'Lucretia's shrug.'

'Yes, I was always Lucretia inside Auschwitz. There was no reason to think the birth certificate was anything other than a properly registered document, and that was quite important. Officialdom ruled in Germany: if you didn't have the right papers you couldn't work or find anywhere to live or travel. So I thought the name would have to stay until I could reach England and have it legally changed. But I called him Alan – I thought it was sufficiently anonymous.'

'In Pedlar's Yard he was known to most people as Al.'

'Al.' She appeared to consider it. 'It suggests a completely new persona, doesn't it? Tougher and more masculine.'

'Yes.' A pause. 'My mother knew who he was, didn't she? She knew about Auschwitz.'

'From what you've told me about her I think she must have known quite a lot. I used to talk to him about the Vienna years when he was very small – about meeting Conrad – the serving girl and the rich aristocrat. I tried to make it into a fairy-story for him.'

'My mother knew all that. She told it to me as a fairy-story. But not Auschwitz.'

'I never talked to Alraune about Auschwitz,' said Alice. 'But he lived there until he was almost four, and he would have had memories.'

'I think my mother knew about Auschwitz, though. But she used to say there were dark places in the world, and that we would only ever make stories about the good places. The places full of light.'

'When you tell me things like that about her, I regret very much that I didn't know her,' said Alice, rather sadly.

'I wish you had known her. She was a bit like you – I don't mean to look at. But when she talked – she could make you remember that there might be really good things waiting in life ahead of you. She could make you forget the bad things in life.'

'That's a very good quality to have,' said Alice at once. 'I think she's passed it on to you.'

'Do you? She hadn't got it full-pelt, turbo-charged, like you have. But it was there.' A pause. 'D'you suppose that's why he married her?'

'Because she reminded him of me?'

'Yes.'

'It's possible. I'm sorry he made her so unhappy, though. I'm sorry she died like that – and I'm more sorry you had to be there when it all happened.'

'She hated him in the end. I hated him as well. The brutality—'

Speaking very slowly, almost as if she might be fighting some inner battle, Alice said, 'But you should try to forgive some of what he did, Michael. He was not entirely to blame.'

CHAPTER THIRTY-ONE

The cruel promise of spring was stirring beyond Auschwitz's grim gates, and somehow Alraune had survived those first few months.

But it was as if there was a sullen core of smouldering hatred inside him, and there were times during those months after his birth when the dark eyes seemed to rest on Alice with unchild-like anger. And were they Leo Dreyer's eyes? Or were they perhaps the eyes of the young officer who had made that faint gesture of apology? There would be a faint far-off comfort to be derived if the young officer could be his father, but could that blue-eyed Saxon have sired this black-visaged scrap of humanity? Please God, don't let him be Dreyer's son; please don't let him grow up to resemble the man I loathe and fear most in all the world!

Alraune lived and slept in the hut with the women, and his playground was the recreation yard, where the prisoners could exercise at set times each evening, and where the roll-call took place each morning. His clothes were whatever the women could fashion for him out of odds and ends of their own, and his toys were made from fragments of wood – carved figures or blocks which they stained in different colours with the dregs of the tasteless coffee they drank.

When the Polish women in one of the other huts received food parcels, they smuggled little gifts of food out for him. 'A tin of meat for the baby,' they said. 'And a jar of meat essence – a spoonful to be dissolved in hot water – very nourishing.' Very occasionally there would be a heart-breakingly tiny pot of jam. 'Sweet,' they said, nodding and smiling. 'The little ones like to eat the sweet.'

One of the younger girls who had been brought to Auschwitz shortly after Alice was mourning the loss of a baby brother who had died in the *Kristallnacht* massacres. Her brother would have been the same age as Alraune, she said, and she liked to spend time with him, singing to him the songs she would never now sing to her brother, and telling him the stories her brother would never now hear. Alice could have wept over the pity of that, except . . .

'Every time I look at him,' she said to Ilena, 'I see the faces of the men who raped me that night. Most of all I see Leo Dreyer's face.'

'But Alraune is half yours, no matter who the father was,' said Ilena. 'He has half your qualities – perhaps more than half. You'll feel differently when he's older – when you've grown away from what they did to you that night.'

Alice did not think she would ever feel differently and she was not sure if she would ever grow away from that night, but she did not say so.

The seasons wheeled round once more – and then twice more. The war was still going on somewhere beyond the bleak confines of Auschwitz – occasionally there was news of it, although it was impossible to know how accurate that news was. But certainly battles were fought in the skies over Germany and over England, and certainly ships were destroyed in the oceans, and houses and cities were blown up and men and women made homeless. In Auschwitz the inmates watched the greasy pall of smoke issuing from the tall brick chimneys of the crematoria block, and prayed to their various gods not to be selected for the gas chambers.

But even in such a dark hopeless place there were occasional patches of light. Music was one of these patches. Incredibly, there was music in the camp – small, infrequent concerts given by a group of musicians, most of them members of a Polish radio orchestra, arrested while actually performing and pressed into bizarre service by the camp commandants.

Alice was usually among the prisoners allowed to attend the ramshackle concerts, and it brought a deep twisting agony to hear music that Conrad had once played. But after the third or fourth time, she managed to speak to one of the musicians – a violinist. The music community had always been a tightly-knit one, and it was just possible that she might pick up news of Conrad. She complimented the violinist on his performance, and asked if orchestras such as this one were being formed in the other camps. In Dachau for instance?

The violinist was sympathetic but not very knowledgeable. Certainly there were other small orchestras, he said; this was generally known, and there might well be just such a one in Dachau – who knew? The Nazis liked to be thought of as people of culture, people who enjoyed such things as good music. This was said as if the words were poison which must be spat out as quickly as possible.

Alice asked the man if he had ever known the composer Conrad Kline. The Gestapo had taken him to Dachau.

The violinist had not known Herr Kline, but had heard him play once in Vienna – ah, a privilege that had been! A maestro indeed! He had not heard what might have happened to Herr Kline, but the baroness should keep in mind that the musicians in the camps were not being so harshly treated as some other inmates.

'So that they can play as we do here,' he said. 'He has a good chance of surviving.'

Alice was heartened by the thought that Conrad might have his beloved music around him. (And one day, my dear love, we will dance together in that Viennese ballroom again, and I will be wearing a Parisian gown and perfume from Mme Chanel, and you will have evening clothes from Savile Row . . .) She had been soothed, as well, by the lyrical Mozart concerto that had formed the afternoon's programme, but when she thanked the man for playing so beautifully, he only said, 'If we don't play well, we go to the gas.'

And then in the spring of 1943 a new chief physician came to Auschwitz.

The man whom some called the Angel of Death, and whom others called the Nazi Mystic. Dr Josef Mengele.

A web of sinister speculation seemed to surround Mengele almost within hours of his arrival. There were whispers about the work he was here to perform – rumours of experiments with twins or dwarfs; whispers of tests to establish the boundaries of human endurance, and grisly procedures aimed at observing the results of bone transplant and nerve regeneration.

Ilena, with her medical background, was assigned to work in one of Mengele's clinics. 'I had been naïve enough to think I might spike his guns,' she said to Alice and the others after the first few days. 'I had visions of stealing morphine and secretly administering it to the victims. After all these months in this place, I really thought that might be possible, can you believe that!'

'Isn't it possible?'

'Everything is locked and guarded,' said Ilena bitterly. 'You couldn't smuggle so much as a needle out of the place.'

'For God's sake don't put yourself at risk,' said Alice, frightened.

'I won't,' said Ilena with her slanting smile. 'One day, Lu, we're going to walk out of here – perhaps when the Russians liberate us, or the British or the Americans. Perhaps we shall even find a way of escape for ourselves before that. But walk out we will, Lu. All of us. And you and I will go out together, arm in arm.'

Somehow, some day, they would walk out, because somehow they would survive.

Ilena had been working in the medical block for several weeks when she sought out Alice one night after the meagre bread-and-margarine supper. Her face was white and pinched, and she said, without preamble, 'If they suspect I'm telling you this, Lu, they'll probably hang me but I can't help that.'

'Telling me what?'

'Mengele has noticed Alraune. You know how Alraune likes to sit in the recreation yard in the afternoons. Well, Mengele has noticed him.' She paused and then said very gently, 'I think they have earmarked him for one of their experiments.'

The iron stove was burning in its corner – there was the usual tin cup of water heating on it, and there was the warm scent of hot metal from the stove's interior. But Alice felt as if an icy hand was closing around her heart. One of their experiments. One of their grim inhuman explorations into the human body or the human mind . . .

'How do you know?'

'They have a schedule of their week's work pinned on a board inside the main administration room in the medical block,' said Ilena. 'Names and numbers of prisoners to be brought in, and who is to be seen by whom. I keep a close eye on that, of course, in case any of our own people are on it. And then this morning—'

'Alraune's name was there,' said Alice in a whisper. 'That's what you mean, isn't it? Oh God.'

'Yes. One of the annexes – Annexe VI. Dr Josef Mengele's patient.'

'When?' said Alice after a moment. 'I mean – was there a date?'

'Wednesday. The day after tomorrow.'

The day after tomorrow. So soon, thought Alice in panic. Less than two days. That's all the time I've got to find a way to save him. 'What kind of experiments are they doing in that annexe?' she said. 'Ilena, please tell me.'

'Several different ones. But Mengele's main interest at the moment,' said Ilena unhappily, 'is to pinpoint the breaking point in the human mind – to understand precisely how much pain and how much fear a man can endure before his mind splinters. They are trying to establish if pain or fear is the dominant factor – and that means applying both to their victims, and then observing the results.'

'We could hide him,' said the Russian girl some time during the night. 'Some of the others have done that with children. Hidden them under clothing.'

'But they're always caught,' said Alice.

'And where could we hide him?' said Ilena, with a swift angry gesture around the bare wooden floors of the hut and the narrow bunk beds.

Alice was dizzy with exhaustion and fear, but she was managing to force her mind to concentrate because there must be a way out of this. The women had not even tried to sleep; they had talked for hours, sitting up in their narrow beds, several of them grouped around the iron stove for warmth and comfort, all of them trying to think of a way to save Alraune from Mengele.

'What about the SS jeeps?' asked one of the older women hesitantly. 'Could the two of you get into the boot of one? You might even be taken out through the gates without them realizing. I know it's been tried, but—'

'The guards are very aware of that trick,' said the Russian girl. 'They search every inch of every vehicle that goes in and out of here. Lu and Alraune would be found and shot.'

'Then,' said Alice, 'it looks as if all I can do is take him out of here now – tonight – and go on the wire.' She felt the shiver go through them at this. 'On the wire' meant, quite simply, walking up to the electric fence surrounding the camp and trusting to God or the devil that you could get through it before the guards saw and fired. Even if the guards, by some fluke, did not see you, you ran the risk of being electrocuted by the wire itself. But there was still that tiny chance of success that had driven a few prisoners to try it.

'Impossible,' said Ilena. 'I'd tie you up before I let that happen.'

'I know we can't actually hide Alraune,' said one of the women, speaking slowly as if she was examining each word before letting it go. 'But is there any way we could confuse the guards – and Mengele's people – by moving him around?'

'From hut to hut?' asked Alice.

'From hut to kitchens, from kitchens to laundry, wherever we can find a corner that might go unchecked for an hour or two,' said the woman. She was one of the quieter occupants of the hut, but when she did speak she was always listened to with respect. She was a little older than most of them; she seldom talked about herself, other than to say rather offhandedly that she had been a teacher. She said, 'Auschwitz is so huge it might be days – weeks, even – before he was found.'

'But they would find him in the end. And then they would certainly hang Lu,' said one of the other women. 'I don't think it would work for more than a few days.'

'But a few days might be all that's needed. And if we could keep one step ahead of the Gestapo—'

'To what purpose?'

'I don't know exactly. But it would gain us time, and in that time there might come some opportunity to get him safely out.'

'The Polish lot would help us to hide him for some of the time,' said someone from the stove.

'Yes, they would, *and* their hut has that bit of a space where the roof slopes upwards,' said the Russian girl eagerly.

'And some of the Poles work in the laundry – they might be able to smuggle him in for a while, inside a linen basket or something—'

'Can we trust the Poles? There aren't any spies in their hut, are there?'

'I don't think so. Yes, I believe we could trust them.'

I don't think I can bear this, thought Alice, listening to them. I don't think I can bear the thought of a child – my own child, never mind how he was conceived – being shunted around this appalling place to avoid being the subject of some grotesque experiment that might maim him physically or mentally . . .

'We'd be questioned,' said Ilena. 'About where he was.'

'Interrogation,' said a very young girl, shuddering and glancing uneasily towards the door. 'It'd be awfully dangerous.'

But several of the women had turned to look at the corner of Alice's bed, where Alraune was asleep. The dark hair fell forward over his forehead, and there was a sheen of moisture on his eyelids. Alice felt again that stir of deep protectiveness.

'We'd just say he had disappeared – that he had wandered off. As somebody said – oh, it was you, wasn't it, Bozena? – Auschwitz is so big he could be lost for days.'

'Yes, we could say that.' They seized on this suggestion gratefully. 'We could be very convincing and we might get away with it.'

'Lu, you'd have to be the most convincing of us all – you'd have to be distraught. But you could do that, couldn't you? You acted in films and you could do it?'

'Yes, I could,' said Alice.

'The rest of us will pretend we're rather glad Alraune's gone – we'll let them believe he's been a nuisance, getting in our way, having to be looked after and fed, keeping us awake by crying—'

The Russian girl said, 'It would be the most terrific gamble, but if we kept our heads and our nerve we might get away with it,' and at once Alice's mind snapped to attention, and she thought: a gamble! All a question of keeping your head! I know better than anyone about taking gambles, about keeping your head!

The tiredness sloughed away from her, and she sat up straighter. 'I think it might work,' she said. 'But only if you are all prepared to risk the danger – the questioning. If even one of you is unhappy or fearful, I won't attempt it.'

'We're all prepared to risk it,' said several voices, and the rest nodded.

'We're all frightened, of course,' said one of them. 'Personally I'm absolutely terrified – but it's unthinkable that Mengele should make use of a child in his experiments. I'll do whatever's needed along with the rest of you.'

Alice was fighting not to cry. She thought: if I live to be a hundred – if worlds end and the stars falter in their courses – I will never again know friends as good and as true as these women. These remarkable women who have become closer than sisters to me, and who are prepared to lie and to risk their lives to protect Alraune.

The others were already moving ahead, discussing the practicalities. The Russian girl was concerned about Alraune being frightened. 'He might give the game away without realizing it.'

'Not if Lu tells him it's a new game—'

'A version of hide-and-seek—?'

'We could all tell him that; we could pretend it's something we're all playing.'

'When do we do it?'

'Tonight,' said Ilena, looking at Alice. 'We can't delay.'

'But what do we do first—?'

'I'll creep out to the Polish hut now,' volunteered the Russian girl. 'I can dodge the searchlights and the guards won't see me.'

The huts were hardly ever locked any longer, so that the guards could make surprise visits, but patrolling parties moved around the camp all night. The trick was to dodge them and also the searchlights that constantly swept the darkness.

'It'll be quite dangerous,' said Alice uncertainly. 'Maria, let me go.'

'No, I must go first to explain it to them,' said Maria. 'Their English isn't very good, and I've got a smattering of Polish,' said Maria. 'Enough to make them understand that we want them to keep Alraune until tomorrow at any rate. That space over their hut is more than big enough— you stay here, Lu, until I get back.'

'All right. But what about tomorrow? We can't put the Polish hut at risk for more than a few hours.'

'We'll have to plan a couple of hours ahead at a time,' said Ilena. 'Maybe the laundry tomorrow night – maybe the kitchens.'

'We'll manage it somehow,' said Maria, moving to the door.

'I'm ready to go. Can someone watch from the window for the searchlights?'

'I will,' said Bozena. There was the faint ingress of light as a corner of one of the shutters was lifted very slightly. 'All right, Maria? No, wait, they've swung the lights this way – oh no, it's all right, they're going away again – *Now*!'

A thin spiritless dawn was breaking as Alice, carrying Alraune in her arms, slipped out of the hut.

The crematoria chimneys jutted forbiddingly up into the grey-streaked sky and as she walked past them Alice glanced nervously in their direction. A sprinkling of coarse ash covered the roofs of the buildings nearest to her, and a heavy scent clung to the air. Then the ovens had been burning recently. Don't think about it.

When I am through this, thought Alice, walking stealthily towards the Polish hut, and when I look back, there'll never be any colour in these memories. Everything will always be in shades of black and grey.

She went doggedly on, her arms around Alraune, praying that he had understood sufficiently to remain silent. But he was apparently curious about this unknown nocturnal world and he did not make a sound. And it was easier than Alice had dared hope to dodge the guards, partly because they moved in sharp unison, the heels of their boots ringing out on the hard ground, giving warning of their approach.

The searchlights were still swivelling around the camp; in this light they were like huge pale lidless eyes. *And if we find you, we'll hang you or shoot you, my dears* . . . But don't think about that, either. Just think about keeping to the shadows, about staying out of the discs of horrid pallid light. And hide Alraune's head against your shoulder, because he's staring at the searchlights . . .

The women in the Polish hut were waiting for her; they drew her in, exclaiming over the little one who must be hidden from the Angel of Death, whispering volubly of their plans. For what was left of tonight, madame and the baby would stay in the little roof space – it was uncomfortable, but it would suffice. And then tomorrow, after morning roll-call, the small one could be smuggled into the laundry block – they had it all worked out. An armful of linen from the guards' quarters to hide him: no one would suspect. The three who worked in the laundries would keep him occupied in a quiet corner – there were many such places in that block – and no one would know he was there. And after that, perhaps the kitchens.

'No,' said Alice, thankful that despite Maria's warning some of them understood a little German. 'No, I can't impose on you after tonight. We'll take him somewhere else. But your help tonight means more than I can possibly express in words.' She thought they only understood about half of this, but she knew they understood all of the sentiment behind her words.

The space in the roof was smaller than she had been expecting, but it was sufficiently large for the two of them to curl up against the wooden rafters. Someone handed up a blanket, and someone else handed a half-cup of some warm substance; Alice could not tell what it was, but she drank it gratefully and gave Alraune a few sips. Tomorrow, after roll-call, she would set in motion yet another masquerade, and this time lives would depend on it. She would report Alraune as missing to the guards, and she would play the distraught mother. Would it work? Would Mengele be fooled? The timing was not good – it was too pat, too near to those schedules Ilena had seen, but it could not be helped. This was the best they could do. The guards would search for Alraune, and if they did not find him it was possible that Alice would be suspected of some plot, and would be executed.

She glanced down at Alraune, and reminded him that this was part of the new game, and that they must be quiet. Again he appeared to accept this, although his eyes rested on her suspiciously, and when Alice put her arm around him to make him more comfortable he resisted for a moment.

But then he leaned against her, and fell quickly into an apparently untroubled sleep.

CHAPTER THIRTY-TWO

It was the sound of the guards marching across the yard outside that roused Alice from her shallow uneasy sleep. She sat up abruptly, memory returning. I'm in this tiny space over the Polish women's quarters, and Mengele wants Alraune, and I've got to keep him hidden.

It was one of Auschwitz's dreariest days; rain drummed ceaselessly on the roofs of the huts, and the stench of the stagnant wastelands seeped into everything.

Alice had decided to report Alraune's disappearance after the morning roll-call. She considered how she ought to behave. Tears and anxiety, followed by sullen acceptance? Yes, for all of the commandants and most of the guards would probably know what had happened at Buchenwald; they would know that Alraune was not some beloved child of a lost husband, but the living reminder of a violent rape. But not too many tears, thought Alice. I'd better not overdo it; this is real life not a film set. And some annoyance as well, I think – wretched child, I can't be watching him all the time . . . How should I know where he goes or what he gets up to . . . ? I just thought you ought to know he's run off . . .

Yes, that should strike the right note. A little distress, and then a sulky anger.

It seemed that it did strike the right note. Alice squeezed out a few tears, and then grew sullen. No, she had no idea where the child might be. Yes, he had been in the hut with her before morning roll-call. Yes, she would let them know if he turned up. She saw that they thought it relatively unimportant – children were always wandering off; they were inquisitive creatures. Some sort of search might be made later in the day, but for now she was to return to her own part of the camp.

They don't know about Mengele's plans, thought Alice, going cautiously across to the laundry block. That'll be the real testing time. Will Mengele order a thorough search? How interested is he in having Alraune in his experiments?

The Polish women had been as good as their word: Alraune had been carried, unprotesting, in a bundle of sheets, and put into a tiny stone-floored room at the end of a long narrow passage. There was not very much in the room; several scrubbing-boards and two huge mechanical mangles standing over drain-holes. A drum of scouring powder of some kind, smelling faintly of old-fashioned lye soap. Alice thought it a terrible place, but it seemed safe for the moment. The two Polish women would spend as much time with Alraune as they could, and Alice would try to slip back here unnoticed during the afternoon. If the women heard the guards coming there would be time to get him out, they said. They would be very watchful.

Alice returned to the laundry block after the midday meal, doing so openly and unconcernedly, so that any of the guards watching would think she had been assigned to duties there. Concealed in her sleeve she had a slab of bread and a square of rubbery cheese for Alraune to eat. The two Poles who worked in the laundry glanced at her, nodding almost imperceptibly to indicate that all was well, and Alice went down the passageway to the grisly stone room. There was still a trickle of light from the small windows, but the shadows were starting to edge across the floor, and in the gloom the huge mangles took on the aspect of malevolent beasts: creatures that would snap at your hands and ankles, and chomp you up in their rolling maws . . . Your blood would drip through their rollers and down into the drain directly beneath . . . Alraune had been shut in here all day – had he watched those machines? Had he seen their sinister qualities as Alice had, and been frightened?

Alice set herself to create a light-hearted atmosphere; she had brought one of the slates on which Alraune liked to scribble meaningless patterns, and the coloured chalks they had managed to cajole out of one of the guards. She wove cats' cradles for him as well with a length of string, and sang the nursery rhymes of her own childhood, keeping her voice low, although the thick walls of the room would muffle any sound. All the time her mind was considering plans for their next move, thinking that he could spend the night in the kitchen block and that she could slip out again to be with him – he could not be left by himself in the dark. And then the next day was Wednesday, the day Mengele wanted him. She wondered if she dare risk the laundry-basket ploy to get him out after all. How much of a gamble would it be?

There was no means of telling the exact time, but it must just be coming up to the evening roll-call, and she was just thinking that she would have to slip out and be in her place for that, when there was a flurry of activity beyond the stone room. Alice's heart leapt in fear, and she backed into a corner of the room at once, drawing Alraune with her.

'We're still playing the hiding game,' she said. 'So we've got to be quiet – like little mice.' Puzzlement flared in the dark eyes at this. 'But tomorrow,' said Alice, hating herself, 'it'll be our turn to be the big furry pussycats who do the chasing and that'll be a very good game indeed.' Absurd to talk like this – he had never seen a cat in his life. 'You'll have a cat of your own one day,' she said. 'A lovely black furry one with green eyes. It'll be all your own, and it'll purr and curl up in your lap. But until then, we're two little mice, and we won't even make a squeak.'

The guards were outside now – they must have entered so

abruptly that there had been no time for any warning. No time to smuggle Alraune out. It was no one's fault. But would the guards go away or would they search everywhere? Alice clenched her fists. Please God, please God . . . Doors were being opened and closed – had that been the main outer door? Were they going away again? For the space of twenty seconds she dared to believe the guards had gone. And then, like a blow across her heart, came the metallic ring of boots on the stone floor of the passage outside. Hateful sound. She pressed down into the corner behind the largest of the mangles, her arms around Alraune, one hand lightly over his mouth, because there was just a chance – just a faint, faint chance – that even if the guards looked in here they would not see the two fugitives crouching in the shadows. And if they could remain silent, if Alraune did not cry out . . . Don't let them come in here, prayed Alice. But if they do, don't let them see us . . .

She stayed absolutely still, her own heart pounding, aware of Alraune's warmth against her shoulders, pressing back against the wall and trying to shrink the two of them, like people in the fairy-stories of her childhood. Like that other Alice who had fallen down a rabbit-hole, and drunk something that had made her tiny. If only I could do that now . . . If only I could do what children do, and believe that if I close my eyes no one can see me . . .

The door was flung open, and light streamed in. Two guards stood in the doorway, both holding machine-guns. Alice flinched and felt Alraune shiver.

'There she is,' said one, pointing. 'And the child.'

They moved forward and Alice saw that a third man was with them. He remained in the shadowy passage, but when he turned his head a trick of the light caught the side of his face, and she saw the disc of glass over one eye.

'You are such a fool to try to outwit me,' said Leo Dreyer looking down at her. 'I will always – *always* – defeat you.'

He signalled to the guards, and they twisted Alice's arms behind her back and half-dragged her out of the laundry block and across the yard. As she went, she saw Dreyer stand looking down at

Alraune for a long moment, his face unreadable. And then he picked Alraune up and followed them.

Alice was never to know if she had been betrayed, but when she could reason again, she thought she had not. She thought it was more likely that once Mengele heard that the child he had planned to use in his experiment had vanished, he would have ordered a very thorough search. The guards had probably been looking for them for several hours before they were found, and for once they had been stealthy, giving no warning, simply entering the various buildings, and ransacking them.

After the first impact of shock she was not so very surprised to see Leo Dreyer. If he had not known about Alraune's birth at the time, he would have known soon afterwards. Had he been secretly watching Alraune growing up? Perhaps pointing him out to Mengele – saying, Why not use that child in your work? Didn't he care that Alraune might be his son?

Alice had expected to be hanged or shot; at best she expected to be taken to the punishment block and beaten. She had not quite reached a stage where she no longer had any feeling, but she was very close to it. Even so, she was still aware of a deep aching regret that despite everything she had not saved Alraune. And now I will die, and they will be free to do whatever they want to him. And afterwards – if there is an afterwards – it will be up to Maria or Ilena to take care of him.

But she had reckoned without the warped passion that drove much of Josef Mengele's work. Never waste anything, Mengele would say to his team. If there is anything – any situation, any remnant of humanity – that can be utilized, then do so.

And Josef Mengele was about to utilize the woman he thought of as Lucretia von Wolff in one very particular aspect of his work.

Alice was not taken to the yard with the infamous bullet-ridden brick wall, nor was she taken to the dreaded gas chamber. She was taken to a small private office in the medical block, with a large square inner window looking into one of the main surgeries.

An observation room? Yes, of course. The blood began to thud in her temples and every macabre rumour and every fragment of grisly gossip she had ever heard about Mengele rushed through her mind. And he appears to have thrown in his lot with Leo Dreyer, she thought. Between them, what are they going to do to me?

It was not until they brought in two men and strapped them down to chairs resembling dentists' chairs, and it was not until they led Alraune in and gave him a seat facing these two men, that Alice began to understand. There would be no straightforward floggings or starvation punishments for her; the Nazis were being much subtler and much crueller than that.

Ilena had said that Mengele's team was trying to establish whether pain or fear was the dominant factor in the disintegration of a human psyche, and to this end the doctors were inflicting both pain and fear on their victims – adjusting the proportions or the ratio as they went, and measuring the different results.

But tonight they were adding a refinement to their experiment – two refinements. They were putting a child in the same room as the victim, and watching the child's reactions to the inflicting of pain on that victim.

And they were putting the child's mother in an adjoining room, so that she would be forced to see the whole thing.

There was nothing Alice could do. Two guards stood by the door and two of Mengele's assistants were seated by the glass observation panel, with clipboards and pens. As a third entered the room Alice saw that more guards were stationed outside. There were no windows in the room which she might smash and try to climb through, and a second's inspection of the observation panel showed that it was of extremely thick glass. She thought: there is no way out of here. I am shut into this room, and I will have to endure whatever is ahead.

The straps were tightened around the two prisoners' ankles and wrists, and wires were taped to their chests and temples, and then linked to box-like machines. Alice supposed they would measure blood pressure levels, and heartbeats. Brain impulses, even? She had no idea if that was possible.

As a thick iron gyve was passed around the neck of the two men and iron braces tightened around their heads to prevent them from moving, her own heart began to pound with nervous terror, because whatever the doctors were about to do, it was clearly something connected with the men's faces.

Alraune was watching these preparations with faint curiosity, but he did not seem especially afraid. He has never known the ordinary world, thought Alice, only this dark hopeless place. So he may see nothing horrific in whatever they are about to do, and he may be unaffected by it. And then, far down in her mind, she thought: but I don't want him to be unaffected! I want him to be capable of pity and compassion – to be able to put himself in another's place – to feel hurt when a friend hurts.

When Mengele himself entered the room he did so quietly and unobtrusively, and it was difficult to connect him with the monster of the legend. But it's in the eyes, thought Alice. There's a coldness, an emptiness behind his eyes. As if he has no soul.

She was just trying to attract Alraune's attention, thinking that the sight of her might reassure him, thinking that she might somehow signal to him not to be frightened, when the door opened again, and Leo Dreyer came in. At once the menace in the room escalated; icy sweat slid between Alice's shoulder blades, and the palms of her hands were slippery. This is it, she thought. It's about to begin.

Without knowing she was going to do it, she banged hard on the glass partition with her fist, and when the men on the other side of it looked round, she cried out to Leo Dreyer. 'Leo! Let the child go! Keep me, but take him back to the hut – please!'

Dreyer turned his head and smiled. He shook his head.

'He could be your son!' cried Alice, hating having to say it, but doing so. 'There were six of you that night, remember? That's a one in six chance.'

'He's not my son,' said Leo Dreyer at once. 'I am unable to

father a child. I was rendered sterile from an illness in my youth. But,' he said, with a sudden glitter in his eyes, 'I am not impotent, baroness, as you very well know.'

Somewhere beneath the jagged panic, a tiny curl of gratitude unfurled at that. Not Dreyer's son. Not the son of this cold cruel implacable monster. Thank God for that at least, thought Alice.

The men imprisoned in the two chairs were aware of the sudden ratcheting up of the atmosphere, as well. Whether or not they knew what was to happen was not clear, but they certainly knew the stories about Mengele and they renewed their struggles to get free, their eyes bolting from their heads like frightened hares. But the gyves and the dreadful head braces held firm, and neither Mengele nor his assistants paid their weak flailing any attention. Mengele merely pointed to one of them and said, in a harsh voice, that this would be the first subject.

At once the assistants by the chairs bent to the machines, and Leo Dreyer moved quietly to a chair in one corner, his expression impassive. Alraune had not moved; he still had the look of faint, unafraid curiosity, and several times he studied Dreyer as if he found him puzzling.

Josef Mengele moved to a small trolley of instruments, and selected a syringe with an extremely large needle.

'You are all ready?' he said to the room in general, and the assistants nodded. 'And in the observation room?'

'We are ready also, Herr Doctor.'

'Herr Colonel?'

'Yes. Begin,' said Dreyer, and Mengele said, 'So,' and there was a split-second of flashing silver as the needle's sharpness caught the light.

Mengele adjusted the chair's headrest so that the man was tilted slightly back, and then took his upper face in a firm grip with his own left hand, the heel of his hand on the man's chin, the fingers and thumb prising the man's eyelids wide. With his right hand he drove the glinting needle directly into the man's eye.

* * *

Alice heard her own gasp, and she heard the gasp of the other man at the same time. Mengele was standing directly between her and his victim, but when he moved, she saw that the whole right-hand side of the man's face was covered in a dreadful thick fluid, faintly streaked with blood. He was sobbing with harsh dry sobs and flailing at the air as if to fight off further attack.

Mengele looked at the man consideringly, and then, turning to his assistants, said, 'You observe that I have entered the eye through the cornea, avoiding the zygomatic bone. The aqueous chamber is punctured of course, but—'

Alice's German was not up to the medical terms that Mengele was using now, but it did not need complete fluency to understand that he was saying the needle was not going sufficiently deeply into the victim's brain to kill him.

The second man was staring in utter horror at what had been done, his own escape struggles momentarily suspended. Had they been friends, these two men? If not friends, they would certainly be allies in this place, just as Alice and the women in her hut were allies. The assistants were still clustered around the machines attached to both men, noting down figures and comparing them, and adjusting settings. Alice glanced at Alraune again, hoping he would look round and see her, and that she might somehow send a message of love or comfort to him, but he was watching the machines. Alice did not know if he realized she was still there.

The attendants were busy with the machines, scribbling down figures, adjusting settings, and Mengele waited patiently until they stepped back, nodding to him. Then he bent over the first man again, and the needle glinted as it came down a second time.

From out of the tangled confusion of pain and horror and disgust, two things emerged with terrible clarity in Alice's mind.

One of these was the reactions of the still-untouched victim. As Mengele drove the needle into the first man's remaining eye he began to scream. He's realized what's ahead of him, thought Alice, appalled. He's seen his friend cold-bloodedly blinded, and he's guessed that he's about to suffer the same fate.

Mengele turned to the trolley to select a second needle, and the second man's screams increased, shrilling through the small room. As Mengele walked towards him, the screams faded and gave way to a wet retching.

'Wipe his face,' said Mengele impatiently. 'I cannot work with a man's vomit on my hands – you should know that by now.' He lifted the syringe again.

The second thing to strike Alice very forcibly and very clearly, was that Alraune had watched everything with silent absorption. And that he appeared entirely untroubled by any of it.

'So much pain,' said Francesca softly, when Michael finished speaking. 'And yet all that courage and all that humanity throughout. Alice and those women—'

'Remarkable, weren't they?'

'It reminded me a very little of Anne Frank hiding in the attics to escape the Nazis,' said Fran. 'Her diaries are unbearably sad, but the people she described were so brave. Or that Frenchwoman – Odette somebody, who was imprisoned as a spy.'

Michael said, 'And Mahler's niece, Alma Rosé, who led an orchestra inside Auschwitz. Alice met her a couple of times, I think.'

'It's an incredible story, Michael.'

'You believe it, though? You believe what I've told you? I do know how far-fetched it must sound.'

'I believe you now that I've seen your own photo of Alraune,' said Fran slowly. 'Until then I was – well, I was questioning it all. But you couldn't have faked that photograph in your wallet. You couldn't have known I'd find the photo of Alraune as a child, either. And they're unquestionably photos of the same person.'

'The child is father to the man.'

'I had been thinking of Alraune as a girl,' said Fran, thoughtfully. 'Trixie always referred to Alraune as "she". That's because of the film, I suppose. And that photograph could be a girl or a boy, couldn't it?'

'Yes. But if you look at the shot with my mother—'

'She's not pretty exactly, but she has a quality,' said Fran, thoughtfully. 'What happened to her? To both of them? Or am I stepping over the line asking that?'

He hesitated. 'Not exactly,' he said. 'And one day I will tell you. Not yet, though.'

'OK. He – your father – is actually very good-looking.'

'Yes, he was,' said Michael. 'He had a magnetism.'

Fran picked up the photo of the child again. 'Do we need to show anyone this? Is it likely to be connected with Trixie's murder?'

'I don't know. But Trixie was delving into the past, wasn't she? If she found Alraune's photograph, she might have found other things – I can't think what other things they could be, but I do know Alice didn't tell me everything about Alraune. So I suppose there could be something in the past I don't know about.'

'Something to cause her to be killed?' said Fran doubtfully. 'To – to shut her up about something?'

'It's only a wild theory. I don't really think it's likely.'

'Michael, what happened to Alraune after Auschwitz?'

'That's one of the things I don't know,' said Michael. 'I think he lived mostly abroad until the early Sixties,' said Michael. 'Then he came to England – he was in his early twenties by then. He changed his name of course; he lived for a while in Salisbury, so he took the name Alan Salisbury. Very English, isn't it? After I ran away, I shortened that to Sallis.'

He frowned and made an abrupt gesture as if to shake off the past. 'I think I'd better let Inspector Fletcher know Trixie had Alraune's photograph,' he said. 'She can make of it what she wants. And truly, Francesca, that's enough about me. More than enough. Tell me about you. I'd like to know – that's why I drove out here.'

'To see me?'

'To find out about you,' he said. 'You're "Mrs", but you don't wear a wedding ring. That's one of the things that's intriguing me most.'

'There's nothing intriguing about it,' said Francesca. 'It's boringly ordinary. I was married to a rat, and the rat deserted the ship for a blonde.'

'How ridiculous of him. I'm very glad to hear he's no longer around, though.'

Fran did not say she was starting to be quite glad as well. She said, 'I'll make us some coffee, shall I?' and got up to switch on the kettle, running hot water on the plates stacked in the sink. She reached for the washing-up liquid at the same moment that Michael leaned over for the tea-towel; his hand brushed hers, and there was a sharp jab of excitement beneath her ribcage. Ridiculous, of course, but still . . .

But still, when his hand took hers again, there was a soaring delight. Fran discovered that she had turned from the sink to face him. He was standing so close to her that she could see the little flecks of light in his eyes. She was just trying to decide whether to make some light, subtly inviting remark (although she had rather forgotten how to do that kind of thing and she had never been particularly good at it anyway), or to step back and finish the washing-up and pretend nothing had happened.

Before she could decide, she discovered that she was in his arms without quite knowing how she had got there or which of them had moved first. His kiss, when it came, was at first gentle and exploratory, and then was not gentle at all. When finally he released her, his eyes were glowing.

Fran said, breathlessly, 'When you let the barriers down, you do so quite spectacularly.'

'I didn't mean to put up barriers. Sometimes it just happens. But I've wanted to do that ever since I opened the door of Deborah Fane's house and found you on the step,' he said. 'You looked like a defiant urchin – all tousled hair and accusing eyes.'

'I thought you looked like an extremely urbane wolf,' said Fran, involuntarily. 'One who might prowl the groves of academe.'

'A book of Elizabethan sonnets in one hand and the key to the bedroom in the other?'

'Something like that. As a matter of fact, I nearly got back in the car and drove away like a bat out of hell.'

'I'm glad you didn't. Could we have dinner tomorrow night? I'll leave the bedroom key behind, although I can't promise anything about the sonnets. You've got the kind of face that could inspire someone to be quite poetic.'

'I wouldn't mind if you recited limericks,' said Fran. 'And I'd love to have dinner with you tomorrow – oh, blast, no, I can't. I really do have a parent evening tomorrow.' In case he thought this was a put-off, she said, 'I could manage Tuesday or Wednesday, though.'

'Tuesday? Eight o'clock? And we'll try to get to the Italian place this time, shall we?'

Francesca's instant reaction to this was that the Italian restaurant was only a short walk from this house, and that he would bring her home, and that she would almost certainly ask him to come in for a final drink or a cup of coffee . . . Don't plan too far ahead, though. Don't let your mind run away too wildly.

Still, there was no harm in thinking that she could serve the coffee in Trixie's little sitting-room on Tuesday – the furniture was a bit weather-beaten, but there was an open fire and she could lay the fire ready for lighting as soon as she got home from school. She might as well use some of the applewood logs a neighbour had let Trixie have last month. And he liked music, and there was her own CD collection upstairs. Mozart and apple-scented firelight and some really good filtered coffee. Perhaps a brandy with it. She would set the glasses on the little low table, and the firelight would glow on them. I'm sounding like a romantic fourteen-year-old. I don't care.

She would not get too stupidly dreamy, though. For the moment it was enough to smile at Michael, and say, 'Tuesday at eight it is. I'll look forward to that.'

CHAPTER THIRTY-THREE

Since that splintering second of recognition at Quondam, Edmund had struggled to control a scalding jealousy of Michael Sallis. Once you allowed an emotion – almost any emotion – to get the upper hand, you stopped thinking and reasoning, and you lost a certain detachment.

But the angry hating jealousy was threatening to overwhelm him, blotting out all other considerations and making it difficult to focus on anything else.

Alraune's son. That was who Sallis was – Edmund knew it quite definitely. After those first few puzzled moments, he had looked from Sallis to the screen and he had suddenly seen the extraordinary resemblance to the young Lucretia von Wolff. A direct descendant? Was that possible? But Michael resembled Lucretia far too closely to be anything else. So who was he? Whose son could he be?

It was unlikely in the extreme that Sallis was a secret son of either Deborah or Mariana. Those two had lived open and conventional lives, but both of them had been sufficiently Lucretia's daughters not to have troubled overmuch about having an illegitimate son. Deborah, in fact, would probably have relished it. Edmund was inclined to absolve both Deborah and Mariana.

That left the third of Lucretia's children. Alraune. And Alraune had not been a legend as so many people had said, but a real person, born in December 1940 – the birth certificate in Deborah's house had been testimony to that. And so far from dying mysteriously or vanishing without explanation, it looked as if Alraune had grown up and had had a more or less conventional life – marriage presumably, and a son.

Alraune had grown up. This was the thought that was sending the corrosive waves of hatred and jealousy scudding through Edmund's body. Alraune had not been that secret intimate ghost whose presence he had felt so strongly at Ashwood, and whose emotions he had shared. *All you need to believe in is the practice of mord*, Alraune had said that day. And there had been that burst of childish glee. *Remember the eyes, Edmund . . . Remember mord . . .*

Alraune was mine! cried Edmund silently to Sallis. Alraune was that fragile little ghost who guided my hand when I killed Trixie Smith! We shared *mord*, Alraune and I, and we shared that killing! The thought of Sallis knowing Alraune – growing up with Alraune as a parent – was almost more than Edmund could bear.

But it was important to stay in control. To fight that black and bitter tide of hatred that threatened to swamp his reason. He forced himself to think on a practical level. How much might Alraune's son know about Ashwood? Had Michael listened to the stories of the past, as Edmund had? A child 'listed as Allie' had been at Ashwood that day: had it really been Alraune? (*'You don't need to believe in me, Edmund . . . All you need to believe in is the practice of mord . . . The ancient High German word that means murder . . .'*)

How much had Alraune seen and understood that day at Ashwood? Enough to pass it on to Michael, years afterwards? 'Once upon a time, Michael, there was a place called Ashwood where a murder happened, and there was a man called Crispin Fane who committed that murder and no one ever knew . . . But I knew, Michael, I knew because I saw it all . . .'

There was no way of knowing how much Sallis had been told, but Edmund was not going to take any chances. There was also no way of knowing if Sallis, or indeed Alraune, might have talked to anyone about the Ashwood murders, although on balance Edmund was inclined to think not. The police did not seem to know much about Alraune, and Sallis did not seem to have told them anything. And although Alraune's birth certificate had been in Deborah's house, if she had known of Michael's existence she had never talked about it, just as she had never talked about Alraune.

Edmund was not, of course, some vulgar, out-of-control serial murderer who killed for the sake of it, and who was destined for the flashier pages of the tabloids followed by a life sentence inside some grim institution. But the jealous hatred of Michael Sallis was seeping into every corner of his mind, and he could not bear to think of Alraune as other than his own – helping him, encouraging him. '*Go on, Edmund, go on . . .*' Alraune had said that day in Studio Twelve.

And if Michael had grown up with Alraune, as presumably he must have done, even if he had broadcast his parentage to the entire western world, he was still far too much of a threat to be allowed to live.

Edmund remembered that he had never liked the man since the day he came to Deborah Fane's funeral, and it was at this point that he knew he was going to enjoy killing Michael Sallis.

The first step had been to get Sallis somewhere on his own, which Edmund thought he had already achieved rather neatly. Once he might have considered Ashwood for the setting, believing Alraune to be there and trusting to Alraune to help him. But Alraune could no longer be permitted into Edmund's thoughts, and in any case, Ashwood was still the scene of DI Fletcher's murder investigation. Also, Sallis would never go there without a lot of questions.

But accidents could happen in old houses, especially rather

remote old houses that had been lived in by an elderly lady who might not have been as assiduous in having things like electrical wiring or gas pipes checked . . .

It took longer than might have been expected to go through the house, and decide which pieces of furniture would be most useful to the house's new incarnation, but Edmund was meticulous about considering every item.

'We've definitely decided to use the place as a halfway house,' Michael said, as Edmund made diligent notes about wardrobes and tallboys and library shelves, and stuck gummed labels on to each item so that the removal men would not cart them off to the sale rooms by mistake. 'We'll probably put another little bathroom in if the funds stretch to it – that little boxroom on the half-landing might do for that – but other than that we'll just give everywhere a lick of paint . . . oh, and mend some of the tiles on the roof where they've become unseated.' He stood in the hall, looking about him. 'In a way it's rather a shame that it won't be a family house any longer,' he said. 'It's a lovely old place. You and your cousin must have had some good times here.'

'Yes, we did.' You're looking in from the outside, thought Edmund. You'd have liked to share in all that, wouldn't you? You're thinking you had as much right to this place as I did, and you're resenting it like fury. It rather pleased him to identify these fragments of emotion from Sallis, and with the idea of administering a further jab, he said, 'My aunt loved us to stay with her in the long summer holidays. We used to have picnics by the river, and cycle rides through the lanes. And huge Christmas parties – all very traditional. Roaring log fires and spiced punch and presents under the tree.'

'Wonderful for you to be able to look back on those years,' said Alraune's son politely, and Edmund smiled. Last night he had thought that he would know when the moment to set the plan in motion arrived, and he knew that the moment was now. A little hammer-pulse of excitement began to beat in his mind.

Sallis was looking at his watch, and saying something about it being well after one o'clock. 'Before I set off for home I think I'll have something to eat in the village, though. The White Hart does food, doesn't it?'

'Only bar meals at this time of day,' said Edmund. 'But they're quite good.'

'Do you have to be back at your office, or could you have some lunch with me?'

Edmund had not expected this but he took it in his stride. 'I don't see why not. Yes, thank you.' *Now*, said his mind, and at once the little hammer-pulse quickened. As they went out to the hall, as if it had just occurred to him, he said, 'Before we go, would you mind giving me a hand with that box of books in the corner? It's not very heavy – not hernia weight or anything like that – but it's a bit awkward. It's only got to go as far as the boot of my car . . .'

Sallis was entirely unsuspicious. He said, 'Yes, of course. Hold on, I'll prop the door open, and we'll carry it out between us.'

And of course, gentle impractical Mr Fane was not accustomed to humping packing cases around. He was more used to sitting behind a desk, and when he needed something moving or mending or adjusting, he rang a suitable workman. A bit of a wimp, really; hopeless when it came to understanding how you walked backwards when carrying something, or how you manoevred around an awkward corner. It was inevitable that he should dither a bit, and that the dithering should result in him fumbling his hold of the heavy case.

He fumbled it quite badly, in fact. The packing case slithered from his hands just as they were going past the stairs, and Michael Sallis made an instinctive grab to stop it falling against the carved newel post. There was a moment when he took the full weight, and then the heavy corner smashed down with a rather sickening dull crunch. It might have gone on his foot – Edmund had, in fact, been aiming for that, but it went on his left hand as he snatched at the corner. Almost as good. Blood gushed to the surface from a deep gash made by the case's sharp corner, and a huge blind weal rose across the knuckles.

Edmund was instantly and deeply contrite. He could not think *how* he had been so clumsy; he had just been negotiating the jutting wall by the little window recess . . . And oh dear goodness, that looked like a very nasty injury indeed. It might be as well to just run down to the local emergency room to get it looked at.

'Please don't bother. It'll be all right in a minute – I'll put it under the cold tap,' said Michael. But his face was white with pain and he swayed for a moment as if the injury had made him dizzy. Edmund waited, trying to decide if it would further his plan if Sallis passed out or not. Probably not. Fortunately Sallis seemed to regain control, and he went a bit unsteadily through to the kitchen, turning on the tap full blast and wincing as he held his hand under the cold water.

'I am *so* sorry,' said Edmund in the tone of a man wringing his own hands with distress. 'How could I have been such a fool— But just as we turned the stair corner— You know, I do think that ought to be X-rayed. It's bleeding quite badly as well, it might need stitching. And you could have snapped a small bone or cracked a knuckle or something. You really shouldn't take any chances with hands.' He saw Sallis hesitate and he saw that Sallis was in too much pain to think straight. 'I'll drive you there at once,' said Edmund firmly. 'No, really, I insist. I'd never forgive myself if there was any serious damage and we ignored it. Wait a moment and I'll see if there's any ice in the fridge. Oh good, yes. I'll fold some ice cubes in a towel and we'll wrap it round your hand— Yes, like that. That might ease it a bit. It doesn't matter about taking your jacket, does it?'

'Yes. Mobile phone and wallet,' said Michael through waves of pain.

'Oh yes, of course.'

All the way to the hospital Edmund could feel how much Sallis was hating this enforced dependency. Serve you right, he thought viciously. How dare you come out here like this, pretending to be someone you're not! Did you really think you wouldn't be recognized? You're Alraune's son, for pity's sake! Did you honestly expect to get away with that?

They had to wait in the Accident & Emergency Department for two hours before they were seen, and then they had to wait a further hour for an X-ray. Not broken, said the harassed doctor at last, but there was a hairline fracture on the metacarpus – the little finger, and a tendon was badly bruised. No treatment was needed, other than to strap it firmly up, which they would do now, and then to keep it immobile for about twenty-four hours. And they would put a couple of stitches in the cut, which was quite nasty, although luckily not sufficiently deep to have damaged any nerves. Michael's own GP would take them out in three or four days, and would check on the damage to the tendon. And in the meantime, here was a prescription for some strong painkillers which could be got from the hospital pharmacy; they would help Mr Sallis through the next twenty-four hours.

Drive a car? he said, in answer to Michael's question. Good God, quite out of the question. Apart from anything else, with the tendon injury it would almost certainly be impossible to hold the steering wheel.

'I'm sure I could manage,' said Michael a bit desperately.

'I don't think you could. Can't someone drive you home? Oh, London. Oh, I see. But you really mustn't drive yourself.'

'I'll sort something out,' said Michael.

Since Edmund knew the White Hart's number, and since dialling a number with one hand in a sling would be awkward, he phoned them on Michael's behalf to see if there was a room for the night. He accepted the use of Michael's mobile phone to make the call – he was a bit old-fashioned when it came to mobile phones, he said; he found them intrusive and he had never acquired one.

Still, here was an occasion where it was very useful indeed. It took him a moment or two to understand about switching the phone on, and about tapping out the number, and then there seemed to be a problem with getting a signal. Perhaps he should get out of the car to make the call – would that help?

Getting out of the car apparently solved the weak signal problem, but the call itself did not solve the problem of where to spend the night.

'No rooms at all?' said Michael, rather dismayed.

'No. Sorry. It's a very small place – only three or four rooms.'

'What about a railway station? If there's a train to London I could get a taxi at the other end.'

'Well, the nearest station is twelve miles from here, but I do know the last train to London is mid-afternoon, and that'll have long since gone. I'm trying to think where else we could ring for you—'

'Don't bother,' said Michael. 'Why don't I just doss down in Mrs Fane's house – you wouldn't have any objection, would you? I'd be quite all right there.'

'Well, I'm not sure,' said Edmund doubtfully, and added in a reluctant voice, 'I daresay I could ask my cleaning lady to make up a bed in my spare room, only it isn't very—'

The speed at which Sallis refused this offer indicated very strongly that he had no more liking for Edmund than Edmund had for him. But he was perfectly courteous about it. He said, 'Please don't go to that trouble. I really don't want to disrupt you, and I think I'm beyond phoning local hotels to find a room. I'm quite happy to stay at the house. It's warm and comfortable, and the gas and electricity are still on.'

'Oh yes,' said Edmund, his eyes on the road as they drove along. 'The phone's been disconnected, but everything else is on.'

'And I can get a taxi to the station tomorrow morning – I'll phone British Rail presently and find out the times.'

'What? Oh, there's a train around eleven. Straight through to Euston.'

'Good. The car can be collected later – if I still can't drive by the weekend I can probably get the AA to help out.'

'I suppose it would be all right,' said Edmund, still sounding reluctant.

'Believe me, I've slept in worse places than that house,' said Michael smiling. 'Or are you forgetting I work with homeless teenagers for most of the week?'

'I was forgetting that for the moment,' said Edmund.

'But if it's not a nuisance, could you just stop off in the town so that I could pick up some bread and milk – oh, and a toothbrush and a razor—'

'Of course I can,' said Edmund. 'And I'll come into the house with you to make sure you've got everything you're likely to need.'

Edmund bought the bread and milk and other things himself from the local supermarket, waving aside Michael's attempts both to come into the shop, and also his attempts to pay. He felt entirely responsible for what had happened, he said; Sallis must at least allow him to make this small reparation. Was he really sure about staying at the house? Why not let him try a couple of hotels in the adjoining town?

'There's no need,' said Michael. 'I'll be absolutely fine here. Food, drink and shelter. All I need.'

To the modest provisions, Edmund had added a half pound of butter, some cooked chicken from the delicatessen which he had asked them to slice up, some crisp eating apples, a wedge of cheese, and half a bottle of Scotch. Scotch was as good a painkiller as he had ever found, he said.

'That's very generous of you.'

'And you'll be warm enough? The central heating's been on the "Frost" setting, so the house hasn't got really cold or damp since my aunt died. But you can turn the thermostat up, of course. It's in the kitchen, on the side of the—'

'I know where it is. I'll turn it up if I need it. You've been very kind,' said Michael, with an obvious effort.

'Not at all. But at least once you're in the house you won't need to go out again,' said Edmund. 'I expect you'll take the hospital's pills and just crash out.'

'I expect I will,' said Michael.

Edmund had enjoyed that last remark to Sallis – 'Once you're in the house you won't need to go out again,' he had said. In fact, once Sallis was in the house, he never would go out again, not alive, not if Edmund's plan worked.

It would work, of course. He had thought it all out carefully and logically, paying attention to every tiny detail. Crispin had always said that was the essence of a good plan. Never neglect the details, Crispin said.

As well as not neglecting the details, Edmund had made sure that if anything did go wrong he could not himself be implicated. Michael Sallis had been successfully isolated – cut off from all methods of communicating with anyone, including his mobile phone; Edmund had been very cunning about that phone, and he was rather pleased with himself. Everything that was going to happen tonight would afterwards be put down to unfortunate accident. Misadventure.

In a way it was a pity that Alraune's ghost would not be around for Michael's murder; Edmund would have quite enjoyed the irony of that. But since the afternoon at Quondam Films, he was accepting that Alraune might not be a ghost at all; Alraune might be alive and living a normal life somewhere in the world.

But Crispin would be there, and that was really all that mattered. As he drove home, Edmund knew that Crispin would enjoy watching Alraune's son die.

CHAPTER THIRTY-FOUR

Michael had spoken honestly when he told Edmund Fane he was used to far worse sleeping quarters than Deborah Fane's empty house; his work had frequently taken him into the squats and the hostels of London's East End, and from there into deeper, sadder worlds where people lived in shop doorways and tube stations.

But after Fane left, Michael felt vaguely uneasy. There was no logic to this feeling: he had been in this house several times already – once after Deborah Fane's funeral, and two or three times after that, stage-managing the various surveys and reports that had to be prepared for CHARTH. It had in fact been at this house that he had met Francesca. Francesca. Even with his hand a grinding mass of agony Michael felt a smile curve his lips at the thought of Francesca. In a moment he would phone her; he was furious and disappointed at not being able to get back to London tonight for their dinner, but hopefully they could meet tomorrow evening. It would be good to hear her voice – thank goodness for mobile phones.

He switched on the rather old-fashioned electric fire in the small room overlooking the lane and closed the curtains. He liked this room; it had a friendly atmosphere, and it looked as if it had been used as a study; there were bookshelves and a little writing desk and a rather weatherbeaten sofa near the window. Had Lucy and Edmund done their homework in here during school holidays? It was still odd to think that Lucy was his cousin – that Alraune had been half-brother to Lucy's mother. Michael wondered how Lucy got on with that dry stick, Edmund Fane. Had they had a teenage romance, as distant cousins sometimes did? Had people in the family speculated about whether they might one day marry?

Michael's own childhood, once he had left Pedlar's Yard and once he had found Alice, had been extremely happy. He had loved living in the old stone house set amidst the ancient fenlands, and it was a measure of Alice's own charm and energy that there had never been any boredom. But he thought he would have liked to have Lucy as a small cousin, part of his growing-up years. And Edmund, said his mind wryly. Don't forget that Edmund would have been a cousin as well. Oh yes, so he would. Only a distant one, though.

He might as well spend the night in the friendly little study rather than go foraging around for sheets and pillows. The sofa was wide and deep, and there would probably be a travelling rug or an eiderdown somewhere upstairs.

To counteract the rather brooding silence he switched on the radio, tuning it to Classic FM. A request programme was on and the ordinary announcements for music and the breaks for advertisements and news went some way towards dispelling the unsettling atmosphere.

He went along the hall to the back of the house. The kitchen had been more or less completely cleared, but a kettle stood on the top of the cooker. Filling it was awkward – Michael had to disentangle his hand from the sling to do so, and he acknowledged with annoyance that the doctor had been right about not driving. But he managed to make a cup of instant coffee which he drank gratefully, swallowing one of the painkillers with it. The label recommended two every six hours, but Michael loathed the vague muzziness that even an aspirin caused. He would take one pill now, and if necessary he would take the second one later.

Now for the call to Francesca. He smiled again, thinking he would say that if she was free tomorrow evening they would still go to the Italian place, because he could spoon up pasta with one hand. It was good to imagine the two of them in the restaurant, Francesca seated opposite to him, her eyes wary and defiant most of the time, and then suddenly and disarmingly intimate when she smiled.

His jacket was in the hall, flung over the stair rail, and he felt in the pocket for his mobile phone. It was at this point that he remembered Edmund Fane using the phone to call the local pub to book a room for the night. Fane had had to get out of the car to make the call because the signal was weak, but it had only taken a few minutes, and then he had got back in.

But what had happened to the phone?

It took the best part of half an hour, and an awkward, one-handed search of the downstairs rooms, before Michael finally accepted that the phone was not in the house and that it must therefore still be in Edmund Fane's car. Blast Edmund Fane and his spinsterish outlook and his unfamiliarity with mobile phones! Dear me, am I using this right? he had said. I don't possess a mobile phone, you know – I'm afraid I've always found them rather intrusive.

And now Fane's dithering uncertainty had resulted in Michael being stranded out here with no means of communicating with anyone. At the moment he did not much care if he never communicated with the entire western world again, but he did care about not communicating with Francesca. Would she think he had stood her up? Was there any way he could get to a phone? Was he, in fact, sure that the phone in this house really was disconnected? He tracked down the two extensions, one in the largest of the bedrooms and one in the hall. Both were dead. Hell's teeth.

He went back into the study and sat down to review the situation. From what he had seen on his previous visits this house was at least a couple of miles from any other buildings. Could he walk that far in his present state? The painkiller was already starting to kick in, and he was feeling unpleasantly light-headed. And even if he did manage to reach a house, could he be sure he would be allowed in to use the phone? His mind flew ahead, seeing himself knocking on the door of a house where some lone female lived (it was a safe bet that the first place he tried would have a solitary woman there!) and making the classic horror-film request. 'I'm stranded and I wondered if I could possibly use your phone.' And the bandaged hand, and the blood on his shirt-cuff, and his dishevelled appearance all contributing to the sinister image.

How about a public phone-box? He tried to remember if he had seen one along the road, and could not. But how often were phone-boxes working nowadays? How far away was the White Hart? Not far, surely?

This was ridiculous. It was the twenty-first century, and it was possible to contact most of the world with the touch of a phone-pad, or the press of a computer key, or the activating of a fax machine. And here he was, stuck in this old house, as cut off from the world as if he had been transported back a hundred years!

He glanced at his watch. It was coming up to six o'clock. Would Francesca be home from school by now, perhaps taking a shower and deciding what to wear for the evening? Did women bother about that kind of thing these days? Michael had not exactly fought shy of women, and women had not exactly fought shy of him, but he had backed away from the deeper emotional involvements. He did not want to back away from Francesca, however.

Probably most women just took dinner dates on the wing, saying, Oh, this is the first thing that fell out of the wardrobe, and it'll do for a plate of spaghetti and a glass of red plonk.

Francesca had changed her mind about what to wear tonight three times already. She had finally decided to play safe with a black silk sweater (it was fairly low-cut, but not tartily so), a chunky gold necklace, and some rather jazzy silk palazzo trousers that Marcus had once sneeringly said made her look like a refugee from a circus.

It felt peculiar but exciting to be preparing to go out to dinner with a man after so long. Fran thought she would have been nervous if it had not been Michael, which struck her as a peculiar way to think. She had set the bottle of brandy and glasses on the low table, and had laid the fire so that she need only put a match to it when they got in. Would Michael see through the small scene-setting ploy, and would he smile the three-cornered smile that made his eyes slant upwards at the corners?

Just on six. Fran experienced a small lurch of pleasure, because there were only a couple of hours left until he arrived. She would take a long hot bath, with an extravagant allowance of scented bath oil, and after she was dressed she would go back downstairs and wait in the armchair in the bay window. From there she would be able to see him drive up to the house.

Michael had decided to make for the White Hart in his car. He acknowledged that he could not have managed the journey to London, but surely to God he could drive the short distance to the village. Quite apart from contacting Francesca, he needed to arrange a taxi to the railway station for the train journey home tomorrow.

He was glad he had only taken one of the hospital's pills and he thought he could keep the worst of the drowsy light-headedness at bay. Remembering he had had no lunch, he had eaten a clumsily made chicken sandwich and an apple, after which the world seemed slightly less unreal. But it was strange how the house had passed from being a welcoming place – a place that a few hours ago he had been regretting not having known in his childhood – to something quite different. Watchful. Menacing. The kind of feeling you got if you knew you weren't alone . . . The kind of feeling he had had all those years ago, crammed into a dank, bad-smelling cupboard under some stairs . . . Praying that a man whose eyes had been gouged out would not find him . . .

Oh, for goodness' sake stop it! You've had a bash on the hand and it was hard enough to crack a bone and damage a tendon, and your mind's playing tricks from the pain and the pill, that's all!

He turned off the radio and the light and he was about to switch off the little electric fire when he caught a sound from outside. He went out into the hall and listened carefully. Nothing there. Imagination. He was about to go back into the study when the sound came again. And this time it was not imagination. This time it was the soft but unmistakable crunch of footsteps on the gravel path outside.

Michael stayed where he was. Someone was definitely out there. Someone was walking around the side of the house, and whoever it was was moving very stealthily indeed.

Might it be an ordinary, innocent caller? It was only six o'clock in the evening, after all. But local people must surely know that Deborah Fane had died and that the house was empty. A salesman, then? Somebody flogging encyclopedias or religion or canvassing for votes? But the house was a quarter of a mile from the road, and unless you knew it was there you would go straight past the turning.

That left the very sinister possibility that it was a burglar. Someone local who knew the house was empty and was going to take a chance on getting in and grabbing anything valuable or saleable. This was such a strong possibility that Michael felt a chill of fear for his own vulnerable condition. He glanced about him for something to use as a weapon. Or would discretion be the better part of valour, and would it be better to simply beat the hell out of it? His jacket, with the car keys in the pocket, was still in the hall; he could grab it and be through the main front door inside ten seconds. He tried to remember what kind of lock the front door had. An ordinary Yale, wasn't it? Then all he had to do was flip it back and turn the latch. A dozen paces to his car and he could be away.

The footsteps had stopped, but the feeling of an unseen presence was still frighteningly strong. He's still out there, thought Michael, and with the thought came a movement beyond the uncurtained kitchen window that sent his heart hammering against his ribs. A figure, unrecognizable from here, pressed up against the pane, and a hand came up and tapped lightly on the glass – so lightly that only someone near to the window could have heard it.

As an antidote to a damaged hand and a hefty dose of painkiller, the sight of that indistinct figure and the soft, fingernail tapping was electric. Michael forgot about feeling light-headed, and he forgot about the pain in his hand. His mind went into overdrive, because he had been right – there was a prowler out there, and he was looking in and making sure the place really was empty before breaking in. In another minute he would lever open the back door, or smash the window and climb through. Michael was no coward, but in his current state he was not sure if he would be able to deal with some desperate house-breaker, who might be high on drink or drugs.

Was it possible to sprint down the hall and be out through the front door without being seen or heard? He was just considering this when the most chilling sound yet reached him. A key was being turned very slowly and very carefully in the lock of the garden door. As Michael stared in horrified disbelief, the door began to inch open.

That sprint to the front door was no longer an option; Michael stepped back into the study, and got behind the door. There was a heavy pottery vase on a side table; if it came to a fight he could probably make use of it. But with luck the prowler would see the light from the electric fire, and would realize someone was in the house and beat it back into the night.

The small room was hot and claustrophobic and there was a smell of burning dust from the electric fire. Michael's heart was beating so furiously that he had the absurd idea that the burglar would hear it. Like the Edgar Allen Poe story where the murdered heart beat so loudly it betrayed the killer.

He had expected the intruder to come into the hall, and every muscle of his body was tense with anticipation. But the intruder did not. He moved around the kitchen for a few moments, and then there was the unmistakable sound of the garden door opening and closing again, and of the key being turned in the lock. The stealthy footsteps went down the gravel path once more.

Michael let out a huge breath of relief, and after a moment went across to the window, opening the curtain the tiniest chink in order to look outside. Was the man walking down the lane to the main road? There had not been the sound of a car – or had there? The radio had been on and this was an old and solid house; he might not have heard a car driving up.

The intruder had not come in a car, or if he had, he had parked it near to the road. He was just coming around the side of the house, doing so quite briskly as if he had just completed a necessary task, and heading towards the lane. But as he came out of the shadows cast by the old beech trees, he paused and turned to look back. Michael froze, praying not to be seen.

The intruder did not see him, but Michael saw the intruder. The man who had spent barely five minutes inside the house – the house which he had entered by means of a key – was Edmund Fane. But it was an Edmund Fane without the prim, rather spinsterish exterior; this was an Edmund Fane with such malice in his face and with such cold mad brilliance in his eyes that if it had not been for recognizing the jacket, Michael might have believed it to be a complete stranger.

He watched Edmund walk away from the house, and when he judged him to have reached the main road, he let the curtain fall back, and sat down. He was acutely puzzled. Why on earth would Edmund Fane steal into the house in that furtive way, spent those three or four minutes in the kitchen, and then creep out again, locking the door behind him?

Unless Fane had found the mobile phone, and had returned it. Was it possible that he had slipped quietly into the house, not wanting to wake Michael in case he was zonked out after taking the pills? This did not entirely square with Michael's impression of Edmund Fane, but it was the only thing he could think of. In that case his phone should be lying somewhere prominent, perhaps with an explanatory note. This would be very good indeed.

But he had barely taken two steps into the hall when a strong suffocating stench met him, sending him instinctively dodging back into the study. For a moment he was unable to identify it, but whatever it was, it was ringing loud alarm bells in his mind. Something on fire? No, not fire— But something as dangerous as fire—

And then he knew what it was. A strong smell of gas. Inside the kitchen, gas was escaping and filling up the house.

Michael did not stop to think. He tore the sling off his hand and crammed it over his mouth as a makeshift mask. Then he ran into the kitchen, banging the door back against the wall.

Even in those few minutes the gas had built up, and it seized his throat and lungs so that he gasped and breathed in the cotton of the sling for a moment. His eyes streamed, but he realized that the old-fashioned gas cooker near the door was hissing out gas, and that all four rings had been turned full on and the oven door propped wide open. That bastard Edmund Fane had come quietly into the house and turned the gas on!

Keeping the sling across his mouth, he wrenched the switches around and slammed the oven door shut. But his mind had already flown ahead to all the various electrical connections in the house, and then had flown back to the surveyor's head-shaking report on the state of the wiring. Very antiquated, the report had said, in fact downright dangerous, and the whole house needed rewiring. Michael was no electrician but you did not need a PhD to realize that belching gas and faulty electrical wiring were a lethal combination. If the gas fumes were to reach a flawed electrical circuit – or even, dear God, the electric fire that was still blazing in the study—

He wasted several valuable seconds trying to unlatch the garden door before he remembered that Edmund Fane had locked it, and grabbed a large saucepan, flinging it hard at the kitchen window. Several panes of glass shattered at once, and the cold night air streamed in. Michael, still trying to keep the makeshift mask over his nose and mouth, ran back into the study, knocking the switch of the electric fire off, and then dived through the hall, snatching up his jacket on the way. As he half fell through the front door, he was expecting the gas fumes to hit some worn-away section of wiring at any minute and the whole house to blow up.

But it did not. Taking deep shuddering gulps of the cold clean air, he reached his car, and unlocking it, slid thankfully inside. The engine fired at once, and he fumbled for the gears. This was going to be hellishly difficult; his left hand was throbbing with pain, and he would be lucky if he could change gear. He did not care. Adrenaline was flooding his body, and he would drive all the way to the White Hart in first gear with the hazard lights flashing if he had to. He depressed the clutch, knocked the car into first gear with his right hand, and then turned the wheel. It resisted slightly and then turned, but there was a grinding sound from somewhere near the back. Michael tried again, and encountered the same resistance and the same grating noise. Like bare steel on stone. *Steel*— Oh God.

He got out, casting a wary glance towards the house and scanning the dark lane. There were plenty of places for Fane to be hiding, but nothing stirred anywhere and there was no longer that indefinable sense of not being alone. He walked to the back of the car, expecting to find the exhaust pipe on the ground. The exhaust was intact but the cause of the problem was obvious; the tyre on the driver's side was absolutely flat, in fact it was right down to the wheel's rim. Presumably it had been punctured by one of the sharp stones on the lane's unmade surface, or – and this seemed more likely – Edmund Fane had jabbed something sharp into the rubber, as part of his incomprehensible plan.

But I can't help it, said Michael to the car. You've got to be driven: you're the only means I've got of reaching a phone. And I'm certainly not staying out here for Fane to come back and see if I've succumbed to the gas fumes, and maybe have another crack at me when he finds I'm still alive.

The steering groaned again against the weight of the flat tyre, but Michael managed to drag the steering wheel around so that the car was at least facing the right way. The wheel rim screeched like a soul in torment, and it would probably not last for more than a few miles, but providing it got Michael to the village, or, at worst, to a house with a phone, he did not care if he tore the car to shreds.

He switched on the headlights and the hazard warning flashers, bounced the car down the lane, and wrenched it on to the high road in the direction of the village.

CHAPTER THIRTY-FIVE

Edmund was glad to reach his own house, and to feel its clean, well-ordered ambience fold reassuringly about him. He switched on lights and picked up his post, which as usual had been delivered after he left the house. One of the disadvantages of living in a small market town was that you got a very late postal delivery; he seldom saw his private mail until he got home each evening. He had complained a number of times about this, but nothing had ever been done to improve things.

He could not decide when to go back to Deborah's house to check that his plan had worked and that Sallis really was dead. Would early tomorrow morning be better than later tonight? If he was seen going back there late tonight, it might look a bit odd, even with the very good excuse of returning the mobile phone. It might be better to leave it until the morning. Perhaps he would drive out there before going into the office. He had better not leave it any longer than that, though, because presumably there was no automatic cut-off and the gas would just go on escaping. He did not want to end up gassing half the county, for goodness' sake!

He was as sure as he could be that Sallis had not heard him steal into Deborah Fane's house and turn all the gas rings on. If that light careful tapping on the kitchen window had happened to attract his attention, Edmund had had his excuse all ready. He had come to return the mobile phone which he had only just found. And he had tapped at the window first in case Sallis had been asleep – a tap light enough not to disturb a deep sleep but loud enough to alert someone who was awake.

But Sallis had not heard. Presumably he had taken the pills provided by the hospital and fallen asleep, either in the upstairs bedroom or on the deep old couch in the little study – Edmund had seen the glow of the electric fire from that room. It did not much matter where Sallis was because the gas would fill up the house very quickly. Would it affect the old electrical wiring and cause a fire as well? Edmund supposed this was possible.

He switched on the oven and while he waited for the remains of last night's casserole to heat up, he sat down to consider Sallis's mobile phone. He had spoken more or less truthfully when he had said he was not familiar with mobile phones, but it was easy enough to see the principle of making and receiving calls, and to call up the directory of saved numbers. Whom did Sallis phone? What kind of friends and business associates did he have? It might be as well to know: to be prepared for any questions that might come hurtling out of the unknown after Sallis's death was made known. If Michael Sallis had family who might know the truth about Ashwood – who might still talk about it, or hand down the memories – Edmund needed to know.

But when he scrolled curiously through the list of names and numbers there did not seem to be very much of interest, and there certainly did not seem to be any family names, which had been his main concern. There were various hostels and homeless centres and housing associations, which would be connected with CHARTH, and there were several numbers casually listed under first names. Edmund supposed these would be friends. Most were in London, but some were not. A number was listed for Francesca Holland, which was a surprise: Edmund frowned over that for a moment, and then moved on. Doctor, dentist, bank. One or two restaurant numbers, a taxi firm in North London. It was interesting how you could build up a picture of someone's life from their stored phone numbers.

The oven timer pinged, and Edmund went back to the kitchen and ladled his food on to a plate. He liked to have a proper nourishing meal in the evenings. Normally he had a glass of wine or a small whisky as well, but tonight he would not do so in case he did decide to drive back to Deborah's house later on. He was always very strict with himself over not drinking when he was driving.

It was just after seven when the phone in Trixie's house rang, and Francesa's heart sank. Michael was not coming. Probably it had been just a casual invitation that he would have kept if something better had not turned up, and the kiss and the intimacy in Trixie's kitchen had been just casual as well. The something better had turned up, and now he was phoning with a polite excuse.

But Michael had not thought better of it, and he was not phoning with a polite excuse. He explained that he had had to drive up to Deborah Fane's house early that morning, and there had been an accident to his hand which meant he could not drive back. And even if he had been able to drive, his car had been vandalized.

'I'm so sorry, Francesca,' he said. 'I thought I'd be back in London in plenty of time to meet you. But I'm stuck up here, and there's no means of getting back until tomorrow at the earliest. And even then—'

Fran suddenly had the feeling that he was choosing his words with extreme care. She said, 'Michael – is anything wrong? I mean – you are all right, aren't you?'

'I'm furious at being stranded with a ruined car and a mangled hand,' he said. 'And I'm even more furious at not seeing you.'

The thought of Michael being in pain upset Fran so much that she said, without thinking, 'How will you get back? By train? Or shall I drive up there tomorrow?'

There was silence. Damn, thought Fran, I didn't mean that to come out. I've overdone it. He'll say, no, it's fine, thank you, everything's already fixed up.

But Michael was already saying, 'Oh Francesca, you have no idea how much I'd like that. But what about your classes?'

'None until Thursday afternoon. So it really wouldn't be a problem. I could drive you back.' Fran was glad to think she had finally managed to get her car fixed and driven back to London by a helpful local garage. 'It'd be a sort of quid pro quo for you driving me back to London that day, if you remember that.'

'Of course I remember it,' he said softly, and there, without warning, was the sudden slide down of his voice into a caress.

So as not to get too carried away, Fran said in a practical voice, 'If I set off fairly early – around half past seven or eight, say – I'd be there by mid-morning. Where exactly are you? Still at Mrs Fane's house?'

'No, I'm at the White Hart in the village, although God knows how I got the car this far, because— D'you really mean it about driving up? I'd love you to be here, but it's over hill, over dale—'

'Through brush, through brier, through flood, through fire,' said Fran promptly.

'There's a beautiful thought. All right, I give in. We could have lunch somewhere and not start back until evening. Or if you bring a toothbrush and some pyjamas I could even book a room here for you for the night, and we could drive back the next day if you'd like that. You'd still be back for Thursday afternoon and it would give me a bit longer to – sort out the car.'

He doesn't just mean the car, thought Fran at once. Something's happened. But he doesn't want to tell me yet – or at least not over the phone.

Michael was saying, 'I'd better give you directions to the White Hart, hadn't I? Have you got a pen? Oh, and I'll give you the phone number here as well in case you get stuck anywhere.'

'OK, I've got all that,' said Fran a moment later.

'Good. I won't hand you the line about keeping the lamps burning for your arrival, especially if it'll be mid-morning when you get here. But I'll be looking out for you. Drive carefully, Francesca darling. I'll be waiting.'

Edmund read his post while he ate his supper.

There was the quarterly electricity bill – it was criminal how much they charged you for electricity nowadays – and also a circular for a pizza delivery house, which irritated Edmund, who disapproved of the slovenly practice of delivering cooked food to people's houses.

The third letter was not immediately recognizable, but it had a vaguely official look. He slit the envelope and unfolded the contents, and with a lurch of anticipation saw it was from the Land Registry: the results of the search he had requested following Trixie Smith's death. The name of Ashwood's present owner. And an address in Lincoln.

He stared at the sheet of paper, because he had seen that name very recently. He had seen it on Michael Sallis's phone barely half an hour ago. He reached for the phone to make sure. Yes, there it was, along with a number and dialling code. But surely it was simply coincidence. Surely there could not be a link between Sallis and Ashwood's owner? Or could there . . . ?

He took down the BT phone directory, turning to the list of dialling codes for the whole country. It took a few minutes to match the code stored on the phone, but in the end he found it. The code was for Lincoln.

Edmund thought for a moment, and then dialled one of the big, anonymous directory Inquiries services. He gave the name printed on the Land Registry's documentation, and when asked for the address, merely said it was in Lincoln. Within seconds an electronic voice recited a number. The number was the number on Michael Sallis's mobile phone.

How much of a danger might this be? Edmund had no idea, but he did not like discovering this link between Sallis and

Ashwood, he did not like it at all. He considered what he should do. How about phoning the Lincoln number to see who answered? He could dial 141 beforehand so that his own number would not register at the other end, and pretend to have called a wrong number. But a voice on a phone would not tell him much. He needed to see the set-up – he needed to be reassured that it was only some faceless property company, and that there was no threat.

How long would it take to drive to Lincoln? He reached for the road atlas and saw that it would not take very long at all, in fact if he made use of the new bypass near Doncaster it would not take much over an hour. Could he do that tomorrow? It would have to be very early, because there was Michael Sallis's body to discover – at least, Edmund hoped there was – and he must not seem to have done anything out of his normal pattern.

But if he left before seven, he ought to reach Lincoln by eight thirty at the outside. Allow for rush-hour traffic and say nine o'clock. A time when there were plenty of people around, so that he could take a discreet look at the set-up and decide what to do. Probably he would not do anything, but he needed to *know*. He needed to know exactly what and who Ashwood's owners were.

Short of the absolute unforeseen, he ought to get back here for eleven to eleven thirty. That was a bit later than he would have liked for discovering Sallis's body, but there was no reason for anyone to drive along that lane to the house; there would not be any milk delivery or anything like that, and even the post – if there was any – would not be delivered until nearly midday. And even if things had gone wrong – even if Sallis had survived or escaped – there was still nothing to throw suspicion on to Edmund. Yes, it ought to be all right.

He washed up his supper things and then sat down to dial his own office number. No one would be there, of course, but he left a message on the answerphone saying that first thing tomorrow morning he was going out to measure the paths in the right-of-way dispute, and that he also had to call at Mrs Fane's house, which meant he would not be in until later. The measuring of the paths was a perfectly credible story; it was a case that had been going on for a number of weeks now; it was, in fact, the very case Edmund had been working on the day Deborah Fane had phoned to tell him about Trixie Smith's approach. Then he did have his tot of whisky, and finally went to bed.

But despite the whisky and despite having worked everything out so carefully, he did not sleep very well. His mind went over and over the details of what he had done and of what he might have to do tomorrow. Surely he had not missed anything, though?

He got up at six, showered and dressed, and made a pot of tea, carefully not opening curtains or switching on lights, in case of any chance passer-by noticing anything out of the normal pattern. You never knew who might be watching you – several times recently he had had the impression of eyes watching him.

He washed up his tea-cup and put it away as normal – there must be nothing done out of pattern; nothing that his cleaning lady might spot and say, My word, that's unusual. That's not like Mr Fane. After this he dressed as normal in his office suit with a clean shirt. As he put on his jacket, he caught a glimpse of Crispin watching him from the depths of the hall mirror. You're doing very well, said Crispin's expression. But isn't there one more thing . . . ?

One more thing . . .

Edmund went back upstairs to where the syringe lay discreetly at the back of his dressing-table drawer. He had contemplated disposing of it after Deborah's death – he had thought he might throw it into the river or bury it in garden rubbish at the municipal tip – but then he had thought that you never knew what you might need. And today, depending on what he found at the end of his journey, he might need it.

It was a few minutes before seven when he left the house, and by seven fifteen he was heading for the bypass, the syringe in his jacket pocket.

* * *

The traffic was still fairly light at this hour. The map was open on the seat beside Edmund and Crispin was with him as he drove along. Once or twice he thought he could hear Alraune's voice but he pushed it away, because he no longer wanted Alraune. Go away, you're a cheat, he said to Alraune. Two-faced, like the rest of your family. Like that cat Lucretia, whom Crispin had loved so much it had destroyed him – yes it had! And like Mariana Trent – another sly deceiver. 'We're all so sorry for Edmund,' she had said that night. 'We've primed some of the girls to flirt with him, to give him some fun for once . . .' But Mariana had got what she had deserved that night, even though Edmund had not intended her to die in the fire. Still, you might almost say that both Lucretia's daughters had had rough justice meted out to them, first Mariana and then Deborah. The symmetry of this pleased Edmund.

As the road unwound, the years continued to unwind as well, taking him into the night his father had died. I couldn't let you live, he said silently to Crispin's ghost. You understood that, didn't you? After you told me the truth, I couldn't risk you talking. And you would have done. You were losing your hold on sanity fast, and you would have talked.

A mad old man's ramblings, dear boy, said Crispin's voice sadly. *You said yourself I was as near mad as made no difference by then . . . Would anyone have listened or believed . . . ?*

But I couldn't risk it! cried Edmund silently. I couldn't be sure! I needed to kill the past! You do understand that?

Of course I understand, Edmund, said Crispin's voice. *I understand it all . . .* Suddenly it was the remembered, infinitely loving voice of Edmund's childhood, and Edmund frowned because just for a moment his sight had misted over. Stupid! He brushed his hand impatiently across his eyes, and concentrated on the unfamiliar road.

You were afraid I might talk, weren't you . . . ? That was it, wasn't it . . . ?

Yes, said Edmund gratefully. Because you had talked to me, you see. You couldn't stop yourself. ('I just kept on stabbing him, over and over again,' Crispin had said. 'I had to wipe out the words he had said; I brought the knife down on his face – on his mouth – over and over again. And there was so much blood . . .')

So much blood. The words had dropped into Edmund's mind that night, exactly in time with the rhythmic ticking of the old clock on the landing. So-much-blood. Tick-tick-tick . . . Like little jabs into your mind. *So-much-blood* . . .

With the words ticking inside his mind, he had taken his father into the bathroom. 'A nice warm bath – it'll be refreshing. I'll run the water for you, and then you can get in. I'll help you – I won't let you slip. And you'll feel much better afterwards.'

I did all that, thought Edmund. But I did it for *you*, Crispin. And while you were in the bath I came in, and I brought the razor down on your throat, and you died, there in the steam-filled bathroom, and there was so much blood, you were right about that, Crispin . . .

Afterwards I did all the things I would have been expected to do if it had been a real suicide. I felt for a heartbeat and when I was sure there wasn't one, I phoned the doctor.

And while I waited for the doctor to arrive, I sat on the stairs, watching the man I had murdered and the father I had loved and admired grow cold and stiff, listening to the ticking of the clock repeating his words over and over. So-much-blood . . . After a time it changed to *No one-must-know* . . . *No one-must-know* . . .

No matter the cost, no one must ever know that you were a murderer, Crispin.

One of the main problems was actually to find the address. Lincoln was a big place, and Edmund could not risk asking for directions. So before coming off the motorway, he pulled in at a big service station with a self-service restaurant and several small shop units.

Once inside, he wandered casually along the shelves of the shops. Magazines, convenience foods, cans of fizzy drink of all kinds. Ah, local street maps. Lincoln? Yes, there it was. *Good.* He picked it up in a rather absent-minded fashion: a traveller taking a break from his journey, spotting a map he did not possess and thinking it might come in handy sometime. You never knew where you might have to drive. He dropped a pack of sandwiches into his wire basket, along with a can of lemonade, a box of tissues and some peppermints, so that the map would not particularly stand out. He paid for everything in cash, of course.

The voice on Lucy's phone was brisk and businesslike and very apologetic for the fact that the time was a few minutes before eight o'clock in the morning.

Lucy had been snatching a hasty breakfast before setting off for work, and she had taken the call in the kitchen. She said it was quite all right to be ringing; was anything wrong?

'Probably not. But we need your help, Miss Trent, and I'm afraid this might be a distressing call for you.'

Lucy asked what had happened.

'I'm ringing about your cousin, Edmund Fane,' said Fletcher, and Lucy felt a stab of apprehension.

'Nothing's happened to him, has it?'

'Not as far as we know. But we need to talk to him quite quickly.'

'Why?'

A pause, as if the inspector was deciding how much to say. Lucy waited, and then Fletcher said, 'Last night Michael Sallis telephoned me to make a statement. He says that earlier in the evening Edmund tried to kill him.'

For a moment the words made absolutely no sense to Lucy. Edmund tried to kill Michael Sallis. She tried them over again in her mind. Edmund-tried-to-kill-Michael-Sallis. This time the words fell into the proper pattern, but even though Lucy understood them, she did not believe them. But with the idea of trying to establish a degree of normality, she said carefully, 'When you say "kill", do you mean in a car? A road accident of some kind?'

'I'm afraid not,' said the DI. 'It seems that Mr Sallis drove up to your aunt's house yesterday— Your aunt Deborah Fane, I mean—'

'Yes, I knew about that.' Here, at least, was something reasonably ordinary and understandable. 'Some of the furniture was being given to CHARTH – that's the charity Michael Sallis works for.'

'While they were at the house, there was an injury to Mr Sallis's hand. It meant he couldn't drive, and he stayed at the house for the night. He's made a statement, saying that while he was in a room in the front of the house Edmund Fane came in through a back door, very quietly and furtively, and turned all the gas rings of the cooker fully on. And then stole out again, locking the door behind him.'

'Leaving the gas escaping into the house? With Michael locked in?'

'Yes.'

'But that means,' said Lucy, wanting to be sure she had not misunderstood, 'if Michael hadn't realized what was happening, he would have been gassed?'

'Almost certainly.'

'But – but this is ridiculous. For one thing Edmund hardly knew Michael. Why on earth would he try to kill him?'

'We don't know yet that he did, although so far there's no reason to doubt the substance of Mr Sallis's statement – or his integrity. As far as we can make out, he's a perfectly sane person, quite highly regarded by the charity he works for, with no axe to grind against Edmund Fane.'

'But so is Edmund sane and highly regarded,' said Lucy at once. 'He's the most correct, most law-abiding person— It's a family joke, how correct he is. And he's – he's devoid of nearly all the emotions! Aunt Deb used to say he was entirely passionless.' At least Deb had been spared this. 'What's happening now?'

'Well, we've certainly got to talk to Mr Fane as soon as possible,' said Fletcher. 'The immediate problem is that we don't know where he is. I drove up here in the early hours, and we went out to his house shortly after seven. But there's no sign of him, his car's gone, so it looks as if he either went off somewhere very early or he's been out all night. Normally in this kind of situation we'd check with neighbours – perhaps the staff at his office – but I'm loath to do that yet in case there's some innocent explanation for all this. I thought I'd talk to you first.'

'In case I might know where he is?' said Lucy. 'Or in case he might be here? Well, I don't know where he is, and he certainly isn't here.'

'Might he have stayed overnight somewhere? With friends, perhaps?'

But Edmund had never, to Lucy's knowledge, stayed out all night. 'He lives a very quiet life. Beyond the office and his clients he hardly has any social life at all – maybe the odd Rotary Lunch or a Law Society dinner, but nothing else. And even on the rare occasion he does go out in the evening I don't think he stays anywhere much after half past ten.'

'Is he likely to have gone out very early?'

'I shouldn't think so. He's hardly the early-morning jogging type.'

'What about friends? Do you know the names of any of them?'

'I don't think he's got any – not close ones,' said Lucy. 'Just acquaintances and business associates.'

'No ladies in his life?'

'No.' But this was all sounding so sad for Edmund that Lucy tried to qualify it by saying that Edmund was a bit of a loner.

'We do want to find him fairly quickly,' said Fletcher. 'Just to check Mr Sallis's story, you understand. I daresay it'll turn out to be a misunderstanding.'

It would be a misunderstanding, of course. This was Edmund they were discussing, and it was simply not possible to think of Edmund skulking into a darkened house with the aim of killing another human being, or to imagine him on the run from the police. Lucy found this such a disturbing image that she said, 'Inspector – would it be all right if I drove up there?'

'D'you mean right away?'

'Yes. I can set off more or less at once – I'll tell Quondam there's a family crisis and that I won't be in for a couple of days. I've got some holiday leave owing, and I've just finished putting together a project so it won't be a problem. I can get there in a couple of hours if there aren't any snarl-ups – it's practically motorway all the way and I know the roads.' She hesitated, and then said, 'I wouldn't get in the way or anything, but he's my cousin and we more or less grew up together. If he's in trouble, I think I ought to be there. I don't think he should be on his own.'

And there isn't anyone else, said her mind. Edmund really hasn't got anyone else. Was that why he had made that odd approach that night? 'You're footloose and fancy-free, Lucy,' he had said. 'It seemed an alluring idea.' And his hand had curled around hers . . . And his body pressing against her . . .

'All right,' said the inspector, having apparently considered the idea. 'You'd better come straight to the White Hart; I expect you know it, do you? Good. Mr Sallis is still there, and the manager's let us have a little coffee-room as a base to work from. We haven't divulged anything to the staff, of course: we've just said we're involved in an investigation.'

'Edmund will appreciate that when all this is cleared up,' said Lucy, hoping that it would all be cleared up.

'I hope he'll also appreciate what a good cousin he has,' said Jennie Fletcher rather dryly.

'He won't,' said Lucy. 'He never appreciates anyone. But I can't help that.'

CHAPTER THIRTY-SIX

At eight thirty the traffic was pouring into London. Lucy battled doggedly through it, and finally got clear of the M25 and on to the northbound M1. At least this was a familiar journey; there was something reassuring about familiar things when your mind was in turmoil. An hour and a half of motorway, a brief stop at the usual Little Chef just before Nottingham for a break and a cup of coffee and to top up with petrol, then on again.

As she drove, she tried to think what she would say to Edmund – always assuming he turned up – and wondered if he would be grateful to her for coming. If he was his more sneering self she would leave him to stew and drive straight home. No, she would not, of course. Concentrate on the journey, Lucy. There's the new bypass that Aunt Deborah hated because it had churned up so much pastureland, although now it was finished it took miles off the last stretch.

When she reached the White Hart she asked for either Mr Sallis or Inspector Fletcher, and was directed to a small coffee-room.

'Hello, Lucy,' said Michael Sallis. He looked pale and there were shadows around his eyes as if he might not have slept much; one of his hands bore a professional-looking bandage, but he came towards her, holding out his other hand. Lucy took it, relieved to find that there was no awkwardness between them. She had not wanted to discover that she hated Michael for making this accusation and she had not wanted any embarrassment between them. But it was all right.

Without preamble, he said, 'This must be a nightmare for you. I'm very sorry about it.'

'I don't suppose it's been any picnic for you,' said Lucy, and saw him smile.

'Francesca's here,' he said. 'Francesca Holland. Did you know?'

'No.' Lucy did not like to ask why Francesca was here; perhaps she was somehow linked up with Michael, or in the process of getting linked up with him. They had seemed quite friendly at Quondam that afternoon.

'She's just gone to get some coffee – Inspector Fletcher said you'd probably get here about this time.'

Francesca came in as he said this, carrying a tray. She smiled at Lucy. 'Hello. I'm glad I timed the coffee so well. Did you have a good journey or did you have to fight through the rush hour?'

Lucy accepted the coffee gratefully, said the journey had been like traversing one of the minor outposts of hell, and asked if there were any new developments.

'I don't think Fane's turned up yet,' said Michael. He hesitated, and then said, 'But Fletcher's people went out to the house with a warrant about an hour ago.'

Then they're taking the accusation seriously, thought Lucy. She tried to quell a swift unpleasant image of Edmund's fury if the police broke into his house in his absence, and by way of explanation for her own presence, said, 'I thought Edmund oughtn't to be left to face this on his own. I thought he might like someone here who was prepared to bat on his side. Family.'

'Family,' said Michael softly, and Lucy saw him exchange a look with Francesca. She thought Francesca nodded very slightly, as if Michael had asked a silent question, and she thought she had been right about them linking up. They already had that rare mental closeness you occasionally encountered in couples.

Michael said, 'Lucy, it's odd you should use the word family, because—' He broke off as Francesca leaned forward to look through the window to the White Hart's little car park at the front of the building.

'What is it?' said Lucy.

'It's Inspector Fletcher,' said Francesca. 'But it looks as if she's on her own.' She glanced at Michael. 'That means they didn't find Edmund, I should think.'

'I should think you're right.'

Lucy did not know whether to be sorry or glad.

'We've been in the house,' said Jennie Fletcher, who looked tired but as if she still had plenty of energy in reserve. 'Fane wasn't there and his car had definitely gone.'

'You broke in? You mean you really did break the door down?'

'We levered the lock off one door, Miss Trent. But it's a neat job of levering and it's easily repairable. We did get a warrant before we did it.'

Lucy guessed that in view of Edmund's standing as a respectable local solicitor the police were not cutting any corners. 'Did you – find anything in the house? Any clues as to where he might be?'

'We've contacted his office now, and it seems he left a message on the answerphone last evening to say he was going out to take some measurements of a piece of land before going in to the office today – something to do with a boundary dispute. The call was made at a quarter to eight last night, and it was made from Edmund Fane's home phone.'

'Well, couldn't it be true about the boundary dispute?'

'It could, except the client concerned – a local farmer – hasn't seen Mr Fane and wasn't expecting him. We've also spent quite a long time at Deborah Fane's house, and the evidence so far bears out your statement,' she said to Michael. 'We found the window you smashed; it's clearly been broken from the inside.'

'It *was* broken from the inside,' said Michael politely.

'We found a couple of things in Edmund Fane's house, that are – well, curious.' Fletcher delved into her pocket and brought out a mobile phone. 'This is yours, isn't it, Mr Sallis?'

'Yes. Then Fane did have it,' said Michael. 'I wonder if he took it deliberately – to prevent me calling for help – or whether it was just absent-mindedness. Can I have it back, or d'you need it for evidence or anything?'

'You can probably have it later,' said the inspector. 'We've looked at the calls made from it in the last twenty-four hours, and they're all perfectly innocent – oh, except that there's no record of any call to the White Hart.'

'There should be,' said Michael. 'He did phone them. As far as I can remember it was around half past four, and he said they hadn't a room.'

'And yet when you got here last night there were several,' said Fletcher.

'Are you saying Edmund faked a phone call?' For some reason Lucy found this almost more bizarre than the attempted murder accusation.

'That's what it looks like.'

'You said there were a couple of things that were odd,' put in Francesca.

'The other thing is a letter that seems to have arrived by yesterday's post. It was on the dining-table, and it's dated the day before yesterday, so it's a fairly safe bet that it was delivered yesterday – the postal authorities are confirming that later. But we think Mr Fane got home last evening around half past six, found the letter, and made the call to his office at quarter to eight that night.'

'And then went batting off somewhere at crack of dawn next morning?'

'It's a reasonable assumption, Miss Trent. The milk was still on the step – it's delivered about quarter past seven apparently, so it looks as if Mr Fane left the house before it arrived. I don't think he'd have left the milk on the step, do you?'

'No,' said Lucy rather shortly.

'What was the letter?' asked Michael.

'It's from HM Land Registry. It's addressed to Edmund Fane's home, and it's a reply to a request he made about some land. We've contacted them, and they confirm that they do provide a search service for the title to property or land. There's a small fee, but it's a standard service to anyone who writes in.'

'And being a solicitor, Fane would know all that,' said Michael thoughtfully. 'He'd know it would be an unremarkable request to make as well. Well? What did Edmund Fane want to know?'

'The name of Ashwood Studios' owner,' said Jennie Fletcher.

'Ah. And did they give him the name?'

'They did.'

There was a shuttered look to Michael's eyes, but when he spoke he sounded quite calm. 'How about an address?'

'Yes.' She was watching Michael very intently. 'Yes, they gave an address for the owner.'

This time Michael turned so white that for a moment Lucy thought he was going to faint, and she was aware of Francesca making an involuntary movement and then sinking back into her chair.

'Mr Sallis?' said Jennie Fletcher sharply.

Michael was already reaching for his jacket. He said, 'I know where Edmund Fane's gone, and it's desperately important that we head him off.' He glanced at his watch. 'It's coming up to eleven o'clock now, and it's probably about an hour's drive from here. Fane's got a three or four hour start, but I can phone ahead.'

He reached for the mobile phone, and Francesca said, 'Michael, if you're thinking of driving it's out of the question. Even if your car was repaired – which it isn't – your hand isn't up to a long journey.'

'Damn,' he said. 'I'd forgotten the car.'

'I'll drive you,' said Fran. 'To – wherever it is.'

'I'll come too if you want,' offered Lucy. 'We could share the driving.'

'Nobody's going to be sharing any driving, and if anyone's going anywhere it'll be in a police car – two police cars,' said Jennie sharply. She frowned, and then said, 'All right, I'll trust you a bit further, Mr Sallis. We can leave someone stationed at Edmund Fane's house, and you can give my sergeant directions as we go.'

'Can Francesca and Lucy come as well?'

'Certainly not.'

'We could follow you,' said Lucy.

'You can't stop us doing that,' added Fran.

'Oh, for— All right,' said Fletcher in exasperation. 'But when we get to – to wherever we're going, you're both to stay well out of the way, is that understood?'

'Yes,' they said in unison.

'You'll never keep up with the police cars,' said Michael to Fran. 'Where's something to write on – thanks, that'll do.' He scribbled an address and what looked like brief directions on the back of one of the paper napkins from the coffee tray. 'Can you read my writing?'

'I think so.'

'Mr Sallis, you'll have to do some fast talking on the journey,' said the inspector as they went out. 'There are a great many unanswered questions in this affair.'

'We can take my car if you prefer,' said Lucy, as she and Francesca sprinted across the car park. 'I don't mind driving.'

'You've already driven a couple of hundred miles,' said Fran. 'You must be exhausted.'

'So have you.'

'Yes, but I've had a break since then, and something to eat.' Fran settled the matter by opening the door of her car and getting in. 'But I might ask you to take over for a spell – it depends how far it is. Michael said about an hour.'

'He was right about us not keeping up with the police cars,' said Lucy, as Fran drove off the White Hart's car park as fast as she dared.

'Yes, they're out of sight already. But we've got directions of a kind and I've got a road atlas in the glove compartment.'

'Then I'll map-read as we go,' offered Lucy, propping Michael's scribbled notes on the dashboard.

For several miles neither of them spoke except when Lucy gave directions, but once they had joined the motorway, she said, 'Francesca – I'd appreciate knowing what this is about. It's clear that there's quite a lot going on under the surface, and it's also clear that you know more about it than I do.'

Fran hesitated, and then said, 'I don't know why we're going to this place, whatever it is, but I do know some things from Michael. But not everything.' As Lucy glanced at her, she said firmly, 'It isn't my story to tell. I think when you do hear it, it's got to be from Michael. And apart from any other consideration, it isn't a story to tell while we're belting along a motorway at eighty miles an hour.'

'Fair enough. How are we doing for time?'

'It's just coming up to half past eleven.'

'I think we're going to be too late,' said Lucy, and thought: but too late for what?

Edmund was beginning to wonder if the Land Registry could have given him the wrong information, because he had not been expecting to find himself driving into such rural isolation. Still, there was a growing trend for companies to have a country house for sales conferences, or for overworked executives to recuperate. And in the last few years ugly, severely functional industrial estates had sprung up on the outskirts of most towns and cities. He might go round a curve in the road and come to just such an estate at any minute.

He did, in fact, go round several curves in the road, and one of them turned out to be a wrong turning, wasting several miles and time he did not really have. Fortunately he realized his mistake and was able to pull on to the side of the road to check the map. Ah, that was where he had gone wrong – that big traffic island. He should have taken the second exit, not the third. It was infuriating when local authorities did not display clear road signs. He drove back to the island, quelling a stab of concern at how late it was getting.

Left, and then right, and left again at some crossroads. He passed several farms, looking as if they had been dropped down from the sky at random. The road was bumpier now, and narrower, and there were fields with the deep lines of drainage ditches in places. In the dull morning they looked like wounds in the earth.

Edmund drove on, through a couple of villages that interlocked with one another; the houses fronted on to the street and had low-browed windows and the wavy look of extreme age. Then came a village pub and a small village church. Yes, this was the right place; he drove into the shadow of the trees surrounding the church and switched off the engine. He was almost at his destination, and he had better decide what he was going to do.

As he sat in the car he was aware of Crispin strongly with him, and presently a plan began to form in his mind. Crispin's plan was it? It did not matter. Edmund would find the house, and to whoever opened the door he would say he had a client interested in buying odd parcels of land in the south-east, and that he was retained by the man to keep his ear to the ground. After seeing the neglected condition of the Ashwood site, it had occurred to him to find out who the owner was. No, he had not wanted to make an official inquiry through Liam Devlin; he had wanted to keep the thing very discreet, very low-key, in case there was no mileage in it.

And so he had obtained the name and address of the present owner via a standard Land Registry Search, and when a business journey had brought him to this part of England, he had made a spur-of-the-moment decision to call, to see if there was a possibility of negotiations being opened. He rehearsed this several times over, trying out different ways of presenting it, and when he thought he had it as right as he could get, he started the car again and drove along the little street, looking for the address he wanted and then at last seeing the sign that took him out of the village again, and along a hedge-fringed lane.

And then he was there.

* * *

His misgivings increased at once. The house was completely unremarkable; it was the kind of house that might have originally belonged to an estate worker in the days when there were lords of the manor. You saw dozens of similar properties the length and breadth of England, often nicely converted but sometimes crumbling into ruin. This one seemed to have been quite well looked after, but . . .

But surely this could not be right. *Had* he got the address wrong after all, or did the owner of the legendary Ashwood Studios really live in this ordinary house, in this remote Lincolnshire village? Perhaps it was some elderly recluse, or an eccentric industrialist whose private retreat this was. Yes, that was a possibility, and it might explain Ashwood's own dereliction as well. But clearly his carefully rehearsed plan about a client and land purchase was not going to work.

It's all right, said Crispin. *This is clearly a private house, but just remember that Michael Sallis has the phone number, so he must know whoever lives here . . .*

After a moment Edmund got out of the car, and went through the gate and along the little path. The house, seen closer to, was neat and clean, and the gardens were tidy. But there was a quiet feeling to it; the feeling you got from a house that had been empty for a long time, or that had only had one inhabitant for several years. Nothing stirred as Edmund went through the gate and down the path to the front door.

He plied the old-fashioned door-knocker and waited. For several minutes nothing happened and another possibility occurred to him. Perhaps the owners had moved out, and the Land Registry had given him out-of-date information. That would explain a good deal. But then there was a flurry of footsteps from within, and the door was opened.

A plump, no-nonsense lady with short hair and weatherbeaten skin, but with the faint tilt of the cheekbones that suggested a dash of Eastern European ancestry, stood in the doorway, looking enquiringly at Edmund.

She was dressed plainly in a skirt and sweater but there was just the suggestion of hospital starch about her, and of thermometers and stainless steel bowls. A nurse? No, but something close to it. At once the plan that had been shifting its contours in Edmund's mind dropped into place, and he saw his way forward.

'I'm sorry I was a few minutes coming to the door,' said the brisk lady. 'Can I help you at all?' She spoke English smoothly, but there was a slight inflection that emphasized the faint foreign air.

Edmund's whole body was thrumming with nervous anticipation, but he smiled Crispin's smile, and introduced himself as Mr Edwards, apologizing for intruding. A business journey from London to a place just north of Rotherham, he said, and he happened to have mentioned it to his good friend, Michael Sallis, earlier in the week. Michael had suggested he might break his journey here since it was only a few miles out of his way. And, said Edmund, he understood that visitors were always welcome.

'Oh, how very nice,' said the woman. 'I always like to see a new face. Mr Sallis comes up about once a month, but of course he phones as well, just to see if there's any news.'

'So I believe,' said Edmund, picking his way carefully, but thankful that he seemed to be striking the right note.

'A bit of company always helps as well,' said the woman. 'Come along in. There's very little change, of course, but we stay positive. Would you like a cup of coffee? – I was just thinking I would make some for myself.'

'That would be very kind.'

'We've converted one of the downstairs rooms,' said the woman, leading Edmund along the hall. 'Friendlier, somehow, than being tucked away upstairs. And it's at the back of the house, so we can open the French windows on to the garden in summer. I'll take you through.'

It was a large room, and in the summer it would be filled with sunshine from the garden beyond. But on a dark autumnal day the shadows clustered everywhere, and there was a feeling of immense quietness, as if hardly anything had happened here for a very long time. A high, narrow, hospital-type bed stood near the window.

Edmund paused just inside the door, waiting for the woman's footsteps to die away. Had she gone back to the kitchen? Yes, that was the sound of a door opening and closing. Then he was on his own for a brief space.

Except that he was not on his own at all. There was someone lying in the high narrow bed. Someone who lay very still, and whose light papery breathing barely stirred the covers. As his eyes adjusted to the shadows, he began to make out colours, shapes, features . . .

There was no movement from the bed, barely even any indication of life. Sleeping? But as he moved to stand by the bed, he could see that this was deeper than sleep. You're very far away, said Edmund silently. You haven't quite died and I don't know if you're drugged or in a semi-coma, but you're not really in this world any longer. Beneath all these thoughts, an immense tidal wave of emotion was sweeping over him because he knew, definitely and unquestionably, who this was.

The legend. The person about whom all those stories had been told, and upon whom so many of those rumours had focused. Edmund did not understand how it had happened, or how the legend had wound up in this remote corner of England, but he knew who was lying in the narrow bed.

As he stared down, he was strongly aware that Crispin was pouring into his mind, filling him up, so that all the guilt and the fear scalded through Edmund's whole body. He thought he gasped with the pain of it, and he must certainly have made some sound, because the movement he had been watching for came from the bed. A light stirring, and then a half-turning of the head.

You're not yet so far away that you don't sense I'm here, thought Edmund. But is it me you're sensing? Or is it Crispin? Because it's Crispin who's smiling down at you, and it's Crispin who's reaching into the coat pocket for the syringe, and who's saying to me, Isn't it fortunate that we brought this with us, dear boy . . .

It isn't me in this room any longer, thought Edmund. It's Crispin. It's Crispin who's about to sever this remaining link to the shameful past. The voice inside his head was very clear, and he could hear exactly what Crispin was saying.

One last murder to commit, that was what Crispin was saying. One last murder, and then we can be safe.

And this murder, dear boy, is going to be the easiest of them all . . .

As he bent over the bed, the door opened behind him.

CHAPTER THIRTY-SEVEN

Lucy and Francesca had not been able to keep up with the police cars, which had hurtled away at top speed and vanished into the swirling traffic and the snaking network of roads.

'I didn't think we would,' said Fran. 'But I think we're on the right track.'

After they left the motorway the roads narrowed and were harder to negotiate, but the signs were still clear. They were going deep into the fenlands, and if the telegraph poles and the occasional electrical pylon or cellphone-mast could have been blocked out, they could both have believed themselves to have somehow gone back to medieval times.

'I've never been to this part of England before,' said Lucy. 'Have you?'

'Fen country. No, I haven't. But there's masses of history out here and lovely bits of folklore. The Babes in the Wood in Wayland Forest and the *Paston Letters*, and some of the settings for *David Copperfield*. I might set up a project for my sixth-formers on all the associations of the place,' said Francesca thoughtfully. 'Where are we now?'

'We need to go straight across the next traffic island, and then turn sharp right after about two miles.'

'It's quite well signposted,' said Fran, negotiating the traffic island. 'But I'm glad Michael wrote down that list of villages, or we'd have been hopelessly lost.'

The names on the signposts were like something out of an old-fashioned children's fairy-story. Grimoldby and Ludford Parva and Osgodby. A fat little country bus jogged along behind them for a few miles, and then turned off down a lane marked Scamblesby.

'You don't suppose we've fallen into Beatrix Potter territory and not noticed it?' said Francesca.

'It feels like that, doesn't it? Or is it nearer to Lewis Carroll?'

'Straight down the rabbit-hole and through the looking-glass,' agreed Fran.

They were passing through stretches of flat, reed-fringed marshlands now, and once or twice there was a feeling that the skies might be moving downwards, blurring with the land. Lucy thought the winter days would be very short here but memories would be long. All kinds of forgotten secrets might live out here for a very long time.

She had thought they would need to ask for directions, but in the event it was easy enough to follow Michael's hastily-scrawled notes.

'The house must be along there,' said Fran.

'Yes. It isn't quite what I was expecting though,' said Lucy, and as Fran turned the car into the narrow lane she thought: we're going back into the past, I can feel that we are.

But I don't know whose past it is.

Crispin had been furious when the woman attendant came back into the bedroom, just as he was reaching for the syringe. He had whipped round and called her an ugly name – almost spitting it out at her – and Edmund had been horrified. He had wanted to apologize to the woman; to explain that Crispin had been startled, but he found it difficult to make himself heard because Crispin was smothering him. Keep your stupid mouth shut, Edmund – that was what Crispin had said. Keep quiet and let me deal with this bitch. It was worrying to find Crispin so strongly in control and it was also a bit frightening.

But the woman seemed not to have heard the epithet and she seemed not to have noticed that Crispin was glaring at her with his hands curling into claws. She smiled and said the coffee was ready, and perhaps he would like to come into the dining-room to drink it. As she led the way out of the big bedroom, she talked in an ordinary voice, asking about his journey here: had the roads been crowded? It was a nightmare to drive anywhere these days, wasn't it?

After that swift eruption of rage died down Crispin became his normal courteous self once again. He knew how to handle women, and he knew how to charm and flatter – Edmund had always admired that in Crispin. He sipped the coffee which was strong and sharp, and listened to Crispin setting himself out to charm this woman. It was only as the coffee was finished and the cup set down that a faint concern crept in. Was Crispin talking a little too much? There was a slight blurriness to his voice, but every so often a sneering arrogant note came to the fore, which Edmund disliked. Crispin had every right to be arrogant – he was the golden charming young man of Edmund's childhood and everyone had loved him – but it did not do to let that arrogance come to the surface. It was always better to present a deferential façade; to fool people into thinking you were quiet and modest and entirely trustworthy. You needed to be diffident, that was the word.

Edmund tried to remind Crispin to be diffident and modest, but Crispin's voice became louder and louder. It went on and on – like a fly buzzing against a windowpane. Irritating. Edmund had never before found Crispin irritating, but this torrent of words was starting to be very annoying indeed.

He was thankful when the sound of a phone ringing somewhere in the house reached him, and the woman had to go out to answer it, leaving Edmund on his own with Crispin.

* * *

Lucy tried to concentrate on what Inspector Fletcher was saying. They were in a small and rather cosy room in the quiet house; Michael was in a deep armchair and Inspector Fletcher had taken a high-backed chair by the window. Fran had curled up on the window-seat, as if she was trying to give Lucy some privacy but was trying not to be obvious about it. An unknown woman with an efficient manner but kind eyes had let them in, and at a signal from Michael had taken a chair near to the fireplace.

Lucy had asked if Edmund was here, and Inspector Fletcher and Michael had exchanged quick glances. Then the inspector said, carefully, 'Edmund got here well ahead of us, as we thought he would. But I'm afraid that he is – very disturbed indeed. I'm so sorry about it, Miss Trent.'

'Disturbed?' said Lucy blankly, and Fletcher looked at Michael, as if she might be thinking this would come better from him.

With the air of a man taking a run at a high fence, Michael said, 'I don't know how to explain without it sounding utterly bizarre, Lucy. But I've talked to Elsa – I did introduce Elsa, didn't I—?'

'You did,' said the woman with high cheekbones, who was studying Lucy with interest.

'And as far as we can all make out, Edmund believes himself to be Crispin. Or to be under Crispin's influence,' said Michael.

'Crispin? You mean Edmund's father?' said Lucy, not questioning yet how Michael knew about Crispin. 'You do mean that?' She looked at the woman called Elsa.

'When Michael phoned me,' said Elsa, 'Edmund was already here as the inspector has said. But I did not need Michael's phone call – I knew who Edmund was at once. And I did not trust him.' She paused, and then said, 'He is very sick, I think. There is a strong indication of split personality of some kind – I am not enough qualified to go further, but it was very evident to me.'

'What happened?'

'After the first few moments,' said Elsa, glancing at Michael, 'I realized that there was some kind of deep conflict in him. When he talked, it was as if he was trying to stop himself from talking, but could not. In the village where my mother was born they believed in possession of the soul. Nowadays we dismiss such things, but listening to your cousin, Lucy, I could have believed in it very easily.'

Lucy said, in a whisper, 'Go on, please.'

'Coming to this house had – had profoundly affected him,' said Elsa, with a glance at Michael. 'I had offered him coffee on his arrival, but when I realized how unstable he was, I took him into the dining-room and dropped a sleeping pill into his cup. Very easy to do so discreetly and the pill itself was harmless. But it would induce drowsiness, you understand?' She paused, as if considering to go on, and then said, 'I was a little frightened, I admit, but after a very short time the drug took over and he dropped into a deep sleep in the chair. So,' said Elsa, 'I locked the dining-room door and waited for Michael to get here.'

'When we did get here,' said Inspector Fletcher, 'the sleeping pill was starting to wear off, and Edmund was—'

'Lucid?' said Lucy hopefully, because she was not bearing the thought of Edmund – always so correct, and so fastidious – behaving like this, being drugged, being regarded as disturbed and dangerous.

Fletcher hesitated, and then said, 'It was clear that for most of the time he believed himself to be Crispin.'

'But I still don't understand this,' said Lucy. 'Crispin's been dead for years. And even if Edmund is – even if he has this belief about being Crispin, why would he try to kill anyone? Or drive all the way out here?' Wherever 'here' is, said her mind.

'I haven't talked to Edmund for very long,' said Jennie Fletcher. 'And we'll have to defer to the doctors. But if he can be believed, fifty years ago, Crispin Fane killed Conrad Kline at Ashwood Studios. And as far as we can piece it together, Edmund has spent most of his life trying to keep that fact quiet.'

Lucy felt as if she had been plunged into a nightmare. She could not really remember Edmund's father, who had sunk into that sad confused old man and who had died when she was very small, but she knew the stories of the charming good-looking Crispin; and her mother had known him very well. ('Such good company,' she had said. 'He always came to my parties before he went peculiar, poor dear Crispin.' But Aunt Deb, downright as ever, had sometimes said that Crispin Fane had been ominously weak, and that she would not trust him a yard.)

Speaking as if she was afraid of breaking something extremely fragile, Lucy said, 'You're saying Crispin Fane killed Conrad? That it wasn't my grandmother who did it?'

'It doesn't look like it.'

Not Lucretia. After all these years – after all the scandal and after all the books that had been written and the articles that had been published – Lucretia had not killed Conrad Kline. Grandmamma, are you going to turn out to be the victim of scandal, rather than the perpetrator? thought Lucy. And then wondered if it mightn't be exactly like Lucretia to have the last laugh on everyone.

She said, 'Inspector, are you absolutely sure about all this?'

'Not absolutely. Not yet. But we're checking the facts, and it's looking that way.' Jennie Fletcher glanced at Michael, and then said, 'It sounded to me as if there had been some kind of love affair between Lucretia and Crispin, and Crispin killed Conrad in a jealous rage.'

Lucy suddenly felt deeply sad at the thought of Edmund carrying this secret around for so long. She said, 'He always had a horror of gossip – of the family skeletons. And he always hated people talking about my grandmother and the old Ashwood case. I never minded it, in fact I rather enjoyed the stories and the rumours – it all seemed far enough back not to matter.'

'Another world,' said Michael, half to himself.

'Yes. But if anyone ever mentioned Lucretia or Ashwood, Edmund used to change the subject at once. He was—'

'Yes?'

'I was going to say he was almost pathological about it,' said Lucy. 'But I suppose that's precisely what he was.'

'It looks like it. The doctors might get more out of him later on, but I think we'll find that he killed Trixie Smith that day to stop her from getting at the truth about the original Ashwood murders,' said Jennie. 'Although we might never know what else he's done over the years to keep his father's secret.'

So Crispin, the golden charming young man who had died sunk in melancholy and madness, had been a murderer. And Edmund, whom Lucy had known all her life, who had held her hand across a table and suggested it was an alluring idea for the two of them to become close, had been a murderer as well. I'm not going to cope with this, thought Lucy in horror. And then – yes, of course I am.

'What will happen to Edmund?' asked Francesca into the silence.

'I should think some sort of long-term treatment will be necessary,' said the inspector.

'Not – prison?'

'On the present showing, I think it's unlikely that he'd be considered fit to stand trial.'

Edmund guilty of murder, but unfit to stand trial. Edmund shut away in some dreadful asylum. And if only one could get rid of an appalling image of Edmund, madness glaring from his eyes, stalking that poor wretched Trixie Smith, bringing the skewer down on her face, it might be possible to feel deeply sorry for him. To dispel this image, Lucy said, 'Elsa – you said you recognized Edmund. Could you explain that, please?' She was not yet quite sure who Elsa was, but presumably at some stage it would be possible to ask.

'My mother had photographs dating back – oh, many years,' said Elsa. 'Some of them showed Crispin Fane. And Edmund is very like Crispin to look at.'

'Crispin? Your mother knew Crispin?'

'My mother was in a place of hell with the Baroness von Wolff,' said Elsa. 'It forged a bond between them – the kind of bond that never breaks, not even in death. I know a great deal about your family, Lucy.'

'Elsa's mother was called Ilena,' said Michael. 'She was Polish. After the war she became a doctor – a very good one.'

'Medicine is a tradition in my family,' said Elsa composedly. 'Me, I am just a nurse, nothing any grander than that.'

Lucy looked at her. 'You said – a place of hell?'

'Yes. My mother and Lucretia von Wolff were in Auschwitz together.'

Auschwitz.

As if a signal had been given, Michael stood up. 'Francesca, could you and Elsa stay in here for a little while?' he said.

'Of course.'

'Thank you. Lucy, if you're up to it, there's someone I'd like you to meet. It won't be very easy and it might be a shock. But since we're in this house— Well, anyway, I think you'd better know about it.'

'Who is it?' Lucy could not keep the apprehension out of her voice. 'Who am I going to meet?'

'My father,' said Michael. 'Alraune.'

Alraune. The uneasy legend. The smear of darkness on the edge of consciousness. The ghost-child named for the half-mythical mandragora root.

As they entered the big room at the back of the house Lucy was glad of Michael's presence. But her heart was pounding and she felt as if she had been running very fast and very hard. I'm about to see the legend, she thought. The fable, the semi-monster from my childhood. 'A childhood so bizarre and so bitterly tragic that it's best not repeated,' Aunt Deb had once said. 'Alraune, living or dead, is better left in peace . . . '

Living or dead . . .

It was not quite a room for the living, but it was not quite a room for the dead either, not yet. There was a hospital air about it, despite the comfortable furnishings and the large bowl of bronze chrysanthemums on a small table. But it's death's waiting-room for all that, thought Lucy, and then moved to the bed.

For a long time she did not speak. She was distantly aware of Michael nearby, and she thought there were sounds from beyond the room – homely ordinary sounds of crockery rattling and cupboard doors being opened. But the world had shrunk to this room, to this corner of the room, to this person in the bed . . .

And after all, the ghost-child was nothing but a dying man, barely conscious, the skin around the eyes ridged and puckered with old scars, the hair that might once have been dark like Michael's grey and thin . . . Sad. So immeasurably sad.

Speaking almost in a whisper, as if afraid to break into the listening silence, she said, 'So Alraune really does exist.'

'Oh yes.'

'Those scars around his eyes—'

'He's blind,' said Michael quietly. 'My mother attacked him when I was a child, and he lost his sight because of it. He killed her that night, and I thought he was dead as well – I couldn't imagine how he could survive being so badly wounded – but he did. He always was a survivor,' said Michael.

'I think,' said Lucy, in the same low voice, 'that I always knew at some level that Alraune was more than just a publicity stunt. But I thought Alraune was a girl. Everyone did. I found some news footage recently – you could see it if it wouldn't be too upsetting – but I can see now that the shot could have been either a girl or a boy.'

'If you read any of the newspaper articles, they seem to assume Alraune was a girl,' said Michael. 'He was born inside Auschwitz.'

'How dreadful.' Lucy hesitated, and then said, 'And he really is Lucretia's son?'

'Yes.' He smiled at her. 'We're cousins,' he said. 'Half cousins.'

'I rather like that thought.'

'So do I.'

Lucy looked back at the bed. 'Michael, I'm so sorry about all of this.'

'I know quite a lot of his history,' said Michael. 'And what I do know is a very bad history indeed. I suspect that Edmund

Fane knows some of it as well. I think he found out that I was Alraune's son, and he was afraid I had some kind of knowledge – something that Alraune had told me or passed on to me – about Ashwood and Crispin. That's why he tried to kill me.'

'Edmund thought you'd know Crispin killed Conrad Kline?'

'Yes. In fact Alraune never told me anything, and I ran away from home when I was eight.' There was a sudden note of reserve.

Lucy looked back at the figure in the bed. 'Is he – dying?'

'Yes,' said Michael. 'He's in the last stages of cancer. He was gaoled for killing my mother all those years ago, but they released him last year on what they called compassionate grounds. So it was arranged that he came here for the final months of his life. Elsa is marvellous, and there's a local doctor who comes.'

'Do they know who he is?'

'Elsa knows, of course. But local people don't. He's known as Alan Salisbury.' He hesitated, and then said, 'Since we're cousins, Lucy, and since there's already been far too much mystery about all this, in the privacy of this room, I'll tell you that Alraune von Wolff was a violent man and he had been a vicious child.'

'You said he killed your mother?'

'Yes. My mother,' said Michael, 'is one of the good memories I have of my early childhood, though.' He glanced back at the figure in the bed. 'But my grandmother – your grandmother – once told me that I should try to forgive Alraune, because he was not entirely to blame for what he had done.'

Lucy turned to look at him. 'You knew my grandmother?' she said in disbelief, and saw a very sweet smile widen his face.

'Oh yes,' said Michael softly.

Edmund was quite happy to go along with the two men who had turned up at the house, and who seemed so interested in Crispin.

He did not in the least mind talking about Crispin. He was unusually tired after the tension of the day and the long drive, and because of that his mind did not feel as sharp as usual, but it sounded as if there was some research being done into the particular form of melancholia that had afflicted Crispin, and so it would be as well to appear co-operative. Edmund knew a moment's apprehension in case this was a ploy to get at the truth about Crispin – you had to be so watchful for that kind of thing, you could not relax your guard for even a moment. But he had not spent the last twenty-odd years keeping Crispin's secret to fall into a trap now. If they thought they were going to catch him out, if they were planning on sneaking under his defences, they would soon find out they were wrong. Edmund was a foe worthy of any man's steel.

All he needed to do was to get Crispin back in place, and regain control. If he could just do that, everything would be all right and he could handle the situation with his customary efficiency and courtesy.

But Crispin would not go back to his place. Every few minutes, Crispin's words kept bubbling and dribbling out of Edmund's mouth, and Edmund could hear with horror that Crispin was telling these men everything, *everything* . . . Lucretia and the shameful untidy affair – the satin sofa in the dressing-room that had been stained because Crispin had not been able to contain himself that first time— The amused tolerance of Conrad Kline. He laughed at me, cried Crispin to the listening men. I couldn't bear to see him laughing at me.

And then the knife – lying there, ready to hand, part of the film set, sharper than anyone had realized. And Crispin's sudden realization that this was the only way to silence Conrad, the only way to stop him laughing. And it had stopped him. The blood had spurted out and Conrad had fallen back, a look of surprise in his eyes, clawing at the air, emitting dreadful wet cries through the blood that was filling up his mouth . . .

Dreadful admissions, all of them. Shameful and embarrassing, and Edmund could not bear hearing any of them. He could not bear to think of how Crispin had run in fear and panic from the studios, leaving Conrad dying there on the floor.

He began to tell Crispin to keep quiet. Because after all the years of silence, after all the risks and the planning, to hear it all come spilling out like this . . . His voice came out louder than he had intended, but that was all right, because it would drown Crispin's voice. After all I did for you, screamed Edmund at Crispin. All those deaths . . . Trixie Smith, stabbed in Ashwood Studios. Mariana and Bruce Trent, died in that fire that had only been meant to punish . . . And Aunt Deborah . . . The sheer unfairness rose up like bile in his throat, choking him. You shouldn't have made me kill Aunt Deborah, cried Edmund, and to his complete astonishment, he began to sob.

There was the faint whiff of something antiseptic, and then the hurting jab of a needle in his arm, and then of someone counting, and saying, 'He's going.'

And then the counting faded away and Edmund sank thankfully into a deep, soft darkness where he could no longer hear Crispin's voice.

The sun was starting to set in huge swathes of colour as Francesca drove away from the house, with Michael in the passenger seat, and Lucy in the back.

'It's not far,' said Michael, and Lucy heard that his voice held the deep contentment of someone turning homewards after a deeply disturbing journey.

They went past the road signs that many years ago a fearful eight-year-old boy had believed to have been placed by friendly will o' the wisps and darting marsh creatures, mischievously beckoning the traveller into a whole new world.

'Mowbray Fen,' said Fran, picking out a sign.

'Yes. We're almost there.'

A village street, with the glow of the setting sun lighting up the trees and bathing an old grey stone church in fiery radiance. The houses and the shops looked as if they had not altered much in the last fifty years.

Lucy's mind was still in tumult from what had happened in the last twenty-four hours, but as they drove along she was aware of a feeling of immense peace and acceptance. People living out here would have time and inclination to pause and talk to you. When Francesca said, softly, 'It feels as if time stopped here and never got wound up again,' Lucy at once said, 'I was just thinking that.'

The house stood at the end of a little lane, just outside the main village. It was built of grey stone, and there was a white gate. There was a sign on the gate that said, 'The Priest's House'.

As Fran stopped the car, Michael said, 'The house is much older than it looks. It was built in the days when there was a lot of religious persecution, and it's supposed to have been a hiding-place for Catholic priests waiting to be smuggled across to Holland.'

Fran switched off the engine, and looked at Michael for guidance as to what happened next.

'Lucy, would you go ahead of us?' said Michael. 'Francesca and I will wait here.' And, as Lucy looked at him questioningly, he said, 'It's all right. I promise.'

Walking down the path, Lucy once again had the sensation of falling deeper into the past. Or was it Looking Glass Land again? Here was the door, with a nice polished brass knocker. But before she could reach up to it, the door opened, as if whoever lived here had been looking out of a window, or perhaps had been waiting and listening for the car. Lucy's heart began to beat very fast, because of all the things in the world, this could not be possible, it simply could not—

Framed in the doorway was a thin but very upright old lady, with the translucent pallor of extreme age but with smouldering dark eyes and long sensitive hands and the most beautiful smile Lucy had ever seen.

'Hello, my dear,' said this figure, putting out both hands in welcome. 'We've never met, and please don't let's have any vulgar displays of emotion. But I think you must be my granddaughter, Lucy, and I'm very glad indeed to meet you.'

CHAPTER THIRTY-EIGHT

After what seemed to be a very long time Lucy said, 'This isn't really happening, is it? This is a dream, and you aren't actually real.'

'Certainly I'm real,' said the lady with the dark eyes, sounding amused. 'I always have been real, Lucy. And since Michael's phone call half an hour ago, I have been watching for you. But I think we should talk about all this in civilized comfort. Come inside, and tell Michael to bring your friend in as well.'

The inside of the house had the same tranquil feeling as the village, and the lady whom Lucy could not quite think of as her grandmother, but whom she could not quite think of as Lucretia von Wolff either, led the way into a room at the back of the house. There was a low ceiling and an old brick fireplace with pleasantly scented logs burning in the hearth, and there were deep comfortable armchairs. The curtains were partly drawn against the encroaching darkness, but it was possible to see a large garden with lawns and old-fashioned flowers, and chairs where you could sit on summer afternoons. Exactly the kind of house and garden a very old lady might be expected to have. Totally conventional and predictable. But if this really was Lucretia von Wolff, she had never been either conventional or predictable.

Lucretia von Wolff. Lucy could not stop looking at her. Michael and Francesca were in the room as well, but Lucy could not think about anyone except the slender figure in the chair by the hearth. She said, 'I don't understand this. You – you're dead.' And then at once, 'I'm sorry, that was an outstandingly stupid thing to say, never mind sounding rude. It's just that – you're supposed to have been dead for over fifty years. All the reports say you died in Ashwood Studios that day— You killed yourself. There were *witnesses*!' This came out in a confused blur of annoyance and bewilderment, with, under it all, an unfolding of delighted hope, because this was the real heart of the legend; this was the imperious baroness, the adventuress who had snapped her fingers at Viennese society, and had strewn lovers and scandals half across Europe. I'm going to know her, thought Lucy. After I've sorted all this out, I'm going to be able to talk to her. Like touching a fragment of the past. Oh, don't let this be a dream, please let this be really happening.

'My dear Lucy,' said the dark-eyed lady, 'I spent a large part of my life spinning illusions for people. Do you really think I wasn't capable of spinning that last illusion at Ashwood Studios that day?'

Michael said, 'We'll explain everything, Lucy. Alice will tell you it all. She tells a story better than anyone I've ever known. And she still loves an audience, even after all these years.'

They smiled at one another, and Lucy felt a sharp and rather shameful stab of jealousy. But then one of the ring-clad hands came out to her. 'I hope, Lucy, that you'll call me Alice, as Michael does,' said the lady who loved an audience. 'I really cannot support the title of grandmother, you know.' For the first time Lucy heard very clearly the baroness's voice. Half imperious, half mischievous. Underneath it all hugely enjoying being an *enfant terrible*. And she's drawing me into that charm and that warmth she shares with Michael, thought Lucy. I think she might deliberately be weaving a spell, but I think it's probably a good spell, and I don't give a hoot anyway. Alice, that's what she wants me to call her. It's rather nice. Tennyson and Looking Glasses – I *knew* this was Lewis Carroll territory!

'And we'll have something to drink, in fact I think we should have champagne,' said Alice briskly. 'And if you can stay on for supper, that would be best of all. You might not want to do that, but I hope you will. All of you, I mean.' She turned her attention to Francesca. 'Do stay, Francesca. I'd like it if you would.'

'Well, actually,' said Francesca rather diffidently, 'I was thinking I'd leave you to it for a couple of hours. There might be all kinds of family things – private things for you to talk about. And I truly wouldn't mind walking down to the village. It looked so nice when we drove through. I could have something to eat in the pub and come back later.'

'There's no need whatsoever for you to leave,' said Alice firmly. 'And I hope you won't think of doing so. In any case, from what I understand you've been as much involved in this as anyone, so you deserve to hear the explanations and the truth.' She studied Francesca for a moment, and then nodded slightly as if pleased with what she was seeing. 'Most families are usually better for a little leaven, and I think you'd be a very nice leaven in this family tonight, my dear. In fact you'd be—'

She broke off, and turned her head, and Lucy caught the sound of a car drawing up. Was this something else about Edmund? A jab of panic spiked into her. But Alice was saying with perfect equanimity that it would be her other guest arriving. 'Michael, be a dear and let him in.'

'Other guest?' said Lucy as Michael went out.

'Yes. After Michael telephoned me this morning – he was in a shocking panic, the dear boy, in case Edmund Fane came out here. As if,' said Lucretia von Wolff in parenthesis, 'I couldn't deal with Crispin Fane's son. Well, anyway I came to a decision about something, and so I telephoned—'

'She telephoned me,' said a voice, and Lucy turned sharply to see Liam Devlin standing in the doorway, looking as dishevelled as if he, and not Michael, had been the subject of yesterday's murderous attack.

* * *

The ridiculous thing was that for several minutes Lucy was so extremely pleased to see Liam that she very nearly forgot everything else.

He appeared totally unruffled at finding himself confronted with a roomful of people, and he merely looked round like a cat surveying a new territory. But when his eyes lit on Alice he smiled at her. 'Baroness,' he said softly, and crossed the room to take her hand.

Alice regarded him approvingly, but said, 'So you've realized who I am at last, have you?'

'I have. But it wasn't until I saw the film of *Alraune* that I did realize it,' said Liam. 'It's a very remarkable film, of course, and Lucretia von Wolff was a very remarkable lady. But once I had seen her, I couldn't mistake the resemblance. It's the eyes and the bones of the face.'

'The silver tongue of the Irish,' said Alice, but Lucy thought she was secretly pleased. 'And you're here in time for supper, I'm so pleased about that. Come along into the dining-room as soon as you're all ready. Some of the story I'll have to tell you is tragic, and some of it is scandalous,' she said. 'And I think most of it had better be forgotten after today. But scandal always seems gentler when there's food to flavour it, and tragedy's easier to take with wine to smooth the rough edges.' She considered this, and then added, 'Someone once said that to me, but I forget precisely who he was. It's so infuriating to forget things – I know we all have to get old, but you'd think that by now evolution could have worked out a way for us to keep our memories intact—'

'There's nothing wrong with your memory, Alice,' said Michael.

'I know there isn't.'

Supper was an easy, uncluttered affair of salad, thin slices of smoked salmon with lemon wedges, a platter of cheeses, and crusty bread, warm from the oven.

'It's quite a plain meal,' said Alice, surveying the table. 'Because there wasn't much time. But perfectly substantial, I hope.'

The food, in fact, was very substantial indeed, and Lucy realized with surprise that she was ravenously hungry. She was just wondering who had prepared everything, when Alice said, 'I'm no longer as domestic as I used to be, Lucy, but fortunately there are two very nice girls in the village who come in a couple of times a week to deal with cleaning and cooking. So after Michael made his second phone call to say he was bringing you and Francesca here, I rang one of them. Do all help yourselves to whatever you want, won't you. Don't wait to be offered anything, it's so stultifying to have to wait to be offered things.'

Lucy thought: she has dined with crowned heads and exiled royalty and she has entertained the rich and the famous and the fabulous. And she probably half starved inside Auschwitz along with goodness knows how many other poor wretches. But now she's presiding over this quite ordinary table with us. And then she looked at Alice again, and knew nothing she did would ever be entirely ordinary.

'Michael, I don't suppose your injured hand will allow you brandish a corkscrew or deal with a champagne cork, will it? No, I thought not. Then, Mr Devlin, could I impose on you for that small service, please.'

'Baroness, if you are serving us Clicquot, I will open an entire cellarful of bottles for you,' said Liam, and Lucy saw that three bottles of an honourable champagne were standing in a silver cooler but that there was mineral water and fruit juice as well. Style, she thought. That's what she's got, and that's what she's always had. She's over ninety years old, but she'll have style until she dies. If this really is a dream I don't want ever to wake up.

Liam dealt with the champagne competently and filled the glasses, somehow ending up in a seat next to Lucy. 'Are you thinking this is pure gothic?' he said. 'Unknown cousins, and wicked family solicitors turning up?'

'I was thinking it's like something from *The Prisoner of Zenda* or *Rudolph of Rassendyll*,' rejoined Lucy. 'I wasn't expecting the wicked solicitor as well.'

'When this particular client calls, I ditch everything else to obey,' said Liam, and smiled across the table at Alice. 'She never pays my bills, although that might be because I usually forget to send her any. But she's my favourite client.'

'Mr Devlin's been my agent at Ashwood for several years,' said Alice. 'It's a good relationship. He's a very good lawyer.'

'I'm very good indeed,' said Liam, grinning. 'But I'd have to say that until last weekend, I really did think I was acting for a lady called Alice Wilson.'

'You're Ashwood's owner?' said Lucy to Alice. 'No, you can't be, though – Michael said—' She stopped. How acceptable was it to refer to Alraune in this house?

'Over fifty years ago,' said Alice composedly, 'I bought the entire Ashwood site. Land, buildings, cottages, fields – everything. I did so under my real name of Alice Vera Wilson—' She broke off as Lucy looked at her in surprise, and then said, 'My dear, no smouldering silent-film star with any self-respect would have got far with a name like Alice Wilson. And you wouldn't believe how useful it is to have two identities. It meant that when I bought Ashwood no one suspected that the wicked baroness was still alive, and buying up parcels of valuable building land. Explain that part, would you, Mr Devlin.'

'She did own Ashwood,' said Liam. 'But three years ago we transferred the ownership of Ashwood Studios to her son, Alan Salisbury. To comply with HM Land Registry laws I had to formally register the land at the time. So if Edmund Fane really did apply for a search for the title—?'

'He did. We know that.'

'Ah. Well, then, he'd receive a brief report showing that the land had passed from the ownership of A. V. Wilson to Alan Salisbury. Relatively ordinary names,' said Liam, looking at Michael questioningly.

'Yes. But,' said Michael, 'both of those names were listed on my mobile phone – which Fane had taken. We know now that he had spent most of his adult life watching for anything that might reveal the truth about his father and when he received the Land Registry information he already knew I was Alraune's son. Seeing those names – the names of Ashwood's buyer and seller – on my phone must have panicked him. He didn't know who Alan Salisbury was, and he didn't know who A. V. Wilson was, but he saw that I was in some way linked to them, because I had their phone numbers. I should think that was enough to send him hotfoot after one or both of them.'

'Michael's told you that his father was a violent man,' said Alice. 'I won't go into what happened to Alraune inside Auschwitz or the things he saw – at any rate, I won't do so now. For now I'll just say that what he saw and what he experienced scarred him very deeply indeed.' She paused, and Lucy saw that she was thinking back over all the years, to the child born in Auschwitz.

'He was an oddly attractive child,' said Alice. 'Dark and enigmatic – people found that intriguing. Women especially. But after he married, he behaved violently towards Michael's mother, and in the end he killed her.' She paused to take a sip of champagne.

'That was the night I ran away,' said Michael, taking up the story. 'I was eight years old, and I had spent all of my life in Alraune's shadow. I was terrified of practically everything in the world. On the night he killed my mother I thought he was going to kill me as well. So I ran away to Alice.'

'How did you know about her, though?'

'I didn't know then that Alice and Lucretia and my grandmother were one and the same person,' said Michael. 'But my mother knew the stories about a young parlourmaid and her dashing lover.'

'I told Alraune those stories,' said Alice. 'I made them into fairy-tales for him. The serving girl and the rich man. But I never knew whether he would remember them.'

'He did remember them,' said Michael. 'He told them to my mother, and she told them to me. She had Alice's gift for recounting stories, so I grew up knowing about the fairy-tale romance between the rich man and the serving girl. And on the night I ran away, it seemed entirely natural that I should run to the lady in the stories.'

'Michael's mother gave him something to run to,' said Francesca thoughtfully.

'Yes. I've always been so grateful to her for that.'

'But she didn't know who "Alice" really was?' put in Lucy.

'No. It was the early years she knew about,' said Alice. 'That seems to have been all Alraune ever told her. I was a parlour-maid in those years. It was a very wealthy family, and they were very prominent in Viennese society. It was all very gay – in the days when "gay" had a different meaning – and everyone was very self-indulgent and even rather decadent, although I only saw things from below-stairs, of course. But then one night I ran away with the young man who was about to become betrothed to the daughter of the house.' Her eyes took on a luminous look. 'His name was Conrad Kline, and he was gifted and charming, and he was your grandfather, Lucy.'

Lucy leaned forward. 'Will you tell me about him later on? I mean – tell me properly about him?'

'Of course. You're very like him, you know. The same colouring, the same eyes,' said Alice, and Lucy stared at her, and thought: now I really know I'm touching the past. How extraordinary. After a moment she managed to say, 'Thank you. Uh – I didn't mean to interrupt. Go on about Alraune.' And was glad to hear that she had managed to say the name without flinching this time.

'Alraune should have died on the night Michael ran away,' said Alice. 'He was badly injured. But he lived.'

'A survivor,' murmured Lucy, remembering what Michael had said earlier.

'Yes. But not sufficient of a survivor to escape justice for murder. He was convicted, and given a life sentence, but three years ago he was diagnosed with cancer. Last year the doctors said they could do no more for him, and the prison authorities released him on compassionate grounds. It seemed to me that the best help I could give him was to make sure he had sufficient money to die in whatever comfort could be provided. So I transferred Ashwood to him.' She glanced round the table. 'Ashwood isn't only the overgrown fields and the tumbledown buildings,' said Alice. 'There are several houses on the outskirts, which are quite profitably rented, and some of the land is leased to farmers. And if the existing income from that hadn't been enough, Mr Devlin could have arranged to sell the land fairly quickly.'

Liam said, 'Any property developer would snap it up at once. It's a prime site, and I've obtained outline planning permission for building, so it would be a good package for a builder.'

'But,' said Francesca, 'until we saw the film that afternoon, you never knew who "A. V. Wilson" or "Alan Salisbury" really were?'

'No. Only that I was dealing with a widow who had an invalid son.'

'Edmund knew who Alan Salisbury was when he saw him, though,' said Lucy. 'He knew it was Alraune – and he knew Alraune was a real person. How did he know that?'

'Deborah had Alraune's birth certificate,' said Alice thoughtfully. 'Edmund could have found it after she died.'

'Yes, I see.'

'And my father was – is – very like Alice,' said Michael. 'And I'm very like both of them. Even with the disfigurement to the eyes, Edmund must have recognized Alraune.'

There was silence for a moment, and Lucy felt a stir of apprehension, because she sensed they were coming to the real heart of this. In another moment they would know exactly what had happened that day at Ashwood. The silence stretched out, and just as Lucy was thinking she could not bear it any longer, Alice said, 'And of course, the past has always influenced the present.' She stopped, as if waiting for a cue.

It's up to me, thought Lucy, and taking a deep breath, she said, 'Alice, what really happened at Ashwood?'

CHAPTER THIRTY-NINE

'I didn't get out of Auschwitz until the war ended,' said Alice. 'Nineteen-forty-five. We were all exhausted and sick – you can't imagine how sick we all were, my dears. Mind and body and soul – every way you can imagine. But we were free and somehow we had survived, and our lives were our own again. The feeling when we saw the American soldiers march into the camp and when we understood what it meant . . . That was so intense an emotion that I don't think you could experience it more than once in a lifetime. I think you might die of it a second time.'

They had moved back to the comfortable sitting-room with its faint scents of woodsmoke. Michael had switched on a coffee percolator, and Francesca had helped him to hand round the cups.

'I can't imagine how you survived Auschwitz,' said Francesca thoughtfully. 'I can't imagine how anyone could.'

'There was nothing else to do but survive,' said Alice. 'To keep hoping it would finally come to an end. And although it was never said, I think most of us had a private image in our minds, something we held on to, something that would happen when we got out. Simple things – lying in a hot bath perhaps, or reading a favourite book. Ilena, my dear good friend, used to talk about the two of us walking out through the gate arm in arm, and her brother waiting there for us. And it happened,' she said. 'We did walk out arm in arm, and Ilena's brother was there.'

Lucy said, 'Some dreams do come true.'

'Yes.' Alice smiled. 'My dream was that I would one day dance again with Conrad – a waltz, to one of his own compositions.'

For Lucy the words instantly conjured up the image of a well-lit ballroom: men in the sharp black and white formality of evening dress, ladies wearing silks and velvets, the air laden with expensive perfumes . . .

'By the time the camps were liberated,' said Alice, 'Alraune had long since left. A year earlier he had been taken away by a man who was – who had reason to believe himself the father.' She paused to drink her coffee. Lucy had no idea if she was playing for time, or if she was deliberately creating an effect, or if she was simply taking a drink before going on with the story.

'You do not need to know the circumstances surrounding Alraune's conception and birth,' said Alice. 'They were macabre and violent and deeply disturbing, and something no female should ever have to endure. But I will say that there was a young German officer who could have been Alraune's father, and I found that he had constantly tried to see the child. His wife and baby had died in the air-raids on Dresden, and although he had no heart to remarry he liked the idea of having a son. So one day he came to Auschwitz and he took Alraune away with him.'

Lucy said, 'You gave him up?'

'If I had resisted I would have been overruled and Alraune would have been taken anyway. But I didn't resist,' said Alice. 'He was a German and a Nazi, that young man, and he was on the enemy's side. But at that time we had no idea how long the war would last – it could have gone on for many more years. There were stories that Britain was losing – that might have been propaganda or it might have been the truth. Again, we had no way of telling. We were afraid that if Germany won we would never leave Auschwitz, and that meant Alraune might not know any other life. I would have done anything to get him out. The officer was young, and I had seen shame and pity in his eyes at some of the atrocities. I thought he could be trusted. And when you are half-starved,' said Alice with a sudden hardness in her voice, 'and when you shiver through every winter's night, and have only the sparsest of clothes and barely enough water to survive, your values change. What did it matter which country Alraune lived in if he had food to eat and warmth, and the promise of a reasonably normal childhood and some happiness?'

'Yes, I see that,' said Lucy softly.

'The officer promised that Alraune would be known as his nephew,' she said. 'And that the circumstances of his early childhood would never be told. He said Alraune would have everything of the best – everything within reason that money could buy. And so I let him go. But after the war ended – after I got out of Germany, Ilena and I searched for him. Ilena was the finest, truest friend I ever had. Elsa, whom you met earlier, is her daughter.'

'And in the end, you found him,' said Lucy.

'I did. But it took a long time,' said Alice. 'I had very little money, and I had no idea then where Alraune was, or where Conrad was. So I searched for them both, and at the same time I made attempts to re-enter the film world. That was harder than I had expected. There were rumours that I had spied for the Nazis, which meant I was looked on with suspicion and often with derision. They said I had slept with von Ribbentrop and consorted with Göering – all nonsense, of course, but the stories stuck. And as well as that, the competition was much fiercer: there were a great many talented actors and directors who had survived the war in their various ways, and who wanted to resume their careers. But we had to learn new techniques – there were no longer any silent films, for instance. Garbo had talked, and the rest of us had to follow suit. But I was determined to regain what I had lost, so I donned the mantle of the vamp again . . .'

'The black hair and the kohl-enhanced eyes,' said Francesca.

'Illusion,' said Alice, smiling. 'Smoke and mirrors. I did it all on a shoestring, but I was used to that. And quite soon I did find Conrad again which was the greatest joy of all. Or perhaps Conrad found me. He had been in Dachau. Another terrible place, but there was music there – a few small orchestras that the commandants had set up, and Conrad had been part of one of them.'

'I don't understand that,' said Liam, leaning forward.

'The orchestras?'

'Yes. It doesn't square with what the Nazis were doing to you all. The brutality and the mass-killings. Oh wait, though, it would be a kind of egotistic culture-trip for them, wouldn't it? "See how civilized we are"?'

'Exactly,' said Alice. 'The concerts were rather makeshift, but many of the musicians were classically trained and very gifted. And the idea that they were promoting serious music made the Nazis feel very good about themselves. Also it conferred a great prestige on them. Conrad once told me that the music saved him,' she said. 'At the time, he meant it saved his life – there was no death sentence for the camp musicians – but I think it saved him in other ways.'

'It helped him to endure the . . . the hardships?' said Lucy.

'Yes. Music was his one real passion,' said Alice. Her eyes suddenly had a faraway look, and Lucy saw that despite the sharp mind, she really was very old. Ninety? Ninety-three? Yes, she must be at least that.

But then Alice said briskly, 'Too many memories,' and made an impatient gesture as if to brush them away. 'I am recounting a history to you,' she said. 'And we do not need romantic memories getting in the way.'

'Personally I'm in favour of all the romance I can get,' said Liam.

'Well, there was plenty of that. Your mamma was born in those years, Lucy. Mariana. Conrad was going through a gothic period at the time; a dark period. Perhaps none of us had quite shaken off the darkness of the camps – probably most of us never did shake it off. But Conrad had written *Deborah's Song* for Deborah, and now he wanted to write a piece of music called "Mariana in the Moated Grange".'

'Tennyson,' said Liam after a moment.

'What a pleasure to meet an educated man,' said Alice, regarding him with approval. 'Yes, Tennyson. I planned that I would bring Mariana and Deborah up together, of course. That when there was a little more money, we would all live in England. Because I did get back into films, of course. You all know that. I became again the adventuress with a past – and now I really did have a past. And Conrad began to give concerts again, and I made a couple of films that replenished the coffers very nicely indeed, and that were quite well thought of—'

'Erich von Stroheim?' said Lucy. '*The Passion Master*?'

A smile lit Alice's face. 'Oh yes, dear Erich,' she said, and for a moment the smile deepened into mischief. 'Such a volatile man. But so immensely talented that I forgave him the tantrums and the temperaments. Yes, we made a film together, and it was fairly successful, but—' She paused, and then said, 'But somehow, you know, none of it was quite the same as it had been in the old days. And all the time I was trying to find Alraune. Eventually I found him because of an item in a German newspaper.' She glanced at Michael, who spread his hands as if saying what the hell, tell them everything.

'The article was a report of the death of a former German officer at Auschwitz,' said Alice. 'It had some news value because there was a suspicion that the man's young nephew had killed him. I didn't know, not for sure, that it was Alraune – the surname given was an ordinary enough German name. Stultz. But that had been the name of the young officer, and the facts seemed to me to fit and the place was right – a small town in Northern Germany, quite near to the Czech border. And the details of the man's death . . .' She paused, and then said, again, 'I thought it might be Alraune and Ilena thought so as well. And so, since Conrad was away touring, and since Alraune was my concern anyway, Ilena's brother managed to get us tickets for the journey and we travelled to the town named in the newspaper.'

'It's a smaller place than I was expecting,' Ilena said, as the train drew into the little German railway station and they got out. 'But that should make the search easier. What now, Lu? Do we try to hire a car, or what?'

'Certainly we get a car,' said Alice with decision. 'We can't just walk the streets looking for an unknown address.'

'What a good thing there's money in the bank,' said Ilena drily. 'And what a good thing that we've at least got a name to go on.'

'Reinard Stultz,' said Alice. And although she had been trying to shut her mind to the night of Alraune's conception, the young officer's gesture in reaching out to touch her face had stayed with her. She could not remember the colour of his hair or the shape of his features, but she could remember that brief moment of comfort he had given her in the midst of the pain and fear. If he was indeed Alraune's father, then Alraune might not have such a bad heritage after all.

They found the house by the simple method of driving to the offices of the local newspaper, and openly asking for the address. Alice was keeping the baroness's name quiet, but she was not keeping the baroness's arrogance quiet. Within minutes the clerk, awed by this imperious female's manner, supplied the address in full, and became voluble as to the details of the attack. No one had believed that such a small child could have been so violent, he said. And so no official action had been taken. The boy was still in the house, in the care of the housemaid, and no one quite knew what to do about him.

Alice said, 'We are relatives of the child's mother. You can tell us what happened.'

The clerk hesitated, but he enjoyed a gossip as much as the next man, and he did not really mind retelling the story that had provided such good headlines for his newspaper. There had been, they were to understand, some small infraction of a rule. Perhaps homework had not been done for the next day's school. Perhaps a bedroom had not been tidied properly or a house task not performed. And so there had been chastisement. A small smacking of the bottom, or the withholding of pudding after the evening meal perhaps. Certainly it would have been nothing large, for Herr Stultz was known to be a kindly man. Ah yes, once a Nazi, everyone knew that, and it was not a thing for pride. But that was in the past, and Herr Stultz was a man of warmth, always ready to contribute to charity and to give of his time for others. And so proud of his small nephew who had been orphaned in the war. The two of them had often been seen in the little town, said the clerk, the good Herr buying toys for the child, the two of them chattering away together. Uncle and nephew, so good to see.

But the small chastisement, whatever it had been, had created a violent rage. Ungovernable fury. And there had been some form of skewer lying to hand – perhaps meat skewers, the clerk was not too sure of the details. What he was sure of – what everyone living here was sure of – was that the boy had snatched the skewer up and driven it straight into Herr Stultz's face.

'The eyes,' said Alice, almost to herself. 'The boy stabbed Reinard Stultz's eyes.'

Ah yes, it had been so, said the clerk. Shocking.

Fifteen minutes later Alice and Ilena had reached the house and requested admittance. Within half an hour they were driving back to the railway station, with Alraune.

'No one questioned us,' said Alice to the four people listening to her. 'No one tried to stop us. We just walked into the house, and found him. He was in the kitchen, drinking soup that the girl had made for him. We simply said we were his mother's family, come to take him away, and we took him.'

'Did he know you?' asked Lucy. 'I mean – did he recognize you?'

'Not immediately, I don't think. Auschwitz was three years behind him, and he was still very young. But after a while he did recognize me, and he smiled and allowed me to hug him. But he was a detached child – there was always the feeling that he performed any act of affection purely because it was expected of him.'

'You brought him back to England?' said Francesca.

'Yes. It was a circuitous route we took, Ilena and I – we wanted to be sure no one was following or watching. Perhaps we were both a little paranoid after the years in the camp. And I thought Alraune could live with us all, that we could be a family. He had two sisters who would love to have him, I said.' She paused. There was no need to say that beneath everything she had been frightened of the child's self-possession and his dark history. She had thought: This is a child apparently responsible for viciously blinding a man – a man who, according to the reports, had shown him only kindness.

'Ilena stayed in England,' she said. 'By the time I was given the Ashwood contract she had qualified as a doctor, and she obtained a post in a hospital nearby. We were pleased to think of being so near to one another. And I was delighted with the Ashwood deal, which was for two films – interesting work and very profitable. The studios were hoping to rival Alfred Hitchcock's productions – he had already made *The Thirty Nine Steps* and *Rebecca*, and he was only a couple of years away from *Dial M for Murder* – and the films in prospect were glossy murder mysteries, very typical of that era. Quite good screenplays though,' said the lady who had known and worked with von Stroheim and Max Schreck, and sparred with Brigitte Helm and Dietrich. Despite herself Lucy smiled.

'And the thought of living in England again after so long – it was another of those moments of extreme and intense happiness,' said Alice. 'I had money again – not a fortune, but enough to buy a house near to the studios. Ilena stayed with us often, and her family came to England regularly. We travelled a little – it was possible by that time. I took the children abroad for holidays.'

'On Howard Hughes' Stratoliner?' said Lucy involuntarily.

'Yes. How on earth did you know that?'

'I found an old newsreel,' said Lucy. 'Pathé News.'

'There were usually cameras around,' agreed Alice. 'But altogether it was beginning to be a good life again. Conrad was there, of course; he loved the idea of living in England: he thought he would be an English gentleman and he wanted to write music to rival Elgar and Vaughan Williams.' She stopped again, and Lucy felt her heart bump with nervousness. We're coming to it, she thought. We're coming now to what really happened at Ashwood.

But it was Liam who leaned forward, and said, in a voice far more gentle than Lucy had heard him use before, 'Baroness. We know that Edmund Fane's father killed Conrad. But who killed Leo Dreyer?'

For a long time Lucy thought Alice was not going to reply. We've overdone it, she thought in horror. It's been too much for her – she's over ninety, for goodness' sake, and she's relived half her life for us tonight!

But then she saw she had been wrong; the lady who had survived Auschwitz, and who had survived God knew what other hardships and atrocities, sat up a little straighter.

'Michael, dear, I believe I will have a small brandy with my coffee,' she said. And, when Michael had poured it, and had added glasses for himself and Liam, Alice said, 'This is what really happened that day.'

Alraune had been well-behaved and apparently normal after Alice and Ilena brought him to England, and if the killing of Reinard Stultz had affected him he did not show it. Alice had dared to believe him innocent; to think there had been someone else in the house that day – perhaps someone with a grudge against former Nazis, someone who had been in one of the camps, or who had lost a loved one there. There would be plenty such people, for goodness' sake!

He had a bright intelligence that pleased Alice, and he seemed to be fitting into the household smoothly and easily, although he was wary of Conrad. Or was it that Conrad was wary of him?

Alice had not told Conrad about the rape – she had been too afraid that Conrad would hate Alraune because of it, and Alraune had had more than his share of hatred in his life already. And Conrad had appeared to accept Alraune amiably enough. 'One day perhaps you will tell me what happened in Auschwitz,' he said once. 'But only when you wish to and only if you wish to.'

'Will you ever tell him?' Ilena said one day.

'No. He would mount a vendetta or a crusade to find the men who raped me, and challenge them to a duel or something equally ridiculous,' said Alice. 'Whatever he did, he would never be able to look at Alraune without remembering.'

Ilena said, 'And you? Can you look at Alraune without remembering?'

'I can,' said Alice, and thought: I must. And in the meantime was grateful that Conrad seemed perfectly happy for Alraune to be part of the family.

Deborah and the small Mariana accepted Alraune unquestioningly. They called him Alan as they had been told to do, and Alice tried to call him Alan as well, although she found it difficult. And dozens of times during those first weeks in England, she found herself watching the boy covertly, and thinking: have I brought a murderer into the house? A killer who might turn on Deborah and Mariana?

And then she would remember how Alraune had witnessed men blinded in cold blood inside a German concentration camp, and how he had been hidden away in a dank wash-house and in the roof spaces of huts so that Josef Mengele should not find him. She would remember the swivel-eyes of the searchlights constantly raking the compound as she carried him into hiding, and the feeling of fear and urgency because it was vital to dodge the lidless white glare if they were to remain alive . . .

Alice did not often take the children to the studios, but she had taken Alraune with her on that last day, and she had taken Ilena and Deborah as well.

'To shield you from the besotted Crispin Fane?' Ilena had said, grinning.

'Perhaps. It's nothing I can't handle,' said Alice.

'Serve you right for seducing him when you were bored,' said Ilena, who knew Alice very well indeed by this time.

'Well, I couldn't have known he would be so intense.'

'All boys of that age are intense,' said Ilena.

Whatever the reasons, Alraune and Deborah had gone to Ashwood that day. Alice had thought it would be all right; granted it was a murder mystery they were shooting, but no especially gory scenes were being filmed that day, and Deborah, who had been there several times, liked watching the filming and talking to the people who worked at the studios. Alice thought Alraune would like it, as well; she thought he would be fascinated by the bustle and the air of make-believe. And Ilena, who was on leave from the hospital for a couple of weeks, had never been to a film studio; she would enjoy the novelty, and Alice would enjoy giving her this unusual afternoon.

When Conrad said he would come along to collect them all later on, Alice was relieved, because it was unlikely that the besotted Crispin Fane would stage one of his emotional, embarrassing scenes with Conrad around.

CHAPTER FORTY

At first it had seemed all right. Alraune did not say very much, but he sat quietly with Ilena and Deborah, and accepted an orange drink one of the cameramen brought him, and watched everything that was going on with apparent interest.

There was a flurry of extra activity today because visitors were expected. Alice did not take much notice of the flurry; there were often guests at Ashwood – people who must be flattered and given lush lunches. Sometimes local dignitaries from the nearby town were given a guided tour so that they could feel themselves on familiar terms with the exotic world of film-making, and could report favourably on it to local people.

But she did take notice of the fact that Crispin Fane was here, trailing along in the wake of his employer. There must be meetings with the legal department again; Crispin would be here to take notes as he often was. But halfway through the afternoon he found his way to Alice's dressing-room while she was changing for the next scene. They were working in the small Studio Twelve and Alice had been allotted a dressing-room that opened almost directly off the main section. It made quick changes easier to cope with and it meant people did not have to wait about for her. Unfortunately, it also meant Crispin knew exactly where she was.

He came in without knocking, as if he had a right, which annoyed Alice. What was even more annoying was that he had broken into her concentration. She was no disciple of Stanislavskian method or symbolism but it was distracting to be interrupted immediately before an important scene.

But she said, as levelly as she could manage, 'Crispin, dear, it's so nice to see you, but I can't talk just now. I'm due on the set. And the children are here today.'

Despite herself it gave her a sharp pang to see the disappointment in his face – like a child deprived of a longed-for treat. But the disappointment vanished and was replaced by a petulant anger. Why had she no time for him these days? he said. Why, when they had meant so much to each other? He adored her, he would die for her—

He was overwrought, and in another moment he would tip from melodrama into outright hysteria, but somehow he would have to understand that the brief, rather irresponsible little affair was over. I'll let him down gently though, I really will, thought Alice guiltily. Regret, that's the keynote. And renunciation – I can do a good renunciation scene, and it would salvage his pride. She was just saying that they would meet later, when the door opened and Conrad came in.

French farce, thought Alice, torn between despair and a jab of hysteria on her own account. One lover wringing his hands at my feet, another entering upon the scene and registering shock and horror. Except that Conrad would never be shocked at anything and he had known her far too long to be horrified at finding a lovelorn youth in her room. Still, it was to be hoped he would not treat this poor child, Crispin Fane, to one of his grand displays of arrogance and temper.

He did not. He was a professional and he knew that a dressing-room minutes before a performance – never mind whether the performance was on a stage, a concert-hall, or a film-set – was no place for an emotional scene. He said, quite amicably, that he and Crispin should go somewhere else to discuss things; somewhere quiet where they could talk man to man.

It was the 'man to man' that tipped the scales, as Conrad had probably known it would. Crispin squared his shoulders and flung back his head – at one level of her mind Alice noted the gesture as rather a good one – and then marched out, head high.

Alice, deeply grateful for Conrad's tact, got into her outfit for the scene, checked her make-up and her hair, slipped on her shoes, and went out into the main part of the studio. The working lights had been quenched and the heavy spotlights were angled to shine directly on to the small set; they were bright and strong to depict the sunlight of a summer afternoon, and the working areas were swathed in darkness. For a moment Alice had a brief shutter-flash of *déjà vu*: a darting vision of the compound inside Auschwitz when searchlights had lit parts of the camp with just that harsh brilliance, and when it had been necessary to avoid the unblinking stare if you did not want to be caught . . .

The image vanished as quickly as it had come, but Alice glanced uneasily across to where Alraune was sitting. Would the spotlights and the surrounding darkness have sparked a similar flare of memory for him? No, surely he had been too young to remember it. She was about to go across to him, to say something light and frivolous, when she was beckoned across to a group of men standing near the door.

Clearly these were the visitors for whom those preparations had been made earlier, and equally clearly they wanted to meet the infamous Lucretia von Wolff. Bother, thought Alice crossly, now I'm a tourist attraction, but she began to pick her way across the lit set to the far side.

She had reached the edge of the set and was about to step into the dark area outside it, when the tallest of the men turned to face her. Alice stopped dead, half in and half out of the light, because the memories were swooping down again. The hut in Auschwitz, lit by the glow from an iron stove. The sofa in the corner of the room, the men watching her with furtive lechery, and the dreadful awareness of sexual excitement filling up the hut. And all the while a tall man standing behind the stove, so that the firelight turned his eyeglass to a burning disc of flame . . .

The man watching her walk across Studio Twelve was Leo Dreyer.

'It wasn't until a long time afterwards,' said Alice, sipping her coffee, and looking at the absorbed faces of her listeners, 'that I understood that Leo Dreyer was one of the financiers of the film.'

'You knew him?' Lucy could not think why this should surprise her.

'I knew him in Auschwitz and also in Buchenwald,' said Alice. 'He was a vicious man with the greatest ability for hatred I ever encountered. He and I had a – what today you would call a "history".'

'Is that why he came to England?' said Liam. 'To find you?'

'He didn't come for me,' said Alice. 'He considered matters settled between us. Leo Dreyer came to England for Conrad.'

Alice was never able to remember shooting the scheduled scene that day and returning to her dressing-room afterwards. She had no idea what kind of performance she had given for the cameras or whether the scene might have to be reshot; her mind had been jerked back into the memories again, to the night when she had endured Leo Dreyer's brutal rape – the hammer blows inside her body, on and on . . .

When the door was pushed quietly open, and he slipped into the room, she was not in the least surprised. *If you try to touch me this time, I'll shout rape, and see you gaoled*, she thought.

But he was perfectly courteous; he was murmuring an apology for disturbing her, and saying something about wanting a few private moments with an old friend.

'We were never friends, and I have no wish to be private with you,' Alice said, glaring at him. 'What do you want? Why are you here?'

'I'm here entirely legitimately,' said Dreyer, leaning back

against the closed door and studying her. 'I have a number of investments these days – finance is very rewarding, I find – and a few months ago I added Ashwood Studios to their number.'

'You have invested in Ashwood?'

'Very substantially. I am probably paying your salary, my dear,' he said.

There's something here that I'm missing, thought Alice, and said, 'Why would you invest in a film studio? It's a risky business at the best of times.'

'I was curious about you,' said Leo Dreyer, and Alice thought, nonsense. You never possessed such an emotion as curiosity in your life!

After a moment, she said, politely, 'Weren't you content with merely spreading rumours that I spied for the Nazis?' and saw him smile slightly.

'What a hell-cat you are,' he said softly.

'You did spread them though, didn't you? Those stories?'

'Things have a way of getting out,' he said, off handedly. 'Did you know that Nina died last year?'

'I didn't know. I'm very sorry,' said Alice after a moment.

'She committed suicide.'

'That's extremely sad. A very great waste of a life.'

'You were the one who caused the waste,' he said. 'You began it – you and Conrad.' The smile was suddenly and eerily the one from Auschwitz and from *Kristallnacht*, and Alice stared at him in dawning horror. Leo Dreyer had not come to England – to Ashwood – for her; he considered that he had redressed the balance with her in the camps. And although he had sent Conrad – the faithless lover, the betrayer – into Dachau, Conrad had spent the years with his beloved music, and Dreyer had known that. And now Conrad was out in the world again, and looking set to become successful all over again. Dreyer must have felt cheated; he must have felt that Conrad had in some way eluded the punishment he had intended. A tiny part of Alice's mind wondered why Dreyer had not taken the opportunity to deal with

Conrad while he was held in Dachau, but the Nazis had worked on the closed-cell principle – each camp had been a unit unto itself, and unless Dreyer had had friends in Dachau as he had had in Auschwitz and Buchenwald, he might have found it difficult to penetrate the bureaucratic regime.

Had Dreyer known Conrad would be here today? Had he fixed the date of this visit deliberately? But whatever the truth, the two of them must not be allowed to meet, and Dreyer must be got out of Ashwood as quickly as possible. Alice began to say that they could not talk here where anyone might burst in unannounced, when, as if in response to this, the door was pushed open. Alice and Leo Dreyer turned to see Alraune standing in the doorway.

His appearance ought not to have been so startling and so instantly frightening, and the room ought not to have filled up with such choking menace.

But Alraune's face was sheet-white and his eyes – monstrous, swollen insect-eyes, like demon's eyes staring out of hell's caverns – blazed with hatred. Alice saw at once that he knew who Dreyer was: that he recognized him as the man who had dragged the two of them out of the stone wash-house that day, and who had carried Alraune across the compound at Auschwitz and sat by him in Mengele's grisly surgery. Of course he remembers him, thought Alice, horrified. If ever Alraune was to remember anyone from those years, it would be Leo Dreyer.

Hatred and fury were pouring into the room: Alice could feel them, and she could feel Dreyer's fear, as well. He's afraid of a child, she thought incredulously. He's not afraid because of what Alraune knows about him: he's afraid of the black malevolence in Alraune's eyes. For a dreadful moment something she had not known she possessed gripped her, and she thought: let him suffer that fear. Let him experience sheer stark terror, just for a few moments, and let him have a taste of what we all endured during those years.

The feeling lasted barely twenty seconds, but it was so violent that it seemed to print itself on the air. When it released her Alice went forward, meaning to snatch Alraune out of Dreyer's path, thinking she could carry him out into the relative normality of the main studio.

But she was too late. Alraune was already bounding forward and Leo Dreyer, unprepared, fell back with the child on top of him. Something was glinting in Alraune's hand – something that was sharp and cruel and pointed . . . Something that caught the light as he lifted it and then drove the point straight down into Dreyer's eyes, first one and then the other . . .

For a very long time no one in the warm, well-lit sitting-room spoke. The glow from the table lamp had fallen across Alice's face while she talked, making her hair seem darker and smoothing the lines on her face so that it had seemed as if a much younger woman sat there. But when she described how Alraune had attacked Leo Dreyer, the light seemed to retreat and the illusion of youth vanished.

'I never told you,' said Alice, looking across at Michael. 'I never told you what Alraune did that day.'

'You didn't need to,' said Michael. 'I guessed years ago. But what I could never fathom, and what I can't fathom now, is how you foisted that colossal deception on everyone.'

'I notice you ask how it was done, not why,' observed Alice.

'I know why you did it,' said Michael, speaking directly to Alice, as if the others were not there. His voice was extremely gentle. 'Of course I do. You had to protect Alraune.'

'He had had so much tragedy in his life,' said Alice. 'The things he had been forced to witness . . . And he had had so little . . .' A spreading of the hands, the mirror image of a gesture Michael had used earlier. 'I had minutes – barely even that – to make a decision. I could let the law take its course, and allow Alraune to be branded a killer. Or—'

'Or,' said Michael, 'you could save Alraune and let the world believe you were the killer instead.' He did not say, At the expense of your two daughters, but Lucy thought the words hung on the air between them for a moment.

'There was never really a choice,' said Alice. 'Alraune would have been put in some appalling institution – this was over fifty years ago, remember, and such places were grim and harsh. I couldn't do it to him. For most of his life he had had nothing – nothing that normal children have. He had lived on scraps – worn bits of sacking, lived in fear and seen the most unbelievable brutalities. And he had killed an evil man – a man he remembered from Auschwitz. A monster.'

Michael said, 'And Reinard Stultz?'

'Stultz's murderer was never established,' said Alice at once. 'And he had been a Nazi officer – he could have made dozens of enemies. One of them might have sought him out – Alraune might even have seen the murder done—' Again she made the quick impatient gesture with her hands. 'Perhaps what I did that day was wrong – certainly it was unfair to Deborah and Mariana – but that was how my mind reasoned in those few moments.'

Michael said again, 'So how did you do it?'

'It wasn't difficult. Since I was seventeen I had spent most of my life spinning illusions. And on that day at Ashwood, I spun the greatest illusion of them all.'

CHAPTER FORTY-ONE

Alice could not have done it on her own. If Ilena had not been at Ashwood that day – if Ilena had not seen Dreyer, or if she had not followed Alraune into the dressing-room – the plan could never have been made and would never have worked.

Ilena took in the situation at once, of course. Alice was to think later – when she could think again – that any other woman would have screamed, but Ilena, good, trusted friend, had shared the memories; she did not need any explanations and she did not scream. She saw Leo Dreyer lying in a messiness of blood, still moving feebly, clawing vainly at the air while dreadful choking grunting sounds issued from his lips, and she saw the stiletto that had been on the film set, still dripping blood, in Alraune's small hand, and she understood at once what had happened.

Alice had backed against the wall, one hand clamped over her mouth, to stop herself from screaming or being sick or both, and it was Ilena who snatched the stiletto from Alraune and thrust it on to a chair. She bent over Dreyer's body – Alice thought she tried to staunch the flow of blood, and she saw Ilena feel for a pulse and a heartbeat.

Alice had lost all sense of time; she had no idea how long Ilena stayed like that, but at last she straightened up, and came over to Alice, taking her arms and shaking her slightly. 'Listen to me, Lu. We have minutes – seconds, maybe – to think what to do.'

'Is Dreyer dead?'

'Dying,' said Ilena, and Alice remembered with deep gratitude Ilena's medical background. 'The stiletto is deep into his brain and there is nothing I can do for him – there is nothing anyone can do for him. I think he has perhaps ten minutes left of life,' said Ilena. 'After that I hope he goes straight to hell, and I hope he can hear me saying it.'

The world was already steadying. I can deal with this, thought Alice. I am equal to this, just as I have been equal to all the other things in my life. She stood up a little straighter, and said, 'Ilena. This is what we're going to do.'

The two of them knew one another so well that a few hastily exchanged sentences were all that was needed for Alice to explain the plan.

Ilena got Alraune out of the room, and Alice locked the door and then ransacked her make-up drawer. Her mind was racing at top speed, thinking, planning, discarding, wondering what she would do if the items she sought were not here.

But it was all right. Everything she needed was here – even down to the green-tinted face powder she had worn to indicate deep shock after discovering the body of her husband in the film. You could act your boots off to convince an audience you were distraught and despairing, but not even Bernhardt had been able to turn pale on cue. Alice sat down at the mirror and applied the powder, determinedly not looking at what lay in the corner, in its own blood.

She was just putting the box of powder away when there was a faint tap at the door. Ilena? Alice opened the door cautiously, and Ilena slid inside, closing the door and turning the key in the lock.

'All right?'

'Yes,' said Ilena. 'Alraune's with Deborah – they're going

straight home. I asked one of the men to phone a taxi – I thought we might need the car. I told Deb you had been delayed.'

'Had she seen anything, d'you think?'

'I'm sure she hadn't. She had wandered off to talk to some of the make-up girls. She wasn't anywhere near this room.'

'Thank God for that at any rate.' Alice hesitated, and then said, 'Alraune?'

'Perfectly all right. He seemed to have no understanding that he had done anything wrong. And he was so quiet that people will probably not even remember he was here.' Ilena knelt down by Dreyer.

'Is he dead?' asked Alice after a moment.

'Yes,' said Ilena, and there was just a split second when Alice had time to think how curious it was that the man she hated most in the world had died there on the floor while she was putting on her make-up.

Ilena stood up. 'Lu, are you sure about doing this?'

'Yes.' Alice took a final look in the mirror. Marble-white skin, faint bruises under the eyes. She had draped a black silk stole around her shoulders because there had not been time to create the deathlike pallor on her arms. 'Ilena, can you give me at least fifteen minutes before you let them break in?'

'I think so. Yes. The door will be locked, so they'll have to break it and that will take time anyway. Lu, what are you going to do?'

'It's better that you don't know,' said Alice. 'It's better that you're as genuinely shocked as everyone. And Ilena—'

'What?'

'I can't imagine ever having a better friend than you,' said Alice.

'Oh, rubbish,' said Ilena, and whisked from the room.

An illusion, Alice's mind was saying. You're going to create an illusion, and part of that illusion is that you turned a little crazy at being confronted with Leo Dreyer – the man who condemned you to four years of living hell, who arranged that mass rape. That's enough to send anyone temporarily mad, surely.

There was an old property chair in the corner: an elaborate thing – high-backed and ornate, with a glossy green satin covering. Alice pulled it forward and, setting her teeth, hooked her hands under Leo Dreyer's arms and half-dragged, half carried him to the chair. It was more difficult than she had expected to get him up on to the chair and prop him in a sitting position, but eventually she managed it. His head lolled to one side, and blood was still oozing from his eyes, so that Alice had to quench a spasm of revulsion. Don't think about what you're doing, just get on with it. She glanced at her wristwatch and saw with panic that six of the fifteen minutes had already ticked away.

Working swiftly, she lit two candles from the emergency box kept for power-cuts, and when the wax had softened a little she set them on the mirror-shelf, so that they were on each side of the chair. The tiny flames burned up, reflecting in the mirror and casting eerie shadows so that for a moment Dreyer's dead face had life and movement. Dreadful. But it added the final touch of Grand Guignol, and when people broke in they would see Leo Dreyer seated upright in the chair, candles positioned as if for a religious ritual, his eyes torn out. And the baroness sprawled at his feet, the evidence of her suicide clear for them all to see.

There was another thing they would see, if they had the knowledge or the memories: the reproduction of the closing scene from an old film that had flickered shockingly and darkly across the silver screen all those years ago . . . A film that had made Lucretia von Wolff famous.

Alraune, catlike and soulless, tearing out the eyes of a man she hated, and then arranging his body in a macabre sacrificial pose.

There were eight minutes left. She had better concentrate on her own death. She would have preferred to use fake blood – there was probably some in the wardrobe room next door, but there was no time to get it and she dare not be seen. There were, however, two bottles of nail varnish in her make-up drawer, both of them the deep blood-red that were the baroness's trademark. Once out of the bottle the stuff would dry a bit too quickly and the smell would be dangerously distinctive, but the room already stank overpoweringly of Dreyer's blood and there was an acrid tang from the candles as well. She unscrewed the top of each bottle and put them ready.

Six minutes left. She could hear Ilena's voice now, telling people she was worried; Ilena's voice was strident, but it was tinged with panic. Exactly right.

A quarrel, Ilena was saying. A dreadful quarrel between the baroness and Herr Dreyer – no, Ilena did not know the details. But they had locked the door, and certainly Herr Dreyer had been a camp commandant at Auschwitz, and there would be enmity between the two as a result.

Good! thought Alice. And perfectly true. She looked quickly round the room. Was there anything else to be done? Yes. The signs of a fight, of a fierce quarrel. She flung a table lamp hard against the long glass, shattering it, and breaking most of the smaller bulb-lights around its edges, which instantly made the room darker. What else? She swept brushes, make-up boxes – everything – to the ground, and for good measure overturned a small side table. From beyond the door, Ilena let out a screech.

'We must stop them!' shrieked Ilena. 'They are fighting – they will kill each other—'

People were gathering outside the door; someone was calling for a key, but someone else was saying, Oh, leave them to it; von Wolff's famous for her tantrums.

Alice let out a gasping scream, and threw a cut-glass scent bottle at the door. The bottle smashed.

'He is killing her!' cried Ilena. 'I know it! Please to hurry—'

'We'd better break in,' said a man's voice – Alice thought it was the floor manager. 'There's certainly some kind of struggle going on in there.'

She lay down on the floor, near to the chair. Her heart was beating so fiercely that she could have believed it was outside her body altogether. *Beat-beat* . . . *Beat-beat* . . . As if someone was standing outside her head, knocking against her mind. *Beat-beat*, *let-me-in* . . . It would be the people outside trying to get in, of course.

But it was not coming from the door, it was coming from the adjoining room – from the small wardrobe-room next door. A soft light tapping. And a kind of scrabbling against the wall. Could it be mice, or even rats? *Tap-tap . . . Let-me-in* . . . Or was it, *Tap-tap . . . Let-me-out . . . ?*

She had been avoiding the sight of Dreyer, but now she raised her head cautiously to look up at him. Supposing he was not dead, after all? Supposing he was scrabbling to get out of his chair? But he had not moved, and the candles were still in place, casting their uncanny shadows. A sick shudder went through Alice at the sight of his face, the blood forming a crust where the eyes had been. Was there time for her to check for a pulse? Because if he were to be still alive – if he survived long enough to tell people the truth about Alraune . . . ?

But there was no time; people were trying to force the lock, and someone was saying it was no use doing that; they would have to kick the door in.

This was the cue. Alice lay down again, and reached for the nail varnish bottles. Would there be enough? There would have to be. And Dreyer's blood was spattered everywhere, and some of it was on her hands anyway, from arranging him in the chair. From the doorway and in the dim light it should look all right.

At least the oddly sinister tapping had stopped, or if it had not, it had been blotted out by the sounds from outside. A new voice was saying, 'Try kicking. A couple of good slams and the lock should snap. God knows what's going on in there.'

As the second blow fell on the door, Alice tipped the contents of the first bottle over her left wrist, and then the contents of the second one over her right wrist, feeling the thick stickiness ooze over her hands. She thrust the emptied bottles in the folds of her shawl – she could trust Ilena to scoop them up before anyone saw them – tumbled her hair over her face, and thrust her arms straight out so that the glossy crimson fluid would be seen.

At the same moment the lock snapped and the door was flung open. Alice heard the cries of horror, and a genuine gasp from Ilena as she took in the scene. And then Ilena took charge, bossy and firm.

Please to keep well back, Ilena called out. She was a doctor and she would make an examination. It was already plain that Herr Dreyer was dead, and the police must be called, of course. For now the concern was Madame. She bent over Alice – Alice felt the warmth of Ilena's fingers feeling for a pulse at the base of her throat, and then for a heartbeat.

'A faint pulse,' cried Ilena. 'But so very faint— Hand me something to use as a tourniquet – scarf – stocking, anything to stop the bleeding from the arteries. *Quickly*!' Alice felt the tightness of silk being tied over each of her arms, and then something being wrapped around her wrists, covering the now-hardening nail varnish. She heard one of the men saying he would telephone for an ambulance.

'No time for that,' said Ilena brusquely. 'There has been a massive blood loss. My car is outside; I will take her straight to my own hospital. You,' Alice felt the imperious gesture as Ilena pointed to one of the men. 'You will carry her for me, yes? But I must be with you, I must keep her arms well above her head.'

As the man – Alice thought it was the cameraman who had given Alraune a fruit drink – lifted her, someone said, 'But what on earth happened here?'

'I do not have time to speculate,' said Ilena sharply. 'But surely it is clear. The baroness killed a man who tortured her inside Auschwitz. I was in Auschwitz with her, and I know that for the truth. And then she tried to kill herself from remorse.'

'We gave it out that I had died on the way to the hospital,' said Alice to the listeners. 'We walked an amazingly dangerous tightrope over the formalities, of course, but we had got over the first difficulty, which was to get away from Ashwood, and out of reach of the police.'

'They would have insisted that the crime scene remained exactly as it was,' said Liam.

'Yes. And then the illusion would have been ruined, of course. As it was, we left Dreyer's body in position for the police, and later Ilena issued a death certificate for me from her own hospital. She took appalling risks and she would have been struck off if any of it had ever come out, but it never did.'

'But the police would need to see a body, wouldn't they?' asked Francesca.

'Yes, but that was only another formality. They accepted Ilena's death certificate unquestioningly. And Ilena simply gave me a hefty dose of veronal – that's a sleeping drug that was fashionable in those days. Not a fatal amount, but enough to knock me out. The surgeon came in, took a cursory look, and bureaucracy was satisfied. Afterwards I got in a wheelchair and Ilena trundled it out of the hospital, and I drank several gallons of black coffee straight off to get rid of the veronal.'

'What about a post-mortem? An inquest?' said Lucy.

'There never was a post-mortem. Ilena took over again – she could be astonishingly autocratic, and she staged a kind of Eastern European hysteria, and said after all I had been through in the camps, no one should touch my body except herself. She was a qualified doctor and quite well thought of, and the Ashwood police already had more than they could cope with. So they were more than happy to let her go ahead with that part of things. She provided a false report for the coroner – death from loss of blood was given as the cause of death. I forget the technical medical terms used.'

'What about the funeral?' asked Lucy.

'Once the coroner released the body for burial, it was easy enough to say that the funeral was private – that it had "taken place at the baroness's home". No one knew where the baroness had come from – it might have been anywhere in the world. I spent those days in a small hotel just outside Ashwood. Without make-up and with a headscarf on if I went out, no one recognized me. "Alice Wilson" was coming back, you see. Quite soon, my hair dye grew out, and I was—' A smile. 'I was an insignificant grey-haired lady approaching middle age.'

Lucy had been listening intently to all this, but when Alice paused, she said, 'Alice—'

'Lucy?'

'I know you're probably absolutely exhausted by all this—'

'Yes, but it's a satisfying tiredness. Cleansing. I should think it's how Catholics feel after confessing and being absolved. So if you've got any questions, ask away.'

'Deborah knew the truth, didn't she?' said Lucy. 'She knew you hadn't died?'

Alice looked at Lucy thoughtfully. 'What makes you say that?'

'Well, for one thing,' said Lucy, hoping she was not stepping over any lines, 'there were a number of occasions when Deb seemed to be on the brink of telling me something about the family. For another, I don't believe you'd have let her go on thinking you were dead.'

'You're quite right, of course,' said Alice. 'Deborah did know. She was intelligent and she was independent – I had been in the concentration camps for six years, remember, and Deborah had had to develop self-reliance during those years. Ilena brought her out to where I was staying, and I told her everything.' She smiled. 'She was so good about it all. Dearest Deb.'

'And – my mother?'

Alice hesitated for much longer this time. 'Mariana was a different pair of shoes entirely,' she said. 'She was only three at the time of the murders, and she certainly wouldn't have understood. So we made a plan, Deborah and Ilena and I, that Ilena would take all three children – Deb, Mariana and Alraune – to Poland to stay with her family for a time. Later, we were going to explain it all to Mariana – when we thought she was old enough.'

'But you never did,' said Lucy.

'No. Mariana was never like Deborah. She grew up to be

frivolous, a chatterbox. And,' said Alice, 'she couldn't have understood, as Deb could, the – the things Alraune had known in Auschwitz. Deb made allowances for Alraune; Mariana could never have done. I was trying to protect all three of them, you see. And Deb insisted that what I had done at Ashwood – taking the rap for the two murders – mustn't be wasted. At one time we had a plan that I would emerge as Lucretia's elder sister. It was not so wild an idea as it might sound; people were still turning up after years inside the concentration camps. I thought I might be able to step back into the lives of the children.'

'Why couldn't you?' said Lucy.

'For one thing I had under-estimated the press interest. They were on to every scrap of information. They talked to neighbours, Deborah's schoolfriends, people at Ilena's hospital. They dug up every shred of information about Lucretia they could find. Today there's the cult of the celebrity and a huge industry devoted to it, but believe me, for months on end my family had the most relentless press intrusion imaginable. For a time I was afraid they would discover the truth, but they didn't.' She looked at them all. 'And so everyone believed I was a murderess,' she said softly. 'Perhaps also that I was mad. But certainly they all believed I had killed two men and then myself rather than face the consequences. That was the verdict.'

'Two men?' said Liam. 'Conrad was the second victim, wasn't he? It was Conrad you heard tapping on the wall?'

'Yes,' she said, and an infinite sadness showed in her eyes for a moment. 'Later I knew that nothing I could have done would have saved him. He died from loss of blood and shock and Ilena promised me that it would have been very quick.'

'And so,' said Liam, 'you got away with the illusion.'

'Yes. We couldn't have done it today, of course, with all the forensic investigations that go on, and the computer-linked emergency services and so on. But things were much less formal then, and Ashwood was a small village that hadn't progressed much since the 1930s. The police had three bodies – all of them well-known people, all of them dead in bizarre circumstances, and they struggled to cope. The inquest decided that I had committed both murders, of course. It didn't occur to anyone that there could have been two separate murderers inside Ashwood on the same day.'

'But surely,' said Francesca, 'if Crispin had killed Conrad—? Didn't you want to do something about that? To bring him to justice?'

'Until Edmund told his story earlier today,' said Alice, 'and Michael told me about it, I didn't know Crispin had killed Conrad. It simply didn't occur to me that Crispin could have been capable of murder – he was just a rather charming, rather immature boy. Naïve. A bit petulant on that last day. Until today I always thought Leo Dreyer had killed Conrad.'

'And Alraune?' said Lucy.

'Deb and Mariana came back to England when Mariana was five,' said Alice. 'So that Mariana could go to an English school. By that time Alraune was at school in Poland, and he seemed content and settled, so he stayed – he lived with Ilena's family. That's why Mariana hardly knew him, of course. She may have dimly remembered a boy called Alan being part of the family for a time, but probably nothing more than that. And in those years, as far as anyone could tell, Alraune was perfectly normal. When he was seventeen he was accepted at one of the smaller Austrian universities. I arranged for him to live with friends from my Vienna days – a little village just outside the city.'

She paused, and Francesca glanced at Michael, and saw that both of them were remembering the photograph in Trixie's things, and their idea that Trixie had found it while she was on holiday in the Vienna Woods.

'He left the university after one term,' said Alice, 'and I lost sight of him for several years. But he came to England some time later, and we were in touch again. He would never come to visit me, but I used to send him money – that's how Michael knew where I was. He found a letter with my address.'

'Deb was always very cagey about Alraune,' said Lucy

thoughtfully. 'She once said that there had been a great tragedy and it was better to let it all go.'

'Details did get out, of course,' said Alice. 'The reporters never actually got the entire truth of Auschwitz, of what Alraune had been forced to witness in Mengele's clinic, but they knew there was something – something macabre. I don't know how much they knew about Reinard Stultz's death. But what they didn't know, they made up.'

'And so,' said Lucy thoughtfully, 'a legend was created.'

'Yes. And in a way, the more bizarre tales there were about Alraune – Alan as he was by then – the more it hid the truth. Everyone assumed he was a girl, of course, and that concealed his identity even more fully.'

'And you?' said Francesca. 'What did you do?'

'I became Alice Wilson once again. An ordinary lady from an ordinary background. There was money from the films, and also from Conrad's estate – more from that than I had thought. Dear Conrad – he left it all to me. He had even had everything drawn up to cover "Alice" as well as "Lucretia". He always loved the idea of the double identity,' she said softly. 'It was like a game to him. A masquerade. And so I was able to buy the house in Mowbray Fen and to make some careful investments so that the children would be provided for, and I became an unremarkable Englishwoman, active in village life, a pillar of the church, an indefatigable worker for a number of charities.'

'Including CHARTH?' asked Francesca.

'Yes. I had known what it was to be homeless, and I never forgot it. I helped where I could.'

'Deborah knew you, didn't she?' said Lucy, looking across at Michael. 'That's why she left the house to CHARTH.'

'She didn't know me very well,' said Michael. 'There was always a degree of reserve – she could never forget that I was Alraune's son, and it created a barrier between us. But she came to this house sometimes, and we got on fairly well.'

'All that was going on, and I never knew,' said Lucy. 'My mother never knew.' She frowned, and then said, 'I hate saying it, but I think you were right to leave her out of it. She could never have kept it to herself. But I do wish Deborah had told me about you.'

'She always intended to,' said Alice. 'After you had finished growing up. But—'

'But she never found the right moment? No,' said Lucy, 'that's not quite it, is it? It's something to do with Edmund.'

'I don't think she trusted Edmund,' said Alice slowly. 'And he was always around, wasn't he? I think she had a gut feeling that it would be wrong to tell Edmund. Perhaps because of the Ashwood link to Crispin.'

'Edmund always connected Crispin with Ashwood,' said Lucy thoughtfully. 'And Deb always maintained that Crispin's illness affected him very deeply. When Crispin died, Edmund was on his own in the house. He – he had to stay there all night with the body until someone came, I think. He was only nineteen or so – it might have affected him, mightn't it?'

'Certainly,' said Alice at once.

Lucy leaned forward and stretched out a hand to the thin figure in the chair, pleased when the white hand closed around hers at once. 'I'm so sorry you lost all those people, Alice,' she said. 'Conrad, and Deborah and my mother.'

'I have had great sadnesses in my life, Lucy dear,' said Alice. 'And I've lost a great deal. But I've also known some great happiness. Michael's been one of those happinesses, of course.' She smiled at him. 'Since Michael turned up on my doorstep that day, there's been a lot of happiness. And now I've got you, Lucy, dear.' She looked at Francesca. 'I'm rather hoping I'll have you, as well,' she said.

'Tell us about Ashwood,' said Fran, carefully not looking at Michael. 'The site, I mean.'

'Oh that.' It came out carelessly, and Lucy thought only Lucretia von Wolff could sound so casual about the ownership of a large piece of land. 'It was going for the proverbial song after the murders, which was how I managed to buy it,' said Alice.

'People were calling it haunted ground – such nonsense, because Leo Dreyer never had sufficient soul to haunt anything, and Conrad was always very dramatic but really he wouldn't have hurt a living creature.'

'Why did you buy it?' asked Lucy.

'To keep people out,' said Alice. 'To stop inquisitive journalists and sensation-seekers from delving around.'

'And to protect Alraune.'

'Yes.'

'But – you agreed to let Trixie in to delve around?' said Francesca.

'Yes. By then I knew Alraune was dying,' said Alice. 'And I thought perhaps it was time to let the place be exorcized at last. I had already transferred Ashwood to him when they released him from prison – it seemed more straightforward to do that, rather than continually pay out the income to him. That's when you and I met, wasn't it?' she said to Liam. 'I rather enjoyed putting on the unworldly elderly lady act for you.'

'You're a disgraceful old ham,' said Liam, and smiled at her.

'Yes, I must have a dash of Irish blood from somewhere,' she said, deadpan.

'I don't know about Irish blood, I don't think you've ever stopped acting,' said Michael.

Lucy said, very hesitantly, 'You said Alraune was dying?'

'Yes. I don't think he'll live for more than another week or two.'

Alice looked at Michael. 'And then,' she said softly, 'perhaps there will be an end to the—'

'Ghosts?'

'Yes.'

'And Ashwood itself?' This was Liam.

'When Alraune's gone, Ashwood will be Michael's,' said Alice. 'If he wants it.'

'I don't want it,' said Michael at once. 'I'd rather let CHARTH have it. They can bulldoze the whole lot and build something in its place to help those wretched teenagers.'

'Get rid of the ghosts once and for all?'

'Yes.'

'That's rather a good idea,' said Alice thoughtfully. 'Liam, you and I will talk about that.'

'I'm yours to command, Baroness.'

'I suppose,' said Michael after a pause, 'after all this melodrama, you'd like another brandy, would you?'

'Do you know, I believe I would. In fact,' said Alice, 'I suppose we'd all like one.'

As Lucy accepted the brandy, she said half to herself, 'I wonder what's happening to Edmund?'

CHAPTER FORTY-TWO

Now that Edmund had got Crispin more or less under control again, he was rather enjoying talking to these two men who had appeared from somewhere or other, and who had driven him to a large and very quiet house.

He was not absolutely clear about that journey: he hoped he had not fallen asleep during it, because he had always thought it the height of discourtesy to fall asleep in a car. Nor was he entirely clear who the men were, because he was so extremely tired. An odd kind of tiredness it was as well: almost as if he was enclosed behind a glass panel, and as if he was hearing and seeing everything from a distance. Occasionally he had to give his attention to Crispin, who kept forcing his way to the surface and trying to speak through Edmund. It was very tiring to have to keep forcing Crispin down, and it was also rather sad; once upon a time Edmund would have been very glad to let Crispin take over – to sit back and smile to see Crispin handle these men with his customary panache and charm. But in view of what had happened earlier on, it was clear that Crispin could no longer be trusted. Edmund was afraid that Crispin might start to shout those shameful embarrassing details again – how he had made love to that bitch, Lucretia von Wolff, how he had killed Conrad Kline, butchering him like some maniac.

Still, he would try to find out where he was, and just who these two men were who were sitting with him so pleasantly. He realized that he did not even know their names. Had they told him who they were, and had he been too taken up with Crispin to hear? If so, he would have to find out their names in a roundabout way. The trouble was that every time he started to frame a suitably polite question, they seemed to jump in with a question of their own. Not pushy, not discourteous, just interested in Edmund and in Crispin.

Having listened to them for a while, Edmund had discarded his first idea that they were researching into melancholia and began to think they might be planning to write a book. There was no denying that the years of Crispin's youth would make a very good story; Edmund had sometimes thought of writing it all down himself.

He said so to the man who seemed more senior, and the man was at once interested. An extremely good idea, he said. They would very much like to read that. Would Edmund really undertake it? It might be quite a long project, but they could probably fund it – perhaps set him up with a laptop and some research facilities. He might as well stay here to write it, as well – that would not be a problem, would it?

Edmund saw at once that this was one of their sly tricks. They thought they were going to find out about Crispin – about the real Crispin – from him. But he knew a trick worth two of that! He would agree to write the story though – he had always thought he had a book in him. Not one of your bonk-busters, not what they called a sex-and-shopping story – just a plain straightforward tale of a young man who had loved a black-haired seductive adventuress, and who had been deceived by her. Crispin's life story. The more he thought about it, the more he thought it would be the best service he could render Crispin. The story as it ought to have been. Crispin's life story as it would have been if that bitch had not lured him into her bed.

He said, in a rather disinterested voice, that he supposed he could take a swing at the thing. He might be able to leave the office in the hands of his staff for a week or two – although he would have to be in constant touch with them by phone, that would have to be understood at the outset. Legal practices were not things you picked up and put down as the mood took you. There were responsibilities – clients who relied on Edmund.

This foxed them for a moment – aha, they were seeing he was not so easily fooled! – but then they said, how would it be if they found another solicitor to caretake the office until Edmund went back. They could arrange for notes to be made and files to be handed over. Because they were really extremely keen for him to write Crispin's story for them, they said. Could something not be arranged?

Edmund pretended to think for a moment, and then said he did not see why not. He could give notes on all the current cases – some conveyancing work, and some land acquisitions and rights-of-way. He added grudgingly that he supposed his secretary might come in useful; she knew what was going on, and she knew most of the clients. Very well, since they were so insistent, he would do it. But – mark you – he would expect to be given proper facilities. He supposed this room might do; it was fairly comfortable, and they could presumably put a desk beneath that window for him, could they? Oh, and he was used to good meals, served punctually, he said firmly, because he was not going to be fobbed off with cheap, pre-packaged, pre-cooked rubbish.

'I'm sure we can work out something that you'll find agreeable,' they said.

'He'll never be pronounced fit to stand trial,' said the man whom Edmund had identified as the senior of the two. He regarded DI Jennie Fletcher with his head on one side, as if saying, Well? What do the police think about that?

'There was always a whiff of real madness about Trixie Smith's murder,' said Jennie. 'What would your initial assessment of Fane's condition be?'

'It's a bit early to start plastering the poor man with labels, but there's a strong indication of schizophrenia. It was very noticeable that while we talked to him, he kept having to break off the conversation.'

'To fight with the other persona?'

'Yes, almost certainly that. He was struggling to keep "Crispin" down. We're getting him on to writing some of it out – he was keen on that idea, and it'll help him. It'll help us to understand him, as well. He's certainly been through various kinds of hell on his own account.'

'So,' said Jennie drily, 'did his victims. Is he ever likely to be let out?'

'Oh God, no,' said the senior psychiatrist at once. 'He's in here for life.'

'There are two spare rooms,' said Alice, shortly before midnight. 'My room's at the front and Michael's is there as well, and the guest rooms are at the back of the house. I don't mind who stays the night, or who sleeps where. Michael, you can sort out sheets and so on if anyone wants to stay, I expect.'

'Of course.'

'I don't mind, either, if any of you want to drive back to London,' said Alice. 'Or to that place where you were last night—'

'The White Hart,' said Michael.

'Yes.' She studied them thoughtfully. 'A remarkable day, wasn't it? And the first meeting for us all.'

'But not the last,' said Lucy, rather tentatively.

'I do hope not.' She considered Lucy for a moment, and then said, 'I was right when I said you were like Conrad. It's quite uncanny.'

'I can come again, can't I? Properly, I mean, when everything's sorted out. Edmund and everything. There's so much I want to know,' said Lucy.

'I hope you'll come soon and stay as long as you want,' said Alice. 'I want to hear about you, about the family. Tonight it's all been me, but next time we'll focus on you.' She gave them the speculative look again. 'I'll say goodnight. I expect you can sort yourselves out regarding sleeping arrangements.'

'You have to admit,' said Liam, after she had gone, 'that when it comes to exit lines, she's Oscar-level.' He looked at the others. 'Well? Life's full of decisions, isn't it? Who's going and who's staying? And who's sleeping in whose bed, I wonder? I think,' said Liam before anyone could respond to this, 'that as far as I'm concerned, I'd better drive back to Ashwood. I've had a couple of drinks, but I don't think I'm over the limit, and I've got an office to deal with in the morning. So anyone heading south is welcome to a lift. But I don't know who's got a car here and who hasn't.' He looked at Lucy as he said this.

'My car's here,' began Francesca.

'And mine's at the White Hart,' said Lucy. 'As the crow flies it isn't so very far, but it would well after one a.m. by the time I got there – always assuming one of you would drive me – and so I think it would be easier for me to go back to London, and get a train back tomorrow to collect it. If I did that, I could drive over here again and see Alice – would that be all right, d'you think?'

'She'd love it,' said Michael.

'She'll be all right, won't she?' said Lucy slightly anxiously. 'I mean – all this won't have been too much for her?'

Michael smiled. 'Meat and drink,' he said.

'In that case,' said Lucy, suddenly finding the prospect of driving home with Liam very attractive, 'I'll take up your offer if I can, Liam. It means driving into London, though. Would that be all right?'

'Perfectly all right. I should tell you I have absolutely no sense of direction, though, and it's God's mercy I even got to this house. I'm quite likely to land you on the gypsy road to Romany, or the route to the Elysian Fields. Still, that might be rather fun, you know. How about you, Michael?'

'I'd better stay put,' said Michael. 'My room's always more or less ready.' In a voice that was just slightly too casual, 'Francesca? Had you better drive back as well, or can you take one of the spare rooms?'

'Well, if you're sure I won't be in the way if I stay—'

'You won't be in the way,' said Michael.

'I think,' said Lucy, peering through the rain-drenched darkness as they sped through the night, 'that we should get off this stretch of motorway in about another mile.'

'What an efficient lady you are. Will we look for the sign yet?'

'It should be coming up any minute. It'll siphon us off to the left,' said Lucy.

'Siphoning's the right word in this weather, isn't it? It's taking all my concentration to keep—'

'On the straight and narrow?' demanded Lucy caustically.

'Well, I always had trouble with the straight and narrow, and I'd certainly never find it in this downpour. Wait though, is that our turning up ahead?'

'I think so.' Lucy wiped some of the condensation from the windscreen. 'Yes, it is. I thought we'd probably find our way in the end.'

'O Faith that meets ten thousand cheats, yet drops no jot of faith—'

'Do you really not know the way?'

'I do not. Do you?' He took his eyes from the road for a moment to direct a very straight look at her. 'For all I know,' said Liam, 'this could be the road to Mandalay or the pathway to the stars, or even the Golden Road to Samarkand.'

'If you keep straight on from here,' said Lucy prosaically, 'you'll be bound to pick up the M25 eventually.'

'Oh God, that we should end by living in a world where all roads lead to the M25.'

'It's probably better tarmacked than the Golden Road to Samarkand, though.'

'Then we'll make a start there,' said Liam, and took his hand from the steering-wheel to briefly enclose hers. 'You never know, Lucy, we might find the Golden Road just when we'd decided it didn't exist.'

* * *

Michael had led the way to a large bedroom at the back of the house. There was a deep wide bed, and he fetched clean sheets from the airing cupboard.

'And there's a spare toothbrush and sponge in the bathroom,' he said. 'I expect Alice will probably lend you pyjamas or something if you want.'

The thought of sleeping in pyjamas belonging to the infamous Lucretia von Wolff was very nearly irresistible, but Fran said that actually she had brought toothbrush and night things with her, following Michael's original suggestion that they might stay overnight at the White Hart.

'Oh yes, I'd forgotten that. It feels like a hundred years ago now. Would you like a last drink? Or a cup of tea or anything?'

Fran considered, and then said, 'A cup of tea would be nice. Shall I help you make it? Your hand—'

'No, I can manage,' he said, and vanished.

I suppose, thought Fran, it's up to me to give him a signal. Or is it? Oh bother, I'm completely out of practice with this kind of thing. Do I want to give a signal? Oh, don't be stupid, of course I do! She padded into the adjoining bathroom, undressed and washed, brushed her teeth, wrapped herself in a towelling robe that hung on the door and scooted back to the bedroom.

When Michael came back with the tea, the curtains were drawn, and Fran had switched on a small bedside lamp, so that the room was bathed in a soft glow.

His eyes took in the scene at once, and he put the tea down and came over to the bed. 'Nice lighting,' he said with that glint of humour that was becoming familiar. 'Shall I stay while you drink your tea? I've brought a cup for myself, but I can take it to my own room.'

'Well, you could stay,' said Fran carefully. 'Although I'm wondering if I actually want a cup of tea after all.'

'Oh good,' he said, pulling her into his arms.

FINALE

'Vienna gets jam-packed on New Year's Eve,' said Michael, meeting Lucy and Francesca with Liam at Vienna's airport. 'Mostly for the Opera House, of course. It's all terribly traditional – the Radetzsky March, and so on – but I like traditions. And there's always a terrific atmosphere.'

'It's got a terrific atmosphere now,' said Francesca, looking out of the windows. 'I've never been to Vienna before.'

'People say that the pavements thrum with music,' said Michael. 'And that you can feel it.'

'Can you?'

'No idea. That's the Opera House across there.'

Lucy, who was sitting in the back of the car with Liam, said, 'Alice danced there with Conrad, didn't she? It was one of the things she said kept her going while she was a prisoner. That she would one day dance with him again, to his own music.'

'We are going to make a terrific entrance tomorrow night,' said Alice, later that afternoon.

'The baroness's return,' Lucy could not help saying.

'Exactly. Like those films where the villain disappears in the final frame in a burning building or over the Reichenbach Falls, but vows to return.'

'You're not a villain,' said Francesca, smiling.

'No, but I'm returning from the dead.'

'Can you?' said Lucy. 'I mean – you've spent the last fifty-odd years keeping all those secrets—'

'Oh, no one will know who I am,' said Alice at once. 'But they will all think I am a person of immense importance, and they will perhaps speculate a little and I shall enjoy that. Now, show me what you'll both be wearing tomorrow— Oh yes, that's absolutely lovely, Lucy dear. I'm glad you go for those bronze shades – they're exactly right with your hair. Silk? Yes, and it's a *good* silk, isn't it? Francesca, let me see— No, hold it to the light – that's beautiful, my dear, really beautiful. Green's one of your best colours, I think. Show me the back . . . Yes,' said the lady who had been dressed by Schiaparelli and Lanvin and had worn jewellery from Cartier with careless indifference, 'yes, you will both look tremendous tomorrow night and I shall be very proud to be seen with you. I wonder – would either of you be offended if I made you a small gift? Lucy, there is a gold necklace – very plain, very modern – but I think it would go with that neckline. And some jade earrings that I think are just the colour of Francesca's gown . . . Please do accept them. It would give me a lot of pleasure.'

'And what about you?' said Lucy. 'What will you be wearing?'

The mischievous smile showed. 'My dears,' said Lucretia von Wolff, 'I shall be more formal than you can possibly imagine, and I shall make the finest entrance of my life.'

The ballroom was crowded when they finally reached it. Alice walked slowly but unhurriedly, as if she might be saying, I will take my time about this. There is a great deal to absorb, and I am going to enjoy all of it.

She was wearing black, as befitted an elderly lady, but it was black silk, heavy and expensive-looking, and around her shoulders was draped a black stole, with the most exquisite silver bead embroidery Lucy had ever seen. Her hair was immaculately arranged, and she wore what looked like a rope of black pearls.

'Probably priceless,' murmured Michael to Francesca. 'If we aren't mugged and robbed before midnight it'll be a miracle.'

'She looks extraordinary,' said Francesca. 'Like something from an Edwardian painting. Arrogant and elegant. And there's such a – a romance about her and about tonight.'

Chandeliers sparkled and coruscated from the ceiling, illuminating the glittering scene and the shifting throng of people, all of whom had flocked here to observe the tradition of New Year's Eve in Vienna. Champagne stood ready in ice-buckets, and hothouse flowers were banked against the orchestra's platform, the heady scents mingling with the perfumes of the women.

There was a stir of curiosity as they walked forward – they don't know who she is, thought Lucy; not really. But they know she's *somebody*. And she's loving that. I'm loving it for her, as well.

There were seats and a table on one of the balconies, with champagne and glasses set out for them. 'Excellent,' said Alice composedly. 'I can look down at the dancers. You're all going to dance, aren't you?'

'Of course.'

But it was not until shortly before midnight, with more champagne opened, that the conductor tapped his stand and looked across to their table. Lucy thought Michael nodded, and the orchestra slid smoothly into a piece of music that made her skin prickle and her senses race. Before anyone could say anything, Michael leaned forward and took Alice's hand.

'Do you mind?' he said. 'They truly don't know who you are – I contacted the conductor last week while they were rehearsing, and asked if it could be played as a tribute to a lady who would be here tonight, and who had known the composer.'

'*Deborah's Song*,' said Alice, and her dark eyes were shining with something that might have been tears, but that might have been intense happiness. 'Oh, my dear boy—' She sat up a little straighter. 'We'll have no embarrassing sentimentality, but Lucy, it would give me immense pleasure to see you and Michael dancing to this.'

Michael stood up, and held out his hand to Lucy. 'For Lucretia and Conrad,' he said.

'For Lucretia and Conrad.'

The music wound its lovely way onwards, conjuring up the ghosts, summoning the shades of the man who had written it all those years ago, and of the scandalous baroness.

It had not quite reached the final bars when Liam said very quietly, 'Francesca.'

Francesca had been enjoying the music, and she had been enjoying watching Michael and Lucy dancing. She turned to Liam, and then her hand flew to her mouth. 'Liam – oh no. She – she's gone, hasn't she?'

'Yes,' he said, very gently. 'But she died in a glittering ballroom, listening to an orchestra playing the music written by the love of her life, with a glass of champagne within reach of her hand. I can't think of a better way for her to die.'

'Michael will be devastated.'

'I know. So will Lucy.'

Francesca looked at the still figure in the chair again. 'She's smiling, isn't she?'

'Yes.' Liam hesitated, and then said, 'Look down there. I don't know if you see it, and maybe it's just the champagne I've had, but—'

'It isn't the champagne,' said Fran after a moment. 'I do see it.'

Michael and Lucy were still dancing – the floor was crowded, but it was easy to pick them out. As they moved, there was a moment when it seemed to Francesca that two other figures moved with them – like the overlaying of a transparent photograph, or like the superimposing of an old, old film – so that it was no longer Michael and Lucy, but two other figures from a long-ago night.

Lucretia von Wolff and Conrad Kline, together again, dancing beneath the glittering chandeliers of a Viennese ballroom . . .

Fran looked back at Alice who had been watching the dancers and sipping champagne, and who had died quietly and happily, one hand turned palm upwards, as if eagerly reaching out to clasp the hand of someone who had been waiting for her . . .